Other Books by Caroline Ailanthus

To Give a Rose

Ecological Memory

Bifurcation Events

The Elf, the Dwarf, and the Telegraph, Book I

The Elf, the Dwarf, and the Telegraph, Book II

The Elf, the Dwarf, and the Telegraph

Book I

A NOVEL BY
Caroline Ailanthus

ISBN 978-1-62806-433-9 (print | paperback)
ISBN 978-1-62806-434-6 (ebook)

Library of Congress Control Number 2024922121

Published by Salt Water Media
29 Broad Street, Suite 104
Berlin, MD 21811
www.saltwatermedia.com

Cover artwork and interior illustrations by Caroline Ailanthus

For Charles Curtin and W.T. Sherman,

my fellow elf-bloods

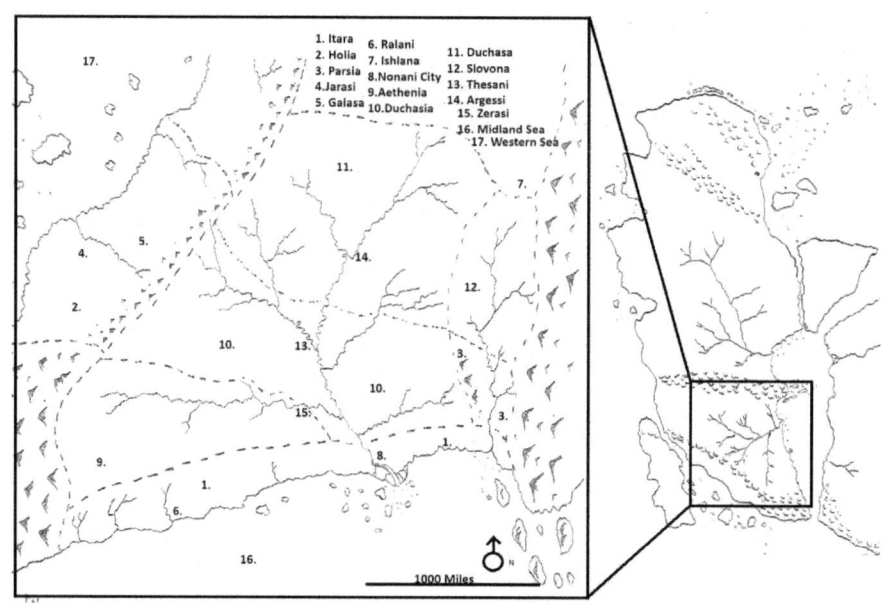

1. Itara   6. Ralani
2. Holia   7. Ishlana   11. Duchasa
3. Parsia   8.Nonani City   12. Slovona
4.Jarasi   9.Aethenia   13. Thesani
5. Galasa   10.Duchasia   14. Argessi
   15. Zerasi
   16. Midland Sea
   17. Western Sea

1000 Miles

Contents

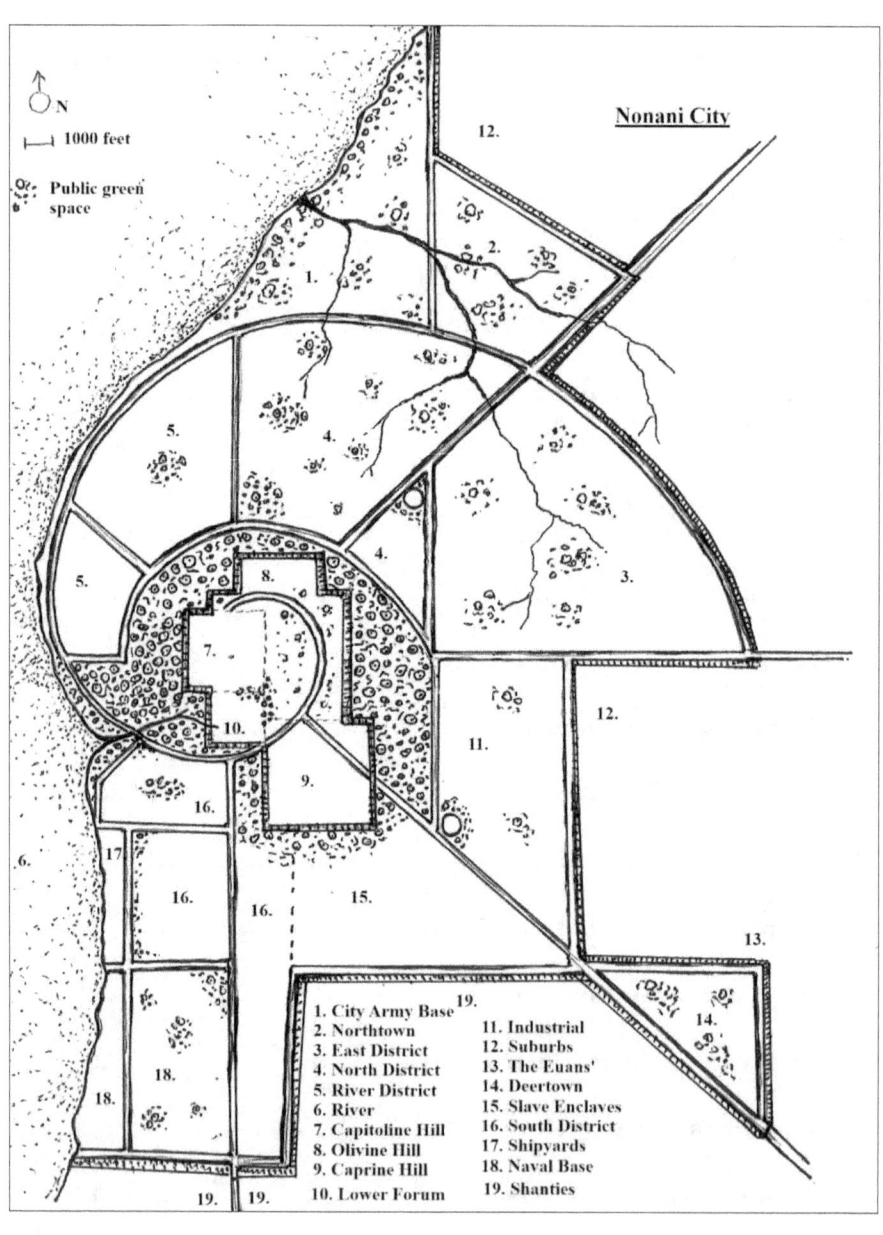

Nonani City

N

⊢——⊣ 1000 feet

Public green space

1. City Army Base
2. Northtown
3. East District
4. North District
5. River District
6. River
7. Capitoline Hill
8. Olivine Hill
9. Caprine Hill
10. Lower Forum
11. Industrial
12. Suburbs
13. The Euans'
14. Deertown
15. Slave Enclaves
16. South District
17. Shipyards
18. Naval Base
19. Shanties

Author's Note

There was once a presidential election whose results the other party did not like—to the point that the outgoing president used his authority to secretly aid and abet a growing armed rebellion. As the votes of the electoral college were being officially counted, the vice president came under extreme pressure to not certify the vote, part of a last-ditch effort to prevent the transfer of power. The vice president certainly did not like the results either, but to his credit he refused to bow to pressure, and so a few weeks later, Abraham Lincoln was sworn in as sixteenth president of the United States.

The more things change, the more they stay the same—until they change.

This book you hold in your hands is not scholarly commentary, historical fiction, or alternative history. It's fantasy, pure and simple. It might possibly count as allegory, or it might be what the author dreamed up to keep from worrying half to death.... It is my fond hope that at least some people will read this book in a far distant future and have no idea what I might have been worried about. For you, it will be just a good story.

What you hold in your hands is half the story. I hope the other half is somewhere nearby, or will be soon, and that you enjoy reading both of them. I think you will. After all, who doesn't love a transmasculine half-elf who wields a katana?

If you've noticed the people I'm dedicating this story to, then you won't be surprised that William Tecumseh Sherman also heads the list of people I've got to thank—but you may be confused. How am I in a position to thank a man who's been dead since before I was born? It's a long story, but it's also a true story, so you wouldn't believe me if I told you. Suffice it to say there are all sorts of reasons I could not have done this without him. If you don't know who he is, some of the books I've included in "Suggested Resources" in the back will tell you. If you *do* know who he is, I suggest reading some of those books anyway, as his story is important but has been seriously obfuscated by propaganda that refuses to die. What you think you know of him might be wrong.

Of Charles, I will admit I've stolen some of his lines. Again. He is another I could not do without, and I really hope I never have to try.

My writing process is heavily dependent on conversation with other people, people who let me bounce ideas off them, people who answer seemingly small but pivotal questions without necessarily knowing why I'm asking, people who just put up with me talking incessantly about whatever my monotropic special interest is at the moment. I can't thank everybody, because I don't keep records of whom I talk with about what, and because it's difficult to define who helped with the book verses simply being in my life in a way that mattered. Should I thank the teacher I had when I was six years old who read us a little book about Abraham Lincoln? Should I thank my mother-in-law who happened to own a book that I picked up when I was bored—a book called *Lincoln's Generals' Wives*?

I don't know. I do the best I can.

Let me then thank, for too many services rendered to specify, Maxfield Sparrow, Jamie Capache, Joel Parthemore, Kass Sheedy (my mother), Chris Seymour (my husband), Fran McMillian, Edina Meiners, Rachel Brice, Andrew Heller, Stephanie Fowler, and Patty Gregorio. If I've left anyone out, please forgive me. It's been something of a confusing year for all of us.

Prologue

Year of Nonani 840, 24ᵗʰ day of First Month,
first hour before noon

A bbas Seras Lian stood in the Curia, at the window of his office, looking out. He couldn't see very much, just the side of the
massive Treasury Building and, beyond it, a sliver of the city stretch-
ing away between the hills and the river. The day was fine and smelled
of spring, and he could hear the mob in the Lower Forum chanting
for blood. His blood, actually. He sometimes heard his name.

He was supposed to be getting sworn in as Speaker soon, a private, all-but-secret ceremony that had always before been public and
festive. The Capitoline Guard had set up barricades around the hill
and deployed behind those barricades, on rooftops with crossbows
and cavalry bows overlooking the Upper Forum, and even in the
Curia itself. There had been talk of calling out the city garrison, but
its legate was nowhere to be found, and anyway the Speaker was the
only one with the authority to do such a thing, and of course outgoing Speaker Canan wouldn't. He'd been down in the Lower Forum
himself haranguing the mob earlier. He still hadn't moved out of the
King's House.

The sound of the mob changed. Abbas stayed at his window,
calmly waiting.

"Sir? It's time." His aide, Jonas Tomas Miran, stood at the door.
Abbas knew he did not mean it was time for the ceremony.

* * *

FOUR MILES AWAY, GWENESSIFYR SHERAS Euan also stood, looking out—out of the door of a tastefully opulent home in a very nice suburb of street-trees, walled gardens, and honey-colored stucco. The house belonged to her foster-father and her father-in-law, who happened to be the same person. She had tried for years to make something of herself, to support her wife and their children like a man—or whatever Gwen was—should. Now she was back under the roof of the closest thing to parents she had. She was almost forty. And the Empire she'd served so faithfully seemed to have lost its collective mind. By the end of the day, the institutions of republican governance would either protect and preserve themselves, transferring power peacefully according to the rule of law, or...?

"Daddy, what if..." Gwen's fourteen-year-old daughter, Ellia, standing in front of her in the doorway, asked.

"I don't know, baby."

The elfin blood ran strong in Gwen. It ran much weaker in Ellia, but both could hear the crowd-noise four miles away. Both heard the moment the roar of the mob in the Lower Forum changed.

There, in the Curia, was Gwen's foster-father, Tomas. There, in the Curia, was her foster-brother, Jonas. And there, in the Curia, was the beating heart of the Nonani Republic.

FORTY MILES TO THE NORTHEAST, Hyras Sylas Dynan, whom most people outside of his family knew of as Ulas Sylas Dynan, sat at a picnic table plunking away at a kalimba. He could not play the instrument, in fact was indifferent to music generally, but his younger daughter, Adna, had left the thing sitting out. There was nothing else for him to do.

Hyras's father was away in town, hanging around the telegraph office there, hoping for news and no-doubt pontificating. His oldest brother was also in town, at work in the nearer of the family's two leather-goods shops. Hyras's other brother was supposed to be at the other shop in the next town over, only he was busy dying of consumption instead. Hyras himself was supposed to be at one or the other shop, helping out, only he was busy not giving a shit about the sale of leather goods because the republic was likely falling today—probably right now, actually, judging by the sun. The new Speaker was supposed to be sworn in at noon. Hyras didn't need the Sight to know that the outgoing Speaker, who did not want to go out, would naturally use his influence on the mob to prevent the ceremony. Speaker Canan publicly called the Speaker-Elect the dwarf-lover. Of course, Speaker-Elect Lian actually did love the derger people and the vast, ancient forests they depended on for their hunting. The truth had been made into an insult because Speaker Canan served those who believed it was their inalienable right to convert the ancient forests, the sacred groves, the wise and wrinkled dryads, to charcoal in order to make steel and, ultimately, money. The proverbial unstoppable force would be meeting an immovable object in the heart of the capital city right about now.

There really were people who thought that way about the relative value of sacred groves, republican government, money, and power—people like Hyras's father-in-law, who had lovingly given Adna the kalimba, an expensive but whimsical imported toy, as a going-away present just a few days ago. It was all very complicated.

But some things were very simple.

Hyras's mother was inside preparing dinner and also hard-boiling eggs with onion skins for the kids' egg-hunt the next day, on Nonalia. The children themselves, Hyras's three and also his dying brother's five, were with his wife, Ilia, off picking spring wildflowers for the holiday. In a few hours, his father would ride home bearing news, the first draft of history, and the news would be that the republic of over three hundred years' duration had fallen before an autocrat employed by oligarchs. And then Hyras would get up, and he would do something about it.

Chapter 1. Abbas

Year of Nonani 796 - 812

Abbas was a desperately poor farm boy who lived on the far edge of the Empire. And yet he was a patrician by birth—his father owned the farm.

Abbas's father, Seras, was a patrician by marriage, but his in-laws weren't wealthy, and anyway he'd moved eight hundred miles away from them to a corner of southern Holia where land was cheap. The land was cheap because so much of it had been abandoned during a plague outbreak years ago, and most of it was still abandoned. Buying a farm with no close neighbors had seemed very grand, but it meant having no neighbors who could help him when Hanna died and left him with two young children.

Seras Ora Calian figured he had nothing going for him besides his ability to work hard. He wore the scars of a soldier and still spoke the poetic, multicultural dialect of the Nonani City slum where he was born. That he owned his own farm in beautiful, green Holia was more than he'd ever thought possible, and now he knew it was the most he'd ever have. He had no more money, no way to earn any money, and now no wife. And he could not get his son, Abbas, to work, though the boy was seven and big for his age.

Abbas spent most of every day playing in the woods. Seras worried constantly about him. There were dangerous beasts in the woods, and maybe even dangerous men—he sometimes smelled wood smoke while he was out hunting, especially near the creek with the beaver dam. But there was no getting through to the boy. Abbas would nod politely and agreeably and then do whatever he pleased. Desperate, Seras would strike the child, sometimes strike him many times. Thus Seras's mother had done. She'd been terrified, too. She was a slave, a former brothel-worker sold to and confined in a textile sweat-shop, allowed to keep her free-born son because love made her vulnerable. She made damn sure Seras behaved. But the same methods would not work on Abbas.

Sometimes Abbas talked about someone named Oboo, an odd name belonging to an apparently fantastical person. Abbas would casually announce that Oboo didn't have to wear clothes in the summer. Oboo was learning Itarish, but he couldn't pronounce certain sounds. Oboo lived in the forest, where his family had three whole houses, all for themselves. Seras played along until the day just after the winter feast of Natalia when Abbas came home with an unfamiliar knife.

"Da, look at this sweet farmer's Oboo gived me!" *Farmer's* was short for *farmer's tooth*, a common kenning for *knife*. The proletarian dialect used lots of kennings and no irregular verbs. "He traded for the business," the *business end*, meaning *blade*, "but he maked the handle himself. It be cool, yeah?"

"Abbas, where ye getted the knife?" Seras asked, very seriously.

"I telled ye, Oboo gived it to me...." Uncertainty crossed the boy's face. "I be in trouble?"

"Not yet. Just tell me who gived ye the farmer's."

"Oboo gived!"

"Oboo be...real?"

"Yes, of course he be, he gived me the farmer's!"

Seras digested this.

"*Who* be Oboo?"

"My friend. He lives in the woods."

Seras pictured armed vagabonds.

"He lives by himself?"

"No, I don't think so. He has a family he talks about sometimes. I haven't met them, though."

"Abbas, I don't want ye playing w' strange people I don't know."

"But he be my best friend!"

And Seras's heart tore. His son had never before called anyone friend. He'd never had a chance. Their closest neighbors lived three and four miles away.

"Tell this Oboo to come to dinner with us here, then."

On the appointed day, Seras went out in the snow and shot a couple of squirrels with his sling so Nara could extend the bean-and-acorn stew. Nara was still not quite eleven, but she had been doing all the family cooking, cleaning, and mending since Hanna died. Seras didn't know how to do women's work, and anyway raising, hunting, or gathering food took all his time. And so his daughter was doing all the work of a woman, and his son was doing no work at all and getting mixed-up with forest weirdos. Everything seemed to be going wrong.

And then a little boy dressed entirely in snow-caked fur followed his son in.

Oboo, for it must be he, stamped the snow from his furs into the hard dirt floor and tipped back the hood of his parka—revealing long red hair as straight as grass, an oddly large face for so small a person, and skin the color of wood rather than of earth. Startling. The boy looked around and up and then, staring amazed at the underside of the tall, conical, thatched roof, said something unintelligible that clicked and clacked and varied in tone in a way no language Seras knew of did. But Abbas grinned.

"He sayed our house be so big!"

Abbas was bilingual now?

And the house? It was a one-room shack! The only reason the roof was so tall was to let the smoke rise up out of people's eyes, and Nara, constantly tending the open hearth, still had a chronic cough. The place barely stayed above freezing, and if the door wasn't open the house was dark, as they had no oil for lamps. But Abbas seemed proud of the place, proud to be showing his friend his amazingly big house. Seras wondered if his son would ever even find out what a big house really was. Probably not.

Oboo liked the bean-and-acorn-mush stew and ate far more than a boy his size normally would, but he did so humbly, with obvious gratitude, and said thank you in mispronounced Itarish. After eating, he sat drinking cup after cup of thuja tea and warming his hands on the earthenware mug that had once been Hanna's. He answered all of Seras's questions. He had perfect manners.

Two of his answers were strange, though.

When Seras asked how many siblings Oboo had, Abbas paused and frowned before translating the question. The answer came as a list, not as a number.

"He sayed 'my family be me, my mothers, my father, my uncles, their wives, and my siblings and cousins.'" *Mothers* plural?

Asking Oboo's age again made Abbas frown, and again the answer wasn't a number.

"He sayed 'I don't suckle at all anymore. But I still suckled a little until just before last winter.'"

Short as he was, the boy had to be seven or eight—and he'd only weaned a year ago?

When Oboo went out to pee, Abbas asked "why don't you like Oboo? What be wrong w' him?"

"Nothing be wrong w' him. I don't say anything be wrong w' him."

"Da...."

"I don't *dislike* him, but he be a dwarf, what they call a, a derger. I've never met a derger before. There not be a lot of 'em. I be just surprised, be all."

"What be a derger?" Abbas asked, but by then Oboo was coming back in, and somehow what he was couldn't be discussed in front of him.

Of course Seras gave his permission for the boys to be friends, insisting only that they both help him on the farm a few days a week and that they stay together when off in the woods.

Abbas hadn't meant to frighten his father, he just hadn't realized that Da didn't automatically know everything important. And he still didn't know what made Oboo different. Was it just that he looked funny? Why should that matter?

A few days later, he had to go meet Oboo's family—apparently, they, too, had assumed their son's friend was imaginary. Their home was only about a half a mile away, but on the other side of the creek. The boys crossed the creek together on an icy beaver dam.

The whole family was funny-looking, like Oboo, with big, open faces, sloping foreheads, and short, stocky bodies. Most had red hair, straight or wavy but never curly. None could say Abbas's name right, nor any ah or ae sound, even those who otherwise spoke Itarish or Galasish fairly well. Their voices were powerful and resonant but nasal, with those of the men just as high as the women's. They had no garden, no fields, no pasture, only a small compound of what looked like burrows in the snow.

They were nervous around Abbas, cautious in a way he didn't understand, but they all welcomed him warmly, asking whether he was cold or tired and what he would like to eat. He shyly told them he'd really like an apple, if they still had any left. Fruit was the only kind of sweet Abbas knew.

"Yeah, we have apples, baby," one of the women told him. "You just wait."

He waited, answering questions and sometimes asking them, while three of the women set up a kind of big, leather bag under a wooden tripod and filled it with water from a large basket. Then they fished hot stones out of the fire and dropped them in, too, more and more stones, until the water boiled. Then the women added more things....Abbas wasn't really paying attention, but the stones puzzled him so he remembered them. The women sang as they worked, and part of the song sounded like a recipe. After a while, everybody squeezed into one of the burrows to eat what turned out to be an acorn mush and bear meat stew heavy with wild onions, crushed prickly-ash and juniper berries, and, yes, apples. Abbas, used to a child's cooking, had not known food could taste so good.

Once inside the burrow, he could see that it was actually a small house constructed of olifant ribs, alder twigs, and clay, an artificial cave perhaps twenty feet long and ten wide, not tall enough to stand up in, but very warm. He could take his coat off! And there were lamps, stone lamps with moss wicks, so that he could see his food and everybody's faces, even though the doorway was blocked with a tarpan skin. Oboo's family was rich!

After they ate, Oboo's father, Benò, sang, a long, quavering song that sounded like no music Abbas had ever heard—but he'd never yet heard much music. He couldn't catch all the words, still being new to the language, but it seemed to tell a story and made him feel sleepy and warm.

Oboo walked Abbas home afterwards.

"Our families don't seem to like us much," Abbas remarked, tramping along through the snow. "I mean, yours doesn't like me, and mine got weird about you." He spoke derger-tongue, not proletarian Itarish.

"Eh, that's normal," Oboo explained. "Ubum don't usually like anybody. They're always making wur and stuff." He meant *war*, but as no such word existed in his language, he'd tried to say it in Itarish. "My father and uncles and mothers and aunts don't *dislike* you, Ubbus, but they're probably worried. They've been hiding from your family this whole time, only I didn't know. The songs say ubum never make wur on us, but still."

"What's ubum?"

Oboo repeated the word more slowly, and Abbas realized it was a form of the word for *newcomer*.

"Yeah, but what *is* it?" he asked.

"Oh. What you are and I'm not."

"I'm ubum? But I like you!"

"I know, Ubbus. Not everybody is the same. It's like how we say squirrels are red, because most are, but there are some black ones. You're a black ubum."

"I look sort of black," Abbas agreed.

Oboo disagreed. The derger language allowed metaphor, but not imprecision. Brown could not be black, and in fact there was no one word that meant all the different shades and hues of brown together.

Oboo rattled off the four or five words that named the colors Abbas was.

"Let's not grow up *like them*," Abbas proposed suddenly.

"We can't not grow up," Oboo told him.

"I know. But let's not grow up like them. Let's be friends forever. Let's pinkie-swear."

"What's that?"

"It's this thing I saw some girls at another farm do, once. I used to think it was stupid, but maybe it's not. Here, we link our pinkies together like this and we swear: we will always be friends."

"We will always be friends," Oboo repeated. "But we would have been anyway."

"I just feel better this way, OK?"

The boys split their time between the two families. Seras taught Oboo how to hoe onions and cabbages, and Benò taught Abbas how to set and check snares, how to track, and how to not give offense to the wild things. He explained that no beast would harm a human who lived within the music, unless the beast was sick or desperate.

"The music?" asked Abbas.

"The way things are properly done. All things, all beings, have their music, and we sing to them and they to us. That is why we do not jump to try new ways of doing."

"New ways? Like using metal cooking-pots?"

"Like using metal cooking-pots. The songs *can* change. We use bronze or steel knives, now, and gold shines for us as for you. But a new song takes time to find, and to live *without* the songs, outside of the music—eventually, the forests and all who depend on them would die, and drought and flood would come, and days too hot and storms too fierce, and the waters and air would lose their virtue and make us sick. To live well, we must live correctly."

The families became neighborly. Seras formally and humbly asked Benò's permission to continue hunting and foraging in the forest, and Benò agreed to look after Abbas and Nara while Seras went away for a while that summer. He did not say where he was going, but he returned with a woman, a laden horse, and two little boys. He introduced the woman as Lara Taddas Cadan—his new wife.

So Abbas's father was a Cadan now, not a Calian anymore, a strange thought. Abbas and Nara remained Calians.

Abbas was never quite clear on whether his father had remarried for love. Seras and Lara certainly got along. They talked and joked and had sex often (something a child in a one-room house can't help but notice). But the courtship must have been extremely short, and the marriage had obvious practical value.

Lara could cook and sew. She had enough money to buy two ewes, a ram, three hens, and a rooster, and she could card, spin, and weave wool as well as make cheese and butter. And she owned the mare. Soon, the family was eating better and dressing better, and by selling the occasional lamb or foal, Seras could raise a little money. Best of all, Lara was a patrician. Had Seras married into a lower-class matriline, he would have joined its class and automatically ceased owning the farm. As for Lara, she was a divorcee estranged from her birth-family, a single mother of two young boys. She needed a husband as badly as Seras needed a wife.

Abbas puzzled over it. Maybe Seras and Lara loved each other. Maybe they only needed each other. Or maybe, when somebody offers you something you need very badly, you love them for it.

Lara taught Abbas and Nara reading, writing, and the use of the base-ten common abacus. She taught them both to ride her horse. And on that horse, starting when he was ten, Abbas rode twenty miles into the town of Sweetmeadow once a week so he could attend the gymnasium, a free mental and physical education center for boys and men. He learned to speak Galesish from the other boys and also to speak their version of Itarish, the kind Lara spoke, irregular verbs included. More importantly, he learned there about a wider world, about cities and heroes and history, everything important happening far away. He intended to go out there and make important things happen himself, someday.

When he was twelve, Abbas talked himself into a job as a shop assistant in Sweetmeadow. Two nights a week, he slept on the floor of the shop wrapped up in his father's old army cloak. He stocked shelves, helped customers, and once a month drove the cart out to meet with the derger family and trade with them, offering knife blades, sewing needles, semi-precious stones, smoked mutton, and bacon in exchange for wild-gathered herbs and mushrooms for cooking and medicine. The shop-owner had been doing that himself for years, but could not speak derger-tongue. That Abbas could was part of why he got the job.

For his labor, the boy earned a few copper coins a week. He gave most of these to his father, but sometimes kept one or two to buy a few sheets of papyrus. He could make ink and his own pen and so write his own poetry or draw pictures of the animals and plants he knew.

Years passed. Abbas grew tall and strong. He became a fair hunter and forager. The family sheep flock grew. Lara bore two more children, a boy and a girl, but the next year the little girl and one of Lara's older boys were lost to a fever. Abbas cut wood for the pyres.

One early spring day when he was fifteen, Abbas struck up a conversation in a pub with a tall, handsome traveler with an extraordinary story to tell. The man started by asking if Abbas had heard of electricity. Well, sure. The stuff lightning's made of. Elves discovered that years ago. Yes, but now there's a device that uses electricity to send coded messages over long, copper threads.

"They're going to build a whole system all over the empire," the man explained. "They already started, two years ago—but there are places where the maps aren't good enough yet to plan the route. So there's a cartographic team out. And *I'm* their leader." And he took a swig of his cider.

"Does this expedition have a guide?" Abbas asked. And the man, whose name turned out to be Jonas Freias Sylan, stopped mid-swig and looked at him.

Abbas could not guide in the sense of navigation, never having been more than twenty miles from home, but he could serve as a hunter, forager, and expert on avoiding the attentions of dangerous animals. From his work at the store, he knew how to cook and how to keep track of supplies. Of course, some of the expedition members could do the same or the group would never have left Nonani City, but none of them could do it as well, and none could speak the derger tongue.

"Derger can talk?" asked b'Freias. "I'm worried about running into them, frankly. We don't have any dwarves back home, but I've heard they run around buck-naked brandishing sticks. They're supposed to be very strong. And clever, you know, the way wolves are."

Abbas looked at him a moment and decided not to say certain things.

"They are very strong," he acknowledged. "And they are generally naked, weather permitting. But they never intentionally hurt anyone. They'd treat you as a brother."

"Huh. Appealingly innocent, then?"

"Oh, no, it's not innocence. They're well aware of our proclivities and can defend themselves. Only—I think there is something in their minds, something in-born, that's different than in ours. They cannot see any human as less than family. Distant family, perhaps, but family."

"'Proclivities,'" quoted b'Freias, chuckling. "You sound like a textbook, you know that, kid? With your accent, you sound like a *hick* reading a textbook."

"Sounds about right," Abbas admitted, chuckling back. He'd worked hard for his new accent.

Two weeks later, on a bright but cold spring morning, six men, one woman, and a tall, angular adolescent rode out of town leading six laden mules. Abbas had no intention of ever living on his father's little farm again.

The woman was a switcher. Abbas had heard of switchers and assumed them to be weird, chimeric men-women, but Jessia Tomas Bentan seemed like a normal, if rather assertive, woman. She was small and wiry, with a pretty, oval face. It was just that she wore men's clothes and did men's work. Professionally, she went by b'Tomas, meaning son of Tomas (Tomas, like Jonas, was a very common name), not the feminine na-Tomas. The men treated her as a little brother. B'Freias even let her share his tent.

The expedition moved, on average, northeast, paralleling the coast, but meandering much. In sparsely-populated areas they took detailed notes that b'Tomas would compile into reports and provisional maps. Sometimes in towns they interviewed locals or even just bought locally-made maps. That a place was not well-known in Nonani City didn't mean it was not well-known at all. Even the genuinely remote places were often inhabited by derger or by forest-dwelling ubum.

Twice the route brought the expedition to the shore of the Western Sea. Abbas had lived his whole life under its breath, but had never before seen it. The gray waves curling and curling against the rocky headlands did something to his heart. He talked with the locals and, by their instruction, was soon climbing on intertidal rocks after oysters and mussels, and padding across mudflats to dig for clams. Then, inland again, they hired boats to take them and their animals across wide rivers patrolled by ospreys, pelicans, and swans. They climbed chalk hills overlooking vast marshes dotted with small, shallow lakes and forested islands. Holia was the only part of the Galasa region to belong wholly to the Empire, a real province, but the telegraph would extend throughout, even into nominally independent ranges where nobody spoke Itarish, but only Galasish, Kelish, or Galish. The three languages were closely related, and Abbas was fluent in Galasish and so could make himself understood in the other two. He often got the group invitations to feasts or dances. At the end of the summer, the expedition attended the autumn Ram Lamb Sacrifice, a ceremony and feast Abbas was familiar with from back home, but in Holia it was done either at home or at temples in towns like Sweetmeadow. These Galish-speakers held theirs at a complex of standing stones set among earthen mounds raised over the graves of their long-dead heroes and kings. Abbas wondered where the standing stones and memorial mounds of Holia had been, before the Itarye people came and made it into just another province of Nonani.

Galasa as a whole was very well-watered and never very hot nor very cold. What wasn't farm field was mostly either semi-wooded sheep pasture or damp, mossy forest. Where the forest was only just growing back after abandonment, like the woods where Abbas had grown up, the trees grew dense and small, mostly orange pine, alder, and the little, weedy, spotted maples, all browsed by an overabundance of roe deer, hares, and rabbits. Large predators and the really big herbivores were as rare as they might be in farmland. Older forests had older trees of more kinds—the mighty star-leafed maple, for example, a few noble maples, ash and beech, two different kinds of linden and four of oak. Predators like wolves and lions were more of a concern. And the big animals, like bison, giant deer, and dicorns, were more abundant. There were even wild olifants, you could tell because of the wild presence of plants whose seeds few other animals spread--apples, peaches, and locust, strychnos-vine, and nut-melon. But these forests, too, hid ruined stone walls or the remnants of vineyards or orchards. Disease, famine, or warfare might depopulate a region and give it back to the forest, but in five years or fifty years or five hundred years, the land would be recolonized and put back under the plow, or at least under the planting stick, a cycle that had been running over much of the continent for something like four thousand years.

But there was another kind of place.

Sometimes Abbas found himself in open woodland or wooded savanna dotted with groves and spinneys of denser trees. Animals of all kinds and sizes moved through these places in almost unbelievable diversity and abundance, their feeding both the cause and the result of the land's open, grassy character. The trees that did manage to grow were big as houses.

Where the trees stood more densely together, the giants grew not wide but tall, airy and close as the columns of the grand temples Abbas had read about but never yet seen, ashes and beeches and lindens, maples and birches, and understories of apple, crab-apple, and dogwood. He knew all the species, but he'd never before seen them like this. Downy oaks and white oaks so gnarled and hollowed that bears could den inside their huge trunks. Yews growing in self-cloning layers, sometimes one inside the other. Hemlocks so old that powdery algae had turned their furrowed bark pale green—and above all of them towered pseudotsugas, false-cedars, and metasequoias two hundred or two hundred and fifty feet tall. All of these trees were draped in tangles of ivy, grape vines, melon vines, and clotted with clumps of mistletoe and arboreal fern. When Abbas climbed up the vines into the canopy, he found gardens of moss and lichens and even blueberry bushes, for fallen leaves resting on the branches had become pockets of soil. It must have taken centuries.

In these places, the ground felt springier, the songs of birds and insects were louder and richer, everything was just *more*. And yet, especially in the larger groves, there was a quality like silence, something that made the human voice want to hush so as not to disturb it. Abbas smiled more when he was in these landscapes, relaxing in ways he hadn't known he was tense. It was something in the air, he decided, something cool and rich and spiced, so that simple breathing felt like listening to derger song, the strange, high, quavering music of his childhood.

How old were these trees? How old were these forests? Abbas didn't know how to tell, but he knew they were older than anything else he'd ever seen. Although humans of three different kinds had lived in these strange landscapes for thousands of years, he could not imagine that they'd ever been cleared.

He remembered something he'd seen once on the teaser board of the newshouse in Sweetmeadow. He'd always avoided the teasers as they had just enough of each story to make you want to pay to go in and read the rest, and he'd never had the money to spare, never would have the money to spare, and didn't like to be reminded of his poverty. But sometimes he couldn't help it. And sometimes the stories were about forests, people trying to protect forests. Once the teaser said something about riots in East Parsia because scientists warned that unless the charcoal harvest was reduced, the ancient forests would be....

And the teaser stopped. But he'd known even then what the rest of the warning was. He'd already learned how you needed charcoal to make steel. And he'd seen, out on the main road outside of town, legions going by, long columns of men, thousands of them, each one bright with steel armor, steel weapons. And then they'd come back the other way, driving thousands of people shuffling along in steel chains. He'd been told these were rebellious provincials or wild, vicious barbarians being relocated someplace their strength and anger could be put to better use. But he'd known what the captives were really for. He knew about his grandmother, a woman kept for male pleasure until she got too old and was sold to a sweatshop to make bed-sheets and table-cloths until she died. He knew about slavery. And he could see that most of the manacled people being marched into servitude were men, strong men, most of them bound for mines and processing centers to make more steel to make more weapons to catch more slaves....

And now Abbas also knew what an ancient forest was.

That anything might really change is hard, very hard, to wrap your mind around when you live in an age of myth and wonder, but Abbas had helped build the pyres for his mother and siblings. He understood that sometimes, when something is gone, you don't get it back.

As autumn began, the expedition turned east and crossed a range of low but rugged mountains capped by dark forests of spruces and firs along their spines. Once on the other side, they were in Ishlana, an entire region officially independent of Nonani, although the Empire maintained a few garrisons there to protect its interests—mostly copper and tin mines. Abbas did not yet have the political sophistication to wonder why Nonani was going to build telegraph lines over land it didn't own, nor did he talk to the locals much. They didn't speak any of the languages he knew, and mostly didn't like foreigners anyway. They built no cities but lived in little stone villages, where they raised sturdy little cattle and sturdier little horses, and spent half their time stealing horses and cattle from each other and then back again, back and forth, back and forth, in pursuit of fame and glory forever.

Averaging east, now, before long the forest looked like it had in the mountains, dominated by spruce, fir, white birch, and rowan. The soil was thin and rocky. There were animals and plants here Abbas did not know. When b'Freias said the winter would be bitter and would come soon, Abbas believed him. Already the goldenrod and the autumn daisies were starting to go to seed. The birch leaves were turning golden.

The original plan had been to head south to the cities of Duchasa, where they could rent rooms and winter safely, but Abbas realized the detour would take weeks, possibly months round-trip.

"Why don't we stay?" he suggested. "We'll be right here when it gets warm enough to work."

"Because we'd freeze to death and die," b'Freias told him. "And then we'd get cold."

"We might even shiver a bit," agreed Abbas, "if we stayed in our tents. But why don't we stay with a derger family? There are some here, I've seen their trail blazes. And all derger everywhere speak the same language."

"Derger don't have houses," b'Freias objected. "They live in those burrow-things they make."

Abbas refrained from rolling his eyes.

Finding a derger family willing to talk wasn't difficult, but the headman Abbas spoke with insisted that he had nothing to share. He said his family was starving.

"We have become few, for you ubum are becoming many," the headman explained. "There is not room for us. Families leave, trying to find room, and the children born are not so many as the elders who die. We no longer have enough men for the great hunts. We have grown poor."

Derger hunters used thrusting-spears only, so their hunts were dangerous and required a lot of people, a temporary convergence of several families. That was why they famously went after such big animals—to kill a bison or an aurochs doesn't take many more people than killing a boar or a tarpan, but there is a lot more meat to go around. A family alone could still forage and could still snare small animals, but neither vegetables nor rabbits had enough calories to get the fast derger metabolism through winter.

"I say this not to complain," the man continued. "We live within the music, and that is enough. I say this only to tell you how it is that we cannot help you. I do not want you to think us ungenerous, inhospitable, but we can spare nothing in gift. And your pretty trade beads will change nothing for us."

Abbas was shocked—he'd known that there was less land for derger than their used to be, but he hadn't realized families could starve as a result. Oboo's family wasn't starving. But then he remembered that Oboo's family spent the winter eating bacon they bought in trade from the store. They sang the songs for the great hunts, but no longer performed them. Benò had said there weren't enough men.

The headman, whose name was Edò, seemed so angry and so sad.

"I know the songs for hunting griffin," Abbas said.

He had to teach the others the songs and how to use them—and why they couldn't just pay for their lodging by hunting elk or deer the Nonanye way. Some didn't even know what a griffin was, imagining some giant bird.

"No, picture a dicorn, but with more hair," Abbas tried to explain.

He also had to ask Edò for permission to use pila, Nonanye-style throwing-spears, instead of derger lances. Ubum just weren't durable enough to risk being thrown by a griffin.

Finally, as pale, yellow leaves fell from the birches, Abbas and b'Tomas set out to find the griffin already selected as quarry—an old jack, of course. Derger never killed jennets or even young jacks who hadn't yet had a chance to breed. They found him browsing spruce foliage on the edge of a small clearing. He was bigger and shaggier than any griffin Abbas had ever seen, but of course this far north he must be of the other subspecies. The hump of muscle over his shoulders stood taller than a man, and the larger of his two horns was almost four feet long.

Abbas began to sing. B'Tomas joined him. The jack lifted his head, pointed his small ears towards the hunters, and sniffed the air. His small, tired-looking eyes could not see much, but he must have disliked what he smelled because he roused himself and ambled away.

Together, the humans followed the irritated griffin. They did not use their pila yet. The idea was to drive the animal to a low, boggy, shrubby place where the bad footing would slow him down and give the hunters a chance. But frightened griffins don't run—they attack. To drive a griffin, one had to just make him a little uncomfortable.

The song contained the instructions for the hunt and had been passed down, unaltered, for nearly twenty millennia, ever since derger perfected the technique. Once derger perfected a way of doing something, they did it that way, and exactly that way, guided by music, until conditions changed and the method was no longer perfect. But the song not only reminded the hunters of the plan, it also told the griffin what he was expected to do, and why it was good and proper for him to do it.

> *Oh, Mighty One, flee from us*
> *Oh, Mighty One, fear us*
> *Oh Mighty One, protect yourself from us*
> *And not from our companions with the lances*
>
> *They are the ones who wait to close your eyes*
> *They are the ones who wait to stop your heart*
> *They are the ones who shall open up your belly*
> *Their scent is disguised from you with dung*
>
> *Oh, Dear One, die today*
> *Oh, Dear One, you must die today*
> *Oh, Dearest One, die and leave all of us here to live*
> *And we will spare your wives and honor your sons*
>
> *For we are the hungry ones*
> *We are the shivering ones*

We are the ones who will love you forever
If you die for us today

It was a slow, careful, undramatic chase, walking along behind the griffin, never getting too close, allowing him to stop occasionally and feed for a while again. He must not be frightened. It was not exciting, and yet you could not let your mind slip into boredom or daydream. That would dishonor the prey and risk the hunter. And so you just carefully ambled, singing, holding your mind, your focus, in a sacred manner.

At last, the drive came to the appointed place, and the six other men of the cartographic expedition, plus Enò and his brother, son, and two nephews, emerged from their hiding places. One of the waiting hunters must attack first, and so b'Freias, as per the song, threw his pilum into the griffin's left eye. Abbas threw his into the animal's right. Ideally, the spears would both break through the skull at the back of the eye socket and enter the brain at an angle and depth to kill the animal instantly, but while Abbas's pilum went through, b'Freias' did not. The griffin screamed and charged.

All thirteen hunters worked together, keeping the dying, terrified animal from finding and focusing on any one of them, while also trying to get in for a jab into some vulnerable place. B'Tomas threw her pilum, but it glanced off the heavy hide at a strange angle, flying up into the blue air and hanging for a moment, and then falling uselessly. Another pilum hit a rib and, though it stuck in the skin, simply hung there, also useless. Enò's son, Ec!o, jabbed in between the ribs and must have punctured a lung because the griffin soon began to bubble pinkish foam, but didn't stop fighting.

The safe thing at that point would have been for all the hunters to run away and wait for the griffin to die of his wounds, but then the meat might be stolen by crocottas, and anyway nobody wanted the jack to suffer any more than he had to. At last, one of the nephews managed to run in close and bury his spear deeply enough to hit the heart. The griffin was dead before he fell over.

The women and children came to skin and butcher the animal and set the meat to dry and smoke. And still the singing went on.

In return for the griffin, the expedition received permission to hunt and forage and also advice on how to make winter clothing and two derger-style houses. The two groups shared the same compound, the same composting privy, and the same outdoor hearth. They often shared meals.

Soon, the nights and then the days turned icy. Snow fell. The new houses were small, with no room for fires, but body heat and lamps kept them warm. And when the weather was clear and dry, the ubum went out and played in the snow with the derger children in the thin, yellow sunlight. Before long, all the ubum knew at least a few words of the derger language, and b'Freias, who worked hard at it, was near-ly fluent. He discovered that the derger knew a great deal about the landscape, not just their own territory but, through their songs, about much of the continent. He wrote up copious notes, which Abbas re-viewed to check translations and b'Tomas transcribed and expanded. The three of them shared one of the houses, and since their fourth housemate was usually elsewhere with Enò's youngest daughter, they had enough room inside to work.

Sometimes Abbas would notice b'Freias looking at him. No one had looked at him like that before. He had to think about it.

His thinking involved no question of sexual orientation, for Nonanye culture assumed all humans to be bisexual. The tricky thing was sexual role, which they considered to be invariably linked to so-cial role and relative status—you were either a top or a bottom, in bed or out. Mostly men were tops and women bottoms, but if you could enact the role, you could have the part. Hence, switchers. The top/bottom binary was considered invariable, so anybody known to have coupled with a top would be assumed to be a bottom and would never get a job outside the home again—that was why female switchers never openly took male lovers. The only loophole was that if the power dis-parity between two men was great enough, say, an adolescent and his adult boss, then being topped would cause no lasting damage to the bottom's masculinity. In fact, sex was a common element of mentorship, a sign and token of tenderness and commitment between men.

Abbas liked b'Freias, and while he'd never particularly wanted the man—or any other man—found him handsome enough. And he did want to put his adolescent libido *somewhere*. To accept a greater closeness with his benefactor? Abbas was over fourteen and therefore a legal adult, free to pursue any kind of mentorship he wanted. And so, one day, when he caught b'Freias gazing at him, he gazed back, smiled, and winked.

B'Freias startled, perhaps unaware his feelings had been visible. After a long moment, he smiled apologetically and shook his head slightly, then glanced away and sighed.

Abbas didn't know why he'd been rejected. He looked around the lamp-lit little burrow trying avoid even looking at b'Freias. He noticed b'Tomas watching the whole interaction carefully. He didn't see how it was any of her business.

In the spring, the expedition members said goodbye to their hosts and continued their journey, all through through Ishlana and the northern Duchasa territories. They wintered in a Duchasa city, one with a large Itarish-speaking population and regular mail service. Abbas exchanged several letters with his stepmother. His father still didn't know how to read. In the third spring of the expedition, they meandered south through long, narrow Slovona. But Parsia Province, the southern-most part of the region, was already thoroughly mapped, so the expedition ended there. They returned, mostly by riverboat, to Nonani City. From there Abbas continued on home alone, taller, perhaps wiser, and no longer so desperately poor.

Abbas only stayed with his family a few months before moving to Sweetmeadow to work for the general store again, now full-time along with another former shop assistant. The owner was stepping back from day-to-day operations. Abbas did not intend to be a farmer again.

Sweetmeadow was one of the market towns built by the legions when they were converting Holia from conquered territory to imperial province, and it mixed the boxy, Itarye architecture and the ornate-ly-carved, octagonal native construction in curious ways. Abbas had not noticed the mixing before, but now he knew what real Itarye cities looked like—and he knew that real Galasye culture had no cities or towns. There had been none in the independent parts of Galasa, only scattered sheep farms and complexes of standing stones and memorial mounds where tribes would gather for trade and ceremony. Evidently, Nonani had wanted to provide places for trade and ceremony that did not affirm tribal identity. The Empire hadn't wanted its newest citizens to remember their old, dead heroes.

Sweetmeadow was a very small town, but it bustled along nicely and was better than living on an isolated farm. He attended the baths, frequented the library, and resumed his studies at the gymnasium, attending lectures and discussions and entering amateur boxing and wrestling matches. Professional athletics was as disreputable as professional sex or acting, but a gentleman could compete as an amateur, and Abbas rather enjoyed winning wreaths and ribbons. He also learned how to dress and speak like a gentleman, not a farm-boy, and how to dance. He was a graceful dancer, when he wasn't flustered by a pretty partner.

At first he slept on the shop floor, as did his co-worker, the tall, quick Justas Juras Jaran, whom everyone called J.J. But working full-time they could soon afford to rent a room together. If they ate nothing but bean stew, they could even put some money away.

"J.J., why am I alive?" Abbas asked one night.

"Because your parents had sex."

"No, seriously. Don't you ever wonder?"

"No."

"Do you think it's a silly question?"

"No."

They were lying in bed in the dark. The evening was still young, but they had nothing to do but go to bed, having run low on lamp oil again. Their room was very small, most of their furniture improvised from packing crates. They had only the one pallet on the floor, and they shared it as two brothers might.

"Oboo doesn't ask why. About anything. I don't think he can. But I can't stop asking."

"Oboo lives within the music," J.J. replied in the derger-tongue.

"I want to know what the music is for me," Abbas answered in kind.

There was no immediate answer, but he attended talks by traveling philosophers, read and reread the few great epics the library had copies of, and borrowed from a friend a good translation of *The Plays of Arianos b'Sharos*. His studies made his father awkward around him. Abbas didn't know why, nor could he bring himself to care. The man symbolized all the limitations Abbas sought to escape. Seras had never even learned to read. But Lara was happy to hear all about it and asked Abbas lots of good, thought-provoking questions, and of course J.J. read right along with him. And every month when he took the cart to trade with the derger and spend some time with his family, he would join Oboo at his work, making tools, household implements, or jewelry with slow, persistent precision. No ubum could match derger craftsmanship, but Abbas learned the songs and did the work as best as he knew how. There were moments, only moments, when Abbas knew himself to be not a singer but a note in a song, a word in the music sung by the universe itself, sung by God.

More prosaically, he started law school, studying mostly from home, by mail. His gold and silver from the expedition and a gift of money from J.J.'s family paid tuition. There was no sense of mission about it, Abbas just didn't want to be poor anymore.

Most men tried to get married young, to get the name-change out of the way, but Abbas dated only casually into his early twenties, and then the death of a friend plunged him into a strange, mental darkness, and all his appetites seemed to die inside him. He barely ate, let alone thought about sex. J.J. covered for him at work so he could put what little energy he had into his studies. Suddenly, becoming a lawyer was the one thing he held on to. He had to hold on to something. Then the death of his sister, Nara, in childbirth—the baby died, too—made him rebel against grief and throw himself into an ill-advised whirlwind romance that he escaped just in time. And so, twenty-three years old and close to passing the bar, Abbas was still single the day he went to a party with J.J. and met a nineteen-year-old woman named Maia Daras Lian.

It was one of the late-summer parties after the annual ram lamb sacrifice. J.J.'s patrician cousins (cousins on his father's side, J.J.'s matriline being plebeian) hosted, and a hundred or so people, including many Abbas didn't know, gathered to dance to the beat of a local band and talk and flirt and eat from platters of lamb and vegetables sauced and grilled and speared on convenient skewers.

"Pretty good crowd, for the edge of nowhere," Abbas remarked to J.J. "Offhand, I'd guess the fashions are only…five years out of date?"

"How would you know?" J.J. asked him. "Anyway, since when do you care about clothes?"

"Since I've been able to *almost* afford good ones." Abbas knocked back the rest of his glass of apple-jack, frustrated. All the windows in the wealthy family's dance-hall stood open to the cooling night air but still the heat from the many lamps and all the dancing bodies was nearly intolerable. A heavy, mingled perfume mixed with the scent of sweat and of burning lamp-oil and beeswax candles.

"You know, there's only two ways to deal with a town like this, long-term," suggested J.J.

"Oh?"

"Yeah. You either move away, try to get closer to the center of the world where the interesting and important things are happening…. Or you decide that this *is* the center of the world, and interesting and important things happen here."

Abbas let his eyes scan the room while he thought about that. Then he stopped scanning.

"I see something interesting now," he murmured.

There were three young women standing together near the punch-bowl, laughing and talking among themselves. Two of them were merely pretty, one tall and angular as a newborn foal, the other medium-height and busty. Both wore Galasye-style finery, wool skirts woven in bold, zig-zag patterns with matching short, light-weight, shawl-like ponchos. But then there was the third.

She was short and curvy, with a round, dimpled face and eyes so black they reflected the candlelight like stars. She was wearing a pale green Itarye-style shift with a white and silver over-dress belted with huge red glass beads that looked like giant rubies and made it more or less impossible not to stare at her hips. A gauzy blue shawl covered her hair and left much of her upper body to the imagination, but one bare, brown arm rather aided the imagining.

"Who is she?" Abbas asked.

"Who? Oh, her? The one in blue? Cousin Maia. You've never met her before?"

"No, I'd remember. Your cousin? So, she's...?"

"The niece of our host tonight. She moved here from Jarasi—three months ago? Had some issue with her step-mother, I think. Nice girl. Headstrong, though."

"I...need some punch."

He ambled over, ladled himself a drink, and struck up a conversation, ostensibly with all three women. He was trying to be polite. But the others were astute enough to excuse themselves and vanish.

"My eyes are up here," Maia told him, but when he adjusted his gaze he saw she was smiling.

"Now, you did that on purpose," he accused, referring to the effect of her beaded belt. She laughed.

"Guilty as charged," she admitted. "Do you have any legal advice for me?" So she'd been making inquiries, too.

"I'm not a lawyer, yet." Abbas was shocked to find himself unable to think up a clever quip. He was all but tongue-tied. The band struck up a popular pair-dance tune and saved him. "Would you dance with me?"

She set down her punch-glass and stepped into his arms. He found her an excellent dancer. He only stepped on her feet twice.

Late that evening, after Abbas and J.J. had left, Maia's friends surrounded her.

"So?" the tall one demanded.

"So, what?" she answered, blithely innocent.

"So you just spent all evening dancing with some guy and looking at him like you want to jump his bones or something!"

Maia had just taken a sip of punch and now smirk-snorted so hard she almost sprayed punch out her nose. She spent some moments laughing, blushing, and flapping her free hand.

"I need a handkerchief. Anybody got a handkerchief?" she managed. "Ah, gods, was it that obvious?"

"No, not at all," one friend replied at the same moment the other said "*Yes!*"

"So who *is* he?" The one who'd said yes continued. "I mean, I know he's the law student at the store and everything, but who *is* he?"

"My future husband, I think," Maia replied, wiping her nose.

"What? He *proposed!*" the first friend exclaimed.

"Oh, no. And if he had I would have said no, I just met him this evening, and I'm not an idiot. But someday."

"Girl, how much punch did you drink?" the second friend asked. Maia started laughing again.

"Oh, not so much," she allowed. "Anyway, you wait and see. He's going to be Speaker of the Senate."

Maia liked to tell herself and everybody else who might care that she had the Sight, but she really didn't. When her predictions came true, it was because she made them come true.

Chapter 2. Gwenessifyr

Year of Nonani 817 - 821

Gwen, fourteen years old, stepped forward in line and watched the registrar's surprise. Now that she wore men's clothes, it always took people a moment to realize she was a girl. Not that it mattered. Switching meant they'd treat you like a man if you acted like one.

The early-spring sunshine streamed in through the high windows of the gymnasium main hall, and the dust in the air caught the light and made of it slanting rectangles of swirling brightness. She could see the light and the dust, but only together. Light alone, or dust alone, was invisible. The registrar asked for her name.

"Gwenessifyr Sheras Lyran."

"Lyran's not a patrician matriline." You could be a girl in the army if you performed like a man, but you couldn't be an officer unless you were of the right class.

"My foster-father told me to give you this." She handed across a small papyrus scroll, rolled neatly and sealed with red wax.

The man clearly recognized the seal. He opened and read the letter.

"Senator Euan has never yet sent us a poor student," he said. Then he collected her family's billing information and her medical exam forms, helped her sign up for electives, and assigned her a squad, a dorm-room, and a student number. Then he told her to please go over there and wait with those others. Another new recruit stepped forward in line, and the registrar began the same conversation all over again.

That her foster-father was a senator wasn't itself remarkable. *Senator* just meant the paterfamilias of a patrician matriline, one of the men allowed to serve in or vote for elected office. Every kid in the room had a father or a grandfather or an uncle or a cousin who was a senator, by definition. But Senator Tomas Salas Euan had been elected to the Ruling Council and had served on it for years. He was rather a big deal. Of course, Gwen didn't intend to go dropping his name all over the place, she intended to earn her own laurels, but this time it had been unavoidable. And kind of fun.

"Hurry up and wait," said a tall, skinny boy next to her. "My dad says that's how it is, in the army. Hurry up and wait."

"Stand by to mill about!" she replied, softly, but in the exact cadence of a centurion shouting orders. They'd all seen centuries drilling outside the headquarters of the city garrison, a fine and thrilling show. The boys around her cracked up.

"Alright, men! Mill about *smartly*!" added a round-faced boy in the same tone, and they all cracked up again.

The last boy in the line got processed. The registrar's assistant handed each new cadet a canteen of water, a block of cheese, a quarter-loaf of good bread, and an apple and said to sit down and finish everything. It would be a long walk to campus.

Gwen regarded the apple.

There was an apple tree in the garden of her foster-father's house, along with several cherry trees, a grape arbor, a vegetable patch, and an herb garden. Tomas was a businessman, not a farmer (he owned a salt-distribution company), but the family grew as much of their own as they could. And that garden also grew children. Two living sons, two daughters, the cousins, Topaz and Euas, whom Tomas and Opal also fostered, Gwen herself, and usually half the other kids in the neighborhood—in good weather, they hardly ever came inside. Hide-and-seek, building forts behind the branches of the weeping cherry trees.... *You be the barbarian princess, and I'll save you from the dragon. No, I don't want to be the princess. I'll be the queen. Make Chalcedony be the princess. No, because she has to be the dragon.*

No fair! I'm not supposed to climb in my good dress. You'll eat all the apples!

And Gwenessyfir suddenly realized she'd left home. She hadn't exactly meant to. She wouldn't really be all that far away, she'd return on leave every nine weeks, and of course they'd all write to each other, so she hadn't thought going off to school was a big deal, really. Except it was. Her childhood was over.

Gwen ate her apple, finding it rubbery with age but still sweet, drank deeply from her jar of water, and introduced herself to the round-faced boy. He was the son of a shipping magnate named Hallas and had read every book she had plus two.

GWEN'S FAVORITE CLASS WAS *ELFIN Numerals and Mathematical Notation*, a required course—you couldn't do higher math with the cumbersome Nonanye numbers, and you couldn't calculate the range of a trebuchet without higher math. At first she'd thought it would be just learning new symbols, like a code, but really it was a whole new way of thinking—a systematic approach to quantity based on groupings of twelve, plus a concept of zero. What did *zero* mean? How could it mean nothing, and how was that different from just not meaning anything? But soon she figured it out.

And yet there were problems. The instructors were not deliberately abusive after the manner of drill sergeants—first-year cadets, though legal adults, were basically still kids and treated as such—but they did have very exact standards that she couldn't always meet. Her bed wasn't made properly. Her uniform wasn't on right. She hadn't said *sir!* in exactly the right tone. And she didn't know why it wasn't right. She didn't even realize that there was a *why* to know, she just thought she had to try harder. Rumors soon surfaced that she was an elf-blood.

She could have denied it. She looked almost elfin, tall, slim, and fair-skinned, very light brown with freckles, not the usual dark brown, but that didn't matter. What mattered was a certain turn of the mind, a way of being. Some people whose elfin heritage was obvious didn't have it. They weren't elf-bloods. Some people whose elfin ancestor was so far back as to have been completely forgotten did have it. Elf-bloods were the weird ones, regardless of color. And Gwen didn't think she was all that weird. She'd learn to wear her uniform right, learn to make eye contact at the right times, in the right ways, and not at other times or in other ways. She'd learn to get it all right. She could do it. But first-generation mixes were always elf-bloods, everybody knew that, and she could not deny her mother.

"WHY ARE YOU ALWAYS STUDYING?" a boy asked.

"So that I can master the material," she replied. She was busy copying over elfish ideograms for one of her electives, sitting on her bunk but tapping one foot rapidly on the floor because she could not be still. With ideograms, you could read scientific journals.

"Why? You're going to pass all your courses anyway."

And Gwen stared at the boy, shocked. She hadn't realized that there were people who voluntarily did less than their best at anything.

"WHY *AREN'T* YOU STUDYING?" THE same boy asked her. A spider spun a web on the ceiling. Boys on their bunks or sitting on the woven-rush floor-mats, all of them busy reading various copies of the same book, a book being a box of scrolls all belonging to the same work. The breeze coming in the window smelled nice, like summer, almost.

"I thought you wanted me not to work so hard?"

"That's not why you're not studying."

"I already read that book," she admitted, after a moment.

"The whole book? That's impossible, it was only assigned today."

"I read it two years ago. My foster-father owns a copy."

The boy laughed.

"Two years ago? That doesn't count! You are so gonna get it in the chapter discussion tomorrow!"

Gwen smiled.

GWEN DID NOT FIT IN. Even just standing around with the other cadets she was subtly but visibly different—like a rock in a creek, in the stream but not of it. And yet they liked her. She had a good supply of dirty jokes, could recite long passages from the heroic epics well, and would help anybody with homework who asked nicely. She could beat anybody at any strategy game ever, but she never gloated, and in fact she happily, even routinely, taught her opponents to improve their play. She seldom broke any rule on purpose but didn't tell on those who did. Her classmates figured that although she was weird and nobody knew what she was talking about half the time, she was basically a good kid.

As long as nothing happened to remind them that she was a girl.

THE FIRST-YEARS HAD BEEN doing stretches and calisthenic routines for weeks, but tomorrow they'd finally begin hand-to-hand combat training. Some of the guys in Gwen's dorm boasted and clowned around, excited, but as usual she didn't join in. She'd torn the seam of her tunic and had to mend it. Unlike the others, she could see well enough to thread a needle by candlelight.

"You can't train with us," one of the boys told her. "Real men train naked."

"I have skin under my clothes, same as you." She didn't bother to look at him. She'd already gotten permission to train clothed.

"But you're a girl, girls shouldn't disrobe around men. Things could happen!"

"If you make free with your sword," she said, still not looking up from her sewing, "then I shall make free with mine."

"Well, *that* escalated quickly," someone remarked.

"Bloody hell, I think she's serious," exclaimed another.

"Of course I'm serious. I'm an elf-blood. We have no sense of humor."

But she laughed telling the story to Chrys, her foster-sister and best friend, a week later, when she went home on her first leave.

"You *didn't*," Chrys said, laughing too. "What did he say to that? Did you get in trouble?"

"Oh, he flipped out, reported me up the chain of command, and I got hauled before the superintendent for threatening a comrade with a deadly weapon."

"Oh, Shepherd preserve us! But you obviously didn't get disciplined?"

"Yes, I did, I got another demerit for 'lack of personal neatness' or whatever." Gwen said it lightly, but she had idly picked up a dead yarrow stalk and now broke it half and flung the pieces, spinning, off into the strawberry patch with some violence. "But the superintendent said that if my comrades don't want me to murder them, then they should simply refrain from raping me, and he told me to carry on."

"That was sensible of him."

"I thought so."

She and Chrys were walking around and around in the garden, filling time until the evening when they would all go to the Caprine to see a new tragedy that was supposed be very good. Spring was getting on, the garden greening, the sun bright enough that Gwen wore a broad-brimmed hat to protect her sensitive gray eyes. The air was still cool, though. Chrys, shortish, narrow-faced, dark as a plum, and blue-eyed, was already dressed to go out in layers of silk and muslin. Being together again felt entirely normal and utterly strange at the same time.

"Are there any others like you there?" Chrys asked after a silence.

"Which of my various eccentricities do you mean? Any switchers? Any elf-bloods? Any redheads?" Totally color-blind, Gwen had been told how unusual her hair was often enough to get self-conscious about it.

"Um...."

"There isn't anyone else like me anywhere."

"Oh, you know what I mean."

"And you know what I mean."

"I'm sorry, I—"

"It's alright, Chrys. I don't feel weird when I'm with you. You're the only one."

"That's 'cause I'm almost as weird as you are." Chrysoberyl plucked a cluster of snow pea pods from a handy trellis and nibbled on the pods one after the other as she walked. "I just say my name and they look at me funny."

"What do you expect?" Gwen told her. "You don't believe in the divinity of the King."

"Neither do you."

"No, I don't believe in the *existence* of the King. There's a difference." There hadn't been a King of Nonani in hundreds of years, but the King had religious significance that nobody was really willing to do without, so everybody from the pontiffs on down went on praising the King and lighting incense to him and so forth just as if he still existed. You weren't supposed to remark on the discrepancy. Chrys giggled.

Chrysoberyl's name marked her as in some way related to the Aethenye pastoralists, who often named girls after minerals. They had been part of the Empire since the Empire had existed, the first barbarian people granted citizenship, and yet they remained outsiders in a way that more recent additions did not. Chrys's maternal grandfather had been Aethenye, but he'd died before most of his grandchildren were born. The family was culturally Itarye, except for the girls' names and their devotion to the singular Aethenye god. That there might be some reason for the tension between the Aethenye and the Itarye besides religious differences had not yet occurred to either teenager.

"I don't see why you don't just follow the Shepherd like we do," Chrys added.

"Because I don't want to."

"You know I'm not going to stop," Chrys warned. "I'm going to keep pushing you to accept the Shepherd your whole life long, if I have to."

Gwen stopped and turned, seizing the last two pea pods and eating them, brooking no protest, her eyes dancing.

"I'm looking forward to it," she told Chrys and then, not for the first time, kissed her.

THE STRANGEST THING ABOUT BEING home on leave was not having any chores. Gwen had always had chores—girl-chores at first, then later boy-chores. Tomas was a man of old-fashioned values, and though he employed servants, he never employed so many as to leave his family with nothing to do. Except now, being on vacation in her own home, Gwen had nothing she had to do. Her second day off, she escaped her feeling of uselessness and went for a walk.

Nonani City was bigger than any other in the known world, but still only six miles long and about four wide, so you could walk anywhere, provided you stayed out of the slums—construction there was so shoddy that four-and six-story tenement buildings would literally fall over with no notice. The soldiers of the city garrison, who functioned as a combined police and fire department, refused to patrol in such neighborhoods for fear of falling bricks, and pick-pockets and muggers gathered to take advantage. But the rest of the city was lovely for walking by daylight, the streets clean and tree-lined, the gardens and other public green-spaces well-kept and numerous. All the buildings were plain, boxy things of white stucco and red roof-tile, but this time of year they were all bright with flowers and foliage in window-boxes and roof-gardens, and in garlands around every door and window. Gwen walked four miles to the river district where Tomas's warehouse stood.

Tomas wouldn't be at the warehouse, the Ruling Council being in session, but Cheras, Cousin Topaz's new husband, and Cousin Euas were learning the business. Gwen went to go chat with them awhile. Then she meandered back more or less towards home, on the way stopping at one of the newshouses on the edge of the market at the Old Forum, where she was surprised to see an article about her oldest foster-brother, Davas, and several other young men being made tribune. Davas had been a tribune three months, and the article got most of his biographical details wrong. So much for *Accurate and Timely*, the motto over the door!

At the edge of the Old Forum, under the three hills at the center of the city, a spring welled up in a marble basin and spilled over, gurgling, into a pipe. The water came out of the pipe over on the other side of the forum as Otter Creek, running strong now after the winter rains. Once this spring had supplied all of Nonani's water, and its naiad, which is to say its soul, was still a friend to the Nonanye people. Gwen greeted the spring and drank with both hands. Then she jogged the long stairway up the steep, wooded embankment of holm oak and stone pine to Capitoline Hill and the aptly-named Upper Forum, the heart of the Empire.

No true market was ever held in the Upper Forum, though people sold snacks, wine, jars of sun-made herbal tea, and various cheap knickknacks from carts. Sometimes festivals were held in the space, often speeches were made, some by persons holding the proper permits, sometimes not. To help feed the spring below, the whole paved plaza graded subtly towards a retention pond surrounded by willows and attended by singing birds. Wind-chimes and sun-catchers hung from cast-iron stands. A big disc of polished granite set flat among the paving stones marked the center of the world, or at least the center of the Nonanye road system, the point to which all the mile-markers on all the properly-paved roads west of the Mountains referred. Huge, becolumned, marble-faced buildings—the Curia, the King's

House, the National Temple, the Treasury, and the National Library, all stood around the perimeter of the Forum, looking down upon gawking tourists, politically-minded gossips, old men playing chess or dominoes at little outdoor tables, and pigeons.

Every day around noon, the doors of the huge buildings would all open, and councilmen and military people, bankers, priests and priestesses, and all the various aides and novices would spill out into the Forum to grab some lunch and maybe a little wine in the warm, spring sunshine. Among them was Tomas.

Gwen found her foster-father, and together they bought pastries and honeyed mint tea.

One particular pigeon got their attention as they sat and talked. He had all-black feathers and no feet. How had he lost his feet? His legs ended only in lumps of calloused, pink flesh. He could walk, though not well, and spent most of his time sitting on the paving-stones as though incubating an imaginary egg. Tomas and Gwen speculated freely on the past and future of the poor bird, who noticed their regard and hobbled over hopefully. Soon, he was gobbling up a generous donation of pastry.

GWEN WOKE AT DAWN, WASHED and dressed for the day, and went downstairs to read in the library for a while. Most of the rest of the family sang hymns to the Shepherd in the garden. The servants came in with the groceries. Birds sang. After awhile she padded out across the cool, blue and white tiles of the atrium under a blue, spring-scented sky to the kitchen where Tomas waited for her. He didn't follow the Shepherd either. He put down his book and went to fetch a scoop of butter. The kitchen-maid, busy grinding flour for the day's bread, let them alone.

Gwen had to return to school that day.

She joined Tomas in making the offering, as she always had. But after he'd thrown the butter in the fire and they'd said the prayer to the guardians of home and storehouse, he held up a finger, a silent gesture of pause. He opened a basket and withdrew a goat kid, apparently dosed with either cannabis or opium to keep it calm and quiet. Handling the little animal gently, Tomas slit its throat and caught a handful of its blood to toss on the fire with a prayer to the Birds Three who had created and continued to guide the humankinds. Nonanye people did not sacrifice to propitiate or bribe their gods—gods do what gods do, whether humans will or no. Sacrifice was the ritual of humane slaughter of animals for food, and to honor both life and death in that way was to attune with the sacred, to offer gratitude, and to celebrate. And so, while the kid's blood hissed and spat on the burning charcoal, Tomas reached out his still-bloody hand and anointed Gwen's forehead, blessing her.

Gwen, the foster-kid who no longer believed she could be important, stood astonished.

GWEN WAS A STARTLINGLY GOOD student in an academic sense, and might have been first in her class, were it not for her growing list of demerits over stupid stuff she could not help, and a boy named Henras Hallas Cullan.

B'Hallas took all the same courses as Gwen, even the same electives, and did better than she at all of them except drawing. He never got any demerits, and so the staff liked him. He wanted the staff to like him, which was why he got no demerits. Everything he did was on purpose. It wasn't Gwen's style to resent his success—she'd always thought that if she were the smartest person in the room, she was in the wrong room—so she spent as much time in rooms with b'Hallas as she could. First-years were confined to their dorms for study period, but second-years weren't, and so in their second year Gwen began inviting b'Hallas to do his homework with her.

He was the round-faced boy she'd introduced herself to on her first day, older than the others because of a bout of polio (besides a slight oddity of his face and speech, he'd recovered completely), but slow to develop physically. Seventeen years old, and he'd only just now begun to sprout.

He lay sprawled across the foot of her bunk reading a history textbook and making notes on a wax tablet. Gwen sat near her pillow, knees curled under her chin, trying to work out a series of algebra problems with a wax tablet and a base-twelve elfish abacus. She wrote with her left hand while using her right to alternately operate the abacus and fiddle with her right third toe, the only one of her joints that could hyper-extend. She also chewed on her stylus.

You're gonna break your stylus, b'Hallas wrote in elfish. He passed his tablet over to Gwen.

Then I'll have twice as many, Gwen replied by the same medium. They often wrote to each other in ideograms, as if it were a secret code. They could have written notes in actual secret codes, they could both handle basic cryptography, now, but it would have annoyed the faculty. B'Hallas wrote I *bet I know one you don't know*, then added another ideogram. He handed over the tablet.

"That's not a real ideogram," Gwen announced, vocally. "There are six hundred and sixty-two, and that's not one of them."

"It's an ideogram, but it's not an *elfish* ideogram," he corrected her. "That's Icthanish. The Icthanye live far to the east of the Mountains in the high steppe there. Supposedly, they're total badasses. They do everything on horseback, and they're building an empire as big as ours. People worth talking to."

"And they're not elves?"

"Nope. They're...like me, I guess." He was savvy enough not to refer to his own species as *normal people* around Gwen, but he did not know a better name. Neither did she.

"So what's it mean?" Gwen asked, examining the symbol.

"Don't know, yet. My father got a book written in Icthanish from one of his clients. I want to learn how to read it. They've got an Icthanish dictionary at the library here, supposedly, but I haven't found it yet."

The Nonanye people had not yet invented a standardized library shelving system.

"B'Sheras and b'Hallas sitting in a tree..." sing-songed another cadet from his own bunk, just as he would have if Gwen were a boy.

"Jealous?" But her blushing—obvious with her pale skin—undermined the retort. The other boy guffawed.

Of course it wasn't like that. She could not be with a real boy, and anyway both she and b'Hallas had girlfriends back home. When she thought she could do so without blushing again, Gwen looked over at him. His dark face was becoming squarish and manly. His eyes were not the typical blue but a very clear brown shot through with light, like the waters of a tannin-rich stream. No, Gwen thought, even if all the other reasons were not present, she wouldn't want b'Hallas in that way—mere sex would ruin it.

B'Hallas gazed back, faintly amused.

DID GWEN HAVE A GIRLFRIEND back home? She and Chrys had never actually discussed their status. And yet who else could either have been with? Each had just always been there for the other. When Chrys caught smallpox while away staying with cousins, Gwen worried herself into a state until she decided—and it felt quite rational—that everything was fine because nothing bad could ever happen to Chrys. The world might be falling apart, and sometimes Gwen convinced herself that it was, but Chrys would always be OK.

When next they saw each other, Chrys gestured sadly at her newly-scarred face and said "if you don't want me anymore, I'll understand." Gwen just told her not to be an idiot.

IN GWEN'S THIRD YEAR, THERE was a new professor with a strange name, Jerioniress ni Saranassiryr. He was pale as moonlight, straight-haired, beardless (not merely clean-shaven), and so slim and slight she wondered if he might be a switcher until she heard his voice. Despite all that, it took Gwen weeks to realize the man was an elf. She had so many questions after that, she dared not speak to him lest they all tumble out at once and make her look a fool.

The other cadets didn't care about Jerioniress's species, nor did they warm to him personally. He seldom encouraged warmth, and when he did, it didn't work. "His timing is off," as b'Hallas put it. That he rarely made eye contact did not help. But he was a more than competent teacher of an interesting group of related subjects, and his passion for his work was infectious.

What was his work?

"He's a scientist," b'Hallas told another cadet, rather tartly.

"Yeah, I know, but what is that?"

"Someone who practices science," b'Hallas explained. Gwen at least could admit to not knowing. The next time the course met, somebody asked.

Jerioniress grinned. He hadn't been hired to teach science, only some of the information science had produced, and he was clearly delighted by the question—which he answered with another question.

"What do you *think* science is?"

The class discussed the matter for a while. Nobody had the right answer, but Jerioniress didn't seem to mind. He liked hearing their thoughts.

"Actually," he said at last, "science might be easier to explain to you than to students in most other schools." He let that sit a moment before dropping one of the counter-intuitive nuggets that seemed to make him happy. "Oh, yes. Science was invented by soldiers."

What?

"Well, science is just a branch of philosophy, and all the first philosophers were retired military in one or another of the Shonye cities on the other side of the Mountains. Think about it. Say someone comes to you and tells you there are barbarians attacking the city gates. Somebody else tells you there aren't. What do you do? Do you debate the symbolism of barbarian attacks, compare the themes and inner meanings of the incident to powerful passages in the great epics? Do you search for truth by noticing which story resonates more deeply with your personal *feelings*?"

The cadets laughed with him.

"No!" he continued. "*You go find out.* Finding out through repeatable, shareable observation and empirical reasoning is just plain intelligent if you're a soldier, and it's the essence of science."

There was a long moment of silence. A cadet spoke up.

"Repeatable, shareable—that means I see something, I can go look at it again to be sure, or I can show somebody else, right?"

"Right. Otherwise, you know nothing. Not knowing's not bad, but the key is to admit to not knowing. Don't just make stuff up."

"But that eliminates most of religion!" objected the cadet.

"I can say an apple's not a citron without speaking against apples, can't I? But if you want a citron, an apple ain't gonna cut it."

After that, it became something of a game among the cadets to start every class meeting by asking if this or that was science. Jerioniress tried to explain that the phrasing of the question made any answer misleading, but he couldn't stop the game, so he played along.

What about Nona?

What about naiads?

I heard the moon is made of water, and all water comes from there.

My grandfather had a dream that if he slept in bed with his girlfriend for a month without having sex with her, his seed would become so potent he could use it to cure his tuberculosis—and he did. He's still alive now. He's not sick. Does that count as empirical?

No, no, no, and not exactly.

"So, I guess trees can't really talk, can they?" asked a cadet one morning, confident in his new and clever cynicism.

"No, actually that one's true," Jeriorniress said, happy to pierce another misconception. "Trees *communicate*, anyway. And forests make weather."

What?

He explained that many plants can communicate with each other through joined-together roots or by subtle scents passed through the air—and by scent they can also communicate with animals, for example calling for help when attacked by caterpillars.

"Other insects, wasps and so forth, smell the call for help and come running. Or, uh, flying, I guess. Humans can pick up many of these scents, by the way. We're in the conversation."

Making weather, though?

"Oh, sure. Everybody knows trees provide shelter, that's a kind of small-scale weather change, but it makes a difference. Streams that lose their forest cover lose most of their fish because the water gets too warm in the summer. But forests also make rain. Soil moisture that would otherwise drain away gets drawn up by plants and released from their leaves as invisible vapor. Water-vapor is what clouds are made of. More clouds, more rain. But each rain-drop in a cloud forms around a tiny particle—too small to see—and a lot of those particles are released by plants and sent up into the sky. More particles means larger clouds. So, again, more rain. In some places, for every ten parts of rain, seven parts would not be there if it were not for large forests."

Nobody asked how Jeriorniress knew about things too small to see. Gwen, for one, did not think to ask because she had another question on her mind—but b'Hallas said it before she could.

"So if a big-enough forest gets cut down…less than half as much rain falls after that?"

Jeriorniress snapped his fingers and pointed at the cadet who'd gotten it right.

Gwen tried to attend at least one of his courses every year. She liked the material, but she also wanted to be simply near him. She wanted to know what being an elf actually meant. But she never asked her many questions. She came close only once, when in her fifth year she approached him after class about one of his books.

"I didn't think that one had been translated," Jeriorniress said.

"It hasn't. I can read elfish ideograms. I can write them, too."

"Good for you. I know they offer reading and writing here as an elective."

"That's how I learned," Gwen explained. "I've taken it every year. I wish they'd teach speaking as well. I know there are multiple elfin languages, but they could just pick one. It would aid comprehension. Learning to write without being able to say what I'm writing is nuts."

"You couldn't say what you're writing anyway. No elfin spoken language is closely related to our written language—it's a written version of intercultural manual sign, completely independent. But your point is well-taken. The academy should teach some of the basics of elfin culture."

"Was that my point?" Gwen asked, fidgeting with the hem of her tunic. "I don't think that was my point. But it's a good point, so I wish I'd made it. I'd like to learn more about elfin culture generally. I don't even know which language my mother—she was the elf—spoke."

Jeriorniress seemed startled, then thoughtful.

"Well, maybe I can help?" he offered. "If I knew a few names from your family, I might be able to recognize what language they spoke."

"My mother was Ellianiine. My brothers were—are—Paracelias and Micalion. Gwenessifyr's an elfin name, too. But I don't know any ni-whatever, like your name has."

Jeriorniress smiled at that.

"The part after the ni is just the matrilinial. Saranassiryr is my mother. So. Ellianiine, Paracelias, Micalion, Gwenessifyr…. That could be Catharish. They mostly speak Catharish in the enclave in southwestern Parsia. Does that sound familiar?"

"I don't know."

"Well, it's going to be either that or Elnarish, and they're related, so if you learn either, you'll be closer to knowing your mother's language than you are now. Or you could learn manual sign. Most of us know at least a little of it."

He made a curious gesture with his hands, and Gwen yelped in recognition. His hands and face had briefly resembled the ideogram for *comprehension* with the second-person interrogative modifier.

"Yes, I do," she replied, vocally.

"They're not all that easy to decipher," Jerioniress said, smiling again, "But you'll get it." He wished her good-day and walked off. But he hadn't answered her question about his book.

FOURTH-YEAR CADETS AND ABOVE were eligible to become "officers" assigned to keep the underclassmen in line, but Gwen's application was rejected. They said she had "poorly-developed leadership and social skills." Really she'd become quite outgoing, but the staff mistook her fidgety weirdness for social awkwardness. Gwen didn't realize she was fidgety or weird, so that wasn't the funny part for her. The funny part was them doubting her leadership skills—because of course they didn't know about the after-hours parties.

Rules were made to be followed precisely, she knew that. Except Gwen had also realized that some rules were quite literally made to be broken. A cadet who had what it took to lead in the field also had what it took to have some fun at the academy and not get caught. The staff played the game for keeps—you could get expelled—but then the game would be for keeps after graduation as well. And so while the parties were never Gwen's own idea, she did help put them together, sourcing supplies, maintaining security, coordinating all the different steps to make the adventure happen. She came close to getting caught only once, when her stash of stolen wine was discovered, but two hundred and fifty teenagers all willingly lost their free time for the rest of the term rather than give Gwen up.

How's that for leadership skill?

WHEN THEY DID HAVE FREE time, the cadets played ball or borrowed horses and went out into the scrub and woodland beyond campus to hunt, explore, or just mess around in small groups. There was a rule against going alone. Most wanted Gwen to be part of their group, partly because they liked her, but also because she never got lost. If in wandering they accidentally covered two sides of a rough triangle, she would lead them back to campus by completing the triangle, even in completely unfamiliar territory, by sheer mental geometry. As a city kid, Gwen had gone on hunting trips with Tomas and the boys, but she'd never had the opportunity to just wander about before. She loved it. In her first two years as a cadet, she even spent some of her leave-weeks backpacking on foot with Jonas and his girlfriend. Now that Jonas had graduated (and married) and was off commanding his century somewhere, she went out backpacking on her leave weeks by herself.

The rule about not going out alone couldn't possibly apply when she was on leave, she'd reasoned that out carefully, and anyway the rule was supposedly because of all the dangerous wild beasts—and Gwen didn't think wild beasts were all that dangerous.

In heroic tales, the red manticores, the laughing crocottas, the dragons whose bites burned like fire and would never heal, all of them had to be *sought out* by the hero. The beasts might prey on unwary children or defenseless old women or the unblemished white buckling the pious farmer had been saving for sacrifice—heroes never went off on heroic adventures without some sort of reason—but a strong, well-armed man made the monsters run away. That's why the hero always needed to procure a net woven by derger, or a spear forged by elves under the light of the moon, or the advice of the dryad of the oldest and wisest tree in the forest simply to catch the beast. If the old stories had any basis in truth at all, the most dangerous species were human.

And so Gwen, a dangerous beast, went out with a pilum, a bow, and a full quiver, but she never used the pilum as anything but a walking-stick, and the bow and quiver was so she could hunt hares and ptarmigan for her dinner. She went fearlessly, cutting across the summer-dun hills mile after mile, often by starlight, listening to the singing of jackals and wolves and the eerie hoots and shrieks of owls. By day, when the bright sunlight hurt her eyes, she slept or sometimes curled up in the shade of a leaning willow or a spinny of crab-apple or holly and watched, forgetting herself and going, for once in her life, so utterly still that other animals forgot her, too. Mosquitoes did not bite. Birds flew carelessly to their nests. Foxes called their kits to dinner, and a lynx interrupted its very dignified business to scratch its ear with one foot and then play with a dead leaf.

And once a family of aurochs stepped out of their own version of invisible nowhere and made themselves real.

It was a bull, two cows, and three half-grown calves. The cows and calves were a warm, rich brown, except for their pale, narrow muzzles and a long, pale stripe down their spines. The larger of the two cows stood almost five feet tall at the hump of her shoulder, and her horns curved like those of the moon. The bull made the cows look small. He was a foot taller and probably twice the weight, utterly black but for his muzzle and stripe, just as utterly white, his coat sleek and shiny but for the curly lock on his forehead. And for all his size, his long legs, the supreme rightness of his build, gave him a beauty and grace no domestic bovine could approach.

Aurochs were known to be extremely intelligent, bad-tempered, and faster than anything that big had any right to be. These were so close that Gwen could hear the swish of the long grass around their legs as they walked, hear the buzzing of the flies that followed them, flies hunted in turn by four small, gold and white egrets. The aurochs looked up, sniffed the air in her direction, and decided she wasn't there at all. She could hear the rip and snap of grass blades as they bit and chewed.

THROUGH ALL THE YEARS OF her schooling, Gwen remained popular, achievement-oriented, and successful. She gained proficiency with every weapon offered her, but she chose the katana to master. Most officers preferred the spatha, a longer weapon that could be used with a shield. A good spatha-user would beat a good katana user more often than not. But the katana was potentially the faster, more adaptable sword, and Gwen did not intend to be merely good.

She could think and move faster than anybody. She was still taller than most of the rest of her class. The boys soon all out-weighed her and could out-lift her, and beating them at boxing and wrestling got harder and harder, but she still won most of the time because she trained herself mercilessly. Any suggestion that she tone it down for her own health elicited a scoff. Any suggestion that she do so because she was a girl triggered an almost violent rage even she did not understand. Gwen still didn't know the difference between imperfection and failure.

Chapter 3. Hyras

Year of Nonani 822 - 824

Hyras didn't want to join the army, but he did it anyway, as there wasn't really anything else he wanted to do for a living.

Oh, there were things he liked. He liked horses. He liked their warm, comforting largeness, their quirky and variable personalities, their absolute absence of pretense. A cow could plot against you, and might, if you bothered her, but a horse wouldn't. A person might demand something of you, but a horse couldn't. And he liked riding. It was like being alone and having a companion at the same time, the two of you moving along together through the dry, shrubby landscape beyond the farms outside of town, where you could see forever over and through the low, dun hills, and the scents of laurel or rosemary would come up into your face as the foliage brushed against your mount's chest or your own legs. In the winter, when it rained, he liked lying in the hayloft and staring up at the underside of the roof, finding form-fantasies in the knots and swirls of the wood and thinking about things. He liked going down to the river where the laurels grew tall among the oaks and the olives, and the water slipped by, green and cool and slow. The river was never exactly the same way twice. Sometimes he brought a fishing pole or a spear, to justify his excursion, but while he was reasonably good at fishing and certainly enjoyed eating fish, that wasn't the point. The point was to sit on the river-bank and do nothing at all but watch the world happen.

But his father was on his case to make something of himself, and becoming a soldier beat working in the family's tannery where every-thing smelled of blood and chemicals.

And so, one winter day just after Hilaria, sixteen-year-old Hyras Sylas Kylan walked away from the little farm his father rented, the lit-tle three-room house, the cow pasture, the hayfield, the cropfield and the vegetable beds, and the barn and corrals where the family boarded horses as a sideline, and he walked for half the afternoon until he got to the recruiting office in downtown Dalani.

The process proved very simple, just a few forms to fill out, a medical exam, and a hair-cut. Then they issued him uniforms (one to wear, one to wash) and gear and told him to report for training in the morning.

Sitting on his bed in the hostel, he examined his new things—an undyed, sleeveless tunic, a blanket of red, unwashed (and therefore waterproof) griffin wool, and a pair of hobnailed sandals that curled up over the toes. The blanket came with a plain bronze fibula so he could pin it, doubled-over, around his shoulders by day. Drawstring leggings, arm wraps, and stockings would keep him warm. There was also an over-tunic of inch-thick griffin leather with a heavy belt and a mail shirt, greaves, arm-guards, and a simple, cork-lined helmet, all of shiny steel. They'd given him a pack frame, two canteens, and a rucksack, but no weapons. He supposed they'd be issued later.

Hyras had seen soldiers before and always thought them very fine-looking in their red wool and bright armor, but they'd always seemed like creatures from another world, nothing to do with him or with anything real. He reached out a hand and touched his new tunic, almost a petting motion, as he might touch a new, and possibly not entirely tamed animal. His home was only a few miles away, and if he got up now and started walking, he could be there in time to get some sleep before breakfast. He touched the tunic again. Home was a million miles away, and there was no going back.

In the morning, he and a few other recent enlistees walked to-gether out to the training camp on the edge of the local fort. The soldiers escorting them taught them funny songs along the way, and the weather, while cold, was at least dry, so the long walk was not unpleasant.

Basic Training was a calculated brutality. Everything had to be exactly so, and everybody had to be exactly the same. They didn't call it a war machine for nothing. Hyras did not want to become part of a machine, but he understood that the machine had to exist and that he had joined it. He knew, too, that a large part of war must consist of coping with unpleasant things, and that the drill sergeant was being unpleasant on purpose in order to teach them to cope. You just had to detach from your emotions, not let your fear, your anger, or anything else kick out the way your leg used to kick out when your brothers poked your knee on purpose. Hyras had learned that lesson pretty well already. He put up with the drill sergeant.

Over the next days and weeks, he and the others learned the somewhat technical terminology of military orders and got in the habit of obedience. He learned the use of the soldier's primary weapons, the short sword called gladius and the big, rectangular scutum shield, the iron-headed pilum, and the little plumbata darts. He and the others trained their bodies to exhausted excellence and drilled formations until the movements no longer required any thought. He got used to doing everything in a squad of eight (plus two squad-bosses) where each man looked out for his buddies and the whole squad would be either punished or rewarded together. They cleaned and maintained the camp, took turns standing watch, and tried to stay out of the way of the other classes of new recruits at other points in the training process.

Hyras didn't mind the work. For all his dreamy fondness of lying around doing nothing, he was not lazy, and while he was short and still not entirely pubesced, he showed signs of becoming stocky, well-proportioned, and strong.

"Did you notice there was no test?" remarked one of the other guys in Hyras's squad, grinning. They were all busy mopping the huge, wooden floor of the mess hall. "Except for the medical exam, they didn't check anything or ask anything. They'll take anybody. It's because they go through so many soldiers, dying and so forth, they have to have a constant new supply."

"You're probably right," Hyras acknowledged. "Or at least half-right. There may be other reasons."

The young man stared.

"You aren't scared?" The jaded bravado was gone. They were all just teenagers.

"No, why should I be?" answered Hyras. "What good would it do?"

As it turned out, there were tests, they just came in the middle, not the beginning. Guys who couldn't humble themselves enough to follow orders were out. Guys who showed signs of breaking under the verbal abuse were out. Guys who couldn't learn the skills or couldn't think for themselves while also following orders were out. Guys who showed signs of an un-soldierly compassion were out. There was one day when a fellow who'd been caught stealing extra food was hauled before the rest of the class and tied to a post. Everybody had to take the whip once and give a lash. Twenty-three lashes, one from each man, full range of motion, hard as you could hit. That sort of thing causes permanent scars. It can cause organ damage. The petty thief was sent home, but so was every man who'd hesitated to whip him.

Hyras understood that lesson, too. He graduated with his class. As long as he was going to be a soldier, he'd made up his mind to be a good one.

After Basic, they all marched two days to the nearest army base. It looked like a small city, with houses, gardens, orchards, small woodlots, and an outer ring of farmland. There were shops, baths, libraries, a gymnasium, two fora, and a sizable civilian population. At first, it seemed as if the place differed from a normal city only in its name, Lucasi, which honored a man (some war hero, presumably) rather than a founding matriline. But then the new soldiers reached Lucasi's city center and found it a dense complex of tents, tarps, sheds, and unlovely block buildings, the whole thing capable of housing and feeding, besides a permanent garrison, up to two full legions. A legion meant not just soldiers but also baggage managers, animals, blacksmiths, doctors, cooks, prostitutes, and everybody else that thousands of men together might need. The base was all set up in nice, straight lines and run by set procedures and rules that you could look up in your own copy of the manual if ever you forgot. Very well organized. Even the prostitutes were organized through the Prefect's Staff, professionals in every sense of the word, mostly women but also some adolescent boys, beautiful yet discrete, and examined every month by a doctor according to regulation.

Hyras was intrigued by the prostitutes, but didn't think he wanted to go make their acquaintance just yet. He was only sixteen.

Hyras found himself the only new member in a squad of guys all at least two years older than him—the oldest was almost thirty. Most were proletarians and spoke in the fast, poetic creole of the children of barbarians and slaves. The others were plebeians like Hyras, but no two had exactly the same accent. Communication depended on a common tongue of technical jargon and camp slang that Hyras had to learn in a hurry. But the ritualistic abuse of Basic was over, and the guys were basically friendly and helpful, provided you showed proper deference to the bosses and did your work well.

Every morning, they would wake to the sound of horns and hurry through a hygienic routine and mandatory praise of the divine (and imaginary) King—shit, shave, and shout, as they said. Then breakfast of wheat porridge with nuts, honey, and chopped prunes. An army has to stay regular. Then would come a meeting of the whole century, a group of ten squads, to learn the plan of the day from their centurion, who had in turn been briefed by the tribune, who himself took orders from the Legate. The Legate commanded the whole legion, but took orders from one or the other consul, who in turn reported to the speaker of the Senate, who was ultimately responsible to the Nonanye people and to the gods.

Ten squads per century, ten centuries per cohort, six cohorts per legion, with the members of each category numbered in linear order so that any two men meeting would know which out-ranked the other, hopefully precluding any conflict. Your place in the order had to be earned and could be changed, up or down. Hyras belonged to the seventh squad of the third century of the second Heavy-Infantry cohort. He would have preferred one of the Horse Cavalry centuries, but none needed recruits at the time. He rarely spoke to his centurion directly, hardly knew his tribune, and while the name of the Legate, Shaddas Geras Miran, was nearly as important as that of the King would have been, had there been an actual king with a name, he wouldn't have recognized the fellow without the yellow legate's uniform. Being a milite not an officer meant basically not knowing what was going on.

After the meeting was calisthenics, then either a work detail or further training. Dinner was usually bean-and-vegetable stew with bread and posca, then more training or some kind of camp or equipment maintenance. Supper was your own responsibility, if you wanted any, and then you could sit around the fire with your squad, drinking your wine ration, singing or telling stories or dirty jokes, and then, unless you were assigned watch, you could go find your tarp, unfold your cloak and wrap up in it, and sleep on the ground a few hours, if the night wasn't too cold. Next day, repeat.

Hyras didn't know how to make friends, but he kept his head down, did his work, and the others learned they could rely on him. Grimness or sadness seemed to be the default option for his face, but catch his attention somehow and half his face would quirk up into a shy grin. Or an eyebrow—only ever just the one—would go up. A few people could get him to laugh. He had a lovely, infectious laugh, inappropriately loud at first, then dribbling away into wheezes and chuckles. When he wasn't laughing, that usually meant he was telling a joke, and if you didn't get that it *was* a joke, he'd think that was even funnier, and everybody would laugh amiably at what an idiot you must be.

As spring became summer, the work details were more often away from the base. One of the older branches of the telegraph system ran within a few hours' march and needed maintenance. There was a flood-control dam in a nearby town that had failed and needed to be reconstructed. And so on. Every day, one or more centuries of men would march out in this direction or that to do what needed to be done. Keeping order. Maintaining civilization.

But in late summer, word came that a Duchesye city called Argessi was not showing due respect.

Duchasa, the region defined by the use of the various dialects of Duchesh, spread across the whole of the upper Old Mother River watershed. Its southern portions had been conquered and made into the Nonanye province of Duchasia almost two hundred years ago, but the rest, called barbarian Duchasa because its residents weren't citizens, was made up of hundreds of small, sovereign kingdoms to whom Nonani professed peaceful respect and an interest in mutually beneficial trade. With favored trading partners, the Ruling Council negotiated mining and logging concessions and ever-expanding market access. Next came offers to build aqueducts, roads, stadiums, libraries, and other infrastructure at a very reasonable price. And since the world is a dangerous place, Nonani would even offer to build military bases, extending its shield to protect its new friends. Of course, should one of these friends in any way act against Nonanye interests....

Argessi was a major trading hub in one such friendly kingdom. Because it had a large Nonanye expat community, the city received some support services from Nonani and therefore owed allegiance— and taxes—to both the Nonanye Senate and the local king. But just recently the city had gotten seriously behind in its taxes to Nonani. Inquiries revealed that the king was still being paid. The Ruling Council had begun discussing the situation when it received a delegation from the king who, terrified of reprisals, was eager to turn over his share of Argessi's tax revenue and to rat out the little city for having formed its own Senate.

Somebody would have to go and gently remind Argessi who had built its aqueduct and its sewage treatment plant.

The several legions currently stationed near Argessi were all busy, unavailable for reassignment. And so Hyras and the rest of his legion packed up their kits and walked north for two months.

It was not a stroll or a hike but an organized march. Sixteen men walking abreast (two squads), then, behind them, four men (squad leaders and seconds), then sixteen again, each century moving in a block separated from the ones in front and behind by neat gaps. Centurions, standard-bearers, and signal-blowers walked in their own line at the back of their century, but tribunes, the Legate, and their various aids rode horseback where they pleased. The Prefect's Staff and everybody and everything associated with it formed a massive baggage train that started each day's march only after everybody else had left, so they could pack up, then formed a narrower, slightly faster second column that passed the others and ended up in front by the end of the day, ready to make camp before the others arrived.

And as all these people marched, they sang.

Each century sang the same song together, led by the Squad-Second of the first squad in the group, and every song had the same rhythm, meter, and length. The songs helped pass the time, but they also kept everybody marching in step—the simultaneous landing of over five thousand feet formed a vast drumming—and therefore taking strides of exactly the same consistent length at always the same consistent speed. And so each song meant a mile walked. A day's march was twenty songs, from one cramped and crowded fort or base to the next along wide, neatly-paved roads. The Empire was designed for efficient troop movement as well as for commerce.

There were thrilling, patriotic songs for use when walking through settled areas, but where civilians got few, the songs got dirty:

My wife's ass is nice and tight!
If she knew I'd said so, we would fight.
We would fight and she would win!
Success depends on dis-cre-tion

King's men, honor bound
King's men, glory bound

Then they got dirtier:

My wife's cunt is long and deep!
'Cause she fucks other men when I am asleep.
That's OK, cause I hear 'em move,
And I jump right up and fuck 'em, too.

King's men, honor bound
King's men, glory bound
When we arrive, you all fall down!

And so on.

The songs were like the whippings, Hyras decided: educational.

After the first week, they walked out of the aromatic shrublands and the dry, rugged woodlands of laurel and olive, oak and holly and pine, and entered a new landscape, a taller, darker forest of broader, more delicate leaves. They had left Itara and entered Duchasia. Most of the people still spoke Itarish, at least as a second language, and the cities and bigger towns had theaters and stadiums, gymnasiums, and libraries, just as in the heartland. But, except for the garrisons and some of the bases, the cities had no walls, only wide, brick-lined moats around low, brick-faced, earthen mounds. All the public buildings and most of the private ones were built atop low hills or artificial earthen mounds rising above the floodplains of the ropy, winding rivers that once in every generation would jump out of their annual floodplains and cover everything as far as the eye could see in brown, muddy, kelpie-haunted water.

And away from the cities and towns and farms the forest grew, a juicy, riotous, well-watered forest of deciduous oaks and chestnuts and hickories, lindens and beeches and apples, hemlocks and black pines, trees so large that they made a green ceiling over the broad road, trees growing since before Nonani's founding, over eight hundred years ago.

Hyras had grown up in a rural area, but not a wild one. There were deer and boar, bears and wolves in the hills at home, of course, and sometimes someone would lose a few calves to a lion, but the other, larger beasts had mostly been hunted out and become the stuff of legends. The lion-like manticore, with its red fur and long, curved teeth, the yeti, a mostly-vegetarian bear people spoke of almost as a man, even tarpan and bison and the fiercely beautiful aurochs had become rare. They were all myths, fantastic stories, and yet they moved through the forests that Hyras now also moved through, passing behind the huge trunks like dreams.

As autumn came on, the birds stopped singing, reverting to simple cries and occasional cheeps, but crickets played on through the days and half of the nights. The wolves sang, too, moaning, wild songs, rising and falling in irregular chorus, and the trees slowly turned every color in the world.

They passed through and out of Duchasia and then through one after another barbarian kingdom until the forest changed again, the oaks and lindens and hemlocks dropping out, replaced by pale, golden-leaved birches and the tall spires of spruces and silver fir.

At last they reached Argessi, finding it fortified after the manner of Itarye cities. The legion camped in and around the fort nearest the city, settling in for the winter, which came early in this far northern country. If the city did not come to its senses by the summer campaigning season, the legion would tear down its flimsy walls.

That winter, more snow fell than Hyras could ever remember seeing. For months at a time all precipitation was snow, never rain, and it piled up and never melted, and little dry drifts of it would go swirling around the corners of buildings and between the poles of tarp-shelters. The fort's garrison issued straw-stuffed mattresses, not for softness but to insulate the men from the killing cold of the frozen ground. Hyras wore both his sets of clothes and a second cloak to sleep in, and he woke to find that the moisture of his breath had frozen upon the outside of his cloak like snow.

In the snow squads would patrol, walking through whitened, silent spruce forests and stubbly, cut-over fields, looking for people from the city who might be out collecting firewood or hunting hares. These people would be stopped and spoken to, questioned—never unkindly, always politely, just a subtle and pervasive show of force. Sometimes patrols were attacked, not by soldiers but by groups of adolescents or young men frustrated and angry and acting without orders from above. They were well-armed and often fearless, and they knew how to move in the snow. Hyras was in some of these attacks, but he kept his head, protected his squad-mates, and got in his first few kills. He noticed the Legate kept his head, too, not ordering reprisals, not letting gangs of teenagers goad him into a war in bad weather or when war might still be avoided.

Spring arrived. The cold began to abate, the frogs began to sing in icy puddles of snow-melt, and Hyras was made a squad-second, that is, the more junior of a pair of squad bosses. He was absurdly young for it, and had only been in the army for a year, but no one objected or complained.

The weather warmed, herbs and trees and grasses all began to flower. Half the guys in Hyras' squad began to sneeze. Birds sang, sometimes so loudly and so beautifully that you had to raise your voice to be heard, or, better yet, you didn't talk, only listened. And the Legate sent the city a politely-worded ultimatum. Was Argessi prepared to be Nonani's friend or its enemy?

The guard at the gate who took this message said he was empowered to provide his city's response and gave a prepared statement. It wasn't polite.

The attack began with the use of a newly-built trebuchet to lob barrels of water over the city walls. The barrels were the empties from a winter of six thousand people (including the various non-combat personnel) drinking wine and posca, and water is both cheap and heavy. The trebuchet's range exceeded that of the arrows of the defenders by close to two hundred feet, and so the legion could attack with impunity. The men of the city soon poured out of the gates to try to stop the bombardment, and then Hyras got to know what it is to press forward in formation, your shield protecting the man to your left while the man to your right protects you, and you reach forward through the gap and hack at other men with your gladius, the arrows raining down on you all the time making a horrible, singing whistle like the wind of a terrible storm, and men dying all around you fast or slow, the smell of the bloody mud and the sound of the signal-horns near and close, their blasts coded orders keeping everything organized. It was glorious, in a way, being part of something so large and so tight and so terrible that Hyras forgot to be Hyras for a little while and became, simply, a pair of arms belonging to the legion.

Afterwards, of course, he puked and had nightmares and struggled for days not to cry. But you had to harden yourself. You couldn't be the little boy hiding from the scent of death and the sounds of suffering while your father slaughtered bull calves. You just couldn't.

After three days of intense fighting before the city gates, the city's senators surrendered and saved their people.

Everybody expected the Legate to have the false and rebellious senators garroted. That would be the normal Nonanye procedure, but Legate b'Geras made a little speech to the crowds in the main forum about how the city had shown good sense and humility, and so he was pardoning everybody. He explained that he had received authority from the Ruling Council to bolster the local garrison with two of his own cohorts, the senior tribune of which had been made a legate by the Council and would serve as the city's governor until order could be fully restored.

Hyras learned from older soldiers that b'Geras was not being magnanimous, nor was he particularly impressed by the good sense, et cetera, of the city leaders. He certainly wasn't known for gentleness with his own people. Legate b'Geras had simply judged mercy a cheaper way to buy compliance in this instance. Although it wasn't Hyras' place to have an opinion about command decisions, he had opinions anyway, and privately thought the Legate was right.

The legion and the city gathered up their dead, or at least the larger pieces of their dead, competing in their gathering with wheeling flocks of hungry, crying ravens, this being too far north for vultures. Behind and through the birds came, invisibly, the Raven, to guide the invisible aspect of the dead. The living cut wood for pyres and for the wooden coins to give the dead to pay the Ferryman. Great plumes of smoke went up, and the ravens kept crying, circling around the smoke. Then Hyras was made squad-boss, to replace one of those lost. Again, nobody complained. The full legion stayed for a few more months to help rebuild the city and to give injured soldiers time to heal and rest. By the time they got back to Lucasi Base, it was almost winter again.

No new work was pressing, and the legion had been more or less engaged for two years straight, so the men were given leave to go home for the Fallow, that empty period of the year outside the calendar between the festivals of Natalia and Hilaria.

Hyras found it strange to be out of uniform, to sleep in a bed, to be able to go take a shit without having to tell a buddy where he was going. He hadn't realized how his language had coarsened until, on his second day back, he accidentally cursed in front of his mother.

His family was glad to see him, and he them—his brothers, both married and living in town, had come home for a few weeks just to be with him. His father, who had always been fair, if not generous or supportive, praised Hyras' promotion. Everybody asked admiring questions about army life. He relaxed. He went fishing and riding and helped his mother, Ana, dig manure into the garden during a long break in the winter rains. Hyras hadn't had a *bad* childhood, not exactly, but he'd heard other soldiers talk about their families weeping when they went off to war, and no one in Hyras's family had ever wept for him. And he'd forgotten how distant, how prickly, all of them were, all except Ana, who was never cruel or impatient but utterly lacked apparent affection for anybody. Her first words to her son in two years were not even any version of *hello* but, simply, "you want anything to eat?" When his leave was up, he was secretly glad to go.

On his return to Base, he learned that his legion had been reassigned to a base in Parsia, there to receive and train replacements for those either lost at Argessi or left at the garrison. The reason they'd been sent to Parsia was that an industrial village there, short-handed after an outbreak of malaria, had asked for help. So while most of the legion stayed at the base, one cohort—Hyras'—went to camp near and work alongside the villagers.

Hyras thought the forest around the village looked very much like that of Duchasia, but somewhat drier and more open. The soil was very sandy, yet so flat that streams and pools easily spread out into black swamps of water-cypress, tupelo, alder, and willow. Uplands were mostly chestnut and oak, where they hadn't yet been logged off for charcoal. If you could find a high, open place from which to look, you could see the High Mountains in the distance. The people lived in longhouses and mostly spoke Ranish as a first language, but they all had at least some Itarish, and seemed mostly normal, except that they ate horse meat. The village itself had no name but Furnace Complex Three.

Six tall, stone towers—the furnaces—stood in a row along the stream bank. Men would fan out into the surrounding swamps to collect the bog-iron that slowly but continuously formed around springs, while other men made charcoal. The bog-iron, charcoal, and quantities of shells brought up the stream on barges all went into the towers from the top, while the fires inside were continually fed fresh air by bellows powered by water-wheels. Great belches of smoke and flame and heat spouted constantly from the towers, shining in the sweaty faces of the men running up the ramps pushing laden wheelbarrows, and making what would have been a pleasant stream-side spot hellish.

Every so often, a man would open a port at the base of one of the towers, and the molten metal would flow out, glowing, into a trench that fed a series of perpendicular trenches in which the iron would cool into brittle, black pig-iron, so called because the arrangement of trenches reminded somebody of a sow suckling her piglets. The finished pigs would go out on the barges, but where they went next, how they became steel, nobody in the village knew or cared. Why should they? Except for the plebeian shopkeepers and doctor and their families, they were all proletarians, illiterate and powerless. As the weather warmed and the forest greened, clouds of mosquitoes came out of the swamp so dense that the very air hummed and prickled.

Nobody knew what caused malaria, but elfin scientists had confirmed that spending too much time near stagnant water was a major risk factor. So Hyras and the others not only worked with the few healthy villagers to keep the furnace running but also helped rebuild the entire town on higher, drier ground. And still there were so many soldiers that each squad got a day off per week in rotation. The men used their time off to rest, to explore the local area, to buy extra alcohol, and to party.

Hyras had always avoided parties. They were noisy, unpleasant, and unnecessary. Plus there were usually girls there, not the professionals but young locals. Hyras desperately wanted to talk to girls but did not know how, and he worried that standing around at a party, not dancing and not talking to anybody, would only make his awkward reticence more obvious.

But by then some of his fellow soldiers had managed to make friends with him, and so he couldn't avoid the parties without hurting their feelings.

So Hyras started drinking.

A little alcohol made him willing to socialize. A little more made him act goofy and entertaining. A little more after that—it didn't take much—and he began to stumble around and slur his words and get very angry at everybody, and then the next morning he woke up in a puddle of his own vomit. He swore he would never do *that* again, glad to have been cured, by sad experience, of such foolishness. But the next week he was stumbling-drunk again.

"Hey, b'Sylas, time to put on your dancing clothes," announced b'Danas. He was the squad second, Hyras' assistant, a fellow plebeian around twenty years old.

Hyras, who had been trying to sleep late on his day off, groaned and muttered "I don't dance."

"Nor do you talk to girls," b'Danas pointed out, "but I do both, and I've got an invitation from a girl to go to her home for dinner today, and if I go by myself, her father will think I'm serious about her, and he won't approve. If I go with you, we're just two handsome young men trying to angle a home-cooked meal. So, get up."

"Why won't he approve of you?" Hyras hadn't even sat up, yet.

"Because she's a patrician. Her family owns this whole village plus two others."

"Why are you trying to get with a *patrician*?"

"Ever heard of sex? It's supposed to be *quite* the thing."

Hyras rolled his eyes.

"You know, I think I have heard of it," he acknowledged, "and I even heard somewhere that plebeian and prole girls, too, have vaginas, and they *don't* have fathers prepared to bugger you."

Few Nonanye men saw any need to protect their daughters from consensual sex. But adolescent girls of privilege tended to throw temper-tantrums if not allowed to marry whatever handsome nobody caught their eye. Smart patrician fathers kept handsome nobodies away pre-emptively.

"That's where you come in," b'Danas explained. "You're camouflage. Anyway, the girl has two sisters, and I borrowed horses so we don't have to walk."

It was the horses, not the sisters, who induced Hyras to go.

Both men did their best to look impressive and succeeded in the way that young men in excellent physical condition usually do. B'Danas was tall and slim with richly dark coloration and a long, puckered scar across his face that made him look rugged and dashing. Hyras had grown almost six inches in two years, so he was no longer short, plus he'd become broad across the shoulders and chest and very well-muscled. His face still looked very boyish—almost girlish—and his skin, though unusually light, a sort of medium-brown color, was smooth and perfectly clear. His hair, less tightly-curled than typical, had a definite red-amber tinge. His eyes were green and sad.

"Let's get this over with," he said.

The ride was just long enough to be pleasant, the weather warm and lovely. The house, a huge, unadorned block of honey-colored, ivied stucco, sat shaded by huge oaks in an airy parkland patrolled by green and gold chickens. A dog guarding the chickens barked, and people came out to welcome the young men. Hyras found himself led into a jewel-box, for the inside was anything but plain.

The forepart of the building was an atrium, open to the sky, where a fountain murmured among ornate benches, potted plants large and small, and life-size bronze statues of pretty little girls and boys variously posed. The floor was a mosaic playfully depicting the tracks of dozens of animals, while the walls were hung with intricately abstract tapestries. Curtains of beads guarded doorways leading to dozens of rooms both private and semi-public, for the atrium was the heart of the house. Beyond it, occupying well over half the footprint of the house, lay the garden ringed by a rectangular, columned peristyle lined with more doorways. Incense burned and wind-chimes clinked softly now and then. Any grand country estate in Itara and many of those in Parsia were thus, but Hyras had never before been in such a place. He supposed he never would be again.

The lady of the house, a handsomely plump matron named Rossa, greeted her guests, insisted they be seated in the atrium, and then excused herself to go supervise the completion of the meal. The rest of the family sat and chatted while a servant girl brought around wine mixed with honey and then returned with a tray of almond-honey cookies and a selection of cheeses, dried fruit, and nuts. All of them spoke in the precise and musical Ranish accent of Parsia, despite the Itarye style of their house and manners.

The girl b'Danas liked was a seventeen-year-old named Traxa. She sat working on her embroidery and said very little, but she kept giving b'Danas encouraging little glances. The younger girl, Crea, a cutely giggly fourteen-year-old, spoke a bit more while keeping herself occupied with a drop spindle. The third daughter, Ilia, was away staying with relatives. There were two grown sons in the family, one of them already married but visiting for dinner with his wife and their young child. Hyras didn't catch their names. He did catch the name of the father, Jessas Creas Dynan, but it meant nothing to him. The man had a genteel manner, a piercing gaze, and a habit of dominating the conversation only to ensure that everyone got a fair chance to talk. He was always asking questions.

Rossa emerged to announce the meal was ready, and they all moved into the dining room, a long, airy space with a long, low table in the center surrounded by cushions. While Nonanye people used chairs and high tables for convenience, the upper class believed that dinner ought not to be convenient. Dinner should be slow and relaxed and not too easy to get up from.

The food was like nothing Hyras had ever tasted before—multiple courses, multiple dishes per course, everything heavily yet delicately spiced, and most of it exotic. Hand-raised dormice stewed in a sauce of honey, crushed apple, black pepper, and prickly-ash fruit. Toasted locusts sprinkled with salt and lime juice. A curry of lentils, chestnuts, and finely-chopped mustard greens. Small, risen buns baked with butter and onion. Carp roasted with walnuts and silphium. Fruit stewed with spices Hyras couldn't even name (ginger and cardamom, mostly). Baklava drizzled with rose-water syrup. The entire Dynan family soon noticed his quiet amazement and entertained themselves by bringing him more things to taste—fine wines, candies, preserved fruit—just to watch his reactions. All of which suited b'Danas perfectly because, with the family distracted, he could hold hands with Traxa under the table.

But the food was not the best part of the dinner.

The Dynas family *talked* to each other. They were all interested in each others' lives and interested in the world, and Jessas and Rossa addressed each other fondly by pet-names in front of everybody. The grandchild, who seemed to be about three, was allowed to participate in the conversation, and did so intelligently, if not always with complete coherence. Nobody attacked each other, and there were no long, awkward silences. If the conversation began moving in a direction that left somebody out—politics, say, or finance—somebody else would notice and either explain matters or tactfully change the subject.

Hyras didn't know the name for this way of interaction. It was as alien to him as baklava. But he wanted more of it.

The next week, b'Danas asked if he wanted to go back. Of course he did. This time, after dinner, they all sat around in the atrium talking while Rossa worked at her loom and the younger son noodled around on a lyre. B'Danas and Traxa took a long walk in the garden and may have spent some time together in a storage room within the peristyle, but no one seemed overly concerned. Crea gently persuaded Hyras to talk to her, but as she was obviously too young for him— four years makes a difference when one of you is fourteen—it was more like a little-sister vibe. He felt with her, not excited, but safe. Before leaving, he asked Rossa if he might come back even if b'Danas didn't. She laughed and told him he'd better.

After that, Hyras had three kinds of day, instead of just two. There were the days—most days—when he was a soldier and a temporary worker at an iron smelter. There were the days when he was a party-boy and a drunkard. And there were the days he could pretend to be a Dynan, the days when he could go, once a week, sometimes with another soldier or two, sometimes alone, to where people he liked and respected would be glad to see him and would say so.

The Traxa-b'Danas relationship gradually and amicably fizzled— there is only so much time one can spend with the same person in a storage room—but all through the summer Hyras kept up his weekly dinners at the Dynans'. Rossa would hug him. Crea would ask his advice about boys. The younger son, whose name, Hyras finally learned, was Yunas, would talk with him about horses. Jessas would explain why you need to put shells in the smelting towers and what, exactly, is done with the pig iron once the barges come to take it away. Most of it was processed into various grades of steel and sold on to weapons manufacturers, but some went for rails for the wagonways.

As summer turned to fall, Ilia came home.

She was a short, plump girl, sixteen years old and plain-looking, but cute in her own way. She had rather fantastic hair, a richly black cloud of very tight curls apt to take on a mind of its own if she didn't keep it corralled with long, mother-of-pearl combs. She had a lazy eye, to the point that she could not look at the same thing with both eyes at the same time, and so she had a habit of turning her head slightly to look at you more carefully with just the one eye, so that you really felt looked at.

And what did she see when she looked at Hyras? She tried, for propriety's sake, to not make it obvious, but plainly she thought him both admirable and sexy. He'd never been looked at that way by anyone before. And she liked horses. She was a more than competent rider, and the animals liked and trusted her. Soon, and almost without realizing it, he was spending his day off entirely at the Dynans' so that he could explore the forest paths on horseback with Ilia. On his working days, after his duty shift ended, he'd sometimes skip supper to go see her in the evenings, often finding her riding out to meet him halfway with some bread and cheese tied up in a cloth bag.

"I don't know, I just thought you might be coming and might be hungry," she would say.

In this lush, green forest, rain fell any time of year it pleased, even in summer, but if his day off proved to be rainy, Hyras would come anyway, and he and Ilia would sit together in the library where he would read to her. She could read, but it hurt her eyes to do it— she had a serious astigmatism, in addition to the lazy eye, and although Nonanye optometrists could make monocles to address some vision problems, they could do nothing for astigmatism. His visits opened up the world of literature to her—to him, too, as he'd never had access to so large a library before—and together they worked their way through long scrolls of poetry, plays, philosophical dialogues (he would do multiple voices to make her giggle), and histories. He liked the small weight of her head on his shoulder. She liked the sound of his voice.

Twice the moon changed from new to full to new again before orders came to re-deploy. The problem lay to the north, in the part of Slovona that was still semi-independent, though Nonanye colonists had been clearing farms there for almost a generation. But the last several winters had been bad, especially in the foothills, where ice storms coated the pastures, nearly starving the barbarians' horses and sheep. Rather than appeal to Nonani for aid, the foothill tribes had come sweeping down into the plow-lands on horseback, looting and burning and raping, trying to drive the farming families out.

Hyras had not thought about the future with respect to Ilia. He had simply enjoyed each day with her as it came. Now...? He might die, that couldn't be ruled out. And even if he survived the campaign, chances were against the legion ever returning to the same place.

In a barely-contained panic, he spoke to Jessas, dropping some indirect questions. He knew now that this man was paterfamilias of the Dynan matriline, with the power to decide who joined the family and who did not, and a leading steel magnate besides—not a man he wished to anger with an unwelcome request. Jessas smiled a little and encouraged Hyras to visit again before heading out.

That evening, Jessas knocked on Ilia's door as the family was going to bed.

"Come in!" she called, after a pause. She was already in her night-gown, but her candle still burned. "Oh, hi, Daddy. What's up?"

He sat down on her bed. She left her candle burning on her dresser-top where it reflected weirdly on the yellow surface of her bronze mirror, and she sat down beside him, expectant.

"Daughter, are you serious about Hyras?" he asked.

"Daddy, you know I've never been serious about anything," she replied, giggling. She waited, quite deliberately, for relief to show in the set of her father's shoulders, then added "except Hyras." Her father sighed.

"I like him, too," Jessas acknowledged. "He's a good kid. And your mother's very fond. But I had hoped that if you married, you would choose someone who could...bring us something."

"Oh, Daddy, that's what you're worried about? That's not going to be an issue. Hyras will be First Consul someday."

Jessas held very still. He was aware that his middle daughter some-times knew things, things she would state with absolute assurance but could not or would not explain. Unlike some people, she never claimed to have special powers, but while she wasn't always right, she was right far more often than anybody had any right to expect. Hyras as First Consul?

"OK, but you know that's impossible, sweetie." A plebeian could not be a commissioned military officer, and only a commissioned officer could be made a consul by the Ruling Council.

"It's not impossible," she countered, "if he marries me."

Chapter 4. The Lawyer

Year of Nonani 815 - 822

"Um, there's a naked man here to see you, sir," announced Abbas Seras Lian's office assistant.

"Well, did you get his name?" he asked. "Or were you distracted by the glory of his nakedness?"

"Um...."

"Is he a derger?"

"I think so? I've never seen one up close before."

"Isn't it kind of him, then, to arrive so ready for your close inspection? Send him up."

The assistant disappeared, and soon a short, very stocky man walked in. He had a waterskin on a leather strap and some jewelry, mostly carved ivory and jade, but no clothes. His skin was a strange color, like that of half-seasoned maple wood, and his facial features were large, heavy, pleasant, frank. He had a long, broad, flowing red beard almost covering his chest and a long, red braid reaching down his back, all straight as grass, not curly like normal hair. He was clean, healthy-looking, but scarred and weather-beaten, and he glanced about the well-appointed room in diffident curiosity.

"Oboo!" Abbas cried, jumping up from his desk to take his friend's hand. "I thought it was you." He interrupted himself to ask his assistant to bring food and drink, plenty of it, but no cheese or alcohol. "How long has it been? It's been since my wedding, hasn't it? Come in, sit down, how are you? Surely you have not come all the way out here only to greet me?"

"Ubbus!" Oboo replied, smiling hugely, "I have missed you, isn't that enough? But you are right, I do have another reason. I want to hire you." They had been speaking in the derger language, but Oboo said the word *hire* in Itarish, not having his own equivalent.

"Hire me?" Abbas returned to his chair behind his desk. Oboo looked around a little awkwardly and settled into the chair in front of the desk. He wasn't familiar with chairs.

"Yes," Oboo confirmed. "I do not clearly understand what you do, but it is something with fighting with words on behalf of others. I need help fighting."

"Fighting?" Abbas leaned forward. "Fighting whom? Who is attacking you?"

"I don't know their names," Oboo admitted. "None of us have talked with them. They have not hurt our bodies, nor even tried to, but they come into our forest, many together, and cut down the oak and the beech and the alder and the cherry and the apple and the pine. They make big piles of the wood and smolder it until it becomes charcoal, and then they take the charcoal away with them. And then they come back. If they keep cutting so much so quickly, they will cut all our forest. We cannot gather acorns if there are no oaks. We cannot trap squirrels if there are no acorns. There will be no food for us, no clean water.... We showed ourselves to them, but they shouted and shook their fists as though they wanted wur. Ubbus, they do not care that we are there. They know it is our forest, and they do not care. This is new. It is not in the music."

"Oboo, I'm not sure how much use words will be in this situation. I can try, of course."

"What makes words good or not good for fighting?"

"Tradition, mostly," Abbas explained. "My job is to clearly understand the traditions that say to do one thing and not to do another. If someone is wronged, I can see if a tradition has been violated, and if it has, I can try to convince an elder that righting the wrong is the proper and traditional thing to do. Only, I am not sure that tradition has been violated here. Tradition does not address everything."

It is hard to explain legal practice in a language that has no words for *law, judges,* or *orders.*

"Oh, but your tradition has been violated," Oboo insisted. "The songs say that your people have always respected our lands. Only when we leave our lands do your people take them, as we take lands that your people give up. It is only because you rarely give up lands—there are always more and more of you—that the room for us is always less and less. The songs say your people have not used force on us, not in many generations, nor do the songs tell of ubum damaging what they know to be ours. Your tradition is to respect us. But these men are not respecting us or our land. They are in violation."

"They are certainly in violation of something," Abbas agreed. "I will try. I can't promise to succeed. Even fights that should win sometimes don't."

"No one can promise to succeed, Ubbus," Oboo told him. "But your words will be strong and good, I believe that. What can I trade for your labor? You know I have no silver."

"Oboo, I will help you for free, you don't need to trade for my help." But Oboo smiled indulgently.

"My friend, I did not come here to take advantage. You help me, I help you. You make your living by trading your labor. What can I give you?"

"Well, you know I am fond of salmon and of chanterelles, but they are hard to get fresh in town, here. Bring me a share of each in its season, and I will call that a fair trade."

The assistant interrupted with a big tray laden with nuts, fruit, sliced hardboiled eggs sprinkled with mustard powder and salt, a pitcher of water flavored with herbed balsamic vinegar, and two cups. Oboo thanked the man in badly-pronounced Itarish, then ate and drank with a will. Abbas nibbled politely but left most of it for his hungry friend.

"This will not be a quick process," Abbas warned. "To fight with words requires a lot of time and many stages. It will be till next fall, at the earliest, before we can hope to see lasting results."

"I do not think our forest will survive so long."

"I can get a..." *temporary injunction* had no derger-equivalent either. "I will tell an elder that the ownership of the forest is contested. He will say that it must not be cut until the matter is settled. Once that is said, Da and the boys can run the charcoal harvesters off if they intrude."

"Hurry."

"I will, Oboo. I can't promise that I will win the fight. But I can promise to fight for you."

"Thank you. I accept your promise, Ubbus."

Of course Abbas insisted that Oboo spend the night. Maia had gone out, so Abbas asked Oboo to await her return while he closed the office a little early and walked the quarter mile to the old general store, where he bought an abundance of fresh fruit and two young roosters. While the new shop boy caught and killed the birds, Abbas chatted casually with J.J., who had recently been made part-owner.

"Hungry?" J.J. asked.

"Well, I'm having dinner with an important new client tonight."

"Wining and dining a high roller? So who's suing whom this week?"

"Oh, you know I can't tell you, that's privileged information."

"Come on, I won't tell anyone but three or four hundred of my closest friends."

"Well, I really shouldn't. It's just—no, I shouldn't."

"Now you have to. Who is this hungry client of yours?"

"Oboo."

"No shit?" And J.J. covered his mouth with his hands. He hadn't meant to curse at work. "Oh, man, really? He's in town? Wait, is he actually your client? Never mind, I'll ask him myself. I'm leaving the boy in charge and coming to dinner, you know that, right?"

"You and Eria both, that's why I bought the second chicken."

J.J. insisted on bringing two bottles of wine. Eria, his wife, brought two loaves of crusty sourdough. By the time they got back to Abbas's modest rental, Maia was already home and had set the garden table with snacks and candies. While the oven heated for the birds, J.J. opened the first bottle of wine, while Maria mixed a honeyed tea of sumac, lemon balm, and lavender, knowing that derger seldom handle alcohol well. Eria sang and played her lute, and the others talked about everything in the world except Oboo's legal problems. He wanted a break.

Mostly they talked about pregnancy, since both Oboo's wife and Eria were expecting. This would be Oboo's second child, so he was able to reassure J.J. and Eria to some extent. Maia had just had her second miscarriage and wanted some reassurance herself. Eventually, though, they moved on to joking and storytelling.

The birds went into the oven, but as there was little to do while they roasted besides make more food, the rest of the meal got fancier and fancier the longer the diners had to wait. Maia had seasoned the chicken with pepper and salt and an herb mix featuring thyme, marjoram, and tarragon. But she cooked the organ meats separately with onion, carrots, celery seed, and garlic in her own white wine. She didn't need to dip into J.J.'s rosé. The artichokes braised in wine and olive oil with mushrooms and butter was Eria's idea. Abbas picked arugula and butter lettuce from the garden and mixed the mustard vinaigrette while Oboo chopped up red onion for him to add in. They saved the drippings from the chicken for dipping bread. Later, Maia turned out a tart tatin with honey on top.

"If you visit more often, Oboo," Abbas said, "I might finally cease resembling a fence-rail."

Abbas, J.J., and of course Oboo spoke mostly derger-tongue. Eria and Maia could understand enough to follow the conversation, but mostly spoke Itarish sprinkled with Galasish, which Oboo could partially understand in turn. And so they all conversed fairly well.

"Why do you call J.J. 'Yui-Yui'?" asked Eria, who'd only just noticed Oboo was doing so.

"*Yuì!rì- yuì!rì,*" he corrected her, then explained in his broken Itarish, "I no say *Jhuh-Jhuh* right."

"A yuì!rì is a kind of of bird," Abbas explained, in Itarish. "Large songbird, quite cheeky."

"Oh, a jay!" exclaimed Eria, realizing the interlinguistic pun.

"Well, J.J. is large and cheeky," acknowledged Maia. "It fits." And they all laughed.

In the morning, before Oboo left for his long walk home, Abbas suggested that next time he wear clothing.

"But it is summer. I am not cold."

"That's not the point."

Abbas set about working on his new case. While talking with Oboo he had used the derger word for *tradition* to mean *law*, but the respect for derger land occupancy really was only tradition, and a tradition could not be defended in court. Legally, all land belonged either to a patrician family or to the Senate as a whole, and if the owner wanted the land harvested for charcoal, there wouldn't be much, besides public shaming, that could be done about it. But the first step was to stop the harvest.

Abbas filed a criminal complaint against the charcoal harvesters for trespass against his own father—Seras didn't own the land, but throwing doubt on that question got the injunction he needed to buy himself some time. Who did own the land? The most recent record he could find indicated an absentee landlord in Sweetmeadow who had died of plague leaving no heirs. Assuming there hadn't been an unrecorded sale (possible under Nonanye law), that meant ownership had reverted to the Senate, to be managed by the provincial governor. Only, the governor seemed not to have noticed and wasn't managing it.

The governor was another of Maia's cousins and the paterfamilias of her matriline—and now Abbas'. Surely, if Arias were alerted to the problem, he would follow tradition and leave the derger alone? But Abbas only thought that until he found out the price charcoal was going for these days. He didn't know the man well enough to be sure he'd do the right thing, and anyway, even if he did, the next governor might not. The more Abbas thought about it, the more convinced he became that his friends didn't need a benign landlord—they needed legal control under their own names. No derger had ever had such control, though. It wasn't done.

Legally speaking, derger didn't exist. That is, they were not legal persons, neither bound by nor protected by any law. There was good reason for that—no derger could be expected to understand most of Nonanye law because their intelligence had a different shape. But few ubum made a distinction between the shape of intelligence and its size, and in ubum society, people who could not count, use abstract nouns, or understand hatred were simply idiots. Itarish had no word for *disabled person*, only words for idiot, cripple, freak, weirdo, and monster. Such people mostly ended up begging on the streets or worse. Better that the derger stayed in their forests, respected in their separateness. But without legal personhood, they had no recourse if respect failed.

There was a legal mechanism for making a barbarian into a plebeian. It had never been done with derger before, but there was nothing to say it could not be. But plebeians couldn't own land.

"It's too bad they're not patricians,"Abbas told J.J., feeling rather glum about everything.

"Are you so sure they're not?" J.J. asked.

And Abbas saw right away what he could do. First he filed a new criminal complaint, claiming now that Benò was the landowner. The judge objected, saying "this 'man' is not a patrician, he can't be a land-owner."

Benò stood there in court, his beard white with age and spilling across the front of his new Nonanye-style suit. If his elderly knees hurt, standing there, he didn't show it. If he was humiliated by the way the judge spoke about him, he didn't show that either. He just stood quietly, looking directly at the judge, being human. If attacked, derger will fight, and Benò was fighting. Abbas looked at him a moment, then turned back to the judge.

"Your honor, my client *is* a patrician. And he is being trespassed against. If the defense wishes to question his ownership of his land, then we request a temporary injunction against all harvest of woody plants from the property except for immediate subsistence use by residents of the property."

The judge granted the new injunction but said he lacked authority in matters of class identity. He sent the question of Benò's status up to the Provincial High Court in Jarasi.

Abbas went to Jarasi with his client and reminded the justices there that all native residents of barbarian countries became citizens upon their countries becoming provinces, with the leadership of every barbarian society in the new provinces becoming patricians. So, he argued, since derger were obviously native to Holia, at least some must logically be patricians, right?

No law actually said derger should be excluded, they had just always been excluded anyway. And since Nonanye courts fancied themselves bound by legal reasoning and not personal bias, Abbas was able to force the Provincial High Court to admit that not only *could* a derger family be patrician, but that those counted as elites within their society already *were* patrician and had always been so.

But derger didn't have elites. Each family had a headman, but all families were equal. So Abbas next argued that since the oldest of Nonani's patrician matrilines were simply the Itarye families who had founded the city, before they were joined by what became plebeians or proletarians, patrician identity must be the basic form of citizenship, with the other classes as add-ons to the bottom. A society with only a single class, like the derger, must therefore be *all* patrician. This, too, he forced the court to concede.

Finally, the justices officially recognized Benò as a patrician paterfamilias—a senator. He could not only own land, he could also vote.

Next step was to return to the local court and demonstrate that the land Benò's family lived on actually belonged to Benò. There was no proof that it did. But there was no proof it didn't. There was the possibility of an unrecorded sale—Benò had proof that his father had been trading with a wealthy Sweetmeadow resident in the years before the plague outbreak, for the family still had gold and silver goods with Sweetmeadow maker's marks from around that time. That his father had bought land from the same person was plausible, especially as the family had moved to its current home almost as soon as the previous occupants were gone.

"If my client were not derger," Abbas declared, "we wouldn't be having this hearing. When a senator says he owns land because he inherited it from his father, who bought it in turn from sellers dead now these fifty-five years, we believe him! There is no legal basis for questioning Senator Benò's claim, and all the weight of custom says not to. How many senators now serving on the Ruling Council could defend their ownership of their ancestral lands if forced to do so in court? It's a wise man who hesitates before throwing open a pasture gate, because it's never just one sheep that gets out! I propose, your honor, that we keep our sheep where they are, even if one of them *is* a derger!"

The judge finally agreed—unless some other claimant to the land appeared and re-opened the question, Senator Benò owned several hundred acres of forested land.

The criminal trespassing trial then proceeded more typically. The defense did not have much of a counter-argument. The charcoal harvesters themselves received only a few lashes each, but their employer was fined into bankruptcy. Benò, a man who had always made a point of living outside the money economy, was paid his restitution and his share of the fines in gold coin. He kept two coins for making jewelry and gave two each to Abbas and Seras for their help. He used the rest to gradually buy up all the surrounding abandoned land he could, using Seras as his agent so as to get a fair price. Thousands of acres would never be harvested for charcoal again.

Abbas had expected the derger land-rights case to be a one-off, but that was before other derger in similar situations heard about what he'd done. He took on a partner and took as many cases as he could, soliciting donations from sympathetic ubum to fund the work. Representatives of forest-living ubum, some of them outlaws, others remnants of ancient hunter-gatherer peoples, asked him for help. And then came messages from tenant farmers, people who didn't live in the forest but depended on it when crops failed. Abbas could not help them all, so he connected with other lawyers who could. Soon he was directing a network of activist lawyers trading tips and sharing in fundraising efforts.

Abbas had known for years the forest was in trouble—the conservation movement began when he was a child—and he'd known the derger were in trouble almost as long. But now, for the first time he realized the two issues were linked and he could do something about both, something nobody else had tried to do. Only, it didn't seem to be enough.

"You could get a job with Arias," Maia suggested one day, apropos of nothing obvious. Four years had passed since Oboo hired a lawyer, and Abbas lay on the floor in his home library, reading.

"I already have a job," he replied, not looking up from his scroll. He kicked his long, narrow, bare feet. His indifference to shoes and furniture, a legacy of childhood poverty, drove Maia nuts.

"You can keep it," she assured him. "Just be an aide part-time."

"What would I do?" He had to ask because *aide* could mean any kind of staffer at all.

"Something educational or advisory. You can figure out the details, but you'd be his expert on the derger problem."

"There is no derger problem. There's an ubum problem."

"You know what I mean. The point is you'd have his ear. You've been using the law as a tool to make changes. Isn't it time you start changing the laws? This is how you get your foot in the door."

And Abbas looked up from his reading.

The problem was that since the governor didn't think there was an ubum problem, he wasn't going to hire an expert in it. How do you combat indifference? You can't lecture it, it won't listen in the first place. Maia suggested entertainment. And so Abbas talked himself into a job running a public speaker series out of the Governor's House in Jarasi.

Maia had grown up in Jarasi and absolutely loved returning to its fast-paced social whirl. She reconnected with old friends and made lots of new ones, attended dinners and dances, and learned the latest fashions for doing her hair and tying her shawl. Abbas liked city living, too. There was something larkish about it, as if it wasn't quite part of his real life. Though only a hundredth the size of Nonani City,

Jarasi was big enough to be truly urban, with a dazzling variety of everything from take-out places to libraries to public parks. He'd only ever read plays before, but now he could see them staged. He could attend comedy acts and recitations of the epics and see some of the best-regarded public speakers in the empire.

At first he wasn't sure how to book speakers for his own events. By the time he learned he could order catalogs from agents, he was out of time, so he gave the first talk himself. Oboo gave the second, and brought his two wives and three children—J.J. got the family dressed and drove them up in a cart. Oboo made a charming public speaker, his accent notwithstanding, and a sampling of Jarasi high society learned that derger are people. But soon Abbas was booking professional speakers specializing in forest issues. There were many to choose from, for while he'd been the movement's first lawyer, the movement itself was hardly new.

Deep in the psyche of every human culture on the continent was an affection for and a sense of reciprocity with the natural world. Everybody knew that people had responsibilities whose neglect would have real consequences. The details varied from one culture to the next, but the traditional Itarye version, which dominated Nonanye thought, involved friendships with naiads and dryads, surprise encounters with magic fish, sacred groves, numinous wetlands, heroes testing their mettle and winning blessings in combat with beasts and monsters, and a Goddess who continually birthed the world if and only if fertilized by a human man worthy of her. These stories were not meant to be taken as literal fact, but literal fact was beside most of the point for most Nonanye, and the stories and traditional ceremonies suggested relationships that every honorable person took seriously.

Unfortunately, an ethic of reverent respect alone does not make for a coherent conservation policy, or even any awareness that a conservation policy is needed. Knowing that the ancient grove on the edge of your town is sacred doesn't automatically translate into reverence for somebody else's ancient grove (which starts to look like a good source for charcoal) or any curiosity as to why ancient groves are important to begin with. Everyone knew that at least some of the rules were superstitious or overblown, that divine fire wouldn't really come to punish transgressors, and people disagreed on how important the ancient rules really were. And when forced by circumstance to give up something, many people kept the purely symbolic aspects of their religion and gave up the things the symbols stood for, simply because they didn't know any better.

And yet, the ethic remained, a pervasive sense that *something* about the natural world was important, that humans had some sort of responsibility to give as well as to take. So when elfin scientists announced a generation or two ago that forest cover on a continental scale was showing a net loss, that ancient forest particularly was mortal and could be, might be, done away with, the warning found at least some receptive ubum ears. Since then, the speed of the charcoal harvest and the size of the area put under the plow to feed the growing cities had only increased—but so had the number of ubum calling for change.

And so there were activists organizing protests, wealthy people creating protected refuges, philosophers, priests (mostly of the magi, an order concerned with religious education), and essayists discussing ideas and spreading awareness, an ever-growing movement. Some had motivations that could only be called religious, an abstract concern for the green and the numinous. Others appreciated the aesthetics of intact landscapes or felt a sentimental attachment or wanted to protect their personal access to some forest-related resource, from recreational boar-hunting to the gathering of life-saving herbs and mushrooms. Some were concerned about justice for derger or for other people besides themselves who could not do without the forest. There were also plenty of people who couldn't care less, unfortunately.

In eighth-month of the second year, a derger activist named Udùo came to talk. Abbas had not known that there were derger activists. Of course, Udùo was part ubum, so that helped—he could pronounce Itarish properly—but mixed-heritage people usually lived as derger unless their derger blood was very dilute. Abbas had met ubum with light-brown faces and very stocky builds, sometimes red or reddish hair, who had no idea they had derger ancestry at all. People mixed, but their worlds didn't, except for Udùo. He spoke both Itarish and Duchesh like a native and dressed like a Nonanye gentleman, but he wore his brown hair and beard long. Around one bicep he wore a red-dyed leather thong tied with polished rings of ivory and jade, and in his stretched earlobe hung bangles of jade and carved horn. And he called himself a derger and nothing else.

Udùo launched a self-possessed, erudite rage upon his listeners, adroitly shaming any who might offer him less than their full attention and respect, then rattling off facts and figures regarding how much land each derger family needed to survive and how many families needed to be within easy traveling distance of each other, and what would happen to families left without such things. Did he understand the numbers he quoted? Oboo would not have. Udùo certainly knew the numbers' implications, at least. Abbas felt queasy. Those numbers couldn't mean....They didn't...?

"It is a strange thing to take seriously the possibility of one's own people's extinction," Udùo told his audience, speaking quietly now, sadly. "Not merely personal death, but the end of one's kind, the loss of the opportunity to become an ancestor. Our blood may continue in some of you, but our way will be gone. Our songs will stop. You, even those of you who carry our blood in your veins, will not remember us. And the loss will be on your heads, to your shame, because it's not necessary. It doesn't have to happen. Don't think we need your pity. Your pity does not help us. But if you let us go you will be fools, for your children's children will not remember you, either. Who among you even knows your grandfather's grandfather's name? Only we can carry the songs across the centuries, across the millennia. Would you like me to sing one of the songs while I am still here to sing it?"

And he sang. He sang the long, quavering, complex verses in the derger tongue with all its tonal changes and its clicks and clacks, he sang the story of the arrival of ubum on the continent that had previously belonged wholly to derger and elves. No one present besides Abbas understood the words, but nobody interrupted him. The reception was somber.

But afterwards, although all the world was changed for Abbas, nobody else seemed to care. Nobody did anything differently. Not as far as Abbas could tell.

Ninth-month brought a pair of scientists—elves, of course. There seemed to be no rule against ubum being scientists, but none were. Abbas had always heard that elves looked strange, but these two, the first he'd ever met, didn't seem so at first. They were very slim, very pale, and beardless. The taller one was a redhead. The thought that he might be a derger-mix made him seem more familiar to Abbas. The two dressed like Nonanye gentlemen and spoke Itarish with only a slight foreign accent.

But the longer Abbas was in their company, the less normal they seemed. He could not put his finger on why. They were uncanny. Maybe it was just that their eyes were a little too big, or maybe....

"It's largely because elfin kinesics are alien to you," the red-haired one said.

"What?" exclaimed Abbas, startled.

"You were wondering what about us makes you uncomfortable."

"I hadn't known mind-reading was part of your magic." Abbas was joking and yet not joking.

"No magic," replied the shorter, blond elf, "you're just predictable."

Their names were Ultafarion ni Renerian and Jerioniress ni Saranassiryr. They had no titles and used their first names professionally. Ultafarion was the redhead, Jerioniress the yellow. They studied and taught something called ecology, but Abbas had been unable to determine what that might be. He'd tried reading translations of their writings, but it all went over his head, being filled with not only specialized terms and elfin numerals (Abbas knew what those looked like but not how to use them) but also with concepts he found utterly alien. But their actual talk was easy to understand, a clear, accessible description of what might go wrong if too many trees were cut—floods and droughts and the collapse of some game stocks—delivered in a straightforward way, without appeals to emotion that might have felt manipulative and become counterproductive. So adeptly had they simplified their material that the audience members felt smart afterwards for having understood all of it.

Afterwards, at the reception, the socialites seemed to mistake the strangeness of Ultafarion and Jerioniress for mere personal eccentricity, evidence of a charmingly iconoclastic and free-spirited attitude. Women flirted and joked and then laughed merrily when the elves took the jokes literally or failed to notice the flirting. Their popularity rebounded on Abbas, and everybody, including the governor, congratulated him on another event well done. Except....

"It's like they didn't even notice what you were talking about!" exclaimed Abbas afterwards. He and Maia had invited the men home for a late supper, since Maia said elves like to stay up late, like owls do. She made a kind of quick leftover stew and opened a bottle of good red wine.

"They notice," Jerioniress said. "They just don't know how to talk about their noticing. Messages often take several repetitions to sink in. Maybe this is the first repetition for a lot of them. Then, too, you don't have to reach all of them to make a difference." He seemed so calmly assured that Abbas wanted to sit at his feet and learn forever, except....

"Repetition takes time," Abbas said. "How much time do the derger have?" He had almost managed to forget about Udùo's warning, since everybody else had, but now he was thinking about what the elves had said about habitat fragmentation, how a habitat patch that is too small gradually and inevitably loses species the same way a squeezed sponge loses water—and how for the really big animals, the ones derger depend on, any habitat patch less than a significant fraction of a continent is too small. Maybe for such considerations, the derger themselves counted as large animals? The liquid dripping from the sponge in Abbas's mind began to look like blood.

Neither elf seemed at all surprised by Abbas's insight.

"That's a really interesting question," Jerioniress said, "that we don't have an answer to. There has been some really good work on it lately—one study estimated a total derger population of no more than ten thousand. That would make, oh, something like twenty-five hundred fertile women?"

He paused a little and, inexplicably, almost smiled. Neither elf had much in the way of either facial or vocal expression, and yet both seemed totally unguarded. Abbas thought that, with practice, he might be able to read their every thought and feeling in those impassive, boyish faces. Jerioniress's eyes shone with intensity, but Abbas could not read them yet.

"The derger metapopulation has never been large," Jerioniress continued. "They may have developed protections from some of the risks of low population size. But they weren't always so deeply fragmented. By some estimates, there could be as many as fifty entirely separate breeding populations now, wholly isolated from each other—that means an average of fifty breeding-age women each, but some must be smaller. Doubtless, some have dropped below the threshold for long-term viability. They will merge with neighboring ubum populations and drop out of the music, as they say. When that happens, how long can the remaining populations remain viable? I don't know. Nobody knows. And nobody yet knows how to figure it out—except by watching. There are only fifteen or sixteen thousand elves west of the Mountains, incidentally. Maybe twice that many east. Time is moving quickly for all of us. But there are some good ideas being tossed around, now."

He sounded so reasonable. Abbas slammed his hand down on the counter-top, making the wine shiver in its glasses.

"All the good ideas are too slow," he declared.

"That's another good question we don't have an answer to," Ultafarion said. "In the meantime, I see no reason not to pursue the best ideas we've got."

Tenth month rolled around, and Abbas was more than ready for the last talk of the year. The speakers were old friends, of a kind—b'Freias and b'Tomas, from the cartographic expedition.

Abbas had lost touch with all his old teammates after returning home, but he'd found b'Freias and b'Tomas in the catalog. The two had written a book about their journey that did very well in Itara, but the booksellers in Holia had never stocked it. Book-authorship itself could never be profitable in a world without printing presses or copyright law, so writers instead leveraged their books into months or even years of work as paid lecturers. Thus, b'Freias and b'Tomas had discovered an affinity for public speaking and were still at it—except they were no longer talking much about their travel adventures. They were talking about derger.

"Remember when I thought they couldn't speak?" b'Freias asked Abbas. "I was such an ignorant ass." They were catching up, waiting for the audience to arrive while staff-members finished setting up.

"Nobody knows anything until they know it," Abbas replied.

"I should have known it earlier. We all should. We share our world with them, and so many of us are happy to pretend they don't exist."

B'Freias was still tall, slim, graceful, and cocky, now with a little early white at the temples and a short, neat beard. Most Nonanye men were clean-shaven, but b'Freias wanted to stand out. "Kinda like I went native among the barbarians, you know?" he said. Oddly, he was still single. He had become paterfamilias for his matriline anyway. He didn't mind Abbas still addressing him as b'Freias, not Senator Sylan, though—he would have liked being called plain Jonas, but Abbas wouldn't do it, it felt too weird. B'Tomas was still in men's clothes, and the clothes as always made her look smaller, not an average-sized woman but a miniature man. And yet she'd never looked un-feminine and now looked frankly beautiful, dressed elegantly in soft gray tunic and leggings and a gray scapular printed in intricate black. She still largely ignored Abbas, though she was not uncivil. She had not ignored him when they first met. They'd never been close, but she really pulled away midway through the trip. He remembered that now and puzzled over it.

Both b'Freias and b'Tomas proved skilled in rhetoric, and while they were very militant in defense of derger rights, they were also engaging and entertaining. The audience responded well, and the reception afterwards felt glamorous and festive. Cups clinked. Women's jewels glittered. People talked and laughed and flirted while a small band played pleasantly.

Abbas found b'Freias leaning up against one of the refreshment tables and joined him.

"So, all this talking," Abbas asked, "is it doing anything?"

"I happen to think it might be," b'Freias replied. "But it's not all I'm doing."

"Oh?"

"We need a new system. You know it, I know it. The old virtues—honor, modesty, public service—they're falling by the roadside. Why? It's no mystery. Pursuit of money and fame achieves power. Those who will not leave behind their virtue are themselves left behind. Once, most Nonanye were either patricians with a voice in the Senate or plebeians with a voice in the courts and the plebiscite. Now, the cities are filling with proletarians who have no voice at all but that of the mob, and no understanding of anything but free wheat and public games. That's no way to run a republic. It's no way to keep money-grubbers in check. The erosion of the traditions that protect the derger and the forest tribes and the sacred groves, it's all of a piece. We need to expand the Senate radically. Derger representation is a good start, but there is far more that needs to be done."

"You sound like a revolutionary."

"If the sandal fits, I'll wear it. But first step is through the established political process. I'm organizing my own faction."

"Your own faction?" Abbas exclaimed. "But you're not a member of the Ruling Council!"

"Not yet. But how do you think people get elected? With even a plurality on the Council, never mind a majority, we'll be able to push through some important reforms. So that's what I'm working on. It's all underground so far, but it'll come up fast like mushrooms when the weather changes."

"I'm in," Abbas said, surprising himself, "if you'll have me."

"I'll have you," b'Freias said. "You are a man who can make things happen. I've known that about you since you were a kid hustling for copper in a hick-town pub." He took a long swallow of his punch. "That's a beautiful woman you've gotten yourself married to," he added. Together, they watched Maia as she introduced b'Tomas to the governor's economic advisor, flirting with the man just enough to be charming but not unseemly. Just for a moment, Maia swayed a little and touched her forehead as though dizzy or pained, but then she waved away any concern and soon became energetic and charming again. Beautiful was an understatement.

"I'm lucky," Abbas replied. "She has terrible taste."

"To women of terrible taste!" b'Freias raised his cup in salute. "May I find one myself someday."

"You think you will?"

"Nah. I'm already married—to my work." As he spoke, he gazed off into the distance—but in his gaze was b'Tomas. Wherever she was, whatever she did, he was aware of her. Abbas didn't notice. "Besides, no wife could have taste *that* terrible."

Abbas chuckled. He still thought b'Freias quite the catch, but he was no longer an adolescent and could not say so.

"I am married to my work, too, I'm simply bigamous," he joked instead.

"You three must have a nest of children by this time," b'Freias remarked, knowing Abbas was almost thirty. Most men did have four or five kids by then. But Abbas abruptly ceased joking.

"No, no children," he said, and b'Freias knew not to ask further.

In the morning, Abbas slept late, not getting up until nearly noon. He was tired, beyond tired, exhausted from two years of pretending to be happy and sociable while working two jobs, neither of which seemed likely to do any good. Natalia, the celebration of mothers and babies, did not help his mood. When the Fallow began, he took the opportunity to rest and found that once he'd stopped moving he could not start again.

Abbas had never been a happy man. He joked and goofed around, he enjoyed his friends and his books and his wife, but when he was not joking, his face would gradually relax into sadness. He did not know the weight he carried because he'd never in his memory been free of it, but there is weight and then there is weight. There are the days when the world looks black.

"When I do nothing, really nothing, I feel alright," he told Maia. He was lying on the bed, on top of the covers, naked, his arms and legs spread out like the rays of a star-fish. He was so big that he did not fit, and his wrists and ankles hung limply over the sides of the mattress and out into space. Goose-flesh pimpled his bare skin, but he lacked the motivation to get under the covers. Anyway, being cold felt good, calming.

"Do nothing, then," Maia said, sitting on the bed beside him and stroking his forehead. She'd never seen him like this before and did not understand what was happening to him. She'd decided he must be ill, though the several doctors she'd consulted said otherwise.

"There are things that must be done," he objected, but even the thought of doing them made him wince.

"None of them must be done right now, though."

"Mm."

"Do you want a blanket?"

"No."

"Do you want something to eat?"

"No."

"Do you want me to go away for a while?"

"No. Stay."

It was late afternoon, the day outside bright with snow, but the room's one small, glass-paned window was still shuttered, the heavy curtain drawn against the cold. Maia had brought in a lantern and set it on the bedside table. It cast a dim, honey-colored glow through its opaque glass shade and made a circle of brighter light from its chimney upon the ceiling. Abbas lay on the bed and watched that bright circle for a long time.

When Hilaria, the festival of jokes, ended the Fallow, Abbas didn't feel like joking. He could barely keep up with his legal work. Re-starting the speaker series wasn't an option. Maia organized the move back to their old home in Sweetmeadow and reached out to Abbas's parents and to J.J., asking if any of them had any ideas. J.J. remem-bered that Oboo's othermother, Xu!luh was a doctor.

All derger doctors were women, which was only one of several reasons most Nonanye ubum wouldn't even acknowledge derger doc-tors existed, but Abbas had noticed derger rarely got seriously ill, and he didn't think their resilient constitution was the only reason why. Anyway, he remembered that Xu!luh had tried to save his half-sister and step-brother—she'd failed, but she'd tried, and he trusted her.

On a slushy, misty day in first-month, Abbas and Maia togeth-er went to visit the little compound where Oboo's family lived. The examination was swift and thorough and different from what any Nonanye doctor would have done. Xu!luh did not even ask about Abbas's dreams, nor did she draw up his astrological chart. She did feel his pulse (Nonanye medicine didn't actually know what a pulse was, except that a corpse doesn't have one), checked the color of his nail-beds, asked about his diet....

"Is he really sick?" Maia asked, in passable derger-tongue. "The other doctors all said he's not, but I don't know. Something's not right."

"Of course he's sick," Xu!luh snapped. "Idiots, to say he's not sick! Ubbus hates seeing doctors because he wants to take care of ev-erything and everybody himself. *If* he sees a doctor, *then* he is certainly sick. Ubbus, your soul is wandering. I'll give you a song to guide it back. You will know when it has returned, but it will not be swift nor all at once. If you do not start to feel better by the new moon after this next one, come back for vision-caps—but do not use them on your own." She also prescribed plenty of sunlight and exercise, absolute avoidance of alcohol and opium, and dietary changes. She warned him that his was a soul that liked to wander, and that it might try to leave again, but to return if he needed more help.

"You should return even if you do not need help, Ubbus," she added.

Abbas smiled at that. A pine-tit nearby said its name over and over again. Crows cawed to each other in sets of three, as they often did on misty or foggy days. Children, those of Oboo, his brothers, and their various wives, talked and sometimes laughed nearby. As a doctor, Xu!luh was deeply ignorant and her pharmacopoeia extremely limited, but she had the basics down correctly because, unlike the Nonanye doctors, she was not distracted by ideas about how the body *ought* to work.

"Will you see me next?" Maia said suddenly. She wouldn't look at Abbas, though he stared at her. The miscarriages—at least six of them now—her spells of weakness when she couldn't get her breath, her worsening headaches, she'd always said she was fine. He hadn't believed her, but she wouldn't talk with him about it, and when he'd tried to press the issue, she'd snarled at him. Maia had a sometimes literally violent temper, and it had been getting worse. Now she wanted to be examined? Xu!luh ignored the tension and got to work.

She concluded that Maia's blood was "losing its virtue." Anemia, in other words. Nonanye medicine used a similar phrase. But Xu!luh went on, saying that diet was not the cause. "The balance is off, and there is contention at the root." Abbas did not understand that part, but he wrote down the recipe for the tea that Maia would need to drink daily maybe forever.

They spent the rest of the afternoon learning the soul-guiding song so Maia could sing it for Abbas every day. When she had it, Maia sang with Xu!luh and Benò, Oboo, and Oboo's mother, Buhuh joined in. Abbas listened and focused on it and held to it and fancied that he could feel the song guiding him home.

Over the next few months, Abbas lived quietly, doing his work and very little else, and gradually started to feel better. He could get through the day, and every day there was a little more light in the world. And early in the following summer, a year and a half after going to see Xu!luh, Maia, who no longer felt weak or dizzy and no longer had headaches, gave birth to a healthy baby boy. They named him Ardas.

Chapter 5. The Officer

Year of Nonani, 824 - 831

Hyras left for war again, but this time as an engaged man. He didn't return for two years. He wrote letters to his parents, his brothers, and to all the Dynans, but mostly he wrote to Ilia. Of all the people he wrote, she made the least response. He tried not to read anything into her silence but failed.

"I'm not unfeeling, just unthinking," she assured him in one of her few letters. "I'm constantly saying, 'I should sit down and write him,' and I really do mean to do it, but then the next thing I know, it's a week or a month later. Anyway, I think about you all the time."

"I can't hear your thoughts, though," he replied, "unless you write."

She never exactly apologized for being a poor correspondent. She never apologized for anything. He could not tell whether she was self-assured or simply self-centered. He didn't exactly care.

At last, the hill-people were defeated—or maybe just all killed, he honestly wasn't sure. As he'd expected, the legion did not return to the base near Furnace Complex Three, but as soon as he was given leave, he sought the Dynans as eagerly as a rabbit might run from an eagle towards its warren.

He arrived late in the day, foot-sore and disheveled, and still wearing his uniform because he had no civvies. He looked and felt ten years older than he had at his last visit, but Ilia found him standing in the yard and took him in her arms.

He joined the family for supper, a simple leftover stew, but Hyras had had nothing that day but breakfast, and he gratefully ate as much as he was given. He declined wine, so they gave him mint tea. He would have preferred posca, but they had none. They would have asked him questions and made much of him, but his mind seemed muddled. He acted a little dazed.

"Never mind," Rossa said, laughing. "Let me show you your room."

"My...?"

"Well, you didn't think I'd make my future son-in-law sleep on the atrium floor, did you?"

And so Hyras followed Rossa down a long hallway, and Yunas followed both of them, carrying Hyras's bag and a candle—night had fallen while they ate.

Once in the room, which was small but wood-paneled and comfortable, Yunas lit a lamp of two wicks from the candle while Rossa explained where the toilet was and how to use a little bell to summon a maid with wash-water or anything else he might need or want. Then they left him alone. And alone he sat there, on his bed, doing nothing.

Now that he'd had time for food and drink to enter his bloodstream, Hyras was no longer feeling dazed. He felt pretty good, physically. But he'd never had his own bedroom before. Nor had he ever before spent the night in a house with indoor toilets, nor any place at all that wasn't either his parents' home or an army facility. He sat in his room, still dressed, lamp burning, overwhelmed.

Ilia knocked on his door and entered. They hadn't been alone since he arrived, and after two years they were a little awkward with each other. They talked for a long while, mostly about all the things Ilia had been doing but not writing to him about. Their hands touched. She kissed him, almost but not quite shyly, and suddenly in a frenzy he was taking off her clothes. It was not romantic or gentle or skilled. Afterwards, laying more or less still stuck to her and still mostly dressed, he apologized.

"Hmm?" she asked.

"I didn't *ask* you."

"You asked in your own way. I answered."

He hefted one smallish, soft, warm breast. She pulled away slightly, so he stopped and instead traced the length of her right collar bone with his finger and cupped one smooth, dark shoulder.

"It feels so good to touch someone *alive*," he told her. She stroked his face but did not speak. "Can I tell you a secret?" he asked.

"Mmm?"

"That was my first time. A mess I made of it, didn't I?"

"You did alright. But—you basically live with two hundred prostitutes. And my sister's not the only woman who likes soldiers. If that was your first, what have you been *doing* when beautiful women throw themselves at you?"

"If a beautiful woman threw herself at me, I'd have ducked. I don't want beautiful women. I want you."

"Wow, that is *not* a compliment."

"Sorry, that didn't come out right."

"Let's get you out of your uniform. You've got so many layers—do you realize you're still wearing half your armor? I'll ring for a maid, she can bring you water and a towel and a robe. We'll get you in the baths tomorrow."

"But a maid—she'll think—"

"Shhh. It's alright. They are paid to not think. Anyway, we're almost married. I'm not even going to take pennyroyal. If a baby comes just slightly too soon after the wedding, no one will care."

She put her shift back on to go to the door and speak to someone. Returning to bed, she started by unlacing Hyras' hob-nailed sandals, then eased his sweat-damp leggings the rest of the way off. The mail unlaced at his throat and came off over his head like an ordinary shirt, but the thick, leather over-tunic gave her trouble until she found the ties under his arms. He let her undress him, and then, when she had his last layer off and neatly folded away, she looked over his nakedness briefly and touched one of his scars. He flinched.

"Sorry. Does that hurt?"

"I'm all ugly, now."

"You really aren't."

She embraced him again, laying back with him on the bed. He clung to her.

"You're so tense!" she exclaimed.

"I'm always tense, except when I drink. Ilia, I think something's the matter with me."

"Oh?"

"The boy who went off to war four years ago—you never knew him. He didn't come back. They make—they make you kill *yourself* first. Otherwise, you can't do the other."

"Hyras. You're not dead, you're just broken. And I have all the pieces right here." She squeezed him. He squeezed her back. He had no prior conscious memory of ever having been held.

Two weeks later, they were married.

Hyras did not dance at his own wedding, telling Ilia "I am a shy man, not a pushover," when she tried to insist. But he enjoyed the food. He enjoyed the spectacle and the ritual. He enjoyed watching his new wife dance, she all in white embroidered with gold but for the red shawl that all brides wear. He would have enjoyed his wedding night, except for a mild but very unpleasant case of accidental food poisoning. And afterwards he believed he belonged to a family that cared about him.

Over breakfast the first morning of his married life—they'd had almond pastries, soft-boiled eggs, and juice brought to their room— he broached the subject of their future.

"Oh, I suppose we'll set up housekeeping somewhere," Ilia said, quite breezily. She'd planned her wedding meticulously, but her married life not at all. "Daddy wants us to live here, of course, but if we live here we can't visit here, you see. I so love visiting. Don't you?"

"Ilia, you know I have almost no money, right?" He said it with a quirk of a smile.

"Oh, Hyras, you know I don't care about that!"

"Yes, you do. Do you have any idea what it's like to be poor? I could maybe rent us an efficiency in town. Those don't have toilets or kitchens."

She stared at him, then gathered herself.

"So I guess we'll eat take-out a lot," she replied, determined to be cheerful. "They say the simple life has such *grace*."

Hyras laughed at her, very fondly.

"Good thing one of us has sense," he said. "You keep me sane, and I'll keep you in some approximation of the life to which you are accustomed. I'll have to go to school, of course."

"Oh?"

"Enlisted men are plebeians and proles, paid accordingly," he explained, ironic. "Can't have the working folks getting too far ahead of themselves. Now that I'm an honored patrician," and he thickened the irony, "they'll let me try to become an officer. Pays slightly better, anyway. My centurion's already kicked my request for leave up the ladder. All goes well, I'll earn a commission and get to fight like a gentleman or something. I don't know if my five-year minimum service term will reset. Might. But doing five years as an officer beats doing just one more year as sword-bait."

"Oh, I'll like being married to an officer!"

"I bet you will. Now, I'll have to live on campus, which means you'll have to live here for a few years, but I'll get leave every tenth week, and the Fallow off, and that's a damn sight better than going a year or three without seeing each other."

"And worrying every day that you'll be killed or maimed."

"Now you're thinking."

His leave came through pretty quickly, but applying to a school and hearing back took months, months while he lived with Ilia as a married man and as an adopted son of privilege. The haunted look started, little by little, to leave him.

The Empire's officer training programs were all private, tuition-funded institutions, meaning there were more of them than the empire really needed, and Hyras had no trouble finding one just two days' ride from the Dynans', right on the outskirts of a small town with a good pub and a couple of interesting take-out places. He arrived dressed as a civilian so as not to stand out.

"Name, please?"

"Hyras Sylas Dynan."

"Nope, not here," the registrar said, after a moment. He looked up, expectant.

"That's not right. I have the acceptance letter right here."

"Nevertheless."

Hyras leaned over the table to read the list himself. The registrar frowned, obviously uncomfortable, but didn't object. Hyras had learned how to make himself hard to object to. Reading upside-down, he spotted an *almost* familiar name.

"There, that's me," he said, pointing.

"*Ulas* Sylas Dynan?" the registrar read. "But you said...."

"No, that's me."

The registrar shrugged and went with it.

Hyras never attempted to update the record. He knew to choose his battles, and chose not to battle bureaucrats and clerical errors. Outside of his family everybody called him b'Sylas anyway. Curiously, his new name made his initials pronounceable, since in written Itarish the SD combination made a th-sound. UTH. It meant nothing by itself, but featured in many common words. His first week off, Ilia came up and got a room for both of them at the inn, and then, over take-out sesame rolls, they sat together on the bed making lists of all the amusing things UTH might be short for.

Juthero (very big)

Oleutho (sexy)

Aranuthai (freshwater minnow)

Iuthret (unshaven)

As a veteran, Hyras was able to skip large parts of the program and ended up on a four-year plan, not the usual six. Mostly what he had left were academics, such as mathematics and philosophy. He picked up the material fairly well, but his grades remained mediocre because he could not make himself study when he knew he would pass. Instead, he read epics and comedic plays from the school library, wrote letters, or watched clouds go by. Where he excelled was in playing cards, strategy board games, or soccer during free time, or in the school's periodic war games.

That these people played at war—the games were an important part of the program, but they were games—struck Hyras as very weird. In general, the other cadets looked like children to him, even the ones close to his own age, and indeed they nicknamed him Old Man (*uthyas*, in Itarish). But he enjoyed the games, and whichever team chose him as captain always won.

He almost always won most things he bothered to compete in. He paid part of his tuition, after his own savings and the money his father could spare, hustling chess.

In the winter of his third year at school, he finally got Ilia pregnant, a sexy major miracle that did something weird to his belly whenever he thought of it. The child, born in seventh-month while he was at school, was a tiny, black-eyed girl. They named her Rosia. He found her as numinous as a young wild animal.

A commission upon graduation wasn't guaranteed—a legate had to pick your name out of the catalog your school sent around, and there were always more graduates than available spots. Hyras's mediocre grades made him a tight squeeze, but he got an offer immediately. At first he worried that the name Dynan had something to do with it, but no, his new Legate, Tyras Saras Bentan, had served as a tribune at Argessi and remembered him trying alone to retrieve the wounded from beneath the city walls at night. His name had changed, but his record hadn't.

Legate b'Saras wanted everybody ready to go come spring, so he sent Hyras money to update his gear. Hyras was back with the Dynans for the Fallow by then, but the nearest large town had a garrison, so he rode the fifteen miles in to get measured. Two weeks after that, he had to go back and stay for a few days for fittings. And then, after four years in a cadet's uniform, he was back in a soldier's tunic, this time as a centurion.

The new leggings were black, not brown. The tunic was red and had short but definite sleeves. And while his old fibula had been something like a big safety pin, the new one had the shape of an eagle. The new helmet had a fancy-looking crest of feathers, the tail-feathers of a red rooster (for Nonanye, mostly avid cock-fighters, chickens meant bravery). The greaves, shin-guards, sandals, and over-tunic were all as he remembered, but instead of mail he had a cuirass of segmented plates. He'd left his gladius and scutum with his old legion, with his old armor. Now, he was issued a spatha, which was like a gladius but longer, and the round shield known as a parma. Officer's weapons. They fit nicely into his hands.

On receiving his new duds, Hyras put on everything and took a look at himself. He liked what he saw. Rather than change back into his civvies and ride straight home, he went for a walk about town, a one-man parade. He was just starting to enjoy the thought that other people were looking at him when a teenage shop-clerk, probably a proletarian, wearing nothing but a worn, undyed tunic, saw him and laughed.

"Well, you be a pretty little rooster, yeah?"

Hyras managed some sort of retort and fled. Against armed barbarians or frightened, dangerous animals he was a very brave man, but he never in his life took pride in his own appearance again.

After several more weeks at home with his wife and child, he celebrated Hilaria and then left. He visited his parents and brothers for a few days on the way, then reported to his new legion and began his work as a centurion of the Prefect's Staff. He would have preferred an appointment to a Horse-Cavalry cohort, but given his grades he couldn't be choosy. Some people spoke poorly of the Staff, asking how a man could earn glory running a mess-tent, but Hyras did not care about glory, and he had great respect for the people who fed, paid, and otherwise cared for the legions. And he didn't like chopping other men into pieces. So as long as he had a job he could be good at and an opportunity to return home to Ilia eventually, he was pleased with things.

His first assignment was to manage the storage, upkeep, and re-pair of un-issued weapons and armor. His own mostly stayed in his locker in the centurions' bunk-house. That was alright. The legion was stationed at a large base, and so Hyras rented a room for his wife and daughter in one of the civilian neighborhoods. He usually got permission to join them there on his days off and at night after his duties were complete. The room was literally only a room, with a chamber pot behind a screen, but Ilia never complained, insisting that such short-term poverty was a fun adventure. Anyway, it was hardly real poverty. They had no servants but didn't need any, since they could send the laundry out and order food or anything else they needed in. The public baths weren't far, the neighborhood pub had an excellent loaded focaccia, and there was even a playground at the end of the block with a swing set shaded by fragrant laurel trees.

Ilia was pregnant again. He'd seen the first pregnancy only in brief glimpses nine weeks apart while he was in school, but now he was able to dote on his pregnant wife, feel the baby kick, and try to answer Rosia's questions about where babies come from. Nonanye people were normally forthright with their children about sex, but Rosia was two and couldn't keep straight whether it was the vagina that went into the penis or the other way around.

When the due-date got close, Crea came to stay and help out, and Hyras asked for and received leave. The midwife actually had to chase him from the room.

It was another girl. They named her Adna.

Hyras was doing well. While not especially gifted in his work—he did OK—he followed orders conscientiously, didn't cause trouble, and didn't tolerate trouble from anyone else. He rarely raised his voice, expecting those under him to quiet down to listen to him, which they nearly always did. He quickly learned the name of everybody he had occasion to work with, and he used the names in conversation, asking after this one's wife, that one's favorite dog, and this other one's aging mother. Though he had begun as Sixth Prefect's Centurion, he quickly moved up, becoming Second by Adna's birth. And that's why, just before Hilaria, when the first two cohorts were detached and sent on a mission alone, Hyras was one of the two prefect's centurions chosen to go with the detachment.

Putting his family on a stagecoach and watching them drive away was not what he wanted to do, but Hyras believed in doing his duty, and he did it.

The miniature legion marched north for three and a half increasingly wintry weeks to a small kingdom in eastern Duchasa whose king had asked Nonani for help with brigands and highway robbers. There being no fort in the area already, they built their own camp. Unfortunately, while there was no snow left, a spring cold snap had frozen the ground quite solid. The men couldn't pound in tent pegs, let alone fortify the perimeter. The tribune commanding the detachment, a man of about thirty named Henras Hallas Cullan, considered the problem briefly.

"Use hot water to make mud," he decided, "stick the tent pegs in that and let 'em freeze in. Forget fortifications. Just double the watch. The king's friendly, and initial intelligence says the brigands aren't organized. No little band is fool enough to attack twenty-three hundred men."

The initial intelligence was wrong.

Hyras was under one of the equipment tarps when he heard yelling and saw men running by with axes, then heard the signal horns blow as the centurions sought to organize the defense. The brigands ignored equipment and concentrated on people, so they parted around the tarp like a wave goes around a boulder. Hyras, standing more or less in the lee of various boxes and barrels, escaped their notice.

He was not armed, nor did he have his cuirass or helmet. He knew his duty was to find his civilian subordinates and keep them and himself out of harm's way.

Except he could not do that.

A messenger's horse stood saddled and waiting. A small cache of arms, including several cavalry bows and full quivers, sat nearby in boxes. Hyras strung one of the bows, took two quivers of the kind meant to hook on to a saddle, and set about calming the horse, who was not battle-trained and had correctly assessed the situation as very bad.

He did not hurry, showed no anxiety, and paid no particular attention to the ax-wielding men. Before long, the horse quieted, though she was still visibly afraid, and gave him a look like "OK, what do you intend to *do* about all of this, then?"

Good question. And he had an answer.

He mounted the horse, and together they left the tarp and observed matters. The Nonanye men had organized into defensive formations with the brigands chewing into them like ants around drops of honey. Hyras was outside it all, looking in, and no one paid any attention to him. The horse wanted to leave. She was no longer panicking, but she kept turning to go, and he kept having to turn her back.

"There's no point in running away," he told her in a quiet voice. "We just have to face it. We just have to be brave, OK?" He patted her neck. Her slightly shaggy hide felt good and warm under his palm. He could feel the power of her body—still just itching to run away—through his legs. A large fly flew by on business of its own. You hardly ever see flies en route to their next appointment, but he saw that one. He felt the horse calm. He urged her forward a step or two, just to see if she'd do it. "OK, you ready now? You ready to be brave? Good girl. Let's do this."

And he signaled her to gallop, not into the fray but at an oblique angle to it. Once in range and sure of not hitting the wrong targets, he shot arrow after arrow into brigand backs while guiding the horse with his knees. When the survivors turned around to see where the arrows were coming from, he was no longer there but on to the next clump of fighting men, and the next after that. Nobody could find him, so none could stop him. When he'd exhausted his quivers, he circled back around to the equipment tarp and supplied himself for another run. He made three runs in all before his horse needed a break, and by then the battle was ending anyway. His body-count that day, while impressive for a single man, could not of itself affect the outcome of the battle, but the brigands could not concentrate knowing an invisible person with a bow could be anywhere behind them, and they became a lot easier to cut down. Few escaped.

Nobody had gotten a very good look at the man on the horse, and Hyras didn't bother to mention his exploit to anyone, so it wasn't until after supper the next day that a messenger found him and told him to report to the tribunes' tent. There he found the Commanding Tribune and the Acting Prefect sitting in folding chairs, waiting for him. He saluted and stood at attention. Acting-Prefect b'Tardas invited him to relax, but not to sit down.

"Yesterday," began Tribune b'Hallas without preamble, "you took a horse not assigned to you, took weapons not assigned to you, engaged the enemy without orders, and neglected your duty to your own subordinates, some of them civilians. Are you aware that makes five violations of the conduct code?"

"Yes, sir."

"Well?"

"Sir, I acted without orders because the situation had changed since my orders were given, and I had no opportunity to receive new ones. I neglected my duty to my subordinates because in my judgment, Acting-Prefect b'Tardas had the same duty and did not need me to assist, whereas the rest of you did need me."

"Indeed, we did."

"Sir, am I to be punished?" Hyras wasn't worried, he just wanted the lecture over.

"Pff, gods, no. I just wanted to make sure insubordination and dereliction of duty aren't part of your ordinary MO. I don't know you very well."

"Consult my service record, sir. Under ordinary circumstances, such behavior would endanger the men and compromise the mission. I would not do that, sir."

"I see," said the tribune. "Well, I'm putting you in for a medal when we get back to Base."

"I'd rather receive a cash bonus."

"Oh?"

"My wife, sir, she likes pretty things. I'd like to get her a new dress."

One of the men killed in the raid had been a centurion. Hyras was temporarily given command of that century, leaving b'Tardas as the only officer of the Prefect's Staff. Hyras didn't have another opportunity for notable heroism, but his men liked him, and he did his job well. He decided that convincing men to go into battle wasn't all that different than doing the same thing with a horse. You just had to keep them pointed in the right direction. If you knew what you were doing, they'd feel it.

The camp was never again attacked, but twice Hyras took his century against brigand encampments, and squads on patrol sometimes found and fought against small bands. Losses were few, but gradually added up, plus men succumbed to accident and illness at the usual slow but steady rate. After three months, the detachment had lost enough people that b'Hallas reorganized it, making eighteen centuries rather than twenty. And so Hyras lost his century and returned to his duties as b'Tardas's assistant.

A month after that, it became obvious that the brigands were being reinforced somehow. There were never fewer of them. The local king, feeling threatened, appealed to the Ruling Council for more help. Another month after that, a full legion arrived to set up a permanent base. Nonanye military presence in client states, once initiated, only ever increased.

The new legion temporarily subsumed the detachment, with Tribune b'Hallas becoming Second to the Legate and everything else reorganized as needed. Hyras slotted in to the new organization as Third Prefect's Centurion and so was not invited to the debriefing meetings. He had to content himself with listening to gossip about his new boss, who was rumored to be impressive, having increased efficiency by ten percent in just a few months of being on the job. Some also said the Prefect was a woman, but Hyras had a hard time believing that.

But the next day in the officer's mess he spotted a slim, rangy youth in tribune-blue walking the aisles with a laden tray, looking for a good place to eat. After a moment, he realized the "youth" was actually close to thirty years old *and a woman*. The rumors about the new Prefect were true.

She was about six feet tall, not very curvy, with pale, brownish, extremely freckled skin, a brick-red mop of unruly hair, and unusually large eyes. She looked rakish and borderline underweight and had excellent posture.

She spotted him looking at her and came over. He started to stand up in deference to her rank, but she shook her head and sat down. He'd met female switchers before, there were a few on the Staff, but they'd always seemed like ordinary women in men's clothes. This one didn't. Her bearing was that of a man, so Hyras, without thinking about it, accepted her as such.

"I don't know you," she began, quite conversationally but without preamble.

"Ulas Sylas Dynan, sir," Hyras explained. "I'm the new Third Prefect's Centurion."

"Gwenessifyr Sheras Euan. Prefect."

"I gathered."

She blushed—quite visibly, given her complexion—and grinned. There was something uncanny about her he couldn't put his figure on, but that sweet, unguarded grin made her impossible not to like.

"Our not being introduced was stupid," she asserted. "I'll have questions for you—I have to come up to speed on your whole detachment, you know."

"Sir, I await your convenience."

"Eat! I'll await yours, and this ain't it." She took a bite of stew. "Man, what's in this? It's good."

"Bear meat. They killed a calista prowling the trash heap yesterday." Calista was one of the several species of bear on the continent, smaller than the others, usually back-furred.

"Oh, good job," exclaimed b'Sheras, quite genuinely. "See? This is why they should have introduced us. Nobody told me the camp was attracting bears. How am I supposed to look after this place if nobody tells me these things? I'll have to get one of the tribunes to set a watch on the dump or have a stockade built around it or...." She kept talking.

Hyras grunted in acknowledgment and resumed eating. If she wasn't going to stand on hierarchical ceremony, then he wouldn't either.

They ate in silence, briefly.

"So, what's your story?"

"My story?" Hyras asked.

"You don't talk like an officer—I don't doubt you are one."

"Tanner's son. Married a patrician."

"Oh, lucky you. Me, too. The married part, not the tanner part. I think Dad sold vegetables to take-out places or something. Eventually they made him a judge just because he knew everybody."

"*You* talk like a patrician, though."

"I know. Dad died when I was four, so I lost my accent. I'm adopted."

"By patricians?"

"Yeah. Not to be weird about it, but you *have* heard of my foster-father."

"Oh, *those* Euans!"

"Yep. I'm one of *them*." She said it as though her family must be strange and suspicious characters, then laughed.

"So, what do you do," he asked, "when you're not increasing efficiency by 10%?"

B'Sheras blushed and grinned again, then asserted "read books, chase girls, and beat people at spherical chess."

"I bet you can't beat me," Hyras said.

"You play?"

"I win."

"Oh, I'd love to see that! I'll take that bet. A day's wages sound good to you?"

"You *want* me to beat you?" Hyras asked.

"I don't care one way or the other. It's only chess, nobody's life is at stake. I want to find out if you *can* beat me."

"My day's wage against yours, then," Hyras agreed. "When and where?"

"You're serious? Awesome. Not everybody is, and I can't always tell. I'm in meetings all afternoon. Come to the tribunes' tent at supper, the other tribunes will be off supping with the Legate, plotting and planning, you know, but I can get out of it."

That settled, they both finished eating. Prefect b'Sheras abruptly got up and walked away.

That evening, just after dark, Hyras turned up at the new, larger tribunes' tent, finding it brightly lamp-lit and deserted by everybody but the Prefect, who wasn't even attended by an aide. He held up his chess set as a kind of entrance pass, and she grinned and waved him in.

"*Hello,*" she said, quite deliberately. "Sorry about leaving out the goodbye-bit earlier, I didn't mean to, I just forget that sort of thing sometimes. You want some wine?"

"No, thank you. I'll take fruit juice if you have it. Or posca."

"Posca it is, then. Is there enough light? I have, like, super-freaky night-vision, so I don't usually use this many lamps, and I don't have a handle on how many normal people need. You'd think I would know, as I *live* with normal people and have all my life, but, you know, it varies so much with context and so forth. I really should figure out some sort of functional average, the knowledge could come in handy in all sorts of situations, and I will, I just haven't yet. Supper's not fancy, but it'll do."

She indicated a pot of what proved to be an excellent rabbit stew sitting on a little table beside a basket of rolls and a spherical chess set ready for play. She fluttered around the tent in a generally hyperactive manner, manifesting drinks, bowls, spoons, garum, oil, folding chairs, and a bowl of walnuts and raisins, all the while muttering darkly--and occasionally spouting off about--how either the tribunes or their aides had already managed to misplace *everything*, meaning she'd have to re-organize the whole place *again*. Hyras sat down, laid his own chess set aside, and waited, amused.

Chess, in a Nonanye context, could refer to any of several different but closely-related strategy games. Like go and its variations, it was strongly encouraged at all officer training academies, but most people stopped playing the spherical version after graduation, finding it too difficult to be enjoyable.

Rather than a board, it used a ball of intersecting wires set on a stand so it could be rotated. The pieces clipped on to the wire intersections. The wires of each hemisphere formed interlocking sets of golden spirals, five in one direction, thirteen in the other, meeting the spirals of the other hemisphere at the equator in smooth curves. Not only was it impossible to see the whole playing-surface at once, but intersections could be "next to" each other, in the sense of being accessible in a single move, that lay literally on opposite sides of the sphere. There were also dozens of lesser-known rules under which in certain circumstances pieces could exchange places with each other, change identity, hide and reappear, or other such shenanigans. It was designed to be confusing.

Prefect b'Sheras finally took her seat and at once became utterly still and focused except for her left leg, which stuck out to the side away from the table and continually bounced up and down as though she had neither control nor awareness of it.

She was damn hard to beat. She did not make mistakes, seemed to think ten moves ahead or more, and never became so married to one strategy that she could not abandon it and immediately take up another. Hyras sat and watched her think. You can learn a lot from watching people think.

Eventually, Hyras built a trap that b'Sheras could not evade even though she knew perfectly well it was there. She paid up gallantly, then challenged him to a re-match and won most of her money back the following evening.

They played several more games over the following weeks as the legion-and-a-half built the physical structure of the new base. Each won about half the time, though their styles differed radically. But while Hyras lost half of their games, he came out ahead financially—he had specified "my day's wages against yours," and b'Sheras made a lot more in a day than he did. He worried that maybe the fact had slipped her mind when she agreed to the bet. He felt a little guilt about it until his detachment re-detached and went to rejoin their own legion. Prefect b'Sheras's legion stayed where it was, and Hyras didn't think about her much for a while.

That began a bad time. The legion as a whole moved to a remote fort, having finished its local work assignments, and there was no way for Ilia to live nearby. Without her, Hyras did not feel quite real.

At first missing her and the girls was merely difficult. Hyras could deal with difficulty, and things seemed to be otherwise going well for him. B'Tardas, along with a few others, had been assigned to the new base in Duchasa, making Hyras First Prefect's Centurion. When the Prefect had a stroke and abruptly retired, Hyras took his place. He did a decent job and frankly looked good in blue.

But his father was not happy with the promotion, opining by letter that the Prefect's Staff was "the bitch of every legion," and telling him to do man's work "if you can." Hyras knew better, but his father's words worked at him. They always had. And since his legion was stationary and not involved in any sort of combat, his work as Prefect quickly became routine, leaving him too much time to think about other things, such as how it felt to step on a dead body, the way the flesh would give a bit under your sandal, and then the flies would come....

At the same time, the number of letters he got dropped way off. His mother remained consistent, but for months at a time he rarely heard from anyone else, and he didn't hear from Ilia at all. He supposed she must be busy with the baby, but she could at least write him a brief note—about the baby, for example. He'd last seen Adna as a newborn, but she must be learning to sit up by this time, maybe even crawl. She'd learn to talk, soon, and he wouldn't be there....

And then the horrible thought occurred to him that maybe she wasn't doing any of those things because maybe she was dead. Babies died all the time for all sorts of reasons or sometimes for no reason at all. Maybe Adna had died. Maybe Rosia had died. Maybe Ilia had died. He was no longer sure anyone would tell him if such things happened. All the letter-writers had fallen away (except his mother, dependable, if still unsentimental, in that respect). He felt like he lived on the far edge of the world.

Hyras knew very little about mental health, and most of what he did know was wrong. He didn't understand what was happening to him.

Drinking a little applejack seemed to help.

He hadn't had any alcohol in years, but lately his avoidance of it had begun to seem silly, given that everybody around him drank a lot. And a little whiskey poured in his canteen warmed him up nicely, sort of took the edge off. The problem was that he could not stop at just a little. As soon as he got off duty, out the mixed canteen would come.

He was hardly unusual in liking alcohol, most Nonanye did, and Hyras actually consumed much less than the other officers—but he got drunker, having much less tolerance. Anyway, drunk on apple-jack, considered lower-class or barbarian, just seemed drunker to his wine-drinking fellow officers, a more serious symptom of the loss of manly control.

And as sober as he stayed on duty, Hyras drank enough when off that his sweat smelled of stale booze more or less constantly. His stomach hurt. He wasn't sleeping well. The croak of ravens or the sound of the signal horns made him startle. A stiff breeze rustling the trees made him feel queasy thinking of the sound of massed, flying arrows. The nightmares returned. There were days he skipped break-fast because he couldn't bear to get out of bed. He wasn't (usually) hung-over, it was just that the weight of an olifant turd seemed to press upon his chest, a dull miasma of ick.

For seven months he did his work and did it well but miserably. Rumors and grumbles swirled around him, mostly not acrimoniously, but soldiers get bored and need to talk about something. He didn't much care. Ilia wasn't writing. He thought his father must be right about him.

Finally, Legate b'Saras called him in and told him, not unkindly, that he could either resign or be dishonorably discharged.

"But—sir, I don't really drink that much," he protested. "And never when on duty." He wanted to leave the army, but not like this.

"Prefect," b'Saras said, "we both know it's not the alcohol."

Chapter 6. Another Officer

Year of Nonani 822 - 831

Gwen married Chrys over the spring break of her final year at school. They were both nineteen years old and almost comically opposite physically, the one tall, pale, and skinny, the other short, dark, and not plump but solid. People said Chrys looked like a version of her father that had been shrunk by poor washing. Gwen spent the entire day grinning and didn't know it.

They held the ceremony in the Euans' garden. Plywood and straw protected the not-yet planted beds, garlands of flowers climbed the colonnade, tables all but bent under trays of finger-food and bowls of wine-punch. Most of Nonani City's high society attended, for it's not every day someone like the elder daughter of Senator Euan marries. Chrys wore a white shift, a green and gold overdress, and the red veil all brides wear instead of a mantle. Gwen wore the first really nice civilian outfit she'd had since switching, tunic and leggings in a warm yellow and a white scapular embroidered in gold and red. The red was a nod to Gwen's supposed femininity, but like all grooms she wore a botanical crown, in her case hawthorn just coming into bloom.

Tomas sacrificed the goat himself, sanctifying the wedding ground, the couple, and their families, who in this case were one family. Opal laid down a circle of sesame seeds and coriander nine feet in diameter around Chrys. Everyone but the songbirds and bees grew quiet to listen.

"I would enter, if you will it," said Gwen, very seriously and humbly.

"I will it. Enter and stay, if you will it," replied Chrys. Ritual words, said exactly the same way every time, since before the dawn of history.

"I will it."

Gwen stepped into the circle, and there she and Chrys fed each other seed cakes and honeyed wine. It was done. The kissing afterwards was not technically required, but all couples did it.

Then the band struck up a pair-dance tune. Once the seed circle was obliterated by dancing feet, husband and wife could dance where they liked, together or separately. Gwen loved to dance and was good at it. Soon, the goat reappeared, its meat stewed with and bulked up by onions, garlic, figs, juniper berries, and imported tamarind. You didn't need a plate, just a flatbread and some sour cream.

Gwen and Chrys had two special duties besides having a good time. First, they had to give out little bags of candied almonds to everybody. Second, they had to try to sneak away unseen. Of course, they were caught and subjected to a rain of fennel seeds and extremely crude and often quite graphic dirty jokes, as if the couple might not know what to do in bed if they weren't told. That there were children present inhibited nobody. Some of the jokes were traditional and suggested Gwen was anatomically male. Some very clearly suggested that she was not. Nobody really cared. At last, the couple escaped to go do whatever they liked with whatever they had.

That night, afterwards, Gwen and Chrys talked in bed for a long time. Gradually they spoke less and less. Chrys snuggled down in the sheets. Then Gwen stretched like a cat and announced "ah, Chrys, my life, my love, my twin!" in a loud voice.

"SLEEPING," said Chrys.

"Come on, you *can't* be sleepy yet!"

"I can be, and I am!"

"I'm just getting started," announced Gwen, literally bouncing. She could see everything in the room without difficulty, just by the moonlight filtering through the window curtain. She had never been enthusiastic about going to sleep when other people did.

"OK, that's IT" Chrys announced and got up and put on her robe.

"What? Where are you going?"

"If you won't *shut up* so I can sleep, I need cookies."

"That makes no sense!" Gwen protested.

"I don't care. You want some?"

"Sure. Get me some of those almonds, too, they were good."

"No way, almonds make you fart!"

"I'll fart *under* the covers," Gwen promised, but Chrys was already bumbling away through the dark. A while later, Chrys returned, bearing a basket of cookies that she placed between herself and her husband and a cloth bag of almonds that she handed to Gwen.

"Be good," Chrys told her.

"I'm always good," Gwen replied as if stung, then added "in bed," and tossed two almonds into her mouth.

"I look forward to having more data with which to assess that claim," Chrys told her, quite formally, then laughed.

The next morning, sitting on the cool tiles of the atrium floor, the two addressed their pile of wedding presents, mostly notes informing them of gifts of money, real estate, and stock, but there were more personal items, too. Chrys got new strings for her harp, a collection of exotic cooking spices, and a very nice prayer-book. Gwen got a small library of books on the art of war, as well as a very large jar of candied ginger. And then there were gag gifts—among them, sex toys.

"Do they think I married a woman by accident?" Chrys asked.

"Or maybe without knowing?" Gwen suggested, holding up hers by one end as though it might drip. It was impressively large, ceramic, and painted with happy-looking eels. Chrys had a smaller one of sanded wood with interesting bumps and ridges.

"They must think I was so disappointed last night, then!"

"I *definitely* don't need anyone to give me a sword for this mission," Gwen asserted.

"Speaking of which," said Tomas from behind them. Both young people shrieked and rushed to cover their dildos in a panic of embarrassment. "Gwen, I have something for you I didn't want to leave in the pile." He held something behind his back.

Gwen got up and stood before her foster-father at respectful attention. He still towered over her.

"How do you feel?" he asked.

"Proud to be a real Euan at last, sir," she answered.

"You always were a real Euan," Tomas told her, "in all but name. And you remain a real Lyran, in all but name. I honor your origins, son-of-Sheras." He waited while Gwen fidgeted in happy embarrassment, then handed her the present: a katana.

Open-mouthed with astonishment, Gwen took the gift. Its sheath and pommel were leafed in red gold. Its handle was wrapped in real shark-skin. Stepping away from the others for safety, she drew the sword and found that its lightness, balance, and flexibility were everything she could have ever wanted.

"Sir, this is a king's weapon," she said.

"Gwen, you know I am a humble man," Tomas told her. "I would rather live below my means than above them, rather be thought poor than stingy or profligate. But I am rich, and that has its advantages. Do you want to try it?"

Gwen, still awed, stepped farther away, giving herself room, then sheathed her sword and knelt, holding the sword by her hip as though it were fixed to her belt. She became utterly still and centered, then exploded into a rapid series of graceful cuts, thrusts, turns, and blocks, the Tenth-Level Sword Form. Then she mimed wiping the blood off her sword, sheathed it, and returned to centered, kneeling stillness. Of course, Gwen could not stay still very long. She popped up, grinning, and thanked Tomas simply and sincerely.

"You're welcome. But I gave you a sword because I want you not only to fight but also to win. You come back to us, you hear?"

"Yes, *sir!*" Gwen replied.

MARRIAGE SHOULD BE THE DEFINITIVE step into adulthood, when a new husband leaves his parents to go support his wife's family. But if your wife's family IS your own, and you don't have a job yet, and you can't even get your wife pregnant, what, exactly, is the point? She wondered the whole school year and was still wondering when she finished the academy program, threw one last party for her friends, and got so drunk she slept most of the next day and had to stay on campus an extra night and miss her family's Natalia dinner. Great.

"HEY, GWEN, DOES THE NAME Paracelias mean anything to you?"

Gwen almost knocked her wife over to seize the letter. Then she read, completely oblivious to Chrys's repeated questions.

"My brother," Gwen crowed at last. "My own, actual, related-to-me brother! You remember Paracelias, don't you? You don't? How strange, you used to play with us too, or I guess we played with you, we all went over to your house, not the other way around, you really don't remember him? What about Micalion? Anyway, yes, my brother, I thought he was dead or had forgotten about me or something, I never forgot about him, but I didn't know how to get a hold of him, and it turns out he didn't know how to get a hold of me because he didn't remember the Euan name or how to get to the house, but one of my professors, he's an elf, I told him about my family, and he tracked down Paracelias and gave him my contact information, because it turns out Paracelias is famous, or sort of famous, or semi-famous just a little, anyway, he wrote a book, you do that to become a philosopher, it's called a dissertation, and Jeriorniress read it and remembered the name and did this for me, he didn't tell me he was going to do that, ain't that fantastic? He really is a very good man, and so anyway, Paracelias wrote to me, and he's sent me Micalion's contact info, too, do you want to read the letter? He remembers you, and you did used to really get along, do I need to ask your father permission to invite them over to visit, or can they just come?"

Gwen danced and jigged all around the room, her joy and astonishment too great for her slim body to contain. Then, without waiting for Chrys to answer any of her questions, she sped off to find papyrus and pen so she could write back.

Chys looked after the receding back of her husband and shook her head, grinning.

"I was going to tell you, I think your commission came in, too," she said, to the empty air.

GWEN AND FIFTEEN OTHER NEWLY-hired centurions boarded a river-trader bound for a base on an archipelago of islands just above the delta of the Old Mother River.

The weather was fine for the crossing, blue sky streaked with mares'-tail clouds and, it being early in first-month, still a little chilly when the wind blew over the water. For hours they could not see either shore, nor anything else but the vast river. Then the islands appeared in the distance, hills seeming to float above the brownish water in an illusion the oarsmen were used to but could not explain. Gradually the hills grew bigger and rooted themselves to reality, a little archipelago, the buildings and tents among the olive trees on the heights, the water-cypress and willow fringing the little coves and bays and creeks choked with reed and cattail and protected by bars and islets of mud and sand, and as the boat came near, angling for the harbor on the largest island, thousands of white egrets just then starting to nest in the water-cypress rose up crying and little terns dove into the water like black-and-white darts, fishing, and Gwen thought she'd remember the scene forever.

After she met her new tribune, a wiry, middle-aged man named Arras Nyas Eran, the other centurions of the cohort kidnapped her, stripped her naked, and tossed her off the nearest dock and into the muddy river. She emerged furious and shivering and found the others laughing at her.

"Hazing I could do without," she announced.

"No you couldn't," one of them explained, still laughing. "Joining the army's gotta suck or it doesn't count. Come on, let's get you cleaned up."

GWEN HAD JOINED A COVERT operations cohort, but there were no such operations at the moment, so Gwen had plenty of discretionary time. Besides training, she went fishing, climbed olive trees, helped in the farm fields, and attended parties with pretty girls in the civilian parts of the archipelago. When she learned she could rent a room in the civilian village, she did so and sent for Chrys. After that, Gwen still enjoyed flirting with other women at parties, but she saved the last dance for her wife, always.

A LETTER FROM MICALION! HE'D gotten her letter (obviously) and was delighted to hear, etc. He couldn't come visit because he was studying to become a philosopher like Paracelias, and his master would not let him go anywhere yet.

A LETTER FROM PARACELIAS! HE could not visit, either. He was living far away in Holia.

"It's curious, our people have never domesticated animals, perhaps because we do not domesticate each other. But I do like these sheep. They are very contemplative company. And although logic suggests there must be a way to make a living as a philosopher (in as much as there are full-time philosophers who persistently do not starve) I, erm, do not know what it is, yet. Perhaps the sheep will tell me."

He actually spelled out erm, uh, and ah in his letters.

"Regarding our mother, I can assure you, she never forgot you. I remember she sent you a letter the very week she died. I think you would have been five or six? She got sick not long after we got back home. Our word for the disease is pulmonary tuberculosis. She wanted me to look after you. She thought I knew how to write to you, but I did not. You may, ah, blame me for our silence."

Of course she blamed him for nothing.

ON A HOT DAY, IF you jumped off the dock, the river-water would still be cold, but so turbid you usually could not see as much as an inch through it. You could not see your swimming hands. Some days, if you sank below the surface and opened your eyes, you saw only blackness. Gharials did not need to see to find their prey, but fortunately they ate only small fish. Jokes at the expense of swimming men followed. Gwen had an advantage.

GWEN WAS TELLING A STORY and onomatopoeiaized the sound of a whip as "waPU!" The others all laughed at her. Because waPU! was wrong. Whips were supposed to go "crack," apparently. But they sound like waPU! There were lots of rules like that. The other soldiers liked her anyway.

WHEN MOST OF THE LEGION got leave for the Fallow, Chrys insisted on going home. Gwen insisted they were home but to no avail. She didn't want to go spend her vacation with the parents like a superannuated cadet, but somehow Chrys outvoted her.

MORE LETTERS FROM PARACELIAS. SHE replied to every one as soon as she received it. She had so many questions she dared ask none, lest in pumping him for information she exoticize him, treat him as something other than fully, individually human. And yet he was exotic anyway. He was the stranger she'd loved all her life, the myth made real. He was made of words, and she did not remember his face.

GWEN LIKED WATCHING THE SHORELINE slip by. Black-skinned kelpies, bulbous-bodied, yawned at each other in the shallows, and gharials sunned themselves on the banks. Near villages, children ran along the tops of the banks shouting and waving. Gwen always waved back. But pulling rank to stay on deck wasn't her style. After the first day, she yielded her place to a milite and spent the rest of the trip in the hold, getting motion-sick and trying to figure out how a girl might piss in a jar. When she and her men finally unloaded, she found herself in another world, frost-blasted, wind-swept, and tangled. No snow left, but the tall, dense trees everywhere looked dead. Gwen knew about deciduous trees, but had never seen so many before. She was part of a detachment sent to go deal with a rogue base commander in independent Slovona.

Gwen had only thirty men in her century—Covert Ops centuries were always small and few—but she also commanded the Infantry century escort, its centurion acting as her Second, because it was a Covert Ops mission. No other centuries disembarked with them because the plan was for each Covert/Infantry pair to cross the watershed divide into Slovona alone, so as not to attract attention. Gwen ordered her men into armor, friendly territory be damned, she didn't trust it, and had everybody pack up. Her own kit weighed over sixty pounds, and even breathing under it took effort, but she saw neither her rank nor her sex as a reason to carry less than her fair share. Men double her size noticed and shouldered their loads without complaint.

Their second night out, Gwen chose a beaver meadow for a camp—a bit wet, but plenty of water and fuel-wood available, with good visibility on one side. On the other side a dense, young oak and pine forest, so Gwen ordered the watch on that side doubled overnight.

While the men made camp, she strolled along the edge of the woods just under the overhanging boughs wondering if she ought to send hunters out. She didn't have a lot of extra food, but hunting takes time, as does cooking game, and she knew her men needed sleep. She wondered what Jonas would do. He was a tribune, now. She wondered if Paracelias had ever fought, or ever would. She wished she and Chrys could make a baby together and wondered what such a child would be like.

A raven perched on an oak-branch. She felt a thrill of superstitious fear. A raven had a way of reminding a person of the Raven, the great friend to all the humankinds whose help one dearly hopes not to need just yet. Gwen told herself that this was just a bird, only the incarnate shadow of the other, not to be silly. And then she spotted another raven and another. She'd never seen so many in one place, except at a carcass.

Or at a place the ravens expected carcasses to be.

"Company!" Gwen shouted.

Dozens of men jumped out of the forest, their cover blown. One lunged towards her, and she reacted from trained habit. A small, wet sound, a brief rush of air, and nothing else, no scream no grunt, no final words, just a corpse collapsing softly in the old, dead leaves.

"I did it," she said to herself, awed and shocked. "I really did it." But then another barbarian was coming towards her, and then another, and so she had to do it again and again, and again. She didn't think about it so much after that. She never learned who the barbarians were or why they'd attacked. They had nothing to do with the rogue commander.

✳   ✳   ✳

GWEN VOLUNTEERED TO LEAD THE diversion, in part because she could see well at night. The rogue was neutralized. The division went back to base, but before Gwen could send for Chrys, the Covert Operations cohort mobilized again, attaching temporarily to a different legion that didn't have one of its own. It was a busy summer and autumn. Gwen rose quickly in relative ranking, becoming third in her cohort by the end of the year.

But there were problems.

Gwen had always treated everybody more or less the same regardless of rank. She had no trouble following orders and was far from an egalitarian philosophically, but she'd offer unsolicited advice to tribunes, crack jokes with milites, and do whatever she thought needed doing without waiting to be told. It wasn't a great eccentricity to have in the army, but then few eccentricities were, and Covert Ops was considered the refuge of eccentric soldiers. For purely practical reasons, Covert Ops cohorts cultivated people of unusual talents, gave them whatever leeway they needed to perform well, and gave leadership roles to whomever had the skillset necessary for a particular mission regardless of rank. You had to be disciplined, and you had to be good at your work, but you could be weird. Everybody who knew Gwen slightly had assumed she would thrive there, and assumed too that she'd chosen Covert Ops specifically for that reason. Those who knew her well knew better.

Gwen had no idea she was as weird as she was, she just found Covert Ops an appealing puzzle. And she did not ignore hierarchy so much as frequently fail to notice it in the first place. An outfit where status was only loosely associated with rank and changed all the time did not help. Because Covert Ops *did* have a hierarchy—Gwen just couldn't figure out what it was.

When she'd first joined, she'd been unambiguously at the bottom by any measure, so for the first year there had been little trouble. But in her second as she rose in rank, that clarity was lost. She was always stepping on somebody's dignity somehow, and while everybody knew she was just Gwen being Gwen and gave her a pass, she noticed the moments of tension. She knew she was doing *something* wrong, but she didn't know what. And she couldn't fix it.

A certain kind of stress inevitably made all the less desirable of her eccentricities worse. She grew scatter-brained (though never about work), irritable, impatient, and closer to socially clueless. And since Gwen habitually analyzed everything and everybody but herself, she was only dimly aware that she had changed. She thought everyone else had just gotten harder to deal with. She also thought she was about to get in serious trouble, but she didn't know why.

"Hey, b'Sheras, ya got a moment?" b'Nyas said. It was a raw, rainy day late in tenth-month, and he was suddenly walking alongside her. Very few people could sneak up on Gwen, but b'Nyas could. It seemed to amuse him.

"Of course, sir," she replied and turned to face him.

"Oh, we can keep going wherever you were headed," he told her. She didn't realize that he was being kind—he knew she could handle anything better if she were physically in motion. She started walking again, scowling at the mud, as she always did.

"What is it, sir?"

"How are you feeling these days?"

"How am I feeling? I don't know. OK, I guess. I'm healthy."

"Are you? I think you're a nervous wreck."

She startled at that, and he laughed.

"B'Sheras, I'm a psy-ops specialist," he reminded her. "It's my job to know when people are stressed."

"Is anything wrong with my work?"

"No, on the contrary, you're very good for us—but I don't think we're very good for you."

"Sir?"

"Let me guess, you're worried right now that you're in trouble for some vague thing?"

Gwen did not respond.

"You're not," b'Nyas assured her. "Your work is uniformly excellent, and if getting work out of you were the only thing I cared about I'd go toe-to-toe with whomever to keep you in my cohort. But it's not, so I've asked Legate b'Jerras to transfer you to the Prefect's Staff, to take effect in the spring."

"Sir!"

"The fact that you currently feel a rush of fear and shame for no reason at all is exactly why I'm doing this. You don't have to like my decision, but I wanted you to understand."

Gwen didn't like it. And for a long time she didn't understand. She arrived home for the Fallow irritable and morose and inclined to kick things that perhaps should not have been kicked.

Micalion is coming! His letter said so!

She looked for him, perking up almost every time she heard someone walk by outside, for days and days, then got distracted and forgot to even think about it until she heard the maid answer the door. She ran downstairs. There were two young men standing in the atrium.

One of them was Micalion. How did she know that? She'd last seen him when he was six. This man was twenty-something, shortish, slightly plump over a bird-like frame, straight brown hair starting to recede from a high forehead, pale as sandstone, beardless, gray-eyed, with an ironic quirk to his mouth. Gwen squeaked and rushed into his arms, realizing too late that he was on crutches.

"I'm sorry," she said, catching him when he would have fallen. "I don't even normally hug people."

"Neither do I, but it's quite alright," he assured her, steadying himself. She made sure he had his feet under him properly, but then her attention snagged on the other man. It was like looking in a mirror, except for his maleness and his shorter, up-turned nose.

"You," she said after a moment, "you are also my brother. You are another b'Sheras."

"Orpharias Sheras Lyran," he acknowledged. "Or Orpharias ni Ellianiine. Same difference."

"I told you I had a surprise," Micalion said, smiling.

Because of his polio-shriveled leg, Micalion waited in the atrium while Orpharias and Gwen took the bags upstairs. When they came down, they found him out in the garden.

"This," he said. "I remember this. I remember playing here. There were...other children. I used to be able to climb trees.... There was a baby, wasn't there? A toddler?"

"Chalcedony," Gwen confirmed. "You know, she's engaged to marry my friend, Sammas now?"

"That *shouldn't* be surprising...."

"I know. I half expected you to be a lot taller than me."

"Well, I once was. But everything here besides you has shrunk!"

Gwen heard the front door open and close, recognized Tomas's step, and called to him. He met them in the garden.

"Micalion!" he exclaimed, "I don't suppose you remember me?"

"You? *You* are not smaller!" Micalion replied with feeling. Gwen and Orpharias laughed. Tomas looked confused.

"Do you hug?" Tomas asked.

"I do not," Micalion confirmed. Most elves didn't.

"I do!" exclaimed Orpharias, then blushed at his own over-eagerness. But Tomas smiled.

"I have hugs for anybody who wants them," he pronounced, gravely.

As to why Orpharias had been left a surprise, Gwen couldn't get a good answer. Orpharias himself would say only "I was afraid you wouldn't like me." But he was impossible not to like, as bouncy as she but less fidgety and more childlike, a younger nineteen than Gwen had been.

Orpharias, shadow-boxing with Sammas like a pair of puppies. Gossiping with Euas about hot girls. Getting irrationally freaked out about seeing a spider web because he *might* walk into it. Becoming anxious and out of sorts because the soap smelled wrong. He wore a silver fascinus on a string around his neck—he sucked on it to cope with his strange anxieties, apparently unaware of why that looked funny. He was a favorite of all children. One of Topaz's daughters announced her intention to marry him someday.

"You don't want to marry me, really," he told her. "By the time you're of age, I'll be way too old. But you can pretend I'm your boy-friend, if you want."

Orpharias, playing his lute and singing. He had a startlingly beautiful voice, could sight-read music in two languages, and knew all the old standards. Micalion sometimes played with him on a two-headed skin drum. Chrys would get out her harp, and the three would fill the house with sound.

Micalion, sitting in the atrium bundled up in a blanket against the winter chill, reading or chatting with whoever passed by. When it rained, he only moved under the shelter of the eaves. He called the fine white drizzle into the citroen trees and the sheeting of water down the red roof tile pretty.

Micalion and Gwen stayed up together more nights than not, talking fast and intense, an evolving, two-person essay about everything in the world, all properly cited, of course. They even sometimes gestured asterisks in order to foot-note in tangential comments for later exploration. Night-time wasn't dark for him, either. Just like color wasn't real. He literally saw the world as Gwen did.

From Micalion Gwen finally learned the word ubum, a way to say what she wasn't besides *normal*.

A NEW ASSIGNMENT!

Ralani, an ancient and well-respected coastal city at the mouth of a small river, had been reduced to ash and rubble by earthquake and fire. In the spring, after Hilaria, the legion went to rebuild the city and to feed and protect those few survivors who had not yet moved away.

Gwen, now a member of the Prefect's Staff, was in charge of food. To telegraph bases—all of which had their own ring of farms—and order rations for the legion and the survivors was easy, but she quickly realized it wasn't enough. Food alone would not keep the survivors from leaving, let alone get the refugees to return. Without a functioning economy to anchor a real community, Ralani would go out of existence no matter how many buildings the legion put up. Only, nobody else seemed to be doing anything about it.

So while she awaited the first ration shipments, she had her people (in the Prefect's Staff it was called an office, not a century) conduct a thorough inventory of what exactly the survivors *did* and did not have. Then she ordered another month of rations, but also whatever she could get of what the Ralanye had lost—fishing nets, farming equipment, and breeding stock, for although the city's cattle herds were intact, their smaller animals had been in the city when it burned. She placed a similar order the next month, except instead of standard rations for Ralani or the legion, she ordered staple foods the survivors didn't have—then she traded those staples for what the survivors did have: eggs, cheese, honey, beef, and fish. And so a fledgling sort of market opened.

Meanwhile, the legion cleared rubble, sorted through salvaged materials, and began building bunkhouses for the Ralanye who'd been sleeping in donated tents.

After Cerealia and the Bull Sacrifice, the wheat harvest started coming in, then the apples. The city salt-works produced its first new crop. Gwen ordered different goods as the people's needs changed, bringing seeds for replanting gardens, seedling trees for woodlots and the little home orchards. The Ralanye were busy making salable goods—hides, horn drinking cups, straw baskets and hats, wool rugs, firewood, necklaces made of seashells—now that there was something for them to buy. Gwen supported their efforts by asking the legion's commissary not to compete. If the men wanted hats or cups or firewood, they had to buy them in the market and pump cash into the system.

By the end of the year, Gwen was Second Prefect's Centurion.

GWEN'S ANXIETY WENT AWAY. IF she couldn't be Covert Ops, working for b'Nyas, then Prefect's Staff was a fine place to serve, and the structured, rule-bound social environment made sense to her. The only thing she'd ever seriously feared was not being able to do her duty.

RALANYE PATRICIANS LIVING ELSEWHERE SENT messengers to anxiously inquire about their real estate, so Legate b'Jerras had maps made of exactly who owned what. As lots were cleared, he encouraged soldiers to move out of the legion's camp and instead rent tents and tent-sites from the absent land-owners. It was a way to keep the patricians literally invested in the city, and it was Gwen's idea.

She and Chrys got one of the first tents, a small wall-tent with a cook-stove and improvised furniture. That tent felt like home, Gwen's own, real, adult home, in a way their rented room on the base had not. She drew pictures on scrap wood and collected feathers and sea-shells to decorate it. Chrys dug up wild aromatics, such as oregano, lavender, or onion, and grew them in pots. They looked so cheerful, green in a world of ash, charred brick, and tent canvas. With little more than flour, eggs, anchovies, and her houseplants, Chrys could make a feast. After dinner, she'd get out her harp, and everybody in the neighborhood would grow quiet to listen. Gwen, drinking wine in front of her tent in the cool of the evening, watching her wife, the girl born to luxury and privilege, literally making a home in a debris field, felt herself unutterably lucky.

"DID YOU HEAR? MA EUAN is *expecting*!" It was the word up and down the neighborhood and doubtless back in Nonani City as well. *Ma* was the formal honorific for the married daughter (or wife) of a paterfamilias.

"Ma Euan? Pregnant? *How*?"

Except they knew. Everybody knew semen could be transferred without intimacy. And if intimacy had been involved, well, that was Gwen's business. A wife's sexuality belonged to her husband (but not vice-versa), and a husband was free to share. The whispers amused Gwen. Of course she could hear them. She could hear everything.

Later they all started whispering again because the child came out looking like Gwen.

GWEN MADE SURE TO GET one of the first new, real houses, not a bunk-house but a Ralanye-style middle-class dwelling, several large rooms opening onto a courtyard that served as atrium, garden, and kitchen combined. Each room was an apartment, divisible as needed by painted, woven screens, with large windows protected by wooden slats to let the breeze in. In the shade of the wrap-around porch, you could sit and watch the world go by. Gwen split the rent and the wages of a live-in housekeeper with two other officers. Three officers, their wives, the proletarian housekeeper, and her young son, Ricas, made eight. The house sat on the south side of a sandy bluff, near the top. You could see blue water from the front door.

CHRYS HAD WANTED TO RETURN to her parents as the birth grew close, but that would have meant being away from Gwen until the baby was old enough to travel. Instead, Gwen arranged for Tomas and Opal to come to Chrys. They brought housewarming gifts practical and otherwise, for the house was still only partly furnished. There was a lot to do, and Chrys's nesting instinct grew very strong—she was literally scrubbing the walls when her water broke. Tomas ran off to get the midwife while Opal ran off to get last-minute supplies, leaving Chrys and Gwen alone together for possibly the last time in the next fifteen years.

"Are you sure you want to do this?" Chrys asked, joking yet not joking, a towel held awkwardly between her legs. Gwen laughed softly and took her wife in her arms.

And then the midwife arrived and chased Gwen (but not Opal) out of the room.

"But I'm a woman!" Gwen protested. It sounded somehow wrong even as she said it, but she was desperate. Anyway, the midwife didn't care, so Gwen, exiled, paced in the courtyard for hours, barely sleeping, through the day and a half of labor. Tomas sat on a bench, watching her go back and forth like the birdie at a badminton game, until night fell and his ubum eyes could not see.

"Your father was just the same," he told her, around midnight. The night was bright with stars. Gwen could smell both the sea and the nearby river.

"What?"

"When the midwife came to attend your birth, Sheras came over to my house. He didn't know what to do with himself. He wouldn't stop pacing, so I paced with him. We must have covered fifteen miles that night, back and forth across my atrium and around my garden. The Owl comes slowly, the first time, but she does come."

"I'm not nuts to worry, though," Gwen protested. "The Raven attends the Owl, they say."

"Remember how this feels when next Chrys sends you off to battle."

Gwen winced.

It was a girl. The baby was dark as Chrys, but the shape of her face, the size of her nearly colorless eyes, her long, elegant limbs hardly bigger around than a woman's thumb, they all echoed Gwen.

"Leh, leh, leh!" she squalled, her small chin vibrating.

"Leh, leh, leh," Gwen murmured, mimicking her. "She don't sound like she's crying."

"She's not, she's yelling. She's pissed off, like her daddy," Chrys asserted. She offered a breast.

"I'm not pissed off."

"No, I mean you yell *when* you are."

"I do not. I argue intelligently with increased volume and urgency."

"Whatever. Look at her eyes. Is she an elf-blood?"

"No way to tell, yet. Micalion said in the second generation fewer than half are."

"She suckles strong. But she's so light-weight. Gwen, do you suppose she's alright?"

"Of course she's alright. She has to be alright. She's too clever not to be alright. What do you want to name her?"

"A mineral name?" Chrys suggested. "*Jade* is pretty."

"Let's do a family name first. If we have more, we can do mineral names then."

"Ah, don't talk to me about having more right now. If we're going to do a family name, then it had better be for your mother. With mine, she'd get a mineral name anyway."

"Ellianiine? No way, she'll spend half her life just learning how to spell it. How about Ellia?"

"Ellia it is, then," Chrys agreed. "Ellia Gwenessifyr—"

"That's even harder to spell," Gwen interrupted. "Anyway, can my name even make a patronymic?"

"You *are* her father. But you're right, it doesn't sound right. What do switchers who father children normally do? It's not a common thing, is it?"

"Let her be another child of Sheras. Ellia Sheras Euan."

THE FALLOW MEANT WEEKS OF intermittent cold rain, but no frost at all, Ralani was so far south. The house stayed dry inside, though the sheets and clothes got a little musty from the humid air. The rain drummed loud on the wavy glass panes of the skylights.

JONAS STOPPED BY TO MEET his niece and stay for a few weeks in the spring. He had just been made legate, but he wasn't sure he'd stay in the army much longer.

"If I can't find a way to spend more time with Celia and the kids, it's just not worth it."

ALMOST ALL THE RUBBLE HAD been cleared away. The city was a blank ground with paved streets and plazas and a scattering of houses and tents. The legion spent the year constructing more bunk houses to get the last of the survivors indoors, building public baths and government buildings, and planting the wood-lots that would one-day provide the city with much of its charcoal. Private land-owners hired local laborers to rebuild Ralani's grand houses, as well as commercial buildings, the kind that have apartments above workshops or storefronts and rent quickly. Families started moving back into the city, some of them followers of the Shepherd—ethnic Itarye and Odesye converts, mostly--and so Chrys found a group she could sing praises with. With Gwen's only slightly grudging permission, Ellia was formally presented at one of the services and blessed. One of the other couples in the house had their first baby. Their landlord planted medlar and crabapple and red-blooming honeysuckle vine in the courtyard, and the newly-formed neighborhood association put in a line of cypress along the street. The city still looked like a construction site, but it would be lovely when it was finished.

ELLIA'S IRISES TOOK ON COLOR, a light, variable gray, like Gwen's. She grew very slowly—as she approached her first birthday, she still weighed little more than ten pounds—and she was slow to crawl, slow to attempt to talk, a quiet, observant, and clingy baby. Paracelias wrote and said all that was normal for elves and Gwen and Orpharias had been the same way. It was too soon to tell whether she was an elf-blood, though. Gwen said she hoped her child would be normal, healthy, etc., all the things you say. After all, she knew the elfin blood was mild in her, and still she was not quite right, no matter how hard she tried. Orpharias's blood was stronger—all his strange worries and odd aversions, the fact that he never wrote letters because he could barely read (except music)—he had become Micalion's constant traveling companion not only because Micalion was lame. Yes, of course Gwen said she wanted her daughter to be able to live a normal life.

Except she was lying.

Secretly, she longed to have a child like herself, if not Ellia then another. Then neither of them would be so very alone.

CHALCY AND SAMMAS AND THEIR baby came out to keep the Fallow with Gwen and Chrys and Ellia. Upon careful consideration, Chrys decided to invite Orpharias and Micalion to come visit for a while in the spring. The next Fallow after that, their third in Ralani, Chrys gave birth to another girl, tiny but this time compact, with medium-brown skin, baby-blue eyes, and golden-brown hair in tight, wispy, ringlets. But Sherra gave no sign of actually being an elf-blood either.

"THEY WON'T LET ME FIGHT, but can't I at least go see new stuff?" Gwen grumped. She had been writing a report at home after dinner and had just come out to the porch where Chrys rocked serenely, letting Sherra suckle. Ellia lay on the floorboards sucking on candy and scribbling on her wax tablet. Gwen paced rapidly up and down, making the floorboards squeak.

"You do see new things," Chrys reminded her. "You took Ellia camping just last week. Anyway, who could get tired of *that*?" and she gestured out at the blue Midland Sea, ship-dotted, hazy with spray. The breeze smelled of sand and salt and sunshine. Gwen stopped pacing and regarded the view, gray eyes squinting against the glare, her face softening for a moment.

"I am not tired of *that*," she assured Chrys. "That's freaky-gorgeous. Nor am I tired of camping, nor of Ellia, nor of Sherra, nor of you. But I spend all day filling out forms, *the same* forms." She recommenced pacing, trailing two fingers idly along the porch railing. "This city is so figured out now that I've become just a griffin-wool-clad clerk! And with this project being what it is, I could be filling out these stupid forms until I'm thirty, assuming I don't get tuberculosis or sepsis before then and die." Her pacing had morphed into walking upon a single floorboard as though it were a balance-beam, and now, in order to turn without stepping on any other board, she executed a sharp spin on the ball of one foot, an energetic, playful extravagance utterly at odds with the foul mood she was rapidly talking herself into.

"If you feel that way about it, why don't you resign?" Chrys asked. "You've done your five years. Father would get you a job, no problem. You'd probably make more, too." She refused to acknowledge that she had anything to do with Gwen's increasing anxiety about money.

"Oh, then I could have every day exactly the same someplace else," Gwen retorted. "Anyway, I *like* the army. I'm good at this. I might not be as good at something else."

"You're good, but you're bored, so how good is that?"

"Not good." Gwen shoved her hand through her hair. "I ought to try to get myself transferred to another legion, one that actually *does* something. I mean, seriously, is this a good use of my time—or of my pay? A new recruit could handle most of what I do if only provided with a wax tablet and stylus. On the other hand—"

"Um, Gwen, where would I go, if you got a new assignment gallivanting off into some war zone?"

"With me. It need not be a war zone, just something that—"

"Would you really be—"

"Will you stop interrupting my train of thought?"

"No, Gwen, your trains of thought don't end. As I was saying, would you really be satisfied if it wasn't a war zone?"

"No. But...."

"Anyway, am I supposed to go traipsing off all across the empire with babies hanging off my tits like a, a mother bat?"

"No. Well, yes, maybe? I want to be out there—" a flamboyant gesture at the wide world "—*and* I want to be with you and the girls. I don't know how it will work, yet. Maybe if...?" Gwen interrupted herself, chewed on her forefinger for a bit.

"Daddy, are you going away?" Ellia asked. And Gwen's heart did a strange thing in her chest.

"Oh, no, baby," she said. "Not today. Today I'm not going anywhere."

BUT GWEN DID PURSUE A new assignment, straight into another war zone as Acting Prefect for a detachment. The job presented some interesting professional challenges, the chance to explore a new kind of landscape, and the chance to pick b'Nyas's brain about how psy-ops worked or chat with some of his centurions about the arts of sabotage and strategic demolition. She had not yet entirely given up on Covert Ops. Gwen returned to Ralani afterwards happy as a hawk who has caught a pigeon.

BY THE TIME GWEN GOT back to her house, the sun had long since set and everybody had gone to bed. Except Ellia got out of bed as soon as she heard her father's step on the porch.

"Daddy, Daddy, Daddy!" she cried. "Derra said that you haven't been fighting this time, cause you didn't need to, because the barbarians where you went don't want to have a king anymore so they're going to become citizens, and there are kelpies there who poo all over the trees, and they eat pigs all the time, the barbarians, I mean, not the kelpies, and I wasn't sleeping because I knew you'd be home, but Mama said I had to go to bed anyway, so I did, and guess what? Sherra can sit up, now! Did you bring me anything?"

She was still elf-tiny, the size of a toddler half her age, but she carried herself and spoke like an older child.

"Daughter, daughter, daughter," Gwen said, matching the girl's tone, though not her volume. She knelt and responded to each of Ellia's statements, one after another. "....but Duchesye people like pork, maybe because they're barbarians, though I don't think citizen-ship will cure them of it. Of course you were not sleeping, it's night-time, why would any child of mine want to sleep at night? But other people do like to, so we've got to be quiet, now. That's wonderful about Sherra, and yes I brought you a rag-doll made by real barbar-ians with a pretty little barbarian dress and with hair that almost looks real, but don't give this one a haircut as it won't grow back, remem-ber? Did I miss anything?

"Uh-uh!"

"Can I go put my pack down, now?"

"Will you pick me up?"

"Once I put my pack down, yes."

Ellia took her father's hand by one finger (oh, heart-melt!) and led her down the passage, into the starlit courtyard, and then in the door to her own apartment, where the child used the world's loudest stage whisper to tell Mama that Daddy was home.

GWEN'S PLAN TO GO OUT with Covert Ops for a few months every year had a flaw—a Covert Ops cohort was not going to stay attached to a construction project indefinitely. In the spring, b'Nyas and his people were permanently assigned to a different legion.

Gwen asked to be reassigned too.

Putting Chrys and the children on the ship bound for Nonani City, Gwen thought something inside her might break—but something else inside her would definitely break otherwise. She didn't know what else to do. She'd tried to talk her wife into coming with her, but Chrys simply reiterated that she was a woman and not a bat.

"Don't go getting mad at me for a decision *you* made, either!" Chrys added. She had never wanted to leave Nonani City or her father in the first place.

THE PREFECT OF GWEN'S NEW legion had announced his intention to retire, and so she stepped in as his heir apparent. Two months after her arrival, he left, and she put on the blue-dyed tunic shared by prefects and tribunes, not that she could see the difference. Within a month she had improved efficiency by ten percent.

A NEW ASSIGNMENT! A KINGDOM in eastern barbarian Duchasa had been having a problem with brigands. A detachment of two cohorts from another legion had already gone to help, but after four months had made little headway, so the barbarian king asked for more. Gwen's legion was assigned to build a new, permanent base.

Of course, the base had little to do with the brigands and nothing to do with helping the king. It was the next step in a process that only ever moved in one direction and only had one real goal. Gwen knew it, and it bothered her a little that the local king, who had given Nonani an opening by asking for help, did not. He, like every other barbarian who did business with Nonani, thought he was going to be an exception. She actually rather admired barbarians. But Nonani was bound to get bigger, and she was bound to help. She had never been one to question her duty.

*   *   *

THE COMMANDING TRIBUNE OF THE detachment was b'Hallas! She hadn't heard from him in ages!

*   *   *

SHE NOTICED A YOUNG MAN looking at her in the officers' mess.

He was short and stocky, a sort of light, medium-brown color, with short hair. As he wasn't wearing armor and wasn't already familiar to her, she guessed he must be a Prefect's centurion from the detachment, therefore someone she needed to talk with. And the chair next to him was empty. Cool.

"I don't know you," she began.

"Ulas Sylas Dynan, sir," he explained. "I'm the new Third Prefect's Centurion."

"Gwenessifyr Sheras Euan. Prefect."

"I gathered."

"Our not being introduced was stupid. I'll have questions for you—I have to come up to speed on your whole detachment, you know."

"Sir, I await your convenience."

"Eat! I'll await yours, and this ain't it." She took a bite of stew. "Man, what's in this? It's good."

"Bear meat. They killed a calista prowling the trash heap yesterday." The man, b'Sylas, had a slight but definite plebeian accent, a kind of choppy lilt very different from the more even speech common to most patricians. After a bit, she asked him about it.

"Tanner's son," he explained. "Married a patrician."

He used few words, but did not seem to mind talking.

"*You* talk like a patrician, though," he observed.

"I know. Dad died when I was four, so I lost my accent. I'm adopted." Of course she wasn't. Had she been legally adopted, she couldn't have married Chrys. Fortunately, legal adoption was such a pain that

Tomas hadn't bothered except for Topaz, and then only so her husband could be his heir.

"So, what do you do," b'Sylas asked, "when you're not increasing efficiency by 10%?"

"Read books, chase girls, and beat people at spherical chess."

"Bet you can't beat me," b'Sylas said.

"You play?"

"I win."

They agreed to play over supper. Only after leaving the table did Gwen realize she'd forgotten to say goodbye. Or hello.

She worried. Would he think her rude? Or weird? Or....Her last-moment discovery that somebody had moved her stuff didn't help. The night proved warm and muggy, thick with choruses of amphibians and insects, and all the lamps she lit in deference to normal eyes made the tent close and hot. She hadn't had anyone to play with in far too long.

He began conservatively, assessing her style, awaiting mistakes, so she made none. She began a long, carefully-plotted attack, but he moved out of the way as if he could read her mind. She gave him no openings. He barely glanced at the sphere. Instead, he watched Gwen—he wasn't playing against the chess pieces, he was playing against *her*. She felt seen.

She played a flawless game, but b'Sylas built a trap that did not require flaws. She watched him do it, knew exactly what he was doing, but she could do nothing about it.

"'Does true nobility rest with he who fights for the hopeless cause or with he who meets defeat with dignity?'" Gwen quoted, repeating a couplet from a somewhat obscure tragedy, a couplet that rhymed and alliterated nicely in Itarish.

"Don't matter to me, you owe me money," b'Sylas said, "Horias."

Horias was the name of the character in the play who'd said the line. Gwen whooped and clapped her hands, laughing, and b'Sylas, who had sat motionless and inexpressive the entire game, suddenly relaxed and grinned. Gwen went to fetch her wallet.

"OK, but you've got to give me a chance to get you back," she said.

"Any time, any place," he told her.

The next night they played again. Gwen used the exact same strategy on b'Sylas that he'd used on her and was not surprised when he defeated it. While he was busy doing that, she put him in check.

"You must think me an egotist," b'Sylas commented, surveying the damage.

"If the sandal fits.... But really I just wanted to see if I could adopt your moves—and whether you could defeat them. I knew no way to beat what you did yesterday."

"Nor did I, when I sat down to play tonight," b'Sylas admitted. Then once again he dropped his cool, almost bored-looking game face and smiled. It was a sweet, fond, impish smile, and Gwen decided there was not a lot she wouldn't do to see that smile again.

They played a few times a week for the next three months as the legion-and-a-half built the bones of what amounted to a new city. B'Sylas won about half the games—he wasn't the first equal Gwen had played, but he was among the very few. And yet he couldn't explain his strategies. "I figured that would work" was about the closest he would come.

By the terms of the bet, b'Sylas could lose half the games and still come out ahead financially. Had he meant to do that? Gwen didn't object. The first game or two it hadn't mattered. After that—she'd come upon the requisition for a large bonus for b'Sylas and asked b'Hallas about it. So she learned about the Prefect's centurion who had saved several hundred lives—and declined a medal so he could buy his wife a dress.

"She's a steel princess from Parsia," b'Hallas had told Gwen, smirking. "Women like that want rubies, not flowers and compliments. Poor son of a bitch."

After b'Sylas and his detachment left, Gwen thought about him sometimes, hoping he was OK, and wondering what he'd bought his wife with the forty denarii he'd won, and whether she'd liked it.

*   *   *

THE CONSULS NAMED THE BASE Charosi, in honor of King Karoz, who still didn't know he was becoming a puppet. B'Hallas was to be the first commander of the base and also the first Nonanye governor of the kingdom, and for that he was made legate. Gwen was there when he put on his new uniform for the first time, helped him lace his leather over his new, yellow tunic, watched him don the new, pentagonal red cape in place of a soldier's wool cloak. He posed briefly and ironically. He still looked good, despite some middle-aged fleshiness.

"The true symbol of rank is how they'll treat you," Gwen told him, admiring. He spared her a tight smile.

"How I'll make them treat me," he corrected her.

Later, b'Hallas considered what staff he'd need, besides those he was being given by the army.

"I'll need washer-women, cooks, a blacksmith.... Do you think I ought to hire local prostitutes, or send away for Nonanye army women?" He sounded as though he were shopping.

"If you hire local women," Gwen advised him, "they'll have someplace to go when they get pregnant and refuse to abort, as some inevitably will. That's less for you to sort out. And by hiring local, you'll increase the cultural and economic footprint of the base. Plus, mixed children are always an aid to the assimilation process, provided the conception was willing."

"Good points. Of course, what I really need is a library. I suppose that will have to wait until I get my house finished. I'll have to send away for books, too, the locals are illiterates. I've heard they have some interesting mathematics, though, all done with pictures and number-symbols."

Gwen had no doubt he'd learn Duchesye geometry within six months.

GWEN WAS NOT BEING ASSIGNED to Charosi long-term, but her legion would stay another year or two to help with construction, and her rank entitled her to a private house (built cozy and warm in the Duchesye style) while she lived on base. She sent for her family. They arrived with Micalion and Orpharias, who would stay for the winter.

THERE WAS *SO MUCH SNOW*! Piles and piles of it! A foot of the fluffy stuff could fall in a night and then just not melt for weeks. Carts were useless, so everything went about on sledges. Everybody had to wear Duchesye clothing, never mind uniforms, there was no other way to keep warm. Fortunately, Orpharias knew what to do in the snow—jump in it, role around in it, slide down hills on it (a small sledge was ideal for sliding, or a big piece of raw-hide worked until it got wet and soggy), make snow-balls, snow-forts, and even snow-people. He taught everyone who wanted to learn the skills, and soon the whole family and some of the centurions and milites were playing a new version of capture-the-flag that included throwing snow-balls instead of tagging people. Chrys played too, of course, but she also learned, from the native women, how to make snow cream and snow taffy and hot, buttered cider.

"I THINK I'M PREGNANT AGAIN," Chrys said one morning. Hilaria had passed, and Gwen's brothers had gone, but this far-northern country was still snowy. The wake-up horns had blown, but she and Gwen were still in bed. No light entered their Duchesye-style sleeping-cabinet.

"Oh, cool," Gwen said, sincerely but without melodrama. But Chrys sighed.

"I don't know, Gwen. I'll have another baby to fly around with."

"Hey, it's not like I knocked you up by accident," Gwen reminded her, propping herself up on one elbow. "If there's an advantage to my being...like this...that's it. No unwanted pregnancies."

"I know. I *want* another baby. It's just.... Oh, Gwen, why can't you come home?"

"I *am* home. We've talked about this—"

"No, *you've* talked about this. You talk and you talk, but you never listen. What I say doesn't matter."

"Chrys, you know that's not true! I *do* listen. You *do* matter. You're why I say this is home—because you are here! We are here together, us and the girls, and I have my work, therefore, this is home."

"Except *you* know that's not true," Chrys exclaimed. "We're together, and that's great, but this isn't home. We can't plant a garden here, we can't really make friends, the girls won't get a chance to learn the local language because in another month or three you'll get a new assignment, and you'll go somewhere else."

"That's not always how it is, though. There are permanent or semi-permanent assignments."

"Yeah, I know. You had one but you hated it, and now you're here, where winter lasts halfway into first-month, and who knows when I'll get to see my parents or sister next. You know, Mother has a cough, now. And I think she's losing weight. She's not going to be around forever."

"Oh, way to keep me abreast of family news!"

"You shouldn't need to be kept abreast of it!" Chrys was sitting up, adamant, whisper-yelling so as not to attract the attention of the children playing audibly now nearby.

"Chrys...."

"Look, can you really stand to be somewhere else when Sherra starts speaking in full sentences?"

"I *like* being a soldier, though. I'm good at it." Gwen sounded equally adamant, but in fact she was pleading.

"I know. But aren't there other things you can like and be good at? I don't want to keep trying to explain to toddlers where Daddy is."

Gwen winced.

TO FIND A GOOD CIVILIAN job and do all related due diligence was a multi-step process that took months. Then she had to train her replacement. Everything seemed fast and slow and elegiac at once. Just before leaving, she quarreled with b'Hallas over the placement of several storage facilities. He said she was insubordinate, a charge she would not accept as he was not her commander. She was still feeling bruised about it when she left, but expected to forgive him and be friends again eventually.

GWEN WAS A CIVILIAN. SHE felt unmoored and very much alone.

Chapter 7. The Aide

Year of Nonani 823 - 826

Abbas decided that although a speaker series might bear fruit eventually, his soul could not wait so long for evidence of success. Rather than try to convince other people to make changes, he had to make changes directly himself. Unfortunately, he couldn't think of any reason why anybody would appoint him governor of anywhere, and as he wasn't a senator, he couldn't run for the Ruling Council. But he could work for a Ruling Council member.

With Cousin Arias's recommendation and some networking, Abbas got himself a one-month trial with a Senator Euan. Not knowing if the job would work out, he went alone.

Abbas got off the riverboat and looked up. An almost cliff-like embankment towered above the narrow strip of river-front neighborhoods and wharves--Capitoline Hill, so-named for its original skull-like shape, before the top was flattened. Anyway, that was where Abbas was supposed to go. What was that joke? *You can't get there from here*? Abbas decided that he certainly would get there from here, he just had to take the long way around.

He checked into a boarding house, dropped off his stuff, bought a map, and walked a couple of miles in order to end up only a few hundred feet, horizontally, from where he started. It was a pleasant walk, taking him through about half the River District, across a bridge over the mouth of a small, marshy creek, in through one of the unguarded gates of the outer city wall, then gradually uphill through a very nice residential neighborhood to one of the unguarded gates of the much older inner-city wall. Through that gate and Abbas was in the oldest part of the city, three hills in a curving row above a small valley where arose the spring that had once been the city's water supply.

He strolled across the Caprine Hill, once mostly goat pasture but now dense with theaters, music venues, brothels, and so forth, hurried past the mansions and gardens on the Olivine (Abbas felt vaguely that he wasn't rich enough to even be near such places), and finally to the Capitoline Hill, where stood the principle buildings of government, including the King's House and the Curia, all facing each other across the Upper Forum, all polished marble shining in the brilliant afternoon sun.

Abbas had never seen the Curia before, but all coins bore its image, and he recognized it at once. He jogged up its steps, went inside, and went blind.

A moment later his eyes adjusted, and he saw a long, low, windowless hallway lit every few feet by small lamps in wall sconces and lined with doors, all closed. He could smell cool stone and the burning lamp oil. From somewhere he heard the susurration of voices.

"Please state your business, sir?" a soldier beside him asked, firm but deferential.

"I'm Abbas Seras Lian. I'm here to see Senator Euan. Do you know where he is?"

"I do not. He has not yet left, however. May I check you for weapons, sir?"

"Of course. I have none, though."

"I still have to check, if you want to pass me."

"Of course."

The soldier patted him down quite professionally and searched his wallet, though what sort of weapon might be hidden in a wallet Abbas didn't know. He resisted a sudden, intense urge towards inappropriate humor ("hadn't you better search my nose? I could have flammable snot, you know") and was waved on his way toward the end of the hall and a wide double door there.

He stepped through the door and found himself in the debate chamber of the Ruling Council.

It was a big space, though not so big as he'd imagined, except for the fifty-foot ceiling. Stone bleachers set with wooden seats rose several levels at the front and back of the room so that the uppermost level was even with the floor of the balconies that lined the other two sides. Rows of doors, perhaps to offices, opened both below the balconies and onto them, and above the upper level of doors were long, narrow windows through which the afternoon sunlight streamed, playing on smooth, pale marble, dark wood, curtains, cushions, and hangings of red velvet, and the floor of white, red, yellow, and orange tile set in a mosaic depicting the sun as if it were a blooming rose. Groups of men stood here and there talking, while a few others hurried up or down stairs, in and out of doors, some of them carrying scrolls or other small objects, but the room was not crowded, nor did any of the men seem to notice the presence of the newcomer. Abbas felt himself to be an interloper, a hick-town lawyer with long-shot ideals nobody was going to take seriously. He supposed that everybody must feel thus, at least at first. The exceptions would be the people to watch out for.

Since nobody seemed to be paying him any attention, and since he didn't know where to go, Abbas wandered around a bit, noticing details—which cushions looked sat-in, which arm-rests bore wine-cup stains or small bits of graffiti (mostly carved names, some of them ancient and startlingly famous) and so on. Five of the chairs had purple cushions, not red, but they were scattered, not in a group, and not in any obvious pattern. He walked over to one such chair on the edge of the lower-most row and reached out to touch the velvet.

"The First Chair," said a richly deep voice behind him. "Occupied, though not at the moment, by the Speaker of the Senate, one of five persons who collectively replace the King, all hail his royal imaginariness."

"I know who the Speaker is. I did not know he had his own chair." Abbas turned around and faced a man as tall and dark as himself, though older and considerably more robust, less a fence-post and more a tower. He was dressed entirely in charcoal gray except for the gold embroidery on his scapular. His short, tightly-curled hair had gone white on top as though left out at night by mistake and hoar-frosted. His blue eyes smiled although his mouth did not—yet. Abbas introduced himself by name.

"Yes, I'd gathered," the man replied. "Welcome. I'm Tomas Salas Euan. Shall we walk in the garden and talk?"

Abbas joined a staff of six, starting out as a gofer and messenger and then taking on additional duties, such as researching constituents' concerns and reviewing the legal language of bills. After just two weeks, Senator Euan told him that he could consider himself hired.

"You have a wife, don't you? You'll want to send for her."

"And a son. He'll be old enough to travel, soon."

"New father? You may be younger than I thought. One of my sons is newly fatherfied, too."

"I'll have to look for a house before they come up. I'm staying down near the fish-market."

"A house? Not on what I pay you. Half a house, maybe. Or somebody's garret. The prices in this city will make a poor man out of the wealthiest."

"I'll have to become Speaker, then," Abbas joked. "I've heard the job comes with a house, as well as a chair." Senator Euan laughed.

By tenth-month, as the city prepared for Natalia, Abbas had indeed rented half a duplex in a decent neighborhood, and he and Maia and the baby were settling in. But everything, from the climate to the food was different and strange. The city was unimaginably big. When Tomas learned that Maia was disoriented and lonely, he insisted that Abbas bring her and the baby to Natalia dinner at his house.

"I know how tough it can be to get through the holiday without family, so please, borrow mine."

In Itara, they served Natalia dinner late, so it was almost sunset by the time Abbas and his little family arrived at the Euan's door. The place stood at the top of a long, low hill on a quiet suburban street lined with planted poplars. From the street it looked like a plain block of blond stucco, with small windows guarded by security bars, just like almost every other private dwelling in the city.

The Senator answered the door himself, explaining that he had already let the servants go to their own families. He was as well-dressed as ever, this time in red and yellow, but seemed relaxed, and he waved away professional titles for the evening. This night, he would be Tomas. He accepted his guests' gifts of wine and candy and ushered them in.

Inside, the place was not the ostentatious jewel-box of many wealthy Nonanye. The atrium had no statuary or expensive furniture, only four citroen trees in large pots, some smaller potted plants, and a collection of simple benches under the large, open sky-light. The blue-and-white tiled floor and the woven-rush wall-hangings were tasteful, not garish. And yet everything was the best available. Everything was lovely. Water trickled musically into the basin of the fountain and caught the dull, indirect gleam of the last light of the shortest day of the year.

Any warmth of the day was fading fast, but the dining room was warmed by charcoal braziers on brass tripods and lamps bright with many wicks. Green boughs of pine and holly and garlands made of twined-together ivy climbed the walls. The table was set with porcelain and silver and tall beeswax candles scented with pine and rosemary oil, and a small crowd, adults and children both, were already seated on the low benches eating nuts and candies and talking more or less all at once. They all stopped talking at the entrance of the guests, and the lady of the house heard the silence from the kitchen and came out to be introduced. Her name was Opal, and she was dressed elegantly in silks of red, white, and green with enough jewelry for a derger, except hers were all gold arm-bangles and gold ear-hoops, with no stones or gems. She was comfortably plump with age, and her gray hair looked more like yarn than anything else. Abbas wished he were a small child so that he could sit in her lap.

Tomas introduced everybody else, nephew, niece, two daughters, and their various partners and children. The niece, Topaz, was the one with the children and the husband. The husband of the older daughter, Chrysoberyl, was, unexpectedly, not home from school yet. The younger daughter, Chalcedony, had a fiance, Sammas, a law student who embarrassed Abbas by jumping up over-eagerly to shake his hand.

"Oh, sir, I've read everything you've published, you're the reason I'm studying law. I mean, my father's a lawyer, and he's great, but you're the one who showed me a lawyer can change the world. And that's just what I want to do. I'm with you, sir, all the way, I mean it!"

"He's here for you, not me," Chalcedony commented, dryly. Sammas didn't disagree.

The family, except for Tomas, followed the Shepherd, meaning their holiday cooking was influenced by Aethenye cuisine—which ran mostly to meat. There were no distinct courses, only platters of plain, rare mutton of excellent quality. Each type of cut had its own platter, though the smaller organs shared platters, plus there was a sort of pâté-like spread made mostly of marrow, baskets of yeasty rosemary rolls, and little crystal pitchers of olive oil or garum and two tureens of oily fried onion with caraway seed and silfium, all paired with heavily-spiced, hot red wine.

"Just take *a little* of everything," advised Chrysoberyl.

The feast of meat went on for hours while the family talked, mostly about politics, but in an intellectually serious yet recreational way, like how a couple of athletes might play ball casually, just for the fun of it on their day off. Abbas wondered what it was like to be a child in such a family, to eat brains or lungs because they were delicacies not because you'd go hungry otherwise, and to have a father who could read.

Finally, Topaz and Chrysoberyl cleared away the platters and plates and served next a clear bone broth floating with ginger, chives, and little chewy bits that Abbas eventually recognized as slices of sheep's penis. The soup was meant to settle the stomach before dessert, little tarts made of caramelized onion and honey in filo-dough crusts.

By then it was getting very late, but the party wasn't over. Leaving the clean-up until the next day, everybody crossed the chilly, star-lit atrium to the already-warmed library—which was enormous, as it included the space a family who didn't follow the Shepherd would have used for a chapel. There, Chrysoberyl played her harp while Tomas read from the Song of the Mother all about the Three Emanations, the separation of fire, water, earth, and void, and how the first incarnate being, an owl chick, received the spirit-fire on the morning of the first winter solstice that ever there was. Maia and Topaz nursed their babies. Sammas and Chalcedony held hands.

When the reading was done, Chrysoberyl changed to a new tune, and Opal sang the Welcome to the two babies whose first Natalia this was, then gave a basket of baby toys, diapers, and other supplies to Topaz—and another to Maia.

Maia sorted through the basket, pulling out labeled parcels.

"Salted caramel? Lavender lotion? Nipple cream?" she exclaimed. "You didn't need to...."

"It's Natalia," Opal replied, cutting her off gently. "No mother's labor goes uncelebrated today."

For some reason, Abbas glanced over at Chrysoberyl, who was still playing. Tears shone on her cheeks in the lamplight. She did not speak.

Sometime around midnight, the carriage Tomas had arranged for his guests arrived.

"When the Fallow's over, I'll have to have more parties so I can invite you three and introduce you around," he said at the door. "Half of politics is *society*, you know."

Abbas, seriously uncomfortable now with what felt like too much undeserved generosity, stammered, but Topaz laid a hand on his arm.

"Don't worry," she told him, "Uncle Tomas just takes in strays. I am one myself."

Abbas had expected that as an aide his main task would be to convince his employer to become a conservationist, but Senator Euan already was one—perhaps not as passionately as could be hoped, but at least he was on board. By working for him, Abbas learned how to get others on board, too. He learned what was possible, what wasn't, and how to make the impossible possible.

The latter didn't seem to be happening fast enough.

"A ship this big does not turn on a coin," Senator Euan told him. "Particularly not when some of the oarsmen are still pulling in the wrong direction."

"But people are dying!" Abbas replied. "*Right* now. And the families who aren't dying? My best friend's sister can't find a husband, there aren't enough derger men left in the region. So what's she doing? She's casually...*fucking* two ubum men my brother introduced her to. They bring her presents of sewing needles and salt pork, and she doesn't understand they're treating her like a whore. She hasn't born a child yet—mixed matings don't bear well—but what choice does she have, except to not try at all? Senator, there are fewer derger on this *continent* than there are citizens in this city. How many childless women can they afford? I'm sorry to go on like this, I just feel...I feel like a whole people have become grains in a sand-timer. How many run out while we sit here making compromises?"

"Not as many as will run out if we don't compromise," the Senator told him calmly. "You met Senator Dynan, he was up here last week? He's never run for office himself, but he bankrolled the campaigns of three sitting Councilmen. You know what he wants. What would you do if he promised to protect *half* the remaining derger forests, on the condition you let him take the other half—and if you don't agree, he'll take the whole?"

"I don't know," Abbas said, appalled.

"Well, if you figure it out, you tell me, because those are the kinds of questions we need answers to, if we're going to win this thing."

Abbas sat down heavily.

"I used to think if I could just...convince enough people that this is important...."

"Oh, they know it's important. That's why they're fighting so hard—for the other side."

"The derger have a song for everything," Abbas explained. "If you want to know how to do a thing, you learn the song for it, and you sing as you work and the song tells you what to do, all the steps, and all the...relationships. To build a fire, they sing to the wood, to be sure it knows how to burn. To do things the right way in cooperation with all beings is to live in the music. I have sought to live in the music all my life, but there are no songs for what I must do. I don't know what to do."

"There are songs," the Senator assured him. "You just haven't sung them for us yet."

Abbas read the epics, looking for songs for ubum. He talked with philosophers. He wrote to J.J. every week, and through J.J. he wrote to Oboo. He corresponded with his law firm and other lawyers, suggesting strategy and helping with fundraising. He quietly helped b'Freias with the underground growth of the new faction. He joined the lecture circuit—he could use the extra cash, and the exercise of articulating his ideas for an audience helped him develop his thinking. And he attended organizational meetings led by Udùo, the activist derger. The law against political opposition groups was rarely enforced but always might be, so the group met in secret, divided into separate cells, raising money and brain-storming. There hadn't been a protest since Abbas joined. Then, just after Cerealia and the bull sacrifice, Udùo called a meeting.

In Parsia, a few villages of separatist hunter-gatherer ubum had found their land being cut over for charcoal—at the behest of Senator Dynan, though he seemed to have been uninvolved in what happened next. Having nowhere else to go, the villagers decided to fight back, except they were well aware that those who took up arms against Nonani always lost—and losing meant forced migration, slavery, or slaughter. So instead of grabbing weapons, the people, men, women, and children, grabbed trees and refused to let go when the harvesters showed up.

Legally speaking, what should have happened next was clear. Impeding lawful private industry was a misdemeanor, and the villagers were technically citizens. No law allowed violence against citizens for merely committing misdemeanors. The nearest garrison, when summoned, should simply have confiscated movable property equal in value to the maximum allowable fines. Once the miscreants let go their trees and submitted, their property would be returned to them pending trial. What actually happened was that the soldiers captured the entire tribe, killed all those too young or old or ill to walk, and were now driving the rest to Nonani City for sale.

Udùo, furious for people he considered his allies, wanted to block the road into the city.

"As many people as we can get," he insisted, "so many they cannot jail and flog all of us. We can paper the town with flyers the night before so everybody will know what we're doing and why. We'll invite reporters, as many as we can get—but friendly ones—we'll sit in the road before the gate so the people of the city can look down upon us from the walls, all of us, men and women both, armed with nothing but the truth. The shame will force the soldiers to release the illegally-taken prisoners—or the Speaker will order them to do so!"

"You know," Abbas pointed out, "if they treat unarmed citizens like foreign hostiles, they may well treat other unarmed citizens like traitors."

He didn't need to say what the penalty for treason was or how it was typically carried out.

Udùo bowed his head a moment.

"I don't think that will happen," he said, "not with the eyes of the city upon us. But if it does, I know where I'll want to be."

Nearly all the cells were able to take on additional members for the occasion. Many people were outraged. The new volunteers were quickly assigned to teams, and the teams drilled, over and over, to stay seated if attacked, to go limp, to not fight back, no matter what.

"In our apparent helplessness is our only strength," Udùo said again and again. "If we fight them, they will fight us, and we will lose. Only if we do not fight might they stay their hand."

One night a runner came in. By morning the city was covered

in flyers. As the crowd of a few hundred captives and soldiers approached the West Gate, nearly two thousand free citizens converged and sat down on or near the road.

The soldiers stopped. The prisoners stopped. The protesters chanted or sang or shouted slogans. The soldiers did nothing. The prisoners, exhausted and confused, did nothing. For a moment, Abbas felt cheerful, optimistic. The weather was fine, the day felt like a picnic or a festival, it was impossible to imagine that goodness would not prevail. And then he realized why the soldiers were doing nothing—they were waiting for reinforcement from the city garrison.

A full cohort, a thousand armed men, erupted from the gate, and Abbas, looking over his shoulder, saw them coming, grimly efficient, and suddenly everything seemed very real. His heart ran away, but the rest of him stayed put, going passive and limp, as he'd practiced. In a very few minutes he found himself bound and then picked up bodily and moved off the road. The captive villagers were quietly herded into the city, where whatever would happen to them would happen.

There being no pen big enough for the protesters, they were all simply left on the ground for a while, tied up, while several tribunes and the city's Legate discussed what to do. The sun beat down on the back of Abbas's neck. His rope-bound wrists and ankles hurt. His shoulders, pulled into unnatural angles, hurt, and his forehead and knees pressed against the dry dirt on the side of the road. Time went by. He couldn't see anything but the dirt an inch before his eyes.

At last, he heard soldiers giving orders, people getting up and moving. People were being arrested and taken somewhere. Why did they take some but not others? Why not him? More time went by.

Later he heard voices asking for names, reading out formal charges (misdemeanor traffic obstruction and public mischief), and giving out court dates. The soldiers had to know that few would show up for court, but the unresolved charge could then be useful should any of these people get in trouble again or, say, try to run for public office. Abbas decided it was better to show up for court.

But he was never charged. Before his name could be taken, a

voice spoke from somewhere saying "I want this one and...this one." Probably money changed hands, though that wasn't audible. A young soldier cut Abbas's bonds and then walked away without bothering to speak to him. Abbas stood up, rubbing his wrists where the ropes had been, and saw Udùo standing up, also free, some yards away. Abbas was glad—he'd tried to talk Udùo out of participating, not sure what might be done to a derger caught making trouble. Then he turned around to find the man who had come for them. Senator Euan, of course.

Later, in private, Abbas approached the Senator, not sure whether he was going to apologize or offer thanks or what. He ended up saying nothing for so long that Senator Euan spoke first.

"Next time, if you're going to do something likely to professionally embarrass me, come talk to me first?"

"I'm sorry, sir, I..."

But the Senator held up his hand for silence.

"I mean it! About next time. There *will* be a next time. There *should* be a next time. I've been trying to get those poor tribespeople freed since before they were captured. What's been done to them is unconscionable and beyond all standards of law and established policy. Nor am I finished with the issue. Never apologize for doing the right thing. But never forget to consult with your allies, either."

Abbas digested the lecture. He felt stupid. Also, he felt a kind of survivor's guilt—he still didn't know what had happened to the people taken away. Most likely they would be brought before a judge and sentenced to flogging, a lenient punishment by Nonani standards, but it was hard to be sure.

"I was prepared to accept the consequences of my actions," he said.

"I know, but I was not."

"Sir?"

"I wasn't willing to accept the consequences of your actions. I want to see you get that free housing someday."

It took Abbas a moment to figure out what his mentor was talking about. Then his jaw fell open.

Neither Abbas nor Udùo were ever charged, but neither were the men responsible for the massacre of the villagers.

A few weeks later, a telegram came addressed to the entire Ruling Council, alerting them that the governor of Holia had been struck by the gods (that is, had a stroke), and that he lived but could not govern and must be replaced. Abbas told Maia, who took Ardas and went to go be with her cousin. The house seemed very lonely without them. He felt guilty for not going too, and second-guessed his decision to stay a thousand times, but something inside him said that staying was right.

Months later, Abbas learned in a newshouse of Cousin Arias's death from pneumonia. Maia's letter took another week to tell him the same—and to say the matriline wanted him as paterfamilias.

Abbas had never imagined such a thing. Surely Arias had more obvious heirs? But Maia explained that none had the kind of political promise that the family wanted in their leader.

Being paterfamilias came with a lot of responsibility. It made Abbas a senator, that is, a voter, and also made him manager of the matriline's collective fund and put him in charge of approving any additions to the matriline. Adoptees, husbands, and babies all needed his permission—he couldn't imagine ordering a baby exposed, but he now had the authority to do it. Births, weddings, and adoptions didn't happen often, but if he wanted his permission to be informed he had to keep up with everybody's lives pretty closely, which took time. Anyway, they all started asking his advice. Abbas joked that he needed a better-paying job if he was to do all this extra unpaid work— then he realized that there actually was a job he very much wanted and was now qualified to pursue.

Nonanye elections involved no ballots, no secrecy, and no voting districts. The Ruling Council was one-tenth of the Senate, and one-third of its seats came up for a vote every two years, so the votes of thirty senators—any thirty senators—would secure a seat. Getting those votes could require some finesse, since each senator was responsible to his matriline and his plebeian client-matrilines, at least several hundred people whose preferences could influence his vote.

All those people had to be courted too, to some extent, but basically campaigning just meant talking to people. Abbas was good at that.

He could count on the votes of every derger paterfamilias, but very few of them knew there was an election on. The support of the other members of b'Freias's faction was invaluable, but most of them were also running for a seat and would vote for themselves. Some did promise him their second- or third-choice votes. J.J. had a number of patrician friends and got them to talk to their patresfamilias for Abbas. But Abbas's most powerful ally was his wife. Maia seemed to know everybody in Holia and now, thanks to Opal introducing her, almost everybody in Nonani, too. She networked, pulled strings, called favors, and made promises with an assertiveness that many people considered borderline improper for a wife—but she was so charming about it, so prettily feminine, that they forgave her. That she gave birth mid-campaign and thereafter went about her work holding little Obas to her breast only added to her appeal.

There was resistance.

Abbas had not expected to please everybody—he was running primarily on a land-reform platform sure to appeal mostly to people who couldn't vote. He also favored an expansion of the role of the plebiscite and changes to labor contracts and the laws governing credit lines available to farmers, none of which was likely to excite most patricians. But he expected those who didn't like him to simply ignore him, because that's what usually happened to first-time candidates. Instead, he had people speaking out against him and writing negative op-eds. Then rumors began to circulate questioning his mental health, his sexual potency (a paterfamilias had to be a worthy mate to the land), whether he was a real patrician, and so forth. The sudden attention in public places from multiple overly-friendly and very attractive men could not be a coincidence, either. Abbas ceased allowing himself to ever be alone lest one of these admirers take the opportunity to claim to have buggered him.

"I mean, they can't be legitimate, I'm not that attractive," he told J.J. by letter.

B'Freias was having similar problems, for although his platform was quite different, its ultimate result would obviously bother the same people. And the fact that he wasn't married made him more vulnerable to sexual rumor. B'Tomas, who functioned as b'Freias's proxy and attack-dog, made speeches openly accusing a specific incumbent candidate of hiring rumor-mongers. She said that there was a "vast, conservative conspiracy" on the part of "the beneficiaries of the military-industrialist complex," weird, alarmist phrases for which she was roundly mocked in the newshouses—except that Abbas realized she was right.

But as powerful as the organized opposition was, land reform, political reform, environmental protection, and environmental justice all had deep and broad support. Plenty of senators were sympathetic, and those who were not were afraid of plebeian clients who were.

Finally, just after Saturnalia, all the senators registered their choices with the Sisters of the King's Hearth. Even in the age of the telegraph, collecting and counting the votes took a long time, and so the results were not announced until just after Hilaria.

Abbas was in the Curia the night the Sister came in and read the results. The reading took a long time. Abbas heard b'Freias's name and those of several other members of the faction. Finally, he heard his own. He turned to Maia, who was standing next to him in the balcony, and hugged and kissed her, lifting her abruptly off her feet.

"We did it!" he crowed. "You and I, we did it!"

Chapter 8. The Civilian

Year of Nonani 831 - 839

Hyras resigned. That is, he formally asked to be shifted to the reserve list and was put through the ceremony that makes a soldier into a civilian, a kind of reverse Basic Training supposed to be both metaphysically and psychologically effective. But really Hyras just felt dazed. He went home.

That is, he went to the Dynans', where Ilia and the girls had been living. Of course, they were fine, all happy and healthy and glad to see him. He'd been worried for nothing. He arrived on foot, dressed like a civilian and carrying his few things in a leather knapsack, and when the dog barked an alert, the whole household came boiling out to meet him. Ilia hugged him, and he clung to her, feeling safe at home now in all possible senses.

"I thought you'd forgotten me," he murmured into her wild, ticklish, scented hair.

"Never," she assured him. "You're the one thing I won't." She kissed him like she meant it, then added, "you and the girls."

The girls seemed to have forgotten him—they were both frankly alarmed when he tried to hug them—but Ilia explained that he was Daddy, and then, after a long moment of doubt, they took her word for it and leaped into his arms, both talking at once so that he could understand neither of them. They knew exactly who he was, they just hadn't remembered what he looked like.

"We thought *you* forgot *us*," Crea said, after she and everybody else had hugged him.

"What?"

"Not *forgot*," Rossa temporized. "But you didn't write very much, so we all figured you must have a lot on your mind."

"I told them to cut you a break," Jessas said. "A soldier can't spend all his time writing letters to a bunch of women."

"What? I...."

It emerged that some of his letters home had never arrived. And since he'd sent off letters in batches—couriers only left with mail once every few weeks—when a batch went missing, every one of his friends and loved ones, including his parents and brothers, lost a letter or two or more. At least two batches had vanished a few months apart. And when they thought he was writing less often, all of them except his unsentimental mother responded by writing to him less, leading to him writing less....

Hyras could not laugh about the mishap. He wanted to cry, actually, but didn't.

For a while, he lived with the Dynans, doing odd jobs for the family business or working around their estate, which was like a cross between a big farm and a small village. Nobody expected much of him, as they'd decided he'd been ill, and indeed he began to recover. The horses had a lot to do with it. The Dynans raised horses as well as sheep, chickens, and various crops. Being Slovonye, they ate, rather than gelded, most of the colts, a fact Hyras did not like, but at least there was always something to do in the barns and corrals, and their large, accepting presence calmed him. Ilia thought alcohol worked as a poison for him somehow and that he ought not to drink it anymore, and he agreed. Surrounded by his family, his craving lessened a little, and he found he could abstain simply by imagining her disapproval. His stomach pains eased up and went away. His sleep improved. He discovered that if he smoked a little hash now and then, the nightmares dissipated and he stopped jumping at every little thing. The hash never became a problem the way the alcohol had. He felt like he was waking up from a very bad and very long dream.

Hyras was also discovering how to be a full-time, every-day

husband and father. The father part was difficult, as he'd never spent much time around children even when he was one, nor did he want to be anything like his own dad. He decided to let the girls themselves teach him and simply began spending time with them, looking to them for cues on what they needed from him.

Rosia mostly wanted him to listen to her telling him things. She would relate long, convoluted stories that were sometimes true and sometimes not, or lists of interesting facts that were almost always true. She somehow reminded him of both her grandmothers at once. She was close to six years old, now, and so he began teaching her to read, starting with the 33 letters of the Itarish alphabet. In autumn, they drew the letters with sticks in the sandy soil outside while acorns fell in a dry clatter all around them. She learned to write her name and his in the light dustings of snow on the tiled floor of the atrium that winter. When she realized she could form her small body into the shapes of some of the letters, he threw himself into the project, and together they figured out how to dance the whole alphabet.

Adna was harder to talk with because, at not quite two-and-a-half, she still didn't form her words well. He thought of it as an accent from whatever country babies live in before they are born. She loved to be cuddled but would not sit still, unintentionally bruising her father repeatedly. She loved to dance, and would stomp and twirl and wave her arms gracefully in the air.

"Now, clap!" she would command, when she was done, and he always did.

During that first winter out of the army, Ilia got pregnant again.

"What can I do?" he asked Ilia one evening. The girls were already in bed in their own room. He lay, wearing only his brown and yellow tunic, resting his head upon his wife's thigh. She'd already changed into her robe and was combing out her hair.

"Do about what?" she asked.

"My life, my career...I need a job."

"Daddy can get you one."

"I'm not asking him."

"Why not?"

"Ilia, your father doesn't respect me now, asking him for charity won't improve matters."

"Daddy respects you! He let you marry me, didn't he? And it wouldn't be charity. Why do you say it would be charity?"

"Ilia, when has your father ever said no to you?"

"Um, never? Not permanently, anyway."

"He likes me, I believe that. But I'm hardly the son-in-law he wanted."

"Just because he talked Traxa into marrying Grias...." Grias was the son of the owner of a major shipping company.

"And he was very pleased when Crea fell in love with an industrial engineer. Ilia, your father is a businessman. I am not. None of what I have is what he wants."

Ilia had no response. She began brushing his short hair, playfully. After a moment, he brushed her brushing away.

"What can I do, though?" Hyras asked. "All I know is how to follow orders and how to give them, how to kill other men and how to avoid being killed."

"There's lots of other things you could do."

"I could gamble," he suggested.

"You could," agreed Ilia. "But sooner or later you'll lose. All gamblers do."

"They say the same thing about soldiers."

"You're good with horses, you're good with children, you're good at math...."

"I could be a stable-hand, or a woman, or...."

"What you're not good at," Ilia opined, "is seeing your options. But on the battlefield you can. Why is that?"

"I don't know. War is simple. It's complicated, but it's simple. And I understand how the pieces work." He lapsed into silence for a moment, then sat up straight as though he'd just had a brilliant idea. "I could be a prostitute!" he joked.

Ilia smirked, then wrapped her arms around him and gently pulled him back down into her lap.

"I am going to make very sure you have neither the time nor the energy for that," she told him.

He made an appreciative, anticipatory noise.

The problem was that Hyras's memories of civilian life were those of a sixteen-year-old plebeian. Now he was a twenty-five-year-old patrician, no longer a youth by Nonanye standards. He had no clear idea how men of his social station looked for work, or even what sort of work they did. And he had no intention of asking Ilia to live like a plebeian's wife, nor did he want her living with her father indefinitely. So he took his first step into independence by taking his small family to go live with his parents instead, just for a while. Their place was nearer a town, and so he thought he might be able to find some work.

Ilia had been looking forward to meeting her in-laws. She hadn't expected to ever *live* with them, but where Hyras thought he should go, she would follow. Just after the Fallow ended, they took a regularly-scheduled stagecoach two days to Dalani, which had once been a fortified city-state much the same as Nonani had been. But in three hundred years, Nonani had grown and Dalani had not. Alighting from the coach there and looking around—the low, somewhat slumped earth-and-stone perimeter wall at the end of every short street, the single-story timber or brick buildings huddled close, the single, neatly-paved forum where a fountain poured out drinking water for all the people and animals in town—it was like going back in time.

The late winter morning was crisp and fine, with ice clinging to the rim of the fountain's basin and speckling the paving-stones where the spray had blown a little the day before. The blue sky was streaked with mares' tail clouds foretelling cold rain or sleet the text day. Hyras asked around and found somebody with a cart willing to take a drive in exchange for a few coppers. Ilia herded the girls into the back of the cart while Hyras loaded their bags. She wore a hooded cloak of gray wool felt against the cold, but it was clasped in silver and edged in decorative green thread, and underneath she wore her customary winter silks. She felt as though everybody, all the women in rough-spun shawls and undyed aprons awaiting their turn at the fountain, must be staring at her.

With a small jolt, the cart got going, and soon the clip-clop of the horses' shod feet on paving-stones changed to the dull thud-thud of a trot upon a rural road of frozen mud. Before too long, they were pulling up at the rented farm where Hyras had been born.

She looked around at the frozen, straw-covered mud yard, the green-and-gold chickens and white-and-gray ducks, the winter-fallow vegetable beds and the barns not fair off, the small fields for wheat, beans, and hay beyond, and everything ringed by scrubby woodland a dull gray-green. The house, of squared-off timber beams caulked with cow dung and thatched with alder twigs, was smaller than her father's atrium. Its windows were open to the day's thin warmth and had no glass. A brick-lined well with a small, twig-thatched roof sat not far away. In the other direction sat a privy of worn, gray-brown boards. She could smell, but not at the moment see, cows, horses. She knew Hyras's family was not poor as such, merely middle-class, and everything looked neat and well-kept, but the permanent reality of his world, where women kept house without servants and children must earn their keep with chores, briefly appalled her. Hyras glanced at her, self-conscious, and she smiled at him.

And then a woman came out of the house and called to someone else, and a man trotted briskly out of the barn, wiping his hands on his apron. Hyras's parents.

Both must have been in their mid-sixties, but their hair had hardly grayed. Age showed only in their weathered skin, their scarred and knobby hands. They both dressed simply in the old Odye style of most country folk, and both were scrupulously clean despite literally working in dirt. Sylas looked very much like Hyras except that his hair had no reddish tinge, but the feeling of his face was very different. He bowed gallantly over Ilia's hand and kissed it, pronouncing her very pretty. Ana was tall and slim, with strange, gray-blue eyes. She flashed Ilia a brilliant, welcoming smile and explained, without greeting or preamble, "I've been serving on a lot of committees lately."

"Oh, really?" Ilia prompted, and found herself on the receiving end of a long and enthusiastic lecture on all the doings at one of the local temples.

The girls were freed to run off and explore, provided they stayed together and within sight of the house, and Hyras and his father carried the bags inside and unpacked.

"I've bought a bunk bed for the girls," Sylas's voice drifted out through the open window, "and there's a cradle for when the bun comes out of the oven—and I rigged this privacy screen so you can put the next bun in after that, eh?"

"Dad...."

For the next few hours, Ilia followed her mother-in-law around as she did various chores. Ilia helped when she could, and although she didn't know how to do most of the things Ana did, she made clear she was willing to learn. She was peripherally aware of Sylas fussing over the unpacking, making sure everything had a place and that the second bedroom where the young family would stay had everything that might be needed or wanted. "I'll take care of that, Dad," Hyras said periodically, to no avail. But Ana never stopped talking. Ilia didn't mind. She was interested. It was only when she caught Sylas's look of relieved approval that she realized perhaps most people would not be. When Ana took the time to sacrifice a pigeon at the home altar, Ilia recognized the prayer she sang and joined in. The scents of blood-smoke and sage rose from the little bowl of hot charcoal and smelled of piety and home.

Hyras's brothers arrived in time for dinner with their wives and children. Both greeted Hyras by good-naturedly pummeling him, and both more or less ignored Ilia beyond polite greetings and obligatory joshing ("what do you see in my ugly little brother, anyway?"). Which was just as well, as she kept mixing them up because they looked alike, both tall, like their mother, and had very similar names. Nor could she keep track of all the children, six of them between the two families. The kids mostly ignored her, too. The smaller ones took turns riding around on Uncle Hyras's back while he pretended to be a hilariously disobedient horse.

Sixteen people could not fit around the kitchen table, but fortunately the afternoon had turned warmish—the ice melted from the ground, even in the shade—and so the brothers moved two picnic tables into the sun and set those for the meal. The food was simple but plentiful, a thick bean and onion stew dressed up with the meat of the sacrificed pigeon, piles of wheat bannocks, and slices of quiche made with mushrooms and a little smoked beef. One of the brothers had brought a couple of bottles of very good cider, and Ana served it spice-mulled, sweetened, and hot (the children and Hyras drank honeyed lemon balm tea instead). The other brother's wife had brought a pot of baked apples and walnuts for dessert, which Ana heated up and served with fresh whipped cream. Ilia had never before sat down to a family dinner with only four dishes and two courses, but she reflected that there was only one cook, and everything tasted good.

Hyras, as the guest of honor, contributed to the meal by answering questions and telling war stories, though Ilia noticed he seemed unusually uncomfortable doing both. Eventually he was allowed to go quiet, and Ana began monologuing about all the things various cousins and neighbors and temple friends were doing, apparently either unaware or unconcerned that Ilia had no idea who any of these people were and couldn't therefore follow the stories. Ana talked with a piece of bannock in one hand and her horn stew-spoon in the other, but neither hand moved. She could not eat and talk at the same time, and eventually seemed to realize that everyone else had finished while she had barely started. While she ate, Sylas and his older sons chatted about the family business—another topic not everybody present could follow—and the children waited anxiously to be allowed to begin dessert.

Dessert eaten, the children were excused to go play, and Sylas poured more cider for all the adults, including Hyras, who frowned slightly, looked at the cup without touching it, then exhaled in a way that Ilia thought sounded either sad or angry. Nobody else noticed. When his father began holding forth on politics, Hyras quietly excused himself, saying he wanted to get a start on dishes.

"If the bill passes, it'll do in the dergers," Sylas was saying, "they won't be able to keep the charcoal harvesters out. It's a money-grab, is what it is, but nobody says that in so many words. I ask you, how will those bloody patricians keep up their precious boar hunts if there's no forest left?"

"There is plenty of forest for boars," Ilia interjected, diffident but used to lively dinner conversation. "And the charcoal harvest is necessary so we can properly arm our soldiers to *protect our national interests.*"

"Right, protect our national interests is a fancy term for picking fights so we can justify taking slaves."

"Picking fights...?" Ilia was confused. "Anyway, taking slaves requires no special justification. Daddy uses slaves in the subsurface mines and some of his secondary processing centers. Steel manufacture at scale wouldn't be economical otherwise. Military spending would go up, so taxes would have to. Nobody likes taxes."

"My dear," Sylas said. "You seem like a good-hearted woman, and I don't want you to take this the wrong way, but what you just said tells me exactly why you think there is plenty of forest."

Ilia could think of no response, so Sylas went back to pontificating, explaining to a more or less captive audience that since derger and elves and other minorities had no patrician patrons to sue for redress, the matter might have to come down to a plebiscite. He seemed at least slightly tipsy, though he was only on his second glass.

The children, three families of cousins, ran and played and shouted to one another as the short winter afternoon cooled towards sunset and the last of the light turned the bare, stubbly fields copper.

Hyras had some money saved up and, early that spring, used it for a down payment on a nearby tenant farm. The rent from that farm was enough to cover his mortgage payments and the rent on a house with a garden in town. It did not pay for the hired help Ilia clearly needed, so he talked his oldest niece into keeping house more or less for pocket-money. To cover other expenses, he found himself a position tutoring children in geography and history. He liked the work and liked the kids, but it didn't pay enough to be a permanent solution. In the summer, Ilia went into labor two months early and brought forth a miniature stillborn boy. After paying for both the midwife and the necessary temple rites, Hyras missed a mortgage payment. He tried finding better-paying work, but failed.

That winter, his old army buddy, b'Danas came to visit. They had kept in touch, so b'Danas knew Hyras was a patrician now and legally able to buy real estate. He suggested they go into business together. B'Danas could provide the up-front cash, and Hyras could buy the location as soon as they'd earned enough. Soon the two of them had a small shop selling both medicinal and culinary herbs as well as various small animals for use in sacrifices. Hyras found the work horribly boring and felt bad for the animals, and he did not like dealing with customers, but it let him pay his bills and put a little money by. Of course the nascent business could not be expected to turn a profit yet, and so there was nothing to draw on for emergencies. The emergency arrived in early summer when b'Danas' wife died in childbirth. Hyras, hurting for his friend, agreed to sell the business to raise cash to pay for the funeral and so that b'Danas could hire a wet-nurse for the baby. Then Ilia had another miscarriage.

No job really worked out. If Hyras liked the work, he didn't like the pay. If he liked the pay, he couldn't stand the work. Sometimes he quit. Sometimes he got fired or found himself first on the layoff list. Some jobs ended through no choice or fault of his own, and twice he fell victim to fraud. Every year, Ilia had a miscarriage, sometimes two. No midwife could tell her why. Twice, Ilia went behind his back and asked her father for money, just to survive. Hyras didn't want Jessas' money, but didn't feel he could turn it down once he had it. Every year he had to eat a little more pride.

Then Ilia lost another pregnancy, this one very near term, and almost died giving birth to the little corpse. Together she and Hyras decided not to risk another. She had heard that some pennyroyal preparations could make a person sick, so instead she tried tracking her cycle, guessing when she might be fertile and declining sex on those days. Of course Hyras respected that. Sometimes, when she wasn't sure, she said yes but asked him to withdraw. The arrangement satisfied neither of them.

It's not that everything in Hyras's life was bad. One way or another, he kept his family fed and housed, and that was the important thing. The house, though not large, wasn't especially small, either, and Ilia gradually got it furnished and decorated in a cute and comfortable way. It was a timber dwelling, just a block away from the Forum, with three or four rooms on each of two floors organized not around an atrium, as in Nonanye architecture, but in the Dalanye way, around a stairwell open to the sky. A balcony off the back had space for a table and chairs and a garden of potted herbs and flowers, and under the balcony was a shaded area where the girls made themselves a playhouse. A small, fenced yard was big enough for a couple of milch goats whom the girls made pets of. The place had no running water, and there was a chamber pot to empty if you didn't want to go out to the privy in the middle of the night, but the house he'd grown up in was the same way. He would come home, and no matter how discouraged and exhausted he felt, he could leave it all outside and play with his girls or listen to their prattle, and later they'd all take turns reading to Ilia out on the balcony, mostly semi-dramatic readings of plays, usually farces or adventure-romances. Sometimes they'd have friends over for dinner, and there was dancing in the Forum in the summer. Hyras still would not dance himself, but he liked to watch Ilia and the girls have fun.

But Hyras knew he was not the success his father wanted, and the constant worry, how he was going to pay his bills, how he was going to find work next when the latest job inevitably fell through, it wore him down.

Through those years, politics were getting increasingly weird and increasingly ugly. There was, indeed, a plebiscite called on the question of land reform, and the law Sylas didn't like was struck. Around the same time, a series of street protests successfully pressured the local council to abandon a plan that would have cut the publicly-owned riparian forests for charcoal and converted several streams to navigable canals for freight. But none of this forest protection was popular with either the wealthier patricians or the proletarians, both of whom saw their livelihoods endangered by any potential loss of economic growth. When Senator Lian, a radical pro-forest, pro-derger lawyer, was selected as Coordinator of the Ruling Council, the proletarians in town rioted.

Riots for any reason usually evoked a response from the local garrison, but this time the soldiers didn't come out, and several shops were looted. Rumors circulated that the soldiers had been paid off by a shadowy organization called the Iron Eagle, but who funded the Iron Eagle, nobody knew.

Two years after that, a businessman named Tanas Rylas Canan got himself elected Speaker. He was both the cause and the symptom of the weirdness, inflaming the anger of the proletarians, and hence the power of mob violence, and directing it against forest conservation and anyone or anything that needed it or supported it or allied themselves with those who did—derger, elves, educated people, Aethenye, immigrants.... All such people rightly felt attacked and got defensive. Everybody seemed angry and suspicious of each other all of a sudden.

Hyras lost several job opportunities when employers assumed that as his father's son, he must support forest protections. When he insisted that he did not care about politics and did not know anything about forestry or the steel industry, word got out, and then pro-forest employers refused to hire him. Of course, Hyras was not so apolitical as he made out. He visited the newshouses regularly, and he was well-read on history and political philosophy. He and Ilia made a point of talking over current events with the girls in order to develop their minds. But none of his political opinions were worth alienating anybody over, and alienation seemed to be all that expressing opinions could achieve. There was no middle ground anymore, no way for anyone to just talk.

Hyras realized he had to get his family out of Dalani, go some place his father's name wasn't known so he could find work. But that summer was very wet, and malaria swept the town. Hyras got sick and for months could not work at all. He was forced to sell the farm to raise enough money to survive, but then he had no income at all. He knew he could not ask help of his father after denying the man's politics. Reluctantly, he wrote to Jessas. He never heard back directly.

Instead, Jessas wrote to Ilia, who, without having any idea of the letter's contents, asked Hyras to read it to her because her eyes hurt. The letter read, in part:

I do not want to subsidize, speak to, or hear about that loser whose seed makes you sick and who can't hold a job. I have instructed the others of our family to say the same. I know you love him, my daughter, and I shan't ask you to choose between him and me, but I love you, and he forces me to choose between you and him. I choose you.

Hyras looked up from the letter. He had not realized how much that letter hurt until he saw his own pain reflected in Ilia's face.

Not long after, Ilia discovered she was pregnant again. Hyras thought she ought to abort. He didn't want her risking labor and maybe her life. But an abortion meant a large dose of pennyroyal, and she wouldn't risk that. That left only one option. Ilia had to take the girls and go home to her father so that he could pay for the medical care she would clearly need. Hyras had to take the last of his money and go alone to Nonani City, the biggest and richest city in the known world, the place where poor, out-of-luck men always went to try to find work.

Getting off the stagecoach late in the afternoon, sore and weary from travel, Hyras went first to find himself a place in a cheap boarding house and then to buy a little bread. Then he wandered the streets. Unemployment is a strange kind of loneliness, with nothing to do because there is nobody who values your doings. He found himself on the bank of the Old Mother River, facing more water than he'd ever seen before in his life.

The bank was a high brick wall, interrupted in places where ladders or stairways led down to the water so that boatmen could come up, though there were no boats along this stretch of shore at the moment. The top of the wall stood even with a wide river-walk like a linear plaza dotted with benches and, every few hundred feet, handsome-looking date palms. The walk stretched upriver perhaps three quarters of a mile to where a warehouse built partly on land and partly on a wharf jutted out into the water. Downriver, the walk stretched about a quarter mile to a pier where a ninety-oared trader lay tied, her sailors up in the rigging doing something or other to her one wide, furled, square sail. He sat on a bench and looked out.

Hyras had taken river boats on tributaries of the Old Mother, and he'd visited cities on her banks in Duchasa, hundreds of miles to the north, but he'd never before seen the main stem this close to her mouth. The water stretched so wide he could not see the opposite shore and wind-driven waves crashed against the brick bulkhead with a continuous but ever-changing noise. Out in the stream lay islands, forested but ringed about by marsh. Gulls and ducks and watercraft of every possible size and shape plied the waters, doing what Hyras could not guess. As he watched, a vast flock of flamingos rose up from behind the nearer island, flying together, a mass of pink and white particles, heading downstream. Closer to shore, a huge gray heron flew by, going in the same direction, its broad wings flapping like table-cloths. He could hear passersby talking in a variety of languages and dialects, sailor song from one of the boats carrying absurdly far over the water. Pigeons cooed, concerned by a party of Aethenye businessmen in their native dress, then took wing in a rush. He caught a faint whiff of hash from somewhere and wished he had some. A street vendor was grilling rats, and Hyras wished he had some of them, too. When you're broke, all the world is full of things you can't buy.

In a wallet hung on his belt where it wouldn't show under his scapular, he had two silver denarii, his last. In his hand he held a pack of playing cards.

"Every hand's a winner," he said to himself.

The water didn't smell very good, and when he stood up so he could look down directly over the edge of the wall, he saw that the waves tossed against the brick all manner of things, most of them ugly—a scum of floating pollen, bits of broken sedge stem and reeds, blocks of scrap wood, dog and horse turds, an actual dead dog—but when he sat back down on the bench and looked out, he saw the river pristine, a strange, pale, variable gray, an answer to the clouds, always moving.

After a while he realized that if he did not head back to his boarding house soon, the sun would go down on him outside, and he might get lost. He couldn't tell how close sunset might be, because of the clouds.

On his way back, he found the streets quiet, almost empty, but there were still a few people about, including a young man walking towards him on the same side of the street. As they approached each other, the youth spotted him, looked at him curiously, and stopped walking. And Hyras realized that she was neither quite as young as he'd thought nor a man. And also that he'd had the same realization about the same person before.

"B'Sheras!" he cried, suddenly and unreasonably happy. "How the hell are ya?"

"Another day, another denarius," b'Sheras replied, which is more or less what all laborers say the world over when they don't want to say how they're actually doing. "It's b'Sylas, right? I thought it was you. How awesome."

She had been scowling at the ground as she walked along, walking quickly, not appearing to notice her surroundings at all except that of course she noticed everything. But her scowl had dissolved as though it had never been, replaced by her sweet, utterly naked smile. Hyras noticed for the first time that her eyes, slightly too large, were the same pale, strange gray as the river at a distance. He noticed, too, that she was dressed as a civilian, tunic, leggings, and scapular all in green and white, and that, even beyond her old habitual slight dishevelment, her once-expensive clothes were faded and patched. She saw him noticing and grinned, a little embarrassed.

"I guess a legion isn't the best preparation for success in business, is it?" she ventured.

"No, it's not," he acknowledged, well aware that she'd noticed his own faded shabbiness.

"Well, something's bound to turn up," she asserted, but Hyras gave her the look such treacle deserves, and her smile turned rueful a moment. Then she grew serious and grasped his upper arm. "No, listen, really. Everything changes. The good things don't stay, but the bad don't either. So things are out of alignment for us right now. The alignment will change. And when it does, we'll have options we don't now see. The thing will be to recognize and take those options. Yes?"

Hyras grasped her arm in reply and nodded a little. When he could speak again, he clapped her on her other arm in a friendly manner.

"You take care, b'Sheras," he said and meant it.

"You, too."

And they each went on their way.

Chapter 9. The Jonah

Year of Nonani 831 - 835

Gwen the civilian had a job as a warehouse manager all lined up. She returned to Nonani City expecting to pick up her family and head to Thasani to start a new, successful, and altogether more stable part of her life.

Nope.

THE HOUSE WAS VERY CROWDED. Chalcy and Topaz each had a new baby, plus Jonas and his family had moved in for a while—he'd just left the military, too, and had been admitted to the bar as a lawyer. His goal was to get a position as an aide to a Council member. That made thirteen children in the house, plus the adults. And two pet ferrets.

THE ELDER EUANS WERE...OLD. It was shocking, but should not have been. Old is what you get if you don't die first. And yet.

Opal's hair had gone entirely gray, and she seemed strangely tired. Tomas remained vigorous, his mane of hair still mostly black, but his voice had roughened, his posture gone slightly stooped. He'd told Gwen by letter about turning his business over to Cheras, but to actually see him not going in to work was something else. He said he even wanted to step down from the Ruling Council but couldn't, as some sort of political nastiness had been going on. Gwen considered all political things nasty and didn't pay much attention.

WRAPPING UP HER WORK AS Prefect had delayed Gwen's move so long that now Chrys was too pregnant to go anywhere.

The labor this time was very fast, so fast that Chrys was starting to push when the midwife arrived. There was no time to kick Gwen out.

Afterwards, while wife and new daughter slept, Gwen went to the kitchen and found Opal sitting there. The house was very quiet.

"Where is everybody?" Gwen asked.

"They all went to the playground. No sense frightening the children."

"They should have been here," Gwen asserted, pouring herself a cup of wine. Then she poured another for her foster-mother without waiting to be asked. "Everybody attends at least one birth, but we don't remember that one. And so we don't know. I hadn't. I'd never known Chrys was so strong." She sat down and she and Opal clicked their cups together and drank. "I mean, I knew she was *strong*, but I hadn't known..." she amended, waving her hand as though trying to collect the right words.

"Do you ever think of wanting one? Of your own body?"

"One what, a baby?" Gwen considered. "You know, I'd forgotten that's even possible, ain't that strange?" She looked down at her tummy, as though just then noticing that she had ovaries and a uterus in there. "But there are so many reasons why not. I can't even consider it."

"*Can't* is a bad place to start," Opal advised her. "Never mind the reasons, what do you want?"

"To be a good father and husband, like any man," Gwen replied, without hesitation, then frowned, realizing she'd referred to herself as a man. "Talk about *can't*!"

"You are a far better man than most men, Gwenessifyr. I believe you can do anything."

The light streaming in through the windows was going golden in the shortening afternoon. The others would be back, soon, and there would be daughters and nieces and nephews to give news to and to try to keep quiet so Chrys could sleep. Gwen regarded her wine, then looked up and regarded Opal. Chrys was right—the old woman was losing weight. Her coughing had been getting worse. Just now, the cloth in her hand had fallen open, showing blood.

AT THE END OF THE Fallow, Gwen and Chrys headed north with Toma, a compact little yellow-brown baby with frankly golden hair, in a sling across Chrys's chest. The older girls stayed with their grandparents, to be collected later once Gwen and Chrys got settled. Bundled in multiple cloaks against the late-winter cold, they spent days up on deck watching the bank of the river jerk by as the oarsmen fought the current, the water mostly a dull gray clotted with slushy blocks of rotten ice, day after day.

Finally they came upon Thasani, the northernmost city on the main stem of the Old Mother, one of the northernmost cities anywhere in the provinces. Coming upon it from the river made it look more than a little like Nonani City, flat-topped hills densely packed with buildings above a river district of warehouses, sheds, hostels, brothels, and wharves. Except the hills were low and broad and many, artificial platforms of clay raised forty or fifty feet above the level of the upper floodplain, steep-sided and wooded, connected by graceful, timbered bridges and causeways, the palaces and temples and astronomical observatories raised even higher on brick-faced stepped pyramids, and all of it covered by patches and crusts of gray, melting snow. Thasani had an Itarish name, but it was a Duchesye city, founded before Nonani was even a village of goatherds. Its mounds and some of its temples were over a thousand years old.

*   *   *

"ONLY ONE ROOM," SAID CHRYS, of the place Gwen had rented. "What a small house we have."

"All the better to warm you with, my dear," quipped Gwen, paraphrasing a folk-tale. "There's a loft, too—that's where the sleeping cabinets are." The place was furnished and even stocked with tinder, kindling, candles, water, and a week's worth of groceries. Gwen laid a fire and lit it with flint and steel, then lit all the candles in the wheel-shaped chandelier, so she could close the door. The windows were all blocked for the winter, having no glass. Chrys explored.

"Cute," she acknowledged. And indeed the Duchesye people were great ones for decoration, everything intricately painted and carved. The walls were hung with brilliant tapestries of thick wool. "Burning wood, though? Don't they have charcoal here? We're going to live in smoke."

"I guess that's why the roof is so high."

"I was wondering. Won't the heat from the fire all just go up?"

"Take a sniff," Gwen suggested.

"Dung? Cow dung? But...Oh!" And Chrys knelt to bury her hand in the straw. "It's hot!"

"Heated floors, Ma Euan. All winter long!"

The layer of dung and straw on the earthen floor produced substantial heat as it decomposed, a system they'd seen used previously in animal barns. Cow dung does not smell objectionable if well-aerated, and the layer of clean straw and lavender over top helped. A ring of bricks kept the straw well away from the hearth and provided great opportunity for stubbed toes.

The house sat on a mound a few acres in extent and occupied by a single economically mixed neighborhood of mostly rentals with a large open area of perhaps an acre or two inside the ring of wattle-and-daub, thatch-roofed houses—a communal space of animal corrals, vegetable gardens, compost bins, apple trees, and the footprints of dozens of playing children in the crusted snow.

Down the street was a shop that sold every kind of cheese you could imagine, and also all sorts of sausages, bacon, ham, and every kind of pickled or honey-preserved thing. A few houses away in the other direction was a bakery making authentic Duchesye pastries fresh every morning.

THE GREAT THING ABOUT THASANI was that while it had all the exoticism of a real, barbarian city, it in fact was a part of the Empire, and its people were citizens. Some were even followers of the Shepherd. So you could have your pastries, your ancient architecture, your palaces and temples raised to strange gods atop stepped pyramids of patterned brick, but you could also go to the public baths, get books from well-stocked libraries, maybe take in a play. The city had theaters for all four types of drama.

GWEN'S JOB CONSISTED LARGELY OF keeping track of everything that entered or left a pair of big warehouses down by the river. She liaised directly with traders and merchants according to contracts already worked out by her supervisors, managed a small staff of workers, kept the goods physically organized so everything could be found quickly, arranged for security as needed, and generally looked after her employer's interests. The pay was good, she'd been promised multiple annual vacations per year in which to travel, and every week brought some new and interesting problem to solve—how to solve them was entirely up to her.

THERE WERE TOO MANY ARTICLES criticizing Gwen's employer in the newshouses. Not that she had any inherent objection to criticism, but the lies bothered her. The facts bothered her even more—because they hadn't been publicly available.

She did some digging and learned that the articles were being written by a man who rented the office above hers—he was the warehouse company's tenant as well as its enemy, which explained how he'd gotten insider information. Reliable town gossip had it that he, a widower, was engaged to marry a younger woman whose father owned a rival shipping company.

"Of all the duplicitous, dishonorable, mercenary..."

Also, Gwen did not like being spied upon. Her supervisor told her to tell the man his lease was canceled. He replied by quoting the terms of the contract and the relevant law by which his lease could not be canceled. Gwen's employer told her to just deal with it, so one fine spring day she jogged up the stairs.

"Leave now," she said.

"Nope," he replied.

She walked towards him. It wasn't a very big room.

"No, let me explain this," she said. "You go today, through the door or through the window. Your choice." She watched him look her up and down, plainly thinking *woman: no threat*. Gwen took another step forward, looming over him now, and spoke almost sweetly. "Would you like me to show you how pain compliance works?" she inquired. "I *can* put you in a joint-lock before you can do anything about it, and then, I promise you, you will go where I put you."

He saw her point of view, after that.

GWEN MADE FRIENDS EASILY AT work while Chrys befriended the neighbors, and the couple hosted dinner parties at least once a week. Other, quieter evenings, Gwen spent reading or writing to friends and relations while Chrys nursed Toma and then worked on the new summer bedspread she was weaving. The house had come with a good loom. As the weather warmed, they opened the windows and the summer doors for air and light and took out all the winter straw. The bare earthen floor, kept slightly damp, felt nicely cool on bare feet. Once a week, Gwen would stop by the bakery on the way home and pick up an Itarye-style rosemary focaccia to load with cheese, sausage, and onion and bake under an upturned pot. As a rule she did no women's work, but for Chrys she made occasional exception.

"WHERE IS ELLIA?" GWEN ASKED. Chrys had gone to get the girls and come back with girl, singular.

"With Father and Mama," Chrys responded, looking uncomfortable. "She's fine. I didn't write you about it because the letter would have taken longer to get here than I did."

"Write me about what? What's happened?"

"I told you, everything's fine. Father just wants to keep Ellia for a while. She does like it there, she gets to play with her cousins, and he misses us, so he said if he could at least keep her...."

"*Keep* her?" Gwen exclaimed. "Keep her? What is this, do I get my children back if I guess his real name?"

"Gwen, it's not like that. Everything's OK, really."

"Everything is *not* OK. Everything is *not* fine. She is *our* child! I can't believe this—"

"Gwen, it's just how Father is, you know that, he just—"

"Oh, I know how he is, I know what he is, he's the human Uncanny Glen, is what he is!" The Uncanny Glen, an image from another popular folktale, was a place that one could enter but never leave. "You enter the circle of his love, not knowing what it is, and straight away the vines begin to twine around your ankles." Gwen gestured the twining vines with her long, narrow hands and comically twisted expression.

"Good thing for you that he *is* like that," Chrys said, beginning to sound defensive. "And good for me, too, obviously."

"Oh, that is a low blow, it just is. You should be ashamed of yourself for that one, really. He *took our kid*. You never should have let him take her, Chrys!"

"OK, Gwen, *you* go and tell Father he can't have something he wants."

Gwen's reply was a mildly blasphemous oath because she knew Chrys was right.

A RAG SOAKED IN LINSEED oil will spontaneously combust if not allowed to dry properly. Gwen knew that, but one of her workers—she never admitted to knowing who—did not. Fortunately, Gwen had stayed late at the office and was on her way home past the warehouses when she smelled smoke and heard fire. She roused the neighborhood, organized bucket brigades, saved most of the goods in the warehouses, and kept the fire from spreading beyond the property.

But she could not save the warehouses themselves. No trading consortium needs a warehouse manager if they haven't got a warehouse anymore.

She found other work, something well-paying and interesting, but it soon fell through. So did the next one. Everybody she worked with was impressed with her and willing to talk her up to others, so she had no trouble getting suitable job offers, but then something would go wrong—sometimes catastrophically so, as at the warehouses. She never caused the crises, and indeed she was a definite asset whenever disaster struck, but it was unnerving. Things just seemed to go wrong around her. When two river-traders struck reefs and foundered with her on them *in one day*....

"I mean, sooner or later I'm just going to have to get eaten by a big fish," she joked to Chrys, pulling distractedly at her still-damp hair.

"Just do the work He requires of you," Chrys joked back. The man in the story Gwen had referenced was cursed to be bad luck to those around him because he'd ignored a divine assignment. "Stop ignoring the Shepherd, we'll move back to Nonani City, and you can work for Father's company."

Gwen made an exasperated noise.

* * *

THEY FINALLY GOT ELLIA BACK! Micalion and Orpharias had kept the Fallow with Tomas and Opal and convinced them to release the girl. All three arrived in Thesani together.

Ellia, seven years old, was now taller than other girls her age, and Opal had been teaching her to spin, weave, cook, and sing the praise-songs of the Shepherd. Sherra, alternately shy and tempestuous, didn't like suddenly having to share parental attention with her talented older sister. Toma's insistence on being the center of attention at all times didn't help. Orpharias could entertain Toma while Micalion let Sherra explain all the latest doings of her dolls, but when the brothers left, Chrys found herself overwhelmed. Kicking all three girls out of the house to go play with the neighbor children helped, but didn't really resolve the competition. So, Gwen started bringing the girls out on adventures. For long rides on the borrowed buckskin mare, she only ever took one girl at a time, either Ellia or Sherra, so that one of the older girls got special time with Mamma, while the other got special time with Daddy.

The farms and orchards and woodlots of the upper floodplain around the city were open, bright, and, in the summer, green and gold and hot, smelling of grass and dust and flowers. Nobody lived there full-time, because of the mosquitoes and the possibility of flooding, but in the growing season proletarian laborers stayed in huts by the fields they worked and were always happy to sell a good dinner to a girl and her daddy.

The lower floodplain swamps were less appealing—lots of mosquitoes, and you had to watch for kelpies and water-hounds. A water-hound could outrun a horse for short distances. But the swamp-forest had a temple-like quality, dense, dark stands of willow and alder, black poplar, and two different kinds of elm, some of these trees were almost a hundred feet tall and very thick. And the swamps were like puzzles, mazes of oxbows and bayous and natural levies. Nobody lived in the swamp, but there were hunters' camps, tree-stands, and blinds. It was a good place for wild boar. Sherra liked exploring.

On the other side of town rose ridges and natural hills, more good hunting land where few people lived—eastern oak, sessile oak, white oak, some of them were giants. Chestnut, walnut, horse-chestnut...yeti bears liked such places, but they'd leave you alone if you left them. They were mostly vegetarians. Orange-pine, black pine, and hemlock cast black shadows. The understory was mostly apple trees, crabapple, roses. Ivy, grape-vine, melon, and mistletoe clung to the branches. Families of wild olifants moved among them, eating the melons and the apples, noiseless as ghosts.

Sometimes Gwen took all three girls on shorter trips just as far as one of the mosquito-control ponds between the mounds. On the way they'd buy soft pretzels and sausage rolls from street vendors and then sit on benches by the edge of the water and try fishing with hand-lines. They hardly ever caught any fish because the girls would not stop talking, and Gwen lived in terror that Toma would accidentally bounce into the water and drown, but the four of them together had a good time anyway. And Gwen would smile knowing that Chrys sat alone under an apple tree in the neighborhood garden, drinking wine and reading a good book.

IN NINTH-MONTH, CHRYS BIRTHED their first son. He was tiny and plump as a pigeon, with the same nearly colorless irises that Ellia had had as a baby and skin as pale as sandstone. Gwen reached out and grabbed one of his curls, gently pulled it straight gently, and let it spring back. She looked at Chrys.

"It's red," Chrys confirmed.

Gwen smiled, gazing at her son.

"Let's call him Gwenias," Chrys said.

Gwen looked up at her, startled.

"No, it's a great opportunity, the job is a perfect fit for my skills, the pay is great, I'm going to love it, and yes, it's travel, but I'll always come back here!"

"How long is this going to continue? This you leaving temporarily thing?"

The general direction and the types of trade-goods were stipulated by the company, but all the details were up to Gwen, from security arrangements and compliance with local law to the route itself. Once all that was sorted out and she had led the route once, she would turn it over to her assistant and go establish another somewhere else with a new assistant. There would be long breaks between trips and something new to see and do every time. With an advance on her salary, she bought a horse, a mischievous dark bay gelding. She'd never owned her own horse before.

Her first trip was into the Aethenye Steppe, a fertile, open country where many traders already operated. The river-city of Zerasi, which functioned as the region's gateway, had grown wealthy. The problem was that the traders did not trade with the Aethenye people directly. They went through the farmers, mostly ethnic Itarye/Odesye who settled there in ever-greater numbers, cutting the Steppe with the new, steel-bladed plows. They were easy to find and to trade with, and they were seldom far from navigable waters or good roads. Of course, the farmers also took their cut. Gwen's employer wanted to try it without the middlemen, going overland to reach the nomadic Aethenye themselves as trade caravans used to do.

It was a good plan because the Aethenye did not like the farmers and didn't like trading with them. Their representatives on the Ruling

Council had been trying to keep the farmers out for a generation, but kept getting out-voted because only grain produced in the rich, black Steppe soil was cheap enough to be economical to transport long distances—and Nonani City and some of the Empire's other leading cities had grown too big to feed themselves. Instead of banning the settlers, the Councilmen had changed tax policy so as to encourage them. They had instructed the consuls to send legions to dig canals wherever possible and lay iron rails everywhere else (the smooth rails enabled mules to pull four times what they could over an ordinary road), all to hurry ever more grain to the river and thence to the hungry cities. The Aethenye continued to fight in the Council and in the courts, but succeeded only in making themselves unpopular. Gwen thought the nomadic Aethenye lifestyle very noble and admirable, but she also thought it time the Aethenye took up farming for the good of the Empire. She did not say so to the Aethenye, of course.

THE STEPPE WAS A GREAT, grassy vastness where animals, unable to find cover, instead banded together for safety in huge herds. Horse-like tarpan, hydruntine asses, plains bison, the saiga and the spiral-horned antelope, days might elapse while a single mass of any of those species passed by. In among them or on their own moved smaller, scattered groups of red deer, southern griffin, and southern mammoths. It all looked like a hunter's paradise to Gwen, and she saw many four-footed hunters who seemed to agree, including a spotted, cat-like animal capable of covering the better part of a mile in just a few heartbeats. She hadn't known anything could run that fast. But to hunt the Steppe, humans needed Aethenye permission, and it wasn't usually given.

"The animals make the grass," the nomads explained. "The mammoths especially, but all the animals help, eating back the shrubs and the young trees and enriching the soil. And it is the grass that feeds our sheep and cattle."

Mammoths—Gwen had heard of them before, but since she'd always heard them described as miniature, hairy olifants, she'd been prepared not to be impressed. But miniature is relative, and a "mere" ten feet at the shoulder will impress anyone who actually sees such animals. Their long, sparse, blond hair moved in the wind the same way the grass did, and their white tusks curved fantastically.

THE AETHENYE PEOPLE DID EVERYTHING on horseback, men and women both, and so both men and women wore wool trousers, leather chaps, and cotton turbans that could be unwound and used for protection from the elements as needed. In warm weather they wore nothing else, and the gold and ivory arm-bangles of the women and the facial jewelry of the men gleamed plainly against their nearly black skin. When the women were away from their home tents they used the tails of their turbans to modestly cover their faces, everything but the eyes, but that still left their breasts bare. Gwen, who liked all breasts except her own, found Aethenye modesty amusing.

THE OTHER PEOPLE IN THE caravan had some difficulty getting used to their Aethenye trading partners. Aethenye were Nonanye—they spoke Itarish as a first language, all the men and most of the women could read, and many of the men had served in the Empire's cavalry—but they had their strange religion, their strange manners, and they lived almost exclusively on meat, milk, blood, and wild onions—as did their guests. But Gwen had grown up with the Aethenye religion and knew the rhythm of their rituals, the compassionate, introspective basis of their strangely personal morals. She'd eaten their food on holidays and praise-days her whole childhood. She wore around her neck the twist of fleece and bone that Chrys had had blessed for her by a priest.

"Have you heard the Call, then?" the women asked. "Do you sing the praises?"

"Oh, my wife takes care of all that for me," Gwen replied.

"We call old women who can't sleep cows," the old woman said, indicating the mostly sleepless bovines in the moonlit grass. "But you are too young to be a cow.""I've never been able to sleep much at night," Gwen admitted. "Maybe it's an elf thing?"

"I wouldn't know. We have so few elves here. I've never met a full one. Is that how you know of the Shepherd? Do elves know the Shepherd, then?"

"No. My brother, Paracelias, herds sheep in Holia. He is a philosopher. He ponders the questions of his students and his teachers as he rests beside his sheep. He is an elf. But he does not know the Shepherd."

"How, then?"

So Gwen told her, and beginning to speak of her family, she could not stop. She spoke especially of Chrys, smiling foolishly without knowing it.

"She would love it here. That's the really sad part. She'd love meeting you all. She is so deeply of the Shepherd, and yet, apart from following Him, she knows as little of her heritage as I do of mine."

The old woman sat silent for a while, then took three of her bangles from her arms.

"Here, take these," she said, "for your wife, because she had no proper grandmother to give her bangles of her own. Tell her from me that there are women here who sing praise in her name."

Gwen took the bangles, gold and ivory shining in the moonlight. They felt warm.

"You, you walk in His footsteps," she stammered the ritual phrase.

Riding along through hot, windy days when there was nothing else to do or say or think except to watch the world go slowly by, Gwen would take the ivory bangle out and fidget it between forefinger and thumb, thinking of her wife.

GRADUALLY, GWEN'S WAGONS EMPTIED OF gold and gemstones, steel blades, and dried spices. They filled instead with richly-made rugs, worked ivory and horn, and the little vision-cap mushrooms that grew well in the abundant cattle and horse dung. Finally, she led her caravan to a river-town and telegraphed her employer for a boat. Soon, she and her people could send off their purchases, refill their wagons with gold, gems, and steel, and pick up and drop off mail.

Mail! Everybody Gwen kept in touch with had written, some many times.

Chrys, of course, twice a week, stories about the kids and the neighbors, questions about household matters, and her typically incisive comments about everything in the world. Sometimes she included a note or a drawing from one of the kids. Ellia's handwriting was already better than Gwen's.

Tomas reported mostly on family news. Euas's health had become poor? But doctors said drinking less wine should help—an irony, as Euas owned a wine distribution company. He didn't mention Opal's health at all. He must be worried.

Paracelias enclosed copies of philosophy papers, his and others, as well as science papers he thought she'd find interesting. He said he was lonely.

Jonas was happy because the Councilman he worked for had entrusted him to drum up votes for a major bill, the import of which he explained at length. But he ended with a note of warning.

"This is not a good time, by the light of the world, to follow the Shepherd. Three times, now, bills have been introduced to strip followers of our dispensation regarding sacrifice to the King. Such bills cannot pass, but they are repeatedly introduced because multiple councilmen find the introduction pleases their constituents. The purely symbolic effort both clothes the rascals in a certain narrow patriotism, and functions as a rhetorical counter-volley against the Aethenye who keep introducing bills to limit agriculture on the Steppe—bills that also cannot pass. Political shadow-boxing. Be careful, little sister, as an Itarye on the steppe. And be careful as the husband and father of followers everywhere else."

If Gwen could have transported herself home by wishing at that moment, she would have.

GWEN'S CARAVAN PICKED UP AND dropped off goods at several more river-towns, making a big loop through the Steppe so they could turn a profit both coming and going. She thus gave her employers two new routes for the cost of one. Bandits threatened a few times, but never successfully.

AFTER MANY MONTHS, GWEN FINALLY walked back in her own front door. The house—cool and dark after the bright summer day outside—looked empty but for a fat, pale-skinned, eight-month-old baby crawling on the floor. He looked up at Gwen, surprised and concerned by her arrival.

"Gwenias! Look at you! Crawling about like a big boy! Do you remember me?"

Hearing her voice, finally recognizing her, he smiled.

"You're going to miss his first words, you know," Chrys said, appearing at the loft railing.

"Somebody has to earn the money for you to spend," Gwen shot back. They stared at each other a moment. "Is that the only greeting I get?" she asked, finally. And Chrys all but leaped down the stairs into her husband's arms.

THE NEXT TRIP WENT UP the length of Slovona, from the industrial villages and slave-worked mines of Parsia to the barbarian north where they ate horses and the women wore gems in which rested the pride and honor of their families. To return, she moved southwest into equally barbarian Duchasa and telegraphed for a boat to take the whole caravan back to Thesani in time for the Fallow. She found Gwenias had indeed started talking while she was away, though he said very little, communicating mostly in grunts. He had grown almost as tall as three-year-old Toma, who was still elfin-short.

A LETTER FROM MICALION. HE did not write often, unlike Paracelias, who sent a long letter almost every month, but this time Micalion had news.

"Hey, Chrys, can you come look at this ideogram?"

"I *can*. But if you don't know it, I won't."

"I know what it is, I just don't know what it's doing."

"OK, OK, I'll look. Why's Micalion writing in ideograms, anyway? His Itarish is better than your Cathanish."

"I don't know. He does, sometimes. Here, Chrys, look at this, he's talking about Orpharias, *head* and *injury/illness* combined, and then these three radicals...."

"Did Orpharias hurt his head?"

"I thought that, too, at first, but then what would this other mean? It makes no sense."

"Of course it makes sense, this is Micalion, we just haven't yet found the sense it makes." Chrys sat down and examined the letter carefully. They were sitting at the table inside, but all the doors and windows were open to the late autumn breeze. The straw was already down on the floor for winter. A stew bubbled on the hearth for dinner. Some sort of bee, wandered in from somewhere by mistake, bumbled noisily against the ceiling. All the kids were outside. Gwen could hear their voices.

"Well?"

"Gimme a moment!" Chrys said. "Cat-fever, form of, head-injury/illness, the intangibility modifier.... Intangibility and head would be mind, right? Mental?"

"I guess so."

"Mental-illness? But what does that mean? How could a mind be ill?"

"Wait—what would that be in Catharish?" Gwen asked, trying to think.

"Um, ikhainaa? Inhikia? I don't know."

"Inhihikhaa!" Gwen remembered, suddenly. "You have to double the in-fix for mixed-declension words. Inhihikhaa. I've heard that word before. Micalion used it. We were talking about elf-bloods. It means...oh, Chrys, it means crazy!"

"Crazy!"

"Oh, yes. 'Orpharias has been diagnosed with chronic cat-fever, a form of mental illness, treatable but not curable.' Chrys, my brother has gone crazy!"

What Nonanye people knew about mental illness could fit in a walnut-shell, and most of it was wrong. Conditions equivalent to anxiety, depression, PTSD, eating disorders, phobias, and addictions occurred among them, but were usually chalked up to poor choices or bad attitudes. Except in extreme cases, that wasn't considered madness. Sometimes people, for reasons of brain injury or age, showed cognitive decline and some pretty strange behavior, but that wasn't madness, either. To the Nonanye mind, true madness, craziness, meant the unexplained loss of reason and self-control, a terrifying prospect to a people more or less obsessed with maintaining order.

And so, they wouldn't let it remain unexplained. Madness could result from poison, such as the effects of vision-caps or contaminated grain or too much alcohol, or from malevolent magic. Or it could be a punishment by an angry god, never mind that in other contexts Nonanye people insisted that the gods don't punish any more than they reward. But nobody would poison or hex Orpharias, he was too sweet—and for the same reason, no god could be angry with him. That left only one possibility. The madness must be in his blood. Hereditary.

Had it come down only to Orpharias, or was it more of a family curse, like red hair or bounciness? Gwen could hear her children's voices in the yard.

"Gwen...?" Chrys asked.

"I know." And then, in response to the other question Chrys hadn't exactly asked, "I don't know."

They did not invite Orpharias to visit that autumn.

ONE OF HER EMPLOYERS HAD been trying to poison the other's opinion of Gwen, apparently over some tangle of sexual hope and jealously she had not been aware of.

"Were they going to *talk* to me before assuming I'm on the make?" she spouted, then went on at some length about etiquette, proper communication, and how ironic it was that everybody *said* elf-bloods had social deficits when in the overwhelming majority of cases, confusion and drama were caused by *ubum*, and it's not like either of those men are any great shakes to look at, and anyway, did they forget she was a switcher? But she said that to Chrys. What she said to her bosses was shorter: I quit. She had thought they were her friends.

"NO, LISTEN, IT'LL BE GREAT, we'll sub-let the house, six months in Ishlana all of us together, then back here, all of us together. Then maybe someplace else next year. You're not without a sense of adventure, I know you're not, and how many children will be as well-traveled as ours will? Other kids get to *read* about the far reaches of the continent, ours get to *see* them. And really, if you don't like being a trader's agent's wife, I promise I'll look for something else next year."

ISHLANA WAS ALL SPRUCE, FIR, and pine forest, low, rocky hills, and fast, rocky streams. It was not within the Empire, but Nonanye roads and wagonways and telegraph cables spidered across it anyway, all to service the mines and military bases that some of the native tribes welcomed and others did not. The tribes were not organized and so Ishlana had no unified voice with which to say yes or no, and the tribes that said no individually were why the bases had been built.

Gwen and her family rented a small house on one of the bases, and the kids made friends with army brats and natives alike while Gwen spent days and sometimes whole weeks out exploring the countryside, talking to people, visiting markets, drinking hot, raspberry-leaf tea in tiny huts with soft furs for rugs. She was looking for salable goods nobody back in Nonani was importing yet.

Merchants expand empires even more efficiently than legions do. Gwen knew what she was doing. She was proud to be doing it.

"I'VE HEARD OF UNICORNS, BUT I don't really know what they are."

"You know what a dicorn is?" the local trader said. He spoke Itarish, though with a thick, strange accent.

"Yes. Dicorns are like griffins, but they don't leave the forests, as they don't like to graze."

"Well, a dicorn's got two, a unicorn's got one." The Itarish words had prefixes for two and one respectively, just as the English words do. The trader looked entertained.

"I see."

"No, really, a unicorn's like a one-horned dicorn, but...more.

Bigger, shaggier, fiercer, and the horn is much bigger, at least in the males. Their heads are so low-slung they can hardly raise them, they're made to graze only, so they never leave the Steppe. They love the cold."

"What's the horn good for?"

"Well, most often it's used as a powder, to treat sexual dysfunction."

"Dude, everything's supposed to treat sexual dysfunction. Or baldness. Does it really work?"

"I don't know, I've never needed any!" The trader rubbed his very non-bald scalp, grinning. Gwen rolled her eyes. "But it's supposed to work! Now, it's not an aphrodisiac—it won't put desire where none exists naturally. But if you've got the want-to, it'll make sure you get the can-do. So they say, anyway."

"Good enough. What else?"

"A cup made of unicorn horn will purify any water placed in it, make it healthy. And if the water is already pure, it will become medicine, powerful medicine, able to turn around some cases where doctors despair—wash the patient's wound or, for illness, have them drink the water. So they say."

Gwen had her doubts, since the Ishlanye people didn't seem any healthier, as a population, than anybody else, but she understood the appeal of doing *something* when someone you love is sick or injured. And bathing in or drinking clean water is generally good for the health.

"How do you protect the supply? If what you say is true, everyone will want some, and everyone will come—and they won't stop here, they'll go on to the Steppe, killing unicorns."

"And being killed by giants, no doubt. The Northern Steppe is giant country, you know. There are ways to pacify them, but a sword won't do it, and only we know what will. But we never kill unicorns, nor do we permit such sacrilege. Their magic is so strong and so pure that only an evil man could think of killing one—if you'd seen one alive, you'd know that—and such an evil man we'd put down like a mad dog. Beasts only are permitted to kill unicorns. A manticore family can do it. A pack of crocottas, sometimes. Maybe a lion, though I haven't seen any try. Usually, unicorns just get old and die. And neither beasts nor old age have any interest in the horns, so we take them. Same with mammoth ivory. And if you think about it, the amount of horn available is actually greater that way, since killing unicorns can't increase their number, only hasten the harvest, and every day a unicorn lives is a day when his horn gets to grow larger."

THE FIRST TRIP WAS A success but there would be no second. Upon her return to Thesani, Gwen was looking through the company files for something else when she came across evidence of fraud. She tried to talk to one of her supervisors about it, but he wouldn't listen. A few days later, she was not only fired but formally accused of embezzling funds. Chrys was almost literally hopping mad and took it upon herself to start spreading some choice rumors about Gwen's former colleagues. Every businessman in the city would soon have a wife who disliked a certain trading company.

"You're vicious, you know that?"

"Gwen, you know what you told me about why you'd never spear a water-hound?"

"The water-hound's wife, yes. They live in pairs."

"Yes, well. I may not be so big or so good at swimming, but my teeth are just as sharp."

Gwen made Chrys the best loaded focaccia yet. Then she made plans to defend herself in court and to file a countersuit to clear her name. After that she expected to have to move back to Nonani City.

Chapter 10. The Gambler

Year of Nonani 839 - 840

Hyras was done doing things the way he, as a patrician, was supposed to do them. He'd tried, he'd tried very hard, and it hadn't worked. He was simply no good at business. What was he good at? Betting at cards and hustling chess, for starters. And so, on the morning of his first full day in Nonani City, he did without breakfast, saving his last two silvers, and questioned the proprietor of his boarding house and the other residents. Thus informed as well as hungry, he walked the several miles around to the Upper Forum and found, as he'd been led to expect, a vast and beautiful plaza surrounded by grand buildings and occupied along its edges by men playing dominoes, dice, or plain chess, the kind with a square board. He stood about, watching games.

"I wouldn't move there, if I were you." The third time he said something like that, the man he was bothering got mad.

"If you're so good at this, why don't you play instead?"

"Can't. Playing for free's no fun, and the wife says I can't bet anymore."

"That must mean you lose a lot, Big Mouth."

Hyras shrugged.

"Well, then, shut up, will you?"

"Alright. I guess we won't find out, then."

"Find out what?" the man asked, reluctantly. Hyras let him stew a few beats before answering.

"Whether I can really beat him for you. I guess we'll just assume I'm only some big mouth."

Of course they offered him a few copper coins to finish the game, which was several copper coins more than he'd had before. And of course he won. The two men, curious, then each played a full game against him for the same flat fee. He won both.

"Your, ah, wife mind if other people bet on you?"

"No, not at all. Provided I get a cut of the winnings."

Hyras earned enough that day to not only buy himself a decent dinner from a food cart, but also to pick up a pound of toasted wheat, a couple of hard-boiled eggs, and some salt at the market. He had no hearth, but he still had his portable little grinder from his army days and could grind the wheat for flour and so make gruel. He filled his canteen at the fountain after greeting its naiad, whom he had heard of and was pleased now to meet. And he still had his original two denarii.

Not every day went so well. Some days he could not find anyone willing to play him, and some days he actually did lose money. But gradually he scraped together enough that he could do his own betting, both at chess and at the card tables in the gambling dens. He was a very smart gambler, never risking money he could not afford to lose, always keeping back enough of his winnings so that he came out ahead.

Starting from almost literally nothing was very hard, and he had nobody to help him. As a patrician, he was ineligible for the free wheat given monthly to proletarians, although he was really in the same job market they were, and the job market sucked. He got a few paying positions, usually part-time and temporary, and ate little besides cold gruel. It wasn't bad-tasting. It wasn't good-tasting, either. The other men living with him at the boarding house, they ate gruel most days, too. Most of them had eaten it their whole lives

He worked for a while as an assistant rat-catcher, the job being to join several other men using brooms to scare rats out from behind piles of refuse and what-not, towards little dogs who were very good at killing rats and happy to do it. Any rats killed above the number needed to feed the dogs were distributed among the humans, but Hyras never took any, and not just because he had no means of cooking them. He enjoyed the team-work with the men and the dogs and found the hunt interesting, but he felt bad for the rats and, even hungry, could not eat anything so obviously once alive. Back when he'd had access to steak, he'd always had it very well done. Any hint of red juice looked too much like blood.

He delivered charcoal. He delivered laundry. He drove a carriage, picking up party-goers too drunk to walk home and not welcome to stay the night in their host's house. Working with horses again was fun, although the horses were mostly ill-treated by their owners and he could do little about it. Also, all such delivery jobs involved working at night by lamp-light, because of the law against horse-drawn vehicles in the city by day. At night the streets belonged to delivery drivers, street beggars, and criminals.

He kept playing cards, and he kept playing chess. He tried not to think about the future.

He was sometimes able to afford papyrus, ink, and postage, and so he wrote to Ilia. Sometimes she wrote back. She was still pregnant, still healthy, still alive. Rosia wrote him more often. She missed her friends back in Delani. She thought being surrounded by servants was weird, but liked the fancy food and the indoor toilets. She was thirteen, almost a woman, a strange thought for Hyras. Adna wrote less often, but her letters were much longer and covered all over with doodles. There were letters from his parents, from his brothers, his nieces and nephews. His brother, Hanas, the one he actually liked, was sick. He'd been sick for a while, and it wasn't going away.

Once, he got a letter from Crea.

Daddy doesn't know I'm writing. Please don't tell him, and don't write me back. He can tell me to stop talking to you, and I more or less have to listen to him as long as I'm living here, but he can't make me stop loving you like family. Mama says the same.

Hyras could not keep himself from weeping.

He could have looked up b'Sheras. Her father-in-law was still on the Ruling Council, would know where she was, and would be easy enough to find. He never tried. He did not want her to think he was

looking for charity. And yet the thought that she was out there, probably living in the same city, did help him feel a little better.

Hyras's life in Nonani City was not entirely unsociable or unpleasant. He made friends with some of the other guys in the boarding house and went with them to the People's Stadium every week to
watch the chariot races there. A spot in the viewing stands cost money,
unless you were a proletarian, but if Hyras didn't have the copper that
week, one of his friends would, and then he could usually repay them
with his gambling winnings. Betting at the races was easy, a simple
matter of understanding both horses and math. There were programs
at the King's Stadium, too, but Hyras never went to those. The ones
he would have liked—the military review and demonstration battle at
Nonalia—were long over when he got to town, and everything else was
bloody. He even skipped the sacrifice of young bulls at Cerelia, at the
risk of being thought impious. And he didn't want to even hear about
the public executions. People thought he was weird.

Sometimes Hyras's new friends bought him wine or cider. He
didn't refuse. He couldn't remember why he should. The mere presence of the alcohol muddled his mind somehow, destroying any
thought of abstention. And every time he drank he got drunk. It never
took much. His friends thought him very entertaining then, sloppy,
foolish, and affectionate, but when he finally awoke again sober there
was always a while when he liked neither his friends nor himself.

"Why don't you just not drink?" his newest friend asked. His first
name was Jonas, but since that was an absurdly common name, he
usually went by b'Raulas even among his friends. Jonas Raulas Keran.

"I can't. I don't know why. I want to. I went years without it, but
now—it has me again." Hyras was Ulas to b'Raulas, he never had gotten rid of that mistakenly-applied name and was now used to it, but
the man knew it was not his original name as they'd both grown up in
or near Dalani and had heard of each other. Everybody in Dalani had
at least heard of each other.

What Hyras had heard was that b'Raulas was the first of several
bastard children of the innkeeper's daughter and the commanding

tribune of the local garrison, and that although the tribune had cared for his family and tried to support them, he had deteriorated some-how. B'Raulas had raised his younger siblings, put himself through law school, and married the daughter of the tailor. As a lawyer, he'd done some work for Sylas, then helped him in various local political endeavors before moving to Nonani City to make a name for himself. It was Sylas who'd told Hyras he wasn't the only Dalanye man in the city, and that he ought to look b'Raulas up.

Hyras's first impression was of a small, dark, man with brilliantly blue eyes that did not blink. But of course b'Raulas's eyes did blink, and he was slightly taller than Hyras. The illusion of littleness came not only from his wiry build and narrow features but also from his manner, so intense that he must have been boiled down and concentrated from somebody much larger.

It was good to hear the Dalanye plebeian accent again.

"Think he'll win?" Hyras asked. It was early fall, just a few weeks past Hidalia. They were sitting on a bench together, looking out across the river.

"Huh?" The water was very blue today. So was the sky, although they were not the same blue. B'Raulas's mind was on the water just then and nothing else.

"Abbas Seras Lian."

"Oh, yeah. Him." B'Raulas chuckled, embarrassed, then collect-ed himself and turned towards the man he knew as Ulas. "Yes, he definitely will."

"I almost wish he wouldn't."

"Why? You don't like *Canan*, do you?"

"See, *that* is why I'm worried. 'Do I like Canan.' You might as well have asked 'do I eat babies?'" B'Raulas chuckled again, a little ruefully, but said nothing. Hyras continued. "My neighbors speak the same way about Lian. Some probably think his followers *do* eat babies. No, I don't like Canan. But he's survivable. Not so sure about what happens next."

"Not everybody has survived Canan. That's our whole point."

"Theirs, too." Hyras did not look at b'Raulas as they talked. He sat, arms folded across his chest, and looked at a group of diving ducks, disappearing and reappearing among the small waves alternately.

"But they can't actually believe all those lies!"

"Some do, some don't. Most don't know what to believe. But they don't feel the way they do because of what they believe. They believe what they do because of how they feel. And they feel bad. I would, in their place. So would you."

"But Canan is *screwing* with them," b'Raulas objected.

"Yeah, so is everybody else, though. The whole economy depends on a class of men who'll do anything for copper—they can't afford to refuse, because if the job goes to a slave, the prole can't pay rent. Not a lot a man won't do to keep wife and daughters off the streets at night."

"It matters, though. The difference between Canan and Lian matters."

"It matters to you."

"It matters to everybody!" b'Raulas insisted. "Speaker Canan *can't* win re-election, over half the Council are his ideological enemies, so it follows over half the electorate is, too. But the same was true four years ago. How did he win anyway? We know how he won. We know how he could win again. I tell you, the republic is in danger."

"So? Yes, it matters to you, and yes, it matters to me, but proles don't care who wears the purple or why. Why should they? They have no power in the republic, they have nothing to lose from tyranny. At least Speaker Canan throws some charity their way. He listens to them. Or, at least he shares their prejudices. They feel he's on their side."

"Their side," b'Raulas scoffed. "The extinction of the derger will not improve the life of a single prole."

"Will put a few denarii in my father-in-law's pocket, though. Man knows how to invest."

"And thus falls the republic. If Canan is re-elected...."

"And also if he is not."

"You sound so calm about it."

"Would it help anything if I didn't?" Hyras asked. "If the republic falls, I will fight for its restoration. I'm no baby-eater."

A gull strolled web-footed just inside the knee-wall on the very edge of the river. It stopped and regarded the two men.

"I haven't got anything to share today," Hyras told the bird, displaying his empty hands. "Go ask the rat-griller. He's got tails."

"Boo!" said b'Raulas, and the bird flew away. "Have you ever met a derger?"

"Can't say that I have. You?"

"Udùo. You know who he is?"

"I've heard of him. The activist."

"I've met him a few times. Of course, he is only half. Do you suppose that matters?"

"I don't know."

"The river is so blue today," b'Raulas remarked.

"That's because the sky is. The one reflects off the other."

"But which one? Which one starts it?"

"Oh, it has to be the sky. It's bigger. And it has clouds and so forth."

"Yeah, but the river is so very big," said Jonas Raulas Keran.

Gradually, Hyras started accumulating more money than what he needed strictly for survival. He still could not afford to support his family, but if he could put some money away, he'd be able to take some chances, and if the chances paid out, that might get him there. But every week that brought him closer to financial stability also brought him closer to the end of Ilia's pregnancy. He hated not being with her. He hated not being able to do anything to help. He hated knowing that the longer the miscarriage waited, the more likely it became that he'd lose his wife as well as his child.

But the letter he dreaded never came. And just after Saturnalia, his child was born alive—a son. Ilia, very much not dead either, named him Hyras, Hyras Ulas Dynan. The elder Hyras read that letter and thought he might not have to touch the ground for a week. Again he wept, but it was a very different kind of weeping.

By then, the votes were being collected all across the empire. By Natalia, they were all in. The counting began. Just after Hilaria, the announcement came, and there was dancing in the streets in some neighborhoods but not others.

Abbas Seras Lian had won.

Two days later, Hyras and b'Raulas met for their traditional weekly drink. Neither of them seemed very happy that his candidate had prevailed.

"Canan's accused the Sisters of miscounting the vote," Hyras said.

"I know. He can't actually think that, can he? I mean, it's never happened, has it?"

"don't matter. It's a move in the game."

"I know. Oh, I know it. Dammit, Ulas, this ain't how any of this is supposed to work!"

"Nevertheless."

"He's not going to go quietly, is he?" b'Raulas asked.

"No."

"Ulas, I don't like this."

"Mmm. I don't plan to be in the city for the inauguration."

"Where will you go?"

"Home," Hyras said. "Where else can I go?"

"Dalani?"

"Mmm."

"I may go too. It's time I be getting back to Neria anyway." Neria was b'Raulas's wife. She had taken the kids and gone home when she got sick, hoping that getting away from the pestilential influence of the big city might cure her. It hadn't. "What will you do in Dalani?"

"Whatever I can," Hyras replied. "I'll write Ilia, tell her to meet me in Dalani with the kids. My father, or one of my brothers, will give us a place to stay in return for the pleasure of seeing me ask. I may even agree to let them give me a job."

"Where, in that tannery you hate?"

"Or in one of the shops. I'd prefer the shop, but either way I'll hate it and I'll be terrible at it. don't matter much. I don't think I'll stay very long, and I'll need Ilia and the kids living someplace safe I'm allowed to visit. This is the only thing I can think of."

"You don't think you'll stay long? Where will you go?"

"You know where I've got to go, b'Raulas."

"If you can find a way for me to go, too, let me know."

There were only four weeks between Hilaria and Nonalia, when the inauguration would be held, barely enough time for letters to go back and forth between Nonani City and Dalani, let alone between Nonani City and Parsia, so Hyras didn't bother to wait for responses. He simply sent letters off explaining what he was doing and why and making the necessary requests or instructions, then he wrapped up his business in the city, such as it was. B'Raulas did the same and then bought both of them places on the regular stage to Dalani.

The stagecoach, as was typical, was a covered wagon with a couple of bench seats, space for mail and other small, time-sensitive freight, and a professional driver who sat outside the passengers' compartment to provide a level of privacy. What made it a stagecoach was that it changed horses at regular intervals—dividing the journey into multiple stages—so that the coach could maintain the fast speed of trotting horses all day, but its construction was simple, even crude, without much comfort or luxury. It did have leather-strap suspension, which helped to even out bumps and jolts, and of course Nonanye main roads were very good, but every so often there was still a jolt or a bump anyway.

Hyras and b'Raulas were the only two passengers of their coach, not counting the mail and packages, and neither of them talked much on the way. After a while, b'Raulas fell asleep, leaning back against the window. Then a bump half-woke him. He looked about in a bleary way, and soon slept again, this time sitting more or less vertically. Gradually, he slumped and ended up leaning on Hyras's shoulder. After a long moment, Hyras adjusted his posture to make of himself a more comfortable pillow. Much of the trip passed like that.

Chapter 11. Rational Anxiety

Year of Nonani 835 - 836

Gwen went about her court cases mechanically. The lawyer she'd hired was eating up her savings, though if she won the civil suit the judgment would at least reimburse her. And she wrapped up her life in Thesani. She did not want to go back to her in-laws, but she had no immediate job prospects and could not afford to remain unemployed long enough to find something.

In the meantime, she had worries. Some were more serious than others, but all of them occupied her mind, popping up in her consciousness in no particular order, chattering away as she stalked about Thesani, scowling at the snowy ground just a few feet beyond the tips of her moving feet.

- Euas had not stopped drinking. According to Tomas, he seemed to be drinking more, and seemed much sicker. But he wouldn't talk about it with anyone.
- The kids, at least the younger ones, had some sort of weird rash on the backs of their knees and around their mouths.
- Why *did* Gwenias throw weird temper-tantrums all the time? Things would be so much easier if he would talk more.
- Politics was getting scary.
- Opal had consumption, didn't she? Of course she did. Nobody in the family would talk about it, the clearest indication that everybody knew.
- Why had the price of smoked salmon gotten so high all of a sudden?

- Euas had not written to her in a long time. He'd begun pulling away from her years ago, and she'd hoped it would blow over, but it had not, and now he'd stopped writing. He'd never adequately explained the problem—oh, he'd said that she took things too literally and that she yelled too much, but that didn't count as adequate. She took things literally? What metaphors did he think she wasn't getting, and why the hell did he care? And she only yelled at people who did wrong things. So what was his problem? Anyway, she missed him.
- Politics was getting really scary.

Politics had been scary for a while, as Jonas had warned her two years ago. Tomas had tried to warn her two years before that, but she hadn't paid much attention then. Now, it seemed foolish not to pay attention, not to try to understand. When Gwen tried to understand something, her trying took the form of composing an explanation, essentially an essay. She would compose her essay, over and over, with some variation, until she was satisfied with whatever it was, but politics wasn't satisfying ever, so she continued composing her essay. It would leak out, apropos of apparently nothing, in conversations about other things, in letters to friends and family that Gwen had begun on other topics, in response to people who had spoken to her about something else.

THE ESSENTIAL PROBLEM IS THAT.... No, the real problem is that.... No, dammit, I mean the thing of it is.... Originally, at bottom, essentially, no that's not right....

Nonani society has, for over three hundred years now, been a republic based on a stable, hierarchical class structure on one hand and common recognition of the inherent and equal dignity and worth of all humans—or at least of all ubum. As the wife submits to the husband, so the client submits to the patron and the servant to the master, yet no honorable husband, patron, master, um, no strike that whole sentence, it's superfluous and distracting.

For three hundred years, Nonani has been a republic based on a stable, hierarchical class structure on the one hand and on the other a common recognition of the inherent and equal worth of all ubum if not actually all humans. That stability is being undermined by demographic changes, such as voluntary migration of various ethnic groups and the dramatic increase in the proletarian population consequent to the importation of greater numbers of slaves over the past two or three generations and the, the, the, damn.

For three hundred years, Nonani has been a republic based on a stable, hierarchical class structure on the one hand and on the other, a common recognition of the inherent and equal worth of all ubum if not actually all humans. That stability is being undermined by demographic changes, including the dramatic increase in the size of the proletarian population, people who naturally feel themselves rather abused but lack both the economic power and the education necessary to effectively seek redress within the system. Most cannot read. Wealthy men jealous of their power see an opportunity to manipulate the justifiable resentment of the masses to turn them against the plebeian class and against political and social institutions such as the Ruling Council, leading to....

TWENTY YEARS AGO, A COURT case in Holia resulted in five hundred derger and three hundred ubum forest tribesmen being added to the rolls of the Senate and thus able to vote for members and officers of the Ruling Council. As more and more of these new senators have learned how to vote, they naturally vote for the allies of Senator Lian, who won the court case for them. These men, who are becoming all but unbeatable in elections, are hostile to men involved in industry and finance, whose business they constantly seek to limit. Five years ago, a measure passed the Council that would have stripped derger senators of land ownership, but was canceled by a plebiscite. The plebeians are, for the most part, allied with the derger, the forest ubum, and the rural proletarian farm-workers—the coalition of Senators Lian, Sylan, and Euan, among others. The patricians involved in industry and finance have therefore forged a counter-alliance with proletarian industrial workers and with the urban proletarians, people who have no institutional power but can riot.

THIRTY-EIGHT YEARS AGO, ELFIN scientists announced that wood-cutting for charcoal and other uses was not being balanced by new growth, that total forest cover across the Empire was shrinking, and that if the rate of harvest did not slow significantly, communities could start literally running out of forest. It was a strange, shocking thought then, and remains so now. And the rate of harvest only increased. But twenty-five years ago, public demonstrations and outright illegal resistance against the harvest of wood for charcoal increased in support of derger, forest ubum, and tenant farmers. Fourteen years ago, organized activists attempted to free a group of new slaves being brought into Nonani City from Slovona after a clash with soldiers over logging. Hundreds of activists were arrested. Ring-leaders were flogged and fined. The rumor that Senator Euan intervened and freed several of the ring-leaders before they could be identified and arrested has never been confirmed—or denied. Similar clashes continue across the Empire.

OVER THE PAST FIVE YEARS or so, there have been a number of riots that started either as counter-demonstrations to events by pro-forest illegal activist groups or as protests against local land-use reform and environmental protection measures. Such measures help plebeians, who can't vote but do have other forms of institutional power, but they cost urban proletarians jobs. Or at least the urban proletarians think they do, and they literally can't afford to take chances. Many of them would not eat were it not for the free government wheat.

Oddly, the local garrisons respond to these riots late, half-heartedly, or not at all.

THERE ARE PRIVATE CLUBS MADE up mostly of ex-military proletarians, now. When did they start? A while ago, maybe. They call themselves independent gymnasia and meet to train, drill, and discuss politics. They are not exactly legal. They seem to be getting money from somewhere.

FOR THREE HUNDRED YEARS, NONANI has been a republic based on a stable, hierarchical class structure on the one hand and on the other, a common recognition of the inherent and equal worth of all ubum if not actually all humans. That stability is being undermined by demographic changes, of which wealthy men, jealous of their power, are taking advantage by weaponizing the resentment of urban and industrial proletarians—by redirecting their resentment against barbarian immigrants, Aethenye migrant workers, and derger.

NO HONORABLE AND PIOUS MAN would order the destruction of an entire forest. His respect for the dryads should prevent him. His respect for the animals should prevent him. His respect for the derger should prevent him. His respect for his own balls should prevent him, frankly, for each man is, at least potentially, the mate of the Goddess and the father of everything She bears. But you can't legislate morality.

The old values are being forgotten, everybody says so. Money soothes the ache of a wounded conscience, so they say.

THERE ARE PLACES IN NONANI City that have no law enforcement presence because the soldiers responsible for order in the city are afraid that buildings will fall over on them. Four hundred thousand people live in buildings like that.

FOR OVER THREE HUNDRED YEARS, Nonani has been a republic based on a stable social order. If that order falls, can the republic be far behind?

Chapter 12. A Brief History

Year of Nonani 806 - 833

There was once a teenager named Tanas who went to work for his two older brothers. Their father, Rylas, a patrician of only moderate wealth and small influence, owned several take-out places in poor neighborhoods, but the family business would of course be inherited by a son-in-law, not a son. So the sons of Rylas used a family grant to start their own company, selling supplies to the military, mostly specialty goods or perishables so that prefects did not need to order from multiple individual farms.

Tanas had no head for business. He was clever and ambitious but undisciplined and impatient, and while he could be very charming short-term, he basically couldn't keep up the act long enough to build professional relationships. He did very little buying, selling, negotiating, or shipping. His role in the company was to fix problems.

By fixing problems, he kept costs low, suppliers compliant, and inspectors preoccupied.

When Tanas was in his early twenties, both his brothers died from smallpox. That was the first tragedy to benefit him, and the only one of which nobody had suspicions. Lots of people died of smallpox. Tanas became sole owner of the business, and on that strength married a woman of the Canan matriline whose extremely wealthy father and paterfamilias owned a string of bathhouses—not public bathhouses, which were free and run by non-profit concessions, but private ones, the kind where paying members can access special services for additional fees. Tanas sold his supply company and went to work for his father-in-law, fixing problems.

Through his thirties, Tanas used his growing private fortune to offer loans, sometimes at very favorable terms, sometimes not, depending on the recipient. He always got paid back, earning advantages not always strictly financial. He became able to fix a lot of problems. He bought racehorses. He bought gambling dens. He bought brothels. He specialized in the disreputable and the quasi-legal, not because of any specific personal villainy on his part but because he understood the people in such places and how to make deals with them. He knew whom to curry favor with and whom to hurt.

He was a small man, thin and wiry, with large, blue eyes and almost black skin. He wore his long hair combed out full and round, a sphere of hair, which went prematurely gray and then white so that people called him Natiras, *Puff-Ball*, behind his back.

When Tanas was in his late thirties, his wife died in childbirth. He soon married one of her cousins, a daughter of an even wealthier branch of the Canan line. He used the money to buy a string of theaters—professional actors were seen as no better than prostitutes or professional athletes, so however prestigious the front of the house might be, the back was comfortably disreputable. And yet besides plays the theaters could also host lecturers, poets, and comedians, all of whom were big box-office draws and lent an air of respectability to the whole enterprise. On the strength of that air, Tanas succeeded his original father-in-law as paterfamilias when he was forty-two years old.

By then, however, Tanas Rylas Canan, though still lending out money, was also deeply in debt himself. And there were rumors that he'd been engaged in darker dealings and that some of his creditors were aware of the truth of such matters. That's when the lecturers and comedians appearing on his stages acquired a certain political slant, one favorable to the aims of Tanas's creditors.

Proletarians could not read. They got their news from rumors and from comedians.

Chapter 13. Rumors and News

Year of Nonani 835 - 836

Gwen had started hearing about an entertainment mogul turned politician named b'Rylas back before she moved her family to Ishlana. Apparently, he wanted to be Speaker of the Senate, despite having no previous relevant experience. Nobody took him seriously then.

That summer, she was largely cut off from events within the Empire, there being no newshouses in Ishlana, but she did get some news from letters, and she did hear gossip from other people who were receiving news in letters. Everybody was talking about b'Rylas.

"HE'S ALWAYS MAKING SPEECHES TO proletarians. Why is he talking to them? They can't vote!"

"He says he's the proletarians' friend."

"If he were their friend, he'd listen to them. Instead he's talking to them, and the senators are listening."

And:

"Did you hear? He paid off the month's rent *for twenty thousand* slum-dwellers. And on Cerelia, he gave everybody in the free seats a complimentary meal! How can he afford that?"

"You're forgetting how rich he is. He could give a denarius to every citizen in the Empire and still have over ninety percent of his fortune left."

"I thought he was in debt or something?"

"Well, nobody really knows."

And:

"You know what they say, no matter whom the senators vote for, the government gets elected."

"Are you aware that's my father-in-law you're talking about? He sits on the Ruling Council."

"Yeah, and how much has he been able to do? Nothing ever changes."

"Yeah, well, it's about to."

GWEN AND HER FAMILY RETURNED to Thesani. Her legal troubles began. Two out of the three people likely to win the speakership abruptly dropped out. The third turned up dead. That left b'Rylas and just enough less-popular other contenders to split the vote against him. How convenient.

NONANI VOTES WEREN'T ANONYMOUS. FOR each race in a given election, each senator got a lead coin produced by the Sisters of the King's Hearth, the unworldly religious who managed elections for the Empire. One side of each coin the Sisters left blank. That side was to be struck by the senator with the name of the candidate of his choice. But the other side had his name on it—had the name of his family on it. Anybody who wanted could find out who you were.

GWEN COULD NOT VOTE. THERE was no possibility of her ever being able to vote because, not being physically male, she could not be the mate of the Goddess.

WHEN B'RYLAS SPOKE, HE SPOKE against immigrants, Aethenye and followers of the Shepherd generally, derger, elves, mixed-blood persons of all kinds...and the Ruling Council. He presented himself as the champion of the people, promising them freedom and true representation at the expense of the only men who were by law actually responsible to the people (to some of the people, anyway).

"NONANI HASN'T HAD A KING in three hundred years. Not for real."

"We don't have one now."

"People have become complacent of their freedom. They should go to barbarian Duchasa and see what it's like to live under kingship—even a good king can turn bad at will, or by a stroke of the gods. Or try the tribal villages of Slovona where tradition is king, supporting the petty grandeur of the chief, and there is only one narrow way to live. People say the current system don't work for them, but the alternative works for nobody but itself. Three hundred years. I don't know, maybe that's the lifetime of a republic."

"You're exaggerating. We've had some awful speakers before, people complain and catastrophize and cry tyranny, then there's another election, we get somebody new, and we move on."

"The death of Senator Naran has not even been investigated. A lot of deaths haven't. Speak up for any of the surviving candidates publicly, in a loud voice, I dare you."

"If he's that bad, he won't get elected. Or he won't get re-elected, anyway. You have to trust the political process."

"I trust nothing on the strength of its intentions alone. If the political process can't or won't defend itself against force then nothing can defend it but a countervailing force. We haven't had war in, what, three hundred and fifty years, not since we took up steel. We have *brought* war to others, but we haven't actually *had it* ourselves. The problem with civil war is that no matter who wins, Nonani will lose."

"You are such a pessimist, Gwen."

JUST AFTER SATURNALIA, AS GWEN fought in the courtrooms of Thesani and the various harvests drew to a close across the Empire, the votes were cast. They were collected by women in white wearing long, black mantles, each with a disc of bright bronze at her throat.

As families celebrated Natalia and began the Fallow, the count of the votes began in the temple by candle-light. However long the count took—and there were a hundred Council races to count as well as the race for speaker—the Sisters would keep their public silence until after Hilaria.

The court cases wound up, and Gwen moved her family back to Nonani City, a place she always missed and yet did not want to be.

A Sister, a woman clothed in white and draped in black, spoke in the Curia, and the news spread by telegraph across the Empire.

And Gwen lay in bed beside her sleeping wife, unable to sleep herself. This was not merely her odd nocturnal habit but true insomnia, a hard, stark feeling that would admit no rest. She could see in her mind what was going to happen, how it would all play out, who exactly would benefit, and who would finally and forever lose. *But it was such a good country*, she kept thinking.

She hadn't felt this bad since the night her daddy died.

Chapter 14. Abbas Elected

Year of Nonani 826

After almost four years as a Ruling Council aide, Abbas became a Councilman. He wasn't the only new member. B'Freias had won a seat, too, as had eighteen other members of their faction. Several others, both newly-elected and already-seated, joined the faction after the election, bringing their number to forty-three—hardly a majority in a three-hundred-member body, but enough to matter in coalition with other factions. Powerful people began courting their cooperation.

Abbas did not think of himself as a leader, either of the Council as a whole or of the faction. B'Freias led the faction. He chose objectives and priorities, issued marching orders, and begged, pleaded, shamed, and brow-beat the wavering into compliance on important votes. Abbas found a different role for himself. He called in favors, compromised, convinced, traded, and encouraged. He could argue brilliantly and eloquently in the hall, being a lawyer, but he spent most of his time and energy building and maintaining relationships. He did things for others whenever he could (so as to have favors to call in later), listened to gossip, and made friends with the aides and family of his colleagues—he was well aware of the strategic value of such activities, but also he just liked getting to know people. Once a week he hosted a card game. Betting was low-stakes, and the winnings would go to pay for the wine and the food. No discussion of government matters was allowed at those events. People on opposite sides of important issues could just hang out.

The conservationists made progress. Most of their more important legislative proposals were defeated, but they were able to make a few small but real changes to policy. With their support, several conservation-minded men were appointed to governorships, and they could sometimes block both bills and appointments they did not like.

"It's not enough," b'Freias said.

"Of course it's not enough."

"We need to do better."

"If you can tell me what 'better' is, I'll be glad to do it," Abbas said. They sat in the garden of the Curia, a mostly ornamental space of roses, oleanders, and rock-roses, but there were plenty of aromatics, too, and they'd picked lemon balm from the garden for their tea.

"You are always full of so many questions."

"I wish I was full of answers," Abbas admitted. "But I do the best I can."

"We need to be bolder. If we propose more legislation, even if it doesn't pass, at least we'll be *doing* something."

"Will we, though?" Abbas stirred his tea. It smelled good but was still too hot to drink. "In my heart, I am impatient as ever I was, but my feeling now is we have no time to waste with symbolic demonstrations. We have no time to waste in backwards steps. We lack the luxury to turn away any ally, however fallible. I have had to learn patience. My impatience demands it." The irony amused him. B'Freias chuckled, too, then looked up at the sky, thoughtfully. He put his cooling tea down on a little wrought-iron table and clasped his hands behind his head.

"Ah Abbas," he sighed. "Is this what you wanted to be when you were a kid? Before you met me, I mean. We're two of the most powerful, big-deal people in the Empire, and I feel so powerless. Everything feels so damn prosaic and slow. I wanted to be First Legate by the time I was thirty, walk around in a plumed helmet and a cape looking cool. And everybody would do what I told them. I couldn't even make it through officer training. I was such an ass."

Abbas chuckled.

"I didn't know enough about the world to have detailed ambitions," he said. "I was an ignorant, uneducated kid, lucky if I could get to a gymnasium once a week. My father didn't want me taking time off my chores to read at home, either. I barely knew what the Ruling Council was. Hm. But I knew I wanted off my father's farm. I wanted...people to think I was important. I thought that's what making a difference meant."

B'Freias smiled at that, then admitted that his military daydreams had not included any fighting.

"Isn't that funny? I don't know what I imagined I'd be doing in the army, other than looking cool. Now, I fight all the time. Everything is win or lose. Either our side wins or theirs does, and I just pray I know what the right side is so I can be on it!"

"Prayer," Abbas repeated and half-chuckled. "For a long time, I didn't pray or sacrifice—daily sacrifice is not really a thing in Galasia, among the Galasye, and my parents weren't very religious. I sang the derger songs, but their way isn't mine, and can't be. I'm not the right kind of smart. But I have started the practice. And when I do sacrifice, now.... The gods aren't on anybody's side, you know. They are on nobody's and everybody's. And when I offer the butter, the wine, or the blood, and say the prayers, I rise a little above the dust of every-day life, and I can see. I see—a little bit. I see it's never either/or. Never has been. It's both/and, always. And if ever both/and doesn't seem like the answer to me, that means I don't yet understand the question."

"That explains why you're always talking to the damnedest people." B'Freias's tea had cooled enough that he could drink it.

"Everybody has a reason for doing what they do, b'Freias. We all have more in common than we might think."

"Maybe. I don't see how I have much in common with some damned industrialist who would raze a forest to make an az." An az was a copper coin worth about the price of a loaf of bread.

Abbas smiled a little to himself, stirring a little more honey into his tea. Then he leaned forward, his eyes shining.

"Remember when you didn't think derger were human? So are

industrialists human. We all think honey is sweet. We all think kids are cute, we all love somebody. Start by trying to achieve the goals we have in common, and you'll never lack for allies."

Abbas had developed a reputation as a moderate that would have shamed and horrified his younger self, but the modest changes he pushed for passed far more often than b'Freias's more radical proposals. And it was for his success that the opposition targeted him.

Indeed, it was Senator Lian against whom the anti-conservationists coalesced, organized, and became a true opposition. The threat he posed was the thing they had in common.

"'Derger-lover' really isn't the insult they think it is," he told Maia. They were standing in the kitchen of their rented duplex, he leaning against the wall, she frying fish fillets in garlic-butter for dinner. They had a hired house-keeper to do the cleaning and dish-washing, but besides the family body-guard she was their only servant, and Maia did her own cooking and marketing.

"I wish they wouldn't try to insult you at all," she told him. "You're not the only one they're trying to get to."

"Anyone who thinks poorly of me because of 'derger-lover' probably didn't vote for me anyway."

"It's not their thoughts you have to worry about, it's their feelings, the rhetorical effect on their feelings. Hear something that *sounds* bad, and that colors things. That's just human nature." She took a taste of the sauce she was simmering on a cooler part of the cook-top, considered a moment, and added more dried onion. Maia knew more about certain aspects of politics than Abbas did, since she'd grown up among the rich and powerful. "Or it's ubum nature, anyway," she corrected herself. "Elves don't pick up attitudes by proximity, the way dogs pick up fleas."

"Who's got fleas, Mom?" asked Ardas, strolling into the kitchen. He had to stand on his toes to get an apple from the fruit-bowl on the counter-top. He was six years old and had not inherited his father's height.

"Nobody's got fleas, I wasn't speaking literally—don't get an apple *now*, you'll spoil your dinner!" The boy ignored her. He *had* inherited his father's friendly indifference to authority. "Well, if you *are* going to ruin your dinner, ruin your brother's, too. Fair's fair." This time he obeyed and grabbed a second apple.

"What's for dinner, anyway?"

"Fish with mustard and capers, rosemary buns, peas with butter and onions, cheesy baked turnip-coins with black pepper, a green salad, and raspberry custard for dessert."

"Does the fish-mustard have cream in it? Mom, I *hate* cream."

"How can you possibly hate *cream*, you're Galasye by blood," Maia protested. "But, no matter. Your fish I'm keeping plain."

"Oh, OK, thanks, Mom." And Ardas turned to go.

"Wait, Ardas?" Abbas asked. "Where is Obas?" He'd learned to worry whenever either child went silent for too long. He was utterly unable to discipline his children, and Maia only tried to do it when she was angry. Fortunately, Ardas was going to the gymnasium, now, and they seemed to be teaching him some manners there.

"He's with the goat."

"What goat? We don't have a goat." Only, Ardas was neither a fanciful child nor a liar. "OK, *where* is the goat?"

"In the library."

Abbas ran to go save his books.

Abbas spent most of his life working and had since he was eight or nine years old, a poor kid trying to get somewhere. When he wasn't in the debate hall of the Curia or in his office there, he was keeping up with his duties as paterfamilias, advising the activist lawyer network—he no longer directed it but did consult—or giving public talks in the forum or in various area gymnasia or theaters. And he continued his study of the epics, his attendance of talks and recitations, his discussions with philosophers and priests, all of which he regarded as an integral part of his work.

"To live within the music, one must learn the songs," he would say to those few people who knew him well enough to understand what he was talking about.

But he always made sure to be home for dinner with his family and to spend at least a day a week doing things with them—even if it was only taking the boys to the playground down the street. He met with friends at the baths or at the weight-room at the gymnasium or at one or another pub. And he kept up with his personal correspondence.

"Did you get to the post-office today?"

"What, do you think I don't have anything else to do?" Maia said it with venom. She'd always had good days and bad days. This was evidently a bad day. Abbas sighed.

"It was just a question. Yes or no?"

"Yes!" and she went to fetch several scrolls from a basket on the counter-top. "You ought to pay someone to get the mail. Or get it yourself. You were just out." She plopped herself down on a cushioned chair and rubbed her temples.

"We can't afford an extra servant," Abbas explained patiently, hopelessly. "The bath-house I've just come from is in the opposite direction from the post-office, and had I gone there anyway, there would have been no mail there as you'd already been."

"Why can't our mail just be sent here?" Nonani had not invented the street-address and therefore couldn't have home delivery.

"Why are you so grumpy today?"

"I don't know. My head hurts."

"Again?"

"More and more often. And the boys were screaming all day long. That didn't help. So I screamed back at them. That didn't help, either."

"No, it wouldn't," Abbas agreed. He went over and massaged Maia's shoulders and neck. Sometimes that could help with the headaches. She grunted with pleasure. "You should go to the baths. Get a real massage, sit in the steam-bath awhile.... I'll watch the kids."

"Whoop-dee-doo, my hero," Maia grumped. There was no pleasing her when she was like this. Abbas kept rubbing her shoulders. "Who are the letters from? I didn't check."

Abbas left off massaging and investigated the scrolls. Three were work-related. He'd think about them later. Another was from the laundry service, probably a bill. There were four others.

"Buncha work stuff," he reported, "Letter from Lara, letter from Xermas—have I told you about him? We went to law-school together, I haven't heard from him in ages—and two from J.J. One of those will be from Oboo, I'm guessing."

"You'd think J.J. would teach him to write."

"I'm not sure he can learn. I've never heard of a derger who did. Unless they had ubum blood, I mean."

"That makes no sense. They can talk with their mouths, so why can't they talk with a pen? Anyway, what does Oboo have to say?"

"I'll tell you when I've read it."

"You never write to your father, Abbas."

"He never writes to me. Not even through Lara. You'd think *he'd* learn to write."

"Maybe he has no reason."

"He has me."

The conservationist faction continued to grow. Not only had it won more seats at the midterm, but the entire Aethenye voting block recognized common cause in a common enemy and joined in, bringing their total number up close to a hundred. Each one found himself targeted by the anti-conservationists, whose numbers were also growing, and who now had the support of an increasing number of urban proletarians, just as the conservationists had the support of most plebeians and rural proletarians. Never before had so many people who could not vote been so deeply involved in political coalitions. Abbas had very mixed feelings about the development.

The Speaker remained an independent moderate. Speakers usually were. Since they needed a majority of the full Senate to win election, they tended not to be niche-market people but rather capable of appealing in at least a minimal way to a broad swath of the electorate. Anyway, it wasn't the speaker's job to originate policy, only to execute it and to handle emergencies. This particular Speaker was a good man usually willing to work with the conservationists at least to a point, and so Abbas had no trouble campaigning for his reelection and even spent a few months traveling that year, giving campaign speeches and talking to community leaders. Maia and the boys went with him, and he learned a great deal about how a general campaign had to work.

The incumbent was duly re-elected—his victory was announced just after Hilaria, as per tradition, and he was sworn in for his second term just before Nonalia, just in time to preside over the holiday's public displays of patriotism. A few weeks after that, in mid-second-month, Maia gave birth to a third healthy little boy, whom they named Laras, after Abbas's stepmother. And then two months after that, five-year-old Obas died.

No one was really clear on what Obas died of. He had "a fever that settled in his chest and carried him off after some weeks," according to the normal way such things were discussed, if they were discussed at all. There wasn't much that could be done about it anyway. Elecampane tea eased the boy's breathing a little. There was laudanum for pain.

"I should have sent for Xu!luh," Abbas said, "right when he first got sick. Maybe she could have saved him. She saved *me*."

"She couldn't save your siblings," Senator Euan reminded him. "And she couldn't have gotten here in time. She'd be getting here now, if she could come at all."

"It's got to be my fault somehow," Abbas replied, not realizing how irrational that sounded. But Tomas understood. He'd lost a boy between Davas and Jonas. He knew guilt is preferable to helplessness. He rubbed Abbas's back.

"I can't believe he's really gone," the younger man said, weeping. "My boy is *gone*."

It shouldn't have been a surprise. Half of all ubum died before they were ten years old, not counting still-births and miscarriages. There was hardly an older couple who hadn't lost at least one child, and many had lost several. But it's always a surprise. Abbas and Maia could not take comfort in each other, and neither could comfort eight-year-old Ardas, who went away inside himself for a very long time. And for all of them, except for little Laras, who didn't know what had happened, vibrant, flower-filled Nonani City simply had no color in it anymore.

Abbas kept on going. There was nothing else he could do.

At the next midterm, Abbas's seat came up for a vote. He stood for re-election and won. So did many other conservationists. The balance of power in the Council shifted decisively, and the mildly pro-business Coordinator, was subjected to a vote of confidence and lost.

The coordinator was another of the five people who collectively replaced the King. While the Speaker executed the law and served as head-of-state and civilian commander-in-chief, the coordinator presided over the Ruling Council, scheduling votes, assigning committee membership, and generally shepherding bills through the process of passage into law. Unlike the speaker, who was elected by the full Senate, the coordinator was elected by the Ruling Council, often from among their number. And yet the coordinator was not a councilman. When Abbas was made coordinator on the second ballot, the people who had voted for him for Councilman were asked to choose someone else. Of course they chose another conservationist.

"More people on our side!" b'Freias crowed.

"There didn't used to be *sides*, though," Abbas replied, concerned.

And indeed the Council—and Nonani generally—was becoming polarized. There had always been five or six different factions and plenty of independents, an ever-shifting landscape of alliances and mostly ad-hoc coalitions. Now, thanks to years of careful political maneuvering and targeted campaign contributions on both sides, there were only two factions, shifting and cooperation were getting rare, and the number of independents was rapidly shrinking. Once, allies only asked each other's support. Now, to be counted as someone's friend, one had to also be the enemy of their enemy—and the enmity had to be in all things. Attendance at Abbas's weekly card-games started falling off. The polarization wasn't just among politicians, either. There were rumors of marriages failing over political differences.

Concern for loyalty and ideological purity was most intense within the anti-conservationists, but some conservationists were doing it, too. Abbas tried to explain the situation to Oboo in a letter. The reply came back in J.J.'s handwriting, but Abbas "heard" the words in his mind's ear in Oboo's voice and accent.

"The songs say ubum like to play pretend quite seriously, and that one of their favorite things to pretend is that humanity consists of multiple groups, some of which are not human. I have seen this done, the people who think I and my family are not human, that we are not important or are not real. You have helped us against such people. But it sounds now as if Nonanye ubum are pretending that other Nonanye ubum are not human, either. Be careful, Ubbus. Such pretending is a sign of wur."

He was right. Abbas had not allowed himself to think thus before, but Oboo was right. War was coming, and Abbas did not know how to stop it.

There was the polarization. There was the increasingly ugly and bigoted tone of many of the popular comedians and the city rumor-mill itself—in Nonani City and in many other cities and smaller communities across Itara, Parsia, and parts of the other provinces. There were the illegal "independent gymnasia" springing up, little centers of sedition that Abbas could not figure out how to move against without also moving against Udùo's activist cells. There were frightening rumors of a group calling itself the Iron Eagle that seemed to be everywhere and nowhere at once. How or even if these developments might be related, Abbas did not know, but he felt as if he were being out-maneuvered by something nebulous and strange.

And yet, b'Freias was right—if there were sides now, then the side of the conservationists was larger and still growing. They could push through some important reforms now by force alone.

Abbas called an unofficial meeting of whichever of his unofficial advisors happened to be available at the moment.

"So, gentlemen and lady," he began. "It seems I've been given certain powers. The question is what should I do with them?"

Present were b'Freias and Senator Euan, of course, and Maia and Udùo, but also an elfin philosopher named Paracelias whose work Abbas had been reading lately, and Senator Euan's son-in-law, Sammas Tengas Euan, the new head of the activist lawyer network. Senator Euan son, Jonas Tomas Miran, sat off to the side, taking notes on a wax tablet. He had been a member of Abbas's staff for a few years now and had come with him to the coordinator's office.

All of them began tossing ideas around.

"What needs to be done," asserted Udùo, "is we need to stop the charcoal harvest, period."

"That...sounds difficult," Paracelias remarked. He was a tall, thin, pale, awkward man with a rare, quick, lovely smile and a fine appreciation of understatement and irony.

"Difficult?" Abbas replied, "we can't do it."

"Nevertheless," said Udùo.

"The economy would completely collapse. Nonanye military dominance would then collapse, too."

"So?" said Udùo.

"This sounds like a good time for that both/and you like," b'Freias put in. "I mean, we're Nonanye. We *are* wealth, power, privilege. This meal, for example. Do you think we'd be able to have pepper, carda-mom, ginger, dates, limes, if we weren't, relatively speaking, rich?"

"You realize," said Udùo, after a moment, "that many Nonanye are not wealthy or powerful? Most of the people I work with eat gruel two or three meals per day. Have you ever eaten gruel? It's not bad, for a meal or two. Imagine knowing you'll never have anything better, and neither will your kids or their kids.... And not all people who matter are even Nonanye."

"*All* people matter," interjected Maia. Udùo raised an eyebrow at her.

"That's it, though, that gruel," b'Freias exclaimed, "it's free for most of the people eating it. You know why? Because of Nonanye economic and military dominance—because of land-use policy and tax policies that everybody in this room has been rightly fighting against! So, there are lots of people who don't get anything out of the deal other than free flour for gruel, I'm not saying the system's not screwed up. There is a *reason* why the proletarians are angry. But cutting the top off the economy isn't going to magically expand the bottom. The poor will still be poor. They just won't have their free gruel. And they'll suffer as much as anyone when some resurgent Duchessye kingdom or maybe Inan or the delta pirates come sack Nonani City. So, yeah, both/and!"

"I don't know that both are available," said Udùo.

"I don't know that either is available," Abbas cut in, "without the other. Anyway, there is no legal mechanism by which we can shut down an entire industry, and there is no political will to create such a mechanism. So what *can* we do?"

"What do you mean, both, neither, what?" the lawyer, b'Tengas, asked. "I'm kinda lost."

"Economic/military strength verses an intact continental forest," Udùo explained. "You've seen the calculations—military readiness as currently defined simply requires more wood than the woods can spare. Hand me another flatbread, please?"

"Having both economic/military strength *and* an intact continental forest is a mathematical impossibility," Abbas agreed, "but having economic et cetera *without* an intact forest is also a mathematical impossibility. Without a fertile, living landscape—which we know depends ultimately on the forest—we won't be able to feed our armies. Already, farm failures are up, mostly from causes related to deforestation—flooding, erosion, streams drying up, that sort of thing. Worse could happen, too. The effects are localized, so far, and more farms can be founded elsewhere. Yields are still increasing in Aethenia. There is talk of importing grain from abroad. But if you burn a candle at both ends long enough, you're going to end up in the dark."

Abbas spoke in a measured, slow way, as he often did, and he mostly looked, not at the other people at the table, but at the single remaining samosa. He fell silent, but nobody else spoke, somehow sensing that he wasn't done. He spoke again.

"But can we have an intact forest *without* military might? I think perhaps we cannot. After all, ours is not the only society that appreciates a good supply of steel, and Inan, to take one example, does not have a supply of wood adequate to fully exploit their known iron ore stocks. What is protecting our forests from them is our army."

"So that's it, we're screwed," b'Freias said. "No way back, no way forward, we're out of options. By the gods, Coordinator, I hope what you're saying is wrong!"

"Well, logically, speaking, you've skipped a step," suggested Paracelias, with a bit of a smile.

"Oh?"

"You're assuming that military et cetera and an intact forest are each unitary entities, to have or lose entirely, but is that true? Udùo asserted that an intact forest requires absolute protection, but I'm not sure what that's based on. And no one has even suggested that the military and the economy can't be changed. I suggest getting very clear on what the actual *needs* are here—it may be they can all be met if some very fond and taken-for-granted *wants* are, well, let go of." And he made a fluttering motion with one hand, suggesting something flying away.

"Well, I think we have our initial marching orders, then," Abbas said. "I don't know whether it's possible to harvest charcoal at a sustainable rate, so that means there is a high order of priority on finding out. And in the meantime, we can explore ways to limit the harvest and reduce the harm that it does. If it turns out that we really must choose, that there can be no charcoal harvest, though, I don't know what we'll do about that. Neither I nor the Council have the authority to shut down an industry by fiat, nor do I have the authority to ignore the wishes of some forty percent of the electorate. As much as I might wish otherwise, I've been hired by all of Nonani, not just those parts I agree with. I can't keep the faith by breaking it."

Two weeks later, Maia bore their fourth son, and some of the light and color seemed to return to the world. They named him Naras, after Abbas's poor sister, but soon nicknamed him Tenadas, meaning tadpole. It seemed to suit him.

The question of sustainable logging would take a very long time to answer, but the scientists whom Abbas consulted all guessed that some degree of harvest probably was sustainable, provided no more ancient forest was cut. And Abbas figured that until he could get a definitive answer, any movement in the right direction was good.

Over the next two years, Abbas was able to marshal the votes to push through a whole series of landmark legislation, including genuine, albeit limited, forest protections—a system of required permits, fees, and subsidies designed to discourage cutting of older forests or forest in sensitive areas and to encourage replanting and the use of techniques such as coppicing and pollarding to reduce soil disturbance and increase regeneration times. No such comprehensive program had ever been tried before.

"Yes, because this sort of thing isn't going to work," Jeriorniress told him.

"Strictly between you and me, I had hoped for a note of congratulations," Abbas admitted.

"Did you call me here to discuss conservation or to have an emotional or social encounter?"

"Both? It has been some years since we saw each other. I always felt us to be friends, of a kind."

That earned a tight, but possibly fond smile. They were chatting in Abbas's office in the Curia.

"You know why elves don't say hello or goodbye?" Jeriorniress asked. "It's because we're never gone. Time does not matter to us *here*." He touched his chest over his heart. Then he became more businesslike again. "But time does matter to the work we do."

"Alright. Continue explaining the flaw in my successes."

"Your success is that you set interim goals and achieved them. The problem is that your ultimate goals may not thus be served. Why has no one passed legislation like this before? Because the scale is wrong. It's top-down, command-control type stuff. It's going to require a literal army of civil servants to enforce, and if anyone in the chain of command is not on board with your objectives, the control will fail. And even if everything goes right, you're painting with such a broad brush that success will be almost hit or miss." He paused a moment, looking piercingly at Abbas and yet not quite making eye contact. "You did better with your earlier approach, supporting the communities that protect the forest."

Abbas gazed at the elf a moment then sat down abruptly, looking away.

"Oh, I know it, I know it. But I fought one battle at a time as a lawyer, protecting communities, protecting families, and for each one I fought and won, three others were lost for want of attention, and all the while I was constrained by a legal system that leaves all the important things unsaid and therefore unenforceable. It took me two years and much shenanigans to force a single judge to re-interpret the law in such a way as to give a single derger family rights that for one of my species would have gone unquestioned. I have to change the system, Jeriorniress. I have to create more options. But to empower local communities wholly, across the board, would mean disempowering industry and commerce, and that would break the Empire. What *is* an empire but an extraction machine, funneling wealth... well, here? I can't ask the Empire to break itself, it won't listen. What I'm doing...no, it won't work in the long run, but I'm hoping it will buy us some time."

"And then what, Coordinator? Time for what?"

"Time for me to think of something."

Abbas had been Coordinator just over two years when the speakership came back up for election. No man could be speaker more than two consecutive terms, so this time there was no incumbent running. Several powerful, popular moderates declared their candidacy, as did a dozen or so others generally thought to have a snowball's chance in an oven of winning, but there was no formal nomination process, no way that a declared candidacy by anybody could be kept from being official. Usually, everybody just ignored the minor candidates. They went away eventually.

But this time two of the minor candidates could not be ignored, not by Abbas, anyway.

One was b'Freias, whom Abbas felt more or less bound to support, although he wasn't sure the conservationist faction was strong enough yet to win the speakership, and he didn't think b'Freias, a firebrand who didn't play nicely with others, was a good choice for their first attempt.

The other was a businessman named Tanas Rylas Canan. He had no prior experience in governance, and was famous largely for being famous. He boasted of his riches but was rumored to be deeply in debt, and whispers of immoral and even illegal activity followed him. The anti-conservationists seemed to like him, and so did the urban proletarian mob—there were incidents of people who spoke poorly of b'Rylas in public being beaten, and although b'Rylas did not seem to have ordered or even asked for such violent support, he also clearly liked it.

Nobody thought b'Rylas could win. Polling as such didn't exist, but people talked to each other, and no senator outside of the anti-conservationist faction praised him. And it was hard to believe that even the anti-conservationists really wanted someone so obviously unqualified. They were all businessmen—industrialists or bankers—and military types, practical, hard-nosed people. Surely they'd want somebody likely to promote a stable business environment? And indeed, there were three popular moderates in the race, two of whom were definitely pro-business.

But then two of the popular moderates abruptly dropped out of the race with no explanation. The third turned up dead. Most of the other candidates dropped out for more standard reasons, running out of campaign funds and so forth. That left b'Rylas opposed only by b'Freias and by a less-than-popular moderate with a good record but a boring character and no strong vision.

"You need to drop out," Abbas told b'Freias. They were talking over lunch, the two of them and b'Freias's friend and campaign manager, the switcher b'Tomas. Abbas had bought lunch, hoping to take the sting out of what he had to say, but it wasn't helping.

"The hell I do."

"If you don't drop out, b'Rylas will win. We can work with b'Thavan. We can't work with b'Rylas, he's running against everything we've been working for."

"Have you said the same to b'Thavan? Surely you can work with me, too?"

Silence.

"Have you?"

"No, and I won't, b'Freias, I'm sorry. It's true that there are people who like you, who want you in office. They'll vote for you because they want you. And it's true that most people will vote for b'Thavan purely because they don't want b'Rylas. The man has no other real appeal. But nobody *dislikes* him. If you drop out, he'll inherit all your votes because nobody who wants you wants b'Rylas. If b'Thavan drops out…there are people who don't like you. And they won't vote at all."

B'Freias looked as if he'd been slapped.

"I have a lot of support," he objected. "I can win this. It's our time. You as Coordinator, me as Speaker, it's what we've worked for."

"No, what we've worked for is meaningful policy change."

"This is how to get it!"

"Is it, though?"

Silence.

"B'Freias, don't you see it? You haven't been put under any pressure to drop out from anybody except now, from me, have you? You haven't been threatened. You're certainly not dead. B'Rylas wants you to run. He knows he can't beat b'Thavan alone, his support is probably capped to members of his own faction. He might be able to beat you alone, but he can't be sure. But the two of you together, he can beat. He's using you, b'Freias. Don't let him."

B'Freias stared at him a moment, and then his face changed.

"That's just what you want, isn't it?" he said.

"What is? What are you talking about?"

"This whole time, this whole time you've been Coordinator, you've liked that power, haven't you? You've gotten to think it's your faction, not mine, and you can't stand the thought that I'm going to out-rank you again. That's it, isn't it? Well, you just think about where you were when I found you, where you'd still be if I hadn't! If you've forgotten where you came from and what I did for you, you can just fuck *all* the way off!"

Abbas stared at him.

"No, please, b'Freias, I.... Let's stop this! Please. I need you."

But then b'Tomas, who had been silent the whole conversation and who had hardly said a word to Abbas in years, found her voice.

"Oh, you need him, do you?" she half-shouted. "Well, he does not need you. He doesn't even want you. He has me."

And Abbas remembered some things that hadn't seemed significant to him before.

Abbas voted for b'Freias, as did six hundred and eighty-seven others. The boring but reliable moderate received almost eleven hundred votes. B'Rylas won with almost thirteen hundred.

Abbas had expected Speaker Canan's administration to be a roadblock, a delay in a process that already was critically short on time. But reality proved far worse.

Speaker Canan not only didn't actively help the conservationists, he made a point of total non-cooperation, refusing to execute laws and policies he didn't agree with, firing judges and civil servants and either replacing them with sycophants or leaving the posts vacant, and generally not doing his job in a totally unprecedented way. Speakers had always had some wiggle-room to pursue their own agendas, but he took it to an extreme, rendering the government nearly non-functional except on his own occasional say-so. He'd effectively made himself into a monarch, and there was no legal mechanism for deposing him except to vote him out.

Abbas decided it was time to run for speaker himself.

There were other people in the race, at first, but none had the support of the conservationist coalition, and Abbas spoke to each of them privately, offering them places in his administration if they'd only drop out.

"To be clear, if you didn't drop out, and I won anyway, I'd still employ you, but unless you drop out I won't win and won't be able to hire anybody."

It was a nasty, contentious campaign, and the public grew more divided than ever, but Abbas knew how to use the allies and advantages he had. He sent out messengers to make sure all the derger and forest-ubum patresfamilias knew how to vote. He spoke to all the members of his own faction on the Council to be sure that their voters would also vote for him. He traveled widely, making speeches and talking with community leaders, reaching out to people who weren't part of his faction to find out what they wanted and needed in a speaker. Friends and allies of his, acting as his proxies, traveled and gave speeches, and met with community leaders, too. He and Maia had long discussions late into the night about campaign strategy. She wanted him to tell more of his personal story, to emphasize his rise from obscurity in order to present himself as a man of old-fashioned humility and public virtue.

"I mean, you were a *poor* farm kid, that's going to play well in this cycle where everybody wants to connect with proletarians all of a sudden. And it's not all that different from the legends of some of the first speakers, you know, the kind called from their goat-herds to simply and humbly serve the people!"

"OK, can we *not* fetishize my childhood poverty, though?" he asked. "I left that little cabin for a reason."

"Says the man who's always telling charming, Galesye-accented stories about growing up on a sheep farm."

"I *did* grow up on a sheep farm!"

"Uh-huh. Did you run high-lanolin or low-lanolin stock?"

"Um...."

Of course, Abbas had spent as little time as possible actually doing farm work. Maia laughed at him. It was good to hear her laughing again. Lately, her headaches had been getting worse and her dizzy spells had returned. He wasn't sure, but he thought she was getting grumpier, too.

He decided not to tell Maia about the death threats he'd been getting.

It was very strange to think that there were actually people who wanted to kill him. He wasn't sure if any were prepared to carry out the threat, but he couldn't rule it out, and he certainly believed the hatred they expressed was real. There were strangers, people who did not know him at all and whom he had done nothing whatever to hurt, who wanted him to die. He looked at that fact for a while, sat with it, and decided he was OK with it. Better to do the work than not do it. He hired a second body-guard and went about his life.

There had been demonstrations, small riots, various outrages for years, and of course under Speaker Canan's influence such signs of civil unrest had been increasing, but for the most part there hadn't been anything Abbas or the Council could do about it, besides talk. Coping with crises was up to either local authorities or the Speaker. But then, in ninth-month, just before the election, a fight broke out in the street outside of a bar in the working-class neighborhood at the foot of Olivine Hill. The fight was over politics, over the deep and petty hatreds between groups that Speaker Canan's rhetoric had harnessed, evoked, and enlarged. And people on both sides were killed.

There being nothing like an official morgue, the bodies lay in the street, guarded by the owner of the pub, while friends and family were summoned. That took some time, and while it was happening, someone ran the half-mile or so up the Olivine and across to the Capitoline to notify both the Council and the King's House. The King's House did nothing, and indeed there wasn't anything particular that any government officer could be expected to do. But Abbas followed the messenger at a run back the way he'd come and found the families gathering, shouting accusations at each other across the bodies of their dead. The air had turned electric. Some people in the growing crowd were armed.

"STOP!" cried Abbas, and at first they stopped only out of surprised curiosity, not knowing who he was. As he spoke, most of them seemed to figure it out.

He argued, making his case for peace like a lawyer. He lectured, explaining the matter like a teacher. And he preached, using the language of the epics to evoke what held Nonani together. And finally, he sang, sang one of the praise-songs of the followers. He sang of forgiveness. He sang of grace.

Chapter 15. Preparations

Year of Nonani 836

Not much changed after the election, not right away. Gwen got used to pessimistic dread and got on with life. Nonalia, the spring equinox and the city's traditional birthday, came around, and b'Rylas was sworn in, beginning his four-year term. He made a speech, moved into the King's House, and went about governing. He wasn't very good at it, but of course few speakers were, simply by the law of averages. Gwen and her family moved back to Nonani City where Orfarias and Micalion joined them for a few weeks. At least the house was no longer quite so crowded. Both Jonas and Chalcy and their respective families had found places of their own and moved out.

"Nonsense. I don't have consumption," Opal insisted. "Everybody knows consumption is a young-person's disease!"

Except no one had said anything about her having consumption.

"You know, you can just ask me questions, I don't mind," said Opharias. But Gwen didn't feel like she could. He didn't seem crazy, just a little less engaged than he used to. His hyper moods were goofier, but there was a slight dullness to him otherwise. Micalion said the symptoms were well-controlled. What did that mean?

* * *

CHRYS'S VERSION OF HER OWN future was that she would thenceforth live at home with her parents and husband and children, everybody together where they ought to be. Of course, Gwen needed a decent job for that future to play out.

"Why don't you talk to Cheras?" Chrys suggested. "I'm sure he could find you something. And then you and he could walk to work together." They were sitting in the atrium before dinner one lovely afternoon. Gwen was drawing a picture in charcoal on papyrus. Chrys was re-stringing her harp, which she hadn't had time to play very much recently.

"Will you quit trying to control my life!" Gwen startled both of them by raising her voice.

"I am *not* trying to control your life," Chrys retorted, raising hers. "I'm trying to control *my* life, the circumstances of which largely depend on choices *you* make. If you hadn't switched, you'd understand how that feels."

Gwen's interest in shouting went out like a candle.

"Should I not have switched?" she asked.

"Oh, that's silly," Chrys replied, after a long moment. "One of us had to, and I'd make a terrible man. You make such a good one! Why, if only you'd follow the Shepherd, you'd be perfect!"

Gwen made an exasperated noise.

"Just don't be a jack-ass sort of man, is all," Chrys added, ignoring the noise.

"I think a certain amount of jackassery comes with the territory," Gwen offered. The comment sounded so self-deprecatingly yet condescendingly male that Chrys rolled her eyes.

"Why *don't* you follow the Shepherd?" she asked. "It can't be that you don't hear the Call."

Gwen put her drawing down a moment and considered, seriously.

"Actually, I walk in His footsteps pretty closely," she acknowledged.

"And I wish everyone did. It's an excellent program upon which to base a society, though I wouldn't want to ignore the other Powers. But the problem is that you make belief an article of faith. See, it don't matter whether I believe there is literally a spirit-being guarding our storehouse and another guarding our home, I can wake up in the morning and offer butter to the fire in praise and gratitude because our home is real and our stores are real and I am grateful for them. It is good and right to begin each day in an awareness of gratitude. Nobody cares what I believe, nobody speculates, and if the Guardians do exist, they don't care either, just so long as they get their butter! But trusting the Shepherd means believing in him and all the details of cosmology and dogma that I can't wrap my mind around—it all seems like so much mist to me. I can't in good conscience act as though I believe when I don't, when I can't."

Gwen had been sitting with her back to the rim of the fountain, and as she spoke she reached her arm over and idly played with the surface of the water. The house fountain was fed, like most of the other fountains in town, by a system of pipes charged by aqueduct from a lake sixty miles away. It wasn't a spring and had no naiad for Gwen to claim to not believe in, but she seemed to be petting it fondly anyway. Sunlight played upon the water, and Gwen closed her eyes against the glare.

"Just *decide* to believe," Chrys advised. "Then you can pray for help deepening your faith. You're over-complicating it."

"I don't believe that I am."

"So why *don't* you want to talk to Cheras about a job? It seems the perfect solution to me."

"Chrys, I am *not* going to work for your father's company."

"Why not?" she asked, tightening a harp string.

"Because, once again, it is your father's company."

"Why? Don't you *like* Father anymore?"

"Of course I like Father," Gwen snapped. "I love him. I always will. But I want to bring something new to him, to you. That's what I'm *supposed* to do! That's the whole *point* of a husband! And I can't *do* that if I don't establish myself as a man!" This time she didn't notice she'd called herself a man.

"Oh, Gwen, but you bring so much!"

"I do not! Everything I have, everything I am, I owe to *him*. So far, I'm *redundant*. You know, this is probably why people shouldn't marry their sibs."

"We are *not* siblings, Gwen. We're not even the same species."

"Chrys, we just referred to the same man as 'father.'"

"You *fight* like siblings," opined Chalcy, who had come for dinner and was working on her embroidery nearby. Gwen and Chrys looked at each other.

"She started it," Gwen said.

"Oh! I did *not*!"

"Did too."

"Did not!"

"Did too!

"Did not!"

"Did too, did too, did too!"

"Did not, not, not!"

"I'm telling Mom."

They did fight like siblings, but they played like siblings, too. The nocturnal noises coming from their room were as likely to be the sounds of pillow battles and tickle fights as anything else. When their kids were outside or otherwise not paying attention, Gwen and Chrys would chase each other up and down the stairs, steal things from each other, or poke each other. Gwen was usually the instigator, but Chrys held her own. The other adults in the family would roll their eyes. When Chrys's latest pregnancy began to show, Gwen took to calling her Melon Thief.

"*Some* husbands are romantic, sweet, and gallant," Chrys announced.

"Good thing you married me instead, I'm ever so much more fun," Gwen replied.

*　　*　　*

GWENIAS WAS ALMOST TWO, BUT still barely talking. He could be bright and sunny one moment, then angry or frightened for no apparent reason. Gwen was sure the boy *did* have a reason, but he couldn't explain what it was. He'd inherited the ubum early growth pattern, unlike the girls, but he still seemed younger than he was. He liked being near other children, but seldom interacted with them in any obvious way. Gwen bought him a set of painted, wooden toy soldiers, thinking that other neighborhood boys might like the toys and so start playing with him. But he didn't show them his toys.

One morning, he was happily setting up the soldiers in a long and mostly straight line on the floor in the kitchen, when Gwen realized she hadn't gotten to play soldier in far too long. She sat down nearby and watched for a bit. Her son ignored her.

"About FACE!" she barked and turned two of the soldiers the other way.

Gwenias made an exasperated noise, just as Gwen might have, and turned them back.

"OK," she said, "but what if there's a trebuchet on the battlefield?" And she tossed a glass marble into the line.

Gwenias startled her by shrieking. He grabbed the marble, threw it off into the corner with surprising violence, and set the toy soldiers back in their places, all without looking at Gwen.

"OK, OK, I won't mess up your line!" Gwen capitulated. "But can't I play, too?" And she started setting up a facing line.

"No, no, no!" Gwenias shouted, and reclaimed the soldiers.

Gwen held up her hands, palms forward in surrender. Then she realized something. She started using the soldiers to extend her son's line.

For the first time he looked up at her, amazed.

"That's right, I get it now," Gwen told him. "I'm sorry I didn't earlier."

"Get what?" Chrys asked. She was chopping an onion.

"He's *not* playing soldier," Gwen explained. "These ain't soldiers to him right now. They are objects to make a pattern with. don't this line remind you of anything?"

In fact, just the day before, Gwen had been chaperoning a children's party, gotten bored, and, unable to leave or pick up a book, she'd entertained herself by lining up all seven onions from the vegetable basket along the kitchen counter-top, equidistant from each other and ordered by size, with the last and largest onion surrounded by garlic cloves in a sunburst pattern. But though Chrys had taken the smallest onion so as not to disturb the pattern too much, she didn't think of the onions just then.

"Your doll-babies!" she exclaimed instead. "When you first came to live with us! Father got you a set of straw dolls, and you made lines with them! I couldn't think what you were doing. Years later, I figured it must have been a switcher thing. I mean, what does a switcher want with doll-babies?"

"I liked my dolls," Gwen insisted, sounding a little stung. "It's not a switcher-thing. It's an elf-blood thing. He's an elf-blood!"

Gwenias was again making his line of wooden pieces. Gwen curled down on her knees and elbows, the way cats do when they make themselves resemble meat-loafs, and watched her son play.

"You are, you are," she murmured happily. "It's not a bad thing. It's why you're so handsome."

CHRYS AND GWEN HAD JOKED that, because each of their babies had been paler than the last, their next child ought to be albino, the one after that transparent. But the baby born that Fallow came out richly dark. They named her Jade. She looked very much like Ellia had as a newborn, but with blue eyes. That made five. The physical strain was starting to tell on Chrys—she was thirty-three, not young anymore— but in Nonanye society for a woman to have eight to ten children was normal, and she both wanted a large family and took it for granted that she'd have one.

GWEN WORKED FOR COUSIN EUAS, refurbishing several defunct wineries he'd bought and wanted to run as rental properties. The job was both temporary and grueling, but she was grateful for it. But he was drinking. Not that he seemed drunk often or was in any way irresponsible, but his sweat smelled always of stale wine. He looked sick. Once, they had been close, but Euas had pulled away. She still didn't know why. She couldn't talk to him about his drinking, not anymore, and the whole thing made her sad.

GWEN STRODE ALONG THROUGH THE River District on her way to Euas's office. He wouldn't be there this close to sundown, but she'd agreed to double-check some of his records for him overnight. The day was cloudy, unusual for summer, and muggy, and she scowled as she walked, staring at the paving stones just ahead of her feet, peripherally aware of everything around her while her attention danced among half a dozen mostly unpleasant topics all a million miles away.

There was hardly anybody out and about now, but one man walked towards her, and so she glanced up at him, largely to make sure they did not collide. Except he looked familiar....

She saw him notice her, then recognize her.

"B'Sheras!" he cried. "How the hell are ya?"

B'Sylas, the chess-hustling centurion! He'd grown his beard out, and of course wasn't in uniform, but it was him alright. They chatted very briefly. He looked anxious and thread-bare, but even as she noticed his clothing, she realized he'd noticed hers. She'd been paying all her own family's expenses, for she could not bear to let Tomas subsidize her into her thirties, but there wasn't enough left for fancy clothes. She grinned, embarrassed.

"I guess a legion isn't the best preparation for success in business, is it?" she ventured.

"No, it's not," b'Sylas acknowledged.

Gwen offered what encouragement and advice she could. Her words seemed to matter to him. Maybe they mattered a lot. He closed his eyes briefly and nodded a little. And she believed her own optimistic words—because she had said them to him.

B'Sylas clapped her arm in a friendly manner with his free hand.

"You take care, b'Sheras," he said and clearly meant it.

"You too," she answered.

Seeing him was somehow the best news she'd had in months.

BUT WHAT WAS SHE GOING to do for work? The thing for Euas was temporary, and nothing else seemed to stick. Knowing Chrys wouldn't like it but at a loss for other ideas, Gwen wrote to her two former legates asking if she might get back into the army. B'Jerras, who was still at Ralani, wrote back, saying that he didn't need a new prefect and didn't think she'd want to be a centurion again, but he did have an idea. He was going to be in Nonani City for a month and said he'd call on her at home.

B'Jerras at the door. Mostly-gray hair. Missing an eye. It had been eight years. Gwen poured two cups of wine and fixed a bowl of toasted grasshoppers with salt and vinegar. They went to sit in the garden, fading now in the summer dryness, but still well-grown. One of the ferrets hopped about, finding and examining mouse-nests. A toad sat in the shadow of the bench, occasionally pouncing on worms or ants. They chatted for a few. Gwen fidgeted with the hem of her tunic. B'Jerras told Gwen how Ralani was almost done, they were just building the second stadium and the People's House, which is what the Ralanye had always called their version of a curia. He told her that his youngest son was in the army now, doing well in a Covert Ops cohort in a legion up in Ishlana. He didn't mention what had happened to his eye.

"I have a friend," b'Jerras said at last, "starting a school. I think it might be the place for you."

"A school? Why? What sort of school? You mean a military academy? Aren't there too many already? Half of all graduates never get hired, there aren't enough positions available."

B'Jerras laughed at her spill of questions.

"This one's different," he said. "It's for misfits."

"Misfits?"

"Who are the people most likely to drop out of their academies or not finish their five years? Left-handers, elf-bloods, switchers, anybody who's different. The problem is Infantry, everybody's got to be the same, there, a piece in the machine, and who wants to command an outfit where there's nobody else like you? Well, I mean, I wouldn't know, but I can imagine, and they do drop out. People think of Infantry as the military, so if they don't want to do Infantry, that's it. But who do I want for Covert Ops? Who does any legate, really, want for Covert Ops? Left-handers, elf-bloods, switchers, anybody who's different, anybody who will *think* differently than your average soldier. And they're just an after-thought in most training programs. You get a two-week unit in one survey course on special cohorts."

"Is that why you hired me? Because I'm different?"

"Isn't that why you applied?"

"No."

"Well, I'll tell you it didn't hurt. Anyway, you were good, and your record since then, frankly, it suggests you've gotten better. I'm happy to recommend you to b'Hanas, and him to you."

"You think I can teach?"

"I think you can run the place. They need a superintendent. But sure, you can teach, too. Why not?"

DARAS HANAS NERAN WAS A short, somewhat portly man just a few years older than Gwen. His wife had died some years earlier, and he had not remarried. Instead, he'd left his children with their grandparents and served some years as a devotee in a temple of the Hawk, then taken back his name and gotten interested in education. He had a substantial fortune and wanted to do something useful with it. He wore his hair in a single long braid down the back, as if to compensate for not having any hair at all on the very top of his head.

CHRYS, EVERYTHING'S GOING SPLENDIDLY. THE campus don't need much as far as renovation goes, only a few repairs to the older buildings, plus the addition of the new training pavilion and getting the gardens laid out and planted. There are fruit and nut orchards from the previous occupants and the prettiest little pond you can imagine. Every day we get something new sorted out and approved, whether it's the number of cooks we'll need to employ for the mess-hall or the details of the engineering curriculum, and the people I'm working with are really top-notch, intelligent, honorable, and they enjoy a good joke, all of them. Of course, this being the steel-belt, and a lot of them being more or less local, most of them would disagree with your father on certain things, but I don't see that as being a barrier. We agree on the work we're doing together, and that is the main thing.

I'm staying for now in the big house here with some of the others, though that's going to become classrooms and offices. We're designing new faculty housing—ours included. I'm attending to every little thing to make it all as nearly perfect as can reasonably be wanted. Chrys, I really do think you and the kids could come and live here now, even before our house is built, they'll make room for us somewhere, and I wish you would, as you'd love being here, and I want to show you everything. But if you feel that you really must stay with your mother, and I suppose you do, given her condition, know that I intend to come home for the Fallow, and then again around midsummer.

Tell Ellia I got her letter and will write back, only I've been indoors at my desk all day, and if I don't get out for a walk or something after dinner, my poor, dissatisfied mind is going to get up and leave without me, and without my mind I fear I couldn't write her a very interesting letter. Give my love to everybody, or—you know what I mean.

Ever yours,
Gwen

THE SCHOOL WAS GOING TO occupy the former site of a small fort whose garrison had been judged superfluous. Being in southern Parsia, it was geographically isolated—Parsia in general had no cities except for army bases, and even the market towns and shipping centers tended to be small. Most of the population lay scattered in tiny industrial villages, farming collectives, or villas, and there were still a few tribal long-house complexes like what they had up north, the native Slovonye community type. But Parsia was no back-water. Roads and canals and natural navigable waterways crisscrossed the country, including the great and perilous trade routes over the passes of the High Mountains, where caravans risked the displeasure of giants to trade with the peoples of the Great Eastern Steppe without having to go through—and pay tariffs to—the cities of Shoni.

The country about was green and lush, like Duchasia but drier and more open, all grassy woodlands of hickories, walnuts, chestnuts, six species of oaks, four of pine, apples, crab-apples, pears, peaches, plums, cherries, almonds, and ropy vines of sweet-tart grapes. The people bred beautiful and clever horses and sheep. The climate was warm, almost as warm as Nonani City. Gwen went home for the Fallow and then returned, finding that spring had come early to the southeastern forest and was, as she'd anticipated, full of the flowers of fruit trees and white rhododendron.

"NO, I *KNOW* HE'S MY father-in-law, but that don't mean he dictates my political views. Strictly speaking, I *don't* have political views. The protests are ridiculous. Half of the attendees are just kids causing trouble and using trendy ideals as an excuse. But if you think you need b'Rylas to defend yourselves against them, you're honestly just as ridiculous as they are. Look, nobody's coming to take your stuff. Nobody *wants* your stuff. All the progressives on the Council are trying to do is implement common-sense guidelines for the charcoal harvest so that the industry remains sustainable. Nobody's coming for your jobs, your furnaces, your factories, your houses.... The progressives need steel, too, you know."

"But there is no way to substantially reduce the charcoal harvest without also substantially reducing steel output. Without steel, no armies. Without armies, no slaves. Without slaves, the economy grinds to a halt. That's just math."

"You're a good man, b'Hanas, but your math is not better than mine. We're not looking at no steel. We're not even looking at reduced steel production necessarily. Greater efficiencies are possible, and with reduced charcoal supply as an incentive, we will see a burst of new technological development. We may end up not even needing charcoal at all."

"Is it your contention ore can be heated by burning ambition?"

Gwen smirk-snorted. The argument was amiable.

"No. Burn coal, maybe. Stuff comes out of the ground, burns hot, no problem."

HER BAY GELDING WAS WITH her. She could go riding when she liked.

And she'd had kept in touch with her old housekeeper from Ralani—unusually for a proletarian, the woman could read and write and had recently prevailed upon Gwen by letter to employ her son, Ricas, in some capacity. He was sixteen, now, a capable lad, though very much still a lad, and far from sure what he ought to be doing. And so Gwen had a servant of sorts. He acted as a kind of combination house-keeper, secretary, and stable-boy—though he was afraid of the horse, at first, which made things difficult—and Gwen tried to remember to address him professionally as b'Radas, and he tried to remember not to address her as Uncle, as he had back in Ralani when he was two.

The problem wasn't so much what b'Rylas was doing as what he wasn't doing. Speakers, by and large, did not originate policy, except in emergencies and then only until the slower processes of the Ruling Council could draft and vote on guidelines. Policy originated with the Ruling Council as led by and presided over by the coordinator. The speaker executed the will of the Council—but b'Rylas didn't.

Speakers had always tweaked policy a bit through creative prioritization, but b'Rylas was an extreme case. He hadn't even bothered to nominate anyone for half the positions of the King's House offices. At the midterm election, the number of progressives on the Council increased rather than decreased, but it didn't matter. They could do nothing. The resulting breakdowns in governance b'Rylas blamed on the Council.

Elves and derger across the empire, in protest, stopped buying steel products entirely, shifting over to bronze (which required substantially less charcoal to make), or in some cases bone, ivory, or stone, even plain wood. There were elves who would get seriously offended if an ubum even used steel in their presence. More and more ubum joined the boycott, too. Bronze suppliers were happy.

A daily rhythm. Meetings, inspections, writing up work orders, shopping lists, order forms, letters read and written in a professional

capacity. Dinner with the rest of the faculty and whichever of the board happened to be on campus that week. The food was simple, good, plentiful, like what Gwen had had in the army. Familiar. But after dinner, to hell with familiar and with paperwork and meetings as she went for long rides on her dark bay, exploring the woods and savannas through the afternoons and into the evening. On returning, she'd meet b'Hanas for a sweat in the steam-bath, and they'd talk about everything in the world. In the baths, he'd disrobe in front of her quite casually, as though she were his fellow man, which she appreciated. She sweated in an old tunic or a towel because looking down at her own naked body always made Gwen feel weird, but b'Hanas would oil and scrape her back for her, as he would have for a man. It was like having—and being—a brother. Afterwards, back at her room, she'd eat a rosemary roll and some sheep's milk cheese and honey, pour herself some wine, and by candle-light read and write personal letters until far too late at night.

Chrys sent weekly updates.

Ellia wrote almost as often. She said she liked a boy but he didn't like her back. She was almost twelve. Gwen thought her daughter ought to slow down, be a kid a little longer, and not grow up while Gwen was away.

Sherra was still reliably childlike. She rarely wrote. She was too busy teaching the ferrets tricks.

Toma wrote even less, usually a line or two in other people's letters. She was still learning; "deear dadddy we wento the bull sacrifice to day and one of the buls ran away he wasnt brave or pious so I dont think he should have been sacrifised but he was I love you sincerely yor dawter TOMA."

Of course, Gwenias and Jayd were too young to write at all, but they sent pictures. Gwen sent pictures of her own back.

Paracelias had a friend, a younger man interested in shepherding, philosophy, and possibly other things. It amused and irritated Paracelias that ubum men made such a point of relative status in relation to sex. All the complicated rules. He thought doing without the rules and seeing what might happen would be a lot more fun. Gwen told him she was sure it would have been—with another elf. I've never really dated elves, he admitted in his reply. I rarely see any. He enclosed the text of his latest paper.

Opal, Topaz, Sammas, Tomas, Chalcy, plus occasional letters to a dozen or so other people. Micalion rarely wrote, and Orpharias never did. Gwen wrote to them.

Sleep. At least a little. Then, another day.

MIDSUMMER, GWEN WENT HOME TO Nonani City for two months. Orpharias was visiting, playing with Gwenias, Jade, and two of Topaz's kids, the five-year-old and the six-year-old. The kids chattered and laughed, demanded piggyback rides, and all talked at once apparently not realizing that made them hard to understand. Gwen spotted the exact moment Orph had had enough. He stopped smiling, looked confused or overwhelmed, but did nothing about it, only sat on the atrium floor, looking dazed. The six-year-old, an eager, assertive girl, spotted the change too and laughed. Noticing that he barely reacted to her laughter, she screamed playfully in Orpharias's face. He froze, paralyzed like a frog shown a lantern at night. The girl giggled and screamed again. Then suddenly both the cousins and little Jade were crawling all over Orpharias, screaming at him, touching him, blowing on him and laughing at his funny reactions. Gwen stood up, ready to rescue her brother, when Gwenias, assessing the situation, preempted her.

"Stop doing that to him!" he shouted, and when that had no effect, he waded into the fray, bodily disrupting the other children. "I'll save you, Uncle Orpharias! I love you!" the little boy cried. "You leave him alone, I'll cut your damn heads off!"

"Well, that escalated quickly," Gwen commented, much impressed.

THE SCHOOL'S SOFT OPENING! A dozen or so cadets were joining the program mid-year. Gwen had moved into her new house, though the garden wasn't planted yet and most of the rooms were not furnished. She kept trying, by letter, to talk Chrys into joining her.

NEWS! GWEN HAD A COPY made at the newshouse in the nearest town. A group of proletarian ex-soldiers, hundreds of them, now openly associating with the Iron Eagle, had planned to invade and destroy a neighborhood of ethnic Aethenye laborers in Zerasi. The article didn't quite say that—what it said was that the ex-soldiers had planned a demonstration for jobs and economic protections, but who takes a peaceful political demonstration through somebody else's quiet residential community? Gwen could read between the lines. Everybody could. Anyway, activists had learned of the ex-soldiers' plans, and thousands of non-Aethenye allies turned out to protect the neighborhood with sticks and stones and their own bodies. But the veterans had a permit to march, and so the city garrison deployed to re-open the approved route. The soldiers and activists fought in the streets. The soldiers fought with clubs, unwilling to use blades against civilians, but they were out-numbered. Eventually, they dispersed lime dust from a cart parked upwind of the activists. The caustic dust effectively dispersed the crowd, but as the dust remained hanging in the air for much of the rest of the day, the permitted march couldn't go ahead either.

"Hey, they stopped the attack! The civilians won!" b'Hanas exclaimed, indicating his own copy of the article. He liked b'Rylas but disliked the growing and sometimes violent ethnic tension. He refused to acknowledge that the one had anything to do with the other.

"That's not the good news you think it is," Gwen cautioned. "When civilians fight with soldiers and win, it's a bad day."

"You think the soldiers were *right* to facilitate the murderous vandals?" he asked.

"The Iron Eagle weren't murdering anybody or vandalizing anybody. They had a permit for a peaceful, organized demonstration."

"That's not what they were going to do, though."

"Last time I checked, the army did not have any soothsayer personnel." Gwen said, facetious. Nonanye generally did believe in soothsayers and often hired them, but the army considered their predictions unreliable and never employed any. "Anyway, if a soothsayer *did* predict murderous vandalism, it would be a bad idea to try to oppose it, if the epics have any truth to them."

B'Hanas starred, incredulous.

"They were going after your people, Gwen! Followers! Like your family. The Iron Eagle *could* come for your family next—and *you*, they don't like elf-bloods much, either."

"Or switchers. B'Rylas said last week that people like me ought to be married to men, by force if necessary." She watched b'Hanas turn away from her a moment, his face a complexity of shame, anger, and stubbornness. "It's not my contention that these folks are good, upstanding citizens. They are, by and large, criminals and criminal-sympathizers. But we have a process for dealing with criminals, and that process is *not* for citizens to violently oppose the lawful actions of other citizens whom they happen not to like."

"Do you honestly think the process was going to protect the Aethenye community that day?"

"No. But *that* is the problem, not the duty of the garrison to protect due process and public order. You can't uphold the law by breaking it, let alone by *pre-emptively* breaking it so that other people do not break it afterwards."

"Even if the law itself is a broken, wrong thing?"

"If the law is broken, we've got bigger problems than the rights of Aethenye people," Gwen asserted. "Look, it comes down to what sort of society are we going to be? Who will be our master, the principles of fair process, the law of the Empire, or the personal whims of thirty-five million people?"

"I hardly think 'don't burn Aethenye houses' is a whim."

"Why not? Because you share it? Because I do? Do you support all lawless mobs, or only those you happen to agree with? Consider, there are approximately ten million adult Nonani citizens. Nine hundred thousand or so of them are plebeians, the class that comprises the overwhelming majority of professed progressives. So, considering that not all plebeians are politically alike, but neither are all non-plebeians, we can guess there are about one million adults with some degree of real progressive sentiment. Most of them are self-funded from fortunes of moderate size at best. Applying the same logic gives us *nine million, two hundred thousand* potential supporters of the Iron Eagle, funded by wealthy patrician businessmen who can collectively raise at least twenty million denarii for political action any time they like. Now, do you prefer to live in a Nonani of laws and due process, or a Nonani where each person does exactly as they please?"

"B'Sheras, why aren't you a lawyer?"

"Technically, I am a lawyer." She waved away b'Hanas's shock. "Long story. I never intended to practice."

THE DARK BAY GELDING DIED. It was a long illness, and Gwen could do nothing about it. She finally had to put him down. Poor horse.

FALLOW AGAIN. HOME AGAIN, HOME again, jiggity jig. Why *wouldn't* Chrys move to campus?

BACK TO CAMPUS. FLOWERS AGAIN. The house was fully furnished, now, the garden planted. B'Hanas gave Gwen a new horse, a gentle buckskin mare, a good animal. Poor, lost bay.

THE SCHOOL WAS OFFICIALLY, FULLY open now, with a full compliment of cadets beginning the year. All had completed at least two years at a standard academy and were thus at least sixteen or seventeen years old. None were actually elf-bloods, but there were some switchers—oddly, Gwen felt no particular sisterhood with them. They were girls interested in doing men's work. Some of them performed very well, and all met or exceeded the standard of the boys. But they were not like Gwen. Whatever Gwen was. She did not have a word for herself.

Gwen did teach classes, as well as superintend—she was the katana master, a strict, demanding teacher, but the cadets rose to the challenge and respected her for it. Teaching was a lot of fun.

She also told stories. Sitting with one or another group of cadets at dinner, hanging out with a few of them in the library during study period, or they'd come find her on her porch or by the pond, they'd ask questions. I heard you once did.... What would you do if.... Tell my friend here about the time you.... Some of the stories were about her travels in Aethenia and Slovona or even her own time as a cadet, but most concerned her brief service in Covert Ops. They wanted to know what it was like. They wanted scenes in which they could imagine themselves.

Gwen remembered that back when she was a cadet, some of the professors, the ones who had actually been soldiers, had told stories. At the time, she'd assumed that some professors just liked to talk, but now, looking back on it, she realized that there is only so much that can be imparted in a classroom. Storytelling helps fill the gap.

Also, yes, some professors like to talk.

A MARKET TOWN SAT SOME miles from campus. That's where Gwen

and some of the others would go to get the mail or visit a newshouse, or sometimes to visit one of the modest but pretty temples. It's also where two women, followers, were themselves followed on their way home from a praise-singing and assaulted. People were saying things, too, sometimes openly. Gwen wrote to Chrys telling her *not* to come. They'd wait until after the baby was born and figure out what to do then.

IN THE MOMENT BEFORE AN historical moment, nothing is foreordained. Nothing is obvious, nothing is historical, except in retrospect. And yet something is happening. There is instability. There is fear. Something is different, now. Something has changed.

A SPEAKER SERVES A FOUR-year term, and can serve another and another. There is no limit on the total number, only the stipulation that there be an election every four years and only the first two may be consecutive.

The first two can be consecutive.

B'RYLAS HAD PURGED THE JUSTICE Department soon after taking office, removing every single appointed official remaining from the previous administration. The resulting chaos in the courts had made it harder to investigate environmental crimes and so forth, but gradually he had re-filled the positions, and now, three years into his first term, he finally had a full roster again. Of course, the vast majority were personally loyal to him. None of them objected when he ordered an investigation of potentially disloyal elements.

SENATOR LIAN WAS RUNNING FOR the speakership, a move widely thought to be bad for his health. Gwen read the text of a number of his speeches. They were very good.

"DO YOU REALIZE B'RYLAS HAS bought half the news services? He's bought the comedians, actors, and athletes the proletarians listen to, and now he's bought the news services everyone else relies on. He'll buy every brain he can find for sale."

"You're exaggerating. You're listening to rumor. Anyway, he's a businessman, it's what he does. He can keep that separate from politics."

"Yes, but why would he? Politics is money and power. Business is money and power. Politics is business, business is politics, QED."

"If you feel that way about it, go on relying on rumor for your news, then."

"Can't. He bought rumor ten years ago."

"GWEN, YOU'VE GOT TO GET out of here, you know you're on the list." B'Hanas spoke quietly, urgently, in the steam-room.

"Have you seen such a list?"

"No. Nobody has. But you check all the boxes. They're purging the military. They're going to come after the training academies next."

"I hadn't thought you were so loyal as to fire me, Daras."

"I'm not! I'm not *loyal* at all, I only support b'Rylas now because b'Seras is worse. I don't want my children's inheritance given away to derger and to forest-savages, is that so wrong? But no, I will never fire you. If ordered to, I'd disobey. I'd take up the katana for you,

Gwen, except I'd probably cut my nose off—" that earned a chuckle. B'Hanas was not just untrained but also clumsy "—but, Gwen, not all the people declared enemies of the King are fired. Not all of them are arrested. Some just disappear."

"I can't leave, I've got responsibilities."

"That's exactly why you can't stay."

Gwen sighed.

"I've never had...."

"I know."

"OK, I've got leave coming up for the baby's birth. I'll start wrapping things up and make my resignation effective then."

"No, that won't do, either. If they see you running, that will convict you in certain people's minds. Everyone around here sees themselves as patriots. You've got to get back to Nonani City before anybody knows you're worried. There are more progressives there, you won't be in danger from the mob. But I wouldn't let it get out that you're traveling to go see your child born, either."

"Alright, what do you suggest?"

ONE FINE SUMMER AFTERNOON, GWEN walked into the mess hall for dinner, as she always did, the happy chatter of boys and young men engulfing her. She almost smiled.

"A moment of silent prayer for those who so desire," she called, just as always. The chatter stopped. The moment passed. "Hail to the King!"

"Hail to the King!" came the massed reply. And the chatter started up again. The room smelled of grilled fish, healthy sweat, dill, and caramelized onions. She found herself a place and served herself from the trays and bowls and baskets on the table, like always. She chatted casually with the boys at her table, like always. It was a good meal. She ate heartily. But she skipped the custard dessert and instead shook the hand of every boy at her table, then got up and slowly, casually, wandered the room, shaking hands, squeezing shoulders, exchanging a word or two. It wasn't unusual for her to get up before the end of the meal, nor was it unusual for her to walk around talking with this or that person among the tables before she left, but....

Gradually, the cadets noticed she was talking to, greeting, touching *everybody*. The chatter changed in tone.

At last, Gwen finished her tour of the room. Everyone grew silent. Just inside the half-open door, she stopped and turned back, looking at her cadets. She opened her mouth to speak, but no sound came out. She touched her chest over her heart, a brief, jerky movement, almost as if she hadn't meant to do it, and then she left the room. Waiting for her on the other side of the door was b'Hanas.

"They don't know why you did that," he said.

"Some of them do," Gwen replied. "But I didn't tell them—and they won't tell anyone else."

"Did you tell anyone? Any of the other faculty? Anyone on the board?"

"No. Of course not. We talked about this. My wife don't even know yet."

"Good."

He walked her outside, then down to the barns where Ricas had the buckskin mare and another, a light bay, another gift from b'Hanas, already saddled, their saddle bags packed. Gwen greeted the boy and then the horses, then turned to b'Hanas.

"Telegraph me at the post-office when you get home," b'Hanas said. "I'll have your things sent then."

"Thank you." Was there something else to say? They looked at each other.

"If war comes..." b'Hanas said.

"War has come," Gwen asserted. "This," she indicated the waiting horses, "is a response to war. It's just that my side hasn't started fighting yet."

"If war comes," b'Hanas continued, "we'll be on different sides."

"Only on the battlefield, my friend. Where I trust you will not be, lest you cut off your own nose." That got a smile. They took each other's hands a moment. There wasn't anything left to say.

THE NEW CHILD WAS ANOTHER boy. He looked a lot like Gwenias, but a little smaller, and with chestnut brown hair, not red. They named him Lyras.

Gwen got a job teaching various martial arts at the local gymnasium. It was not her idea of a good career move overall, but it was available, the pay was more than decent, and the commute was wonderfully short.

In the fall came the election. The priestesses kept the Fallow in the temple, counting, and then kept their silence until after Hilaria, when one of their number spoke in the Curia, first reading out the names of the people who had won Council-seats, and then the name of the new Speaker: Abbas Seras Lian.

There was dancing in the streets that night away in the plebeian neighborhoods, a blooming of distant sound, auditory phosphorescence, in the dark.

"WE, THE SISTERS OF THE King's Hearth, do hereby decline to recount the vote. We counted it correctly the first time, the results are not close nor in any way ambiguous, and so we would only recount it the same way again. Further, as the only possible way that the count could be wrong would be if we had miscounted, we resent the implication that we are in this moment out of all the moments in the long history of our order, either uniquely incompetent or uniquely corrupt. And were we either, our counting again would obviously not fix the problem, so we must conclude this request is either political theater or an invitation for us to in fact miscount. We reject both."

The next morning, large rag-dolls made to look like naked women were found scattered across the paving-stones of the Upper Forum, their throats painted yellow in imitation of the Sisters' bronze discs, their crotches painted red.

Jonas met Gwen at the retention pond in the Upper Forum. The morning was unseasonably cool, to the point that Gwen wore a cloak. Jonas did not. He'd left his in his employer's office in the Curia. He was a middling man in height, middling to wiry of build, slim and fit though now past forty, with a handsome, oval face, bushy eyebrows, large, blue eyes, and a complexion somewhat paler than either of his parents, a medium brown. He was said to take after a maternal great-aunt he'd never met. He wore his hair in the same mop-like fade Gwen had always favored or, rather, the other way around, as he'd had it first. His eyes crinkled into a smile even when his mouth did not.

"Thanks for getting me an appointment," Gwen said, by way of hello.

"Don't mention it," he replied. "Come on."

They went up the steps to the front door of the Curia, where the guard took Gwen's pugio and greeted Jonas cordially by name. They made their way to the Coordinator's office, where Jonas rapped on the door.

"Who's there?" asked a voice. It was high and soft, for a man's voice, with a thick Galasye accent.

"It's b'Tomas, sir. I'm here with Gwenessifyr Sheras Euan. She has an appointment?"

"Sure, sure. Come in." They did, and found a man putting a scroll back in its case. "Sorry about the closed door," he said. "But I find if I leave it open, everyone comes in, and then I can't get any reading done." He stood, hands clasped behind his back, and regarded them. He was a tall man, taller than Gwen and almost as thin, with an angular face and ears that appeared to belong to someone else, somebody larger—ears, hands, feet, limbs, like a teenage boy or a newborn colt he seemed to be composed mostly of parts that didn't match. His hair was a collection of narrow, neat dreadlocks of various lengths, a style calculated to not need much upkeep, and his clothing, charcoal gray with gold embroidery, was elegant of make but rumpled. Looking at him, Gwen had the strange impression that he looked younger than he was, although she did not know his age.

"Coordinator Lian, sir," Jonas said. "This is my sister, the son of Sheras."

"Ah, yes, son of Sheras," he greeted her. "Your brother says you have something to tell me?"

"Yes, sir. I am in contact with people from all over the Empire and all across the city here, and all say the same—that more proletarians than not believe that the vote was rigged and that your election was illegitimate. They believe you are a usurper. They are angry and ready to act. Sir, something is going to happen, some violent convulsion, on or before your inauguration. They will try to prevent your taking power, because they honestly think it to be wrong."

"Do you have positive intelligence of this 'something' happening?"

"I do not. I say only what all with eyes to see and a mind to understand know."

"Why are you informing me of what you say only an idiot doesn't know already?"

Gwen blushed and looked away for a moment. She hadn't meant it to come out that way.

"I'm not, sir," she tried to explain. "I'm only letting you know what I'm talking about so that what I have to say will appear in its proper context. It is this: get ready. Your term must, in a practical sense, begin now, as you will not have time to craft your response when the crisis happens. Make what plans you must. And if you need help, I am here. I can return to the army, or I will serve in whatever other capacity you need, if I am able."

The Speaker-Elect looked at her a quick moment, an intelligent, piercing look, as though he'd noticed something. Then he chuckled.

"Well, I thank you for your offer and your dedication. I may call on you. But understand I have a lot of good men around and behind me, and this is not, as they say, my first rodeo. I think we've got things well in hand."

Jonas and Gwen were hurrying down the steps outside on their way to get a bite to eat when Gwen suddenly erupted.

"ALL POLITICIANS SUCK! *All* of them!"

"Present company excepted, I'm sure," muttered Jonas, rolling his eyes, but Gwen ignored him.

"He might as well have said 'don't worry your pretty little head.' Do I deserve that? I don't think I deserve that. My *record* don't deserve that. He must know I'm right, but he blows me off. What the hell. He talks a lot of radical, 'progressive' nonsense during his campaign, and when the inevitable fruits of that tree come ripe, he has no plan to gather and protect them from the crows. Self-serving, hypocritical..." she went on. Jonas had stopped walking, still on the steps, but Gwen could not stop moving just then so, like the fairy in the story who must fly so fast that she makes circles around her slower companions in order to converse with them, Gwen danced around Jonas, up and down the steps, in a hyperactive orbit.

"Gwen." No reaction.

"Gwen!" She did not seem to hear him.

"Gwen, STOP." She finally stopped, mid-sentence. They faced each other. "Not here, not now, and *not so loud*!" Jonas paused a moment to be sure he had her attention. "First, I *am* a politician."

"You have your moments, too."

"Man, it's a good thing I love you, ya know that?"

Gwen dropped her gaze and shuffled one foot.

"I love you, too," she said, grudgingly, like a chastened child.

"Good. Now, I don't think your pretty head has anything to do with it. He can see you're wearing a tunic, and even if he couldn't, his wife was one of his campaign managers. He's not an idiot about women. Did it occur to you that you went in there like you were lecturing a schoolboy? Did it occur to you that you don't have any particular security clearance? What else was he going to tell you, other than to stand by?"

"So there is a plan?"

"I can't tell you that."

"But *you* have a high security clearance?"

"I do."

"So what's the plan?"

"Gwen!"

"Jonas, two of the people I love most in all the world *and* the beating heart of the Empire itself will be in the Curia on Inauguration Day. Tell me there's a plan!"

"There is a plan."

"So, what is it?"

"I can't tell you...yet. When you need to know, I'll tell you. You will have a role."

"Good."

THE NEXT FEW WEEKS WERE uneventful. Normal. The Council announced that because of vague security concerns the exchange of power and the swearing-in would take place indoors at the Curia, before the Council alone. There would be no public event until the following day.

The outgoing Speaker made no attempt to move out of the King's House. He did not cooperate with transition efforts. He continued to insist that he had been re-elected.

"YOU KNOW, I DON'T THINK he actually has an exit strategy. Once he's out of the King's House, there won't be any barrier to the investigation and prosecution of any crimes he may have committed—the disappearance of some of the people on his enemies list, for example."

LYRAS LEARNED TO SIT UP.

IT FELT ODD NOT TO go to the Forum for Inauguration Day. Normally as many people as possible crowded in, thousands and thousands, and Gwen had been among them most Inauguration Days of her life. But this time the event would be private, indoors, the public actually barred from the entire Upper Forum for the day. Had anybody asked, Gwen would have advised just such a departure from tradition, but it still felt strange, and as the morning wore on, she became more and more convinced that something bad was going to happen anyway. Ellia, almost as tall as Gwen now, stood at the front door, listening. Gwen stood behind her, leaning on the doorjamb. No one with ubum ears could have heard anything unusual, but the vast chatter of the city had changed, grown concentrated and mean. The mob, excluded from the Upper Forum, had gathered instead in the Lower.

"Come on, Jonas, what's the plan?" she muttered.

But of course Jonas wasn't there. He was at work, in the Curia. She paced up and down.

The women and children of the household were all present and accounted for, mostly in the garden or the kitchen at the moment, except Opal was upstairs in bed—she was having a bad day—and Chrys was with her. Charas was at his office, which had once been Tomas's office. Tomas himself was at work, meaning in danger, and—

"I know the plan."

She was so startled by the realization that she said it aloud, though nobody was in the room to hear. But she had to be right. If things went severely pear-shaped, the city would become dangerous for the entire family because of their association with Tomas, so whatever else Jonas might have set up, part of the plan must be to move the family somewhere else, somewhere either secret or defensible. He would have location and means of transport already chosen, and would send a messenger if and when it was time. The key would be to get ready.

She called a meeting and briefed the family and the servants. The servants were staying—their choice, they had families of their own and weren't at risk from the mob—except for Ricas, who would follow Gwen. As he put it, she was a good boss, and he had nothing else lined up. She thanked him and sent him off to get the horses from the boarding stable at the end of the street, and from there to go find Charas at the warehouse and find out if he was coming. Euas was too far away to go ask, but Jonas knew that and must have planned for it. Then she deputized both Topaz's oldest and Ellia to keep the younger kids calm and orderly, assigned Sherra to find the ferrets and close them up in a basket for travel, and set Chrys and Topaz to packing necessities. She wished she had a cart available, but wheeled vehicles were illegal on the city streets except at night, so the family did not own one. The backs of people and horses would have to do. Opal, too weak today to walk, would ride. Ricas returned with Charas—he was staying to look after the house and business but would see his family off in person. Everything moved swiftly and smoothly. Nobody panicked or wasted time.

And yet, for all her preparation, when the messenger from Jonas actually arrived—

Gwen ran out in the street and looked west, towards center-city. She could not see the three hills from where she stood, miles of two- and three-story buildings and street-trees being in the way, but—

A black column of thick smoke rose high into the impossible air.

"*Father!*" she cried out, and neither she nor anyone else could say for sure to whom she called.

A Note on Living Things

If you're a natural science geek, like me, you may have noticed something odd about some of the plants in this book. Even if you're not a geek, you've probably noticed something odd about the animals.

First, the plants. As you can probably tell, the subcontinent Nonani occupies ("west of the Mountains") is loosely speaking, a Europe analogue. And yet there are wild plants mentioned that aren't native to Europe. Did I make a mistake?

No.

The deal is that Europe has fewer native plants than either Asia or North America do—in fact, there are a number of plant genera that exist in both North America and Asia but not Europe. I don't know whether the matter has been formally studied, but I have heard at least a suggested explanation. Basically, because Europe has mountain ranges that run east-west, during the ice ages, plants trying to shift their ranges south ahead of the ice couldn't get over the mountains and went extinct. In contrast, both North America and Asia have passages allowing north/south range shifts.

Also, there are a lot of plant species in North America that were once wide-spread but are now either restricted to very small patches or dependent on humans. These include Osage orange, avocado, Joshua tree, and various gourd species. There is some thought that these plants depended on now-extinct megafauna, such as giant ground-sloths or mastodons to disperse their seeds. I assume the same pattern exists on all continents that have lost their megafauna. There are holes in the natural world....

But in the world of my book, the Europe analogue has north-south passageways AND an intact megafauna, so neither of these extinction patterns could have occurred. So I looked for plant genera that North America and Asia, but not Europe, have in common or once had in common, or that existed in Europe before the ice ages and persist elsewhere now. I added these back in to the "European" forests. These include hemlock, baldcypress, Douglas-fir, metasequoia, honey locust, and false-cedar. I also looked for Eurasian plants that have very limited native ranges but do well across much larger areas if humans plant them, especially if they have very large fruits. These include apples, pears, peaches, and melons. I added them in, too. I also added a strychnos species, since that genus is found in Asia and often has very hard rinds, and an imaginary orchid vine, because there are real Asian orchids pollinated by dung beetles. The extinction of the European megafauna almost certainly meant the extinction of insects, such as specialist dung beetles, co-evolved with those large mammals, and likely also plants co-evolved with those insects.

And that brings us to the animals—you hold in your hands a book in which, among other puzzles, both unicorns and griffins appear to be...rhinoceroses? What kind of fantasy book is this!

It's a wonderful kind of fantasy book.

The thing is, unicorns were unquestionably real. The long-extinct Siberian unicorn, a species of rhinoceros, closely matches the original description of the unicorn written by Pliny. He was writing natural history, not fantasy or mythology, and he'd been told these things existed. Is it a coincidence that some ignorant ancient made up a real but extinct animal? No. Nor could it have been an interpretation of fossils; as the horn itself doesn't seem to have fossilized, untrained people would not have known how to recognize the signs that a horn might have been there. No, Pliny was told about unicorns because he was the end of a long chain of people telling stories about an animal that the first person in the chain had seen alive. Humans and unicorns co-existed. We know about unicorns today because somebody saw them and told other people what they had seen—and if you're sitting there disappointed that "unicorns were only rhinoceroses," then you haven't seen a wild rhinoceros. I mean, I haven't either, but I have seen wild deer, and if seeing deer is a magical experience, how much cooler must a *rhinoceros* be?

Unicorns were real. What else might have been?

For the purpose of this story, I am assuming that *all* the fantastic beasts of myths and legend were real animals, were, in fact, the ice-age megafauna. And I'm writing about a world in which these animals aren't extinct. So that's the kind of fantasy book this is. I'm not pretending to live in a world in which magical beasts are possible. They *are* possible. Some still live, though mostly they aren't doing well. I'm pretending that I can see them, and so can you. I'm pretending that we don't live in a world of holes but in a world that is still whole.

Nothing is ever so bad that we can't keep it from getting worse.

The following list is a kind of zoological glossary showing what animals I actually have in mind (I've included a few plants I've had to re-name for various reasons). A few minutes' searching online on both the fantastical names and the scientific ones will show you what I was working with and also give you a sense of what is actually known about these species verses what I made up. Please note that if the scientific name has only one part, that means I made up the species (but not the genus). Also, not all these are extinct. Some just go by unusual names or turn up in unexpected places.

Arctas: Brown bear, *Ursus arctos*, the familiar Eurasian species.

Aurochs: *Bos primigenius*, the wild ancestor of domestic cattle. Very big and very dangerous.

Calista: Asian black bear, *Ursus thibetanus*, a species that in our world is restricted to Asia.

Cattle (cow or bull): yes, domestic cattle, *Bos taurus*, but these have only been domesticated within the past five or six thousand years, so they are much closer to their wild ancestors. They resemble Spanish fighting cattle and can be almost as aggressive if not handled correctly.

Milk yields are low by our standards. Variable, but not separated into different breeds.

Crocodile: *Crocoylus sp.* A species related to the saltwater crocodile, C. porosus, and, like it, capable of living in salty, brackish, or fresh water. Typically grows ten or fifteen feet long, but can get larger.

Crocotta: Cave hyena, *Crocuta spelaea*. Closely related to the African spotted hyena, and similar to them in shape and color, but larger, heavier, and shaggier. The name, crocotta, refers in our world to a mythical being almost certainly based on either this species or its African relative.

Derger: Neanderthal, *Homo sapiens neanderthalis*, a human species or subspecies adapted to ice-age Europe. Whether they are the same species as us or only a different subspecies is unclear, as hybrids were clearly possible, but there are suggestions that the fertility of mixed pairings was low.

Dicorn: either of two closely-related rhinoceros species. The forest dicorn (Merck's rhino, *Stephanorhinus kirchbergensis*) and the slightly smaller steppe dicorn (narrow-nosed rhino, *Stephanorhinus hemitoechus*) have different habitat preferences but are sometimes found together.

Dog: yes, domestic dog, *Canis familiaris*, but the breeds readers are familiar with don't exist in this story. These are generally mutts of six broad types: collies (for herding), sheep-guards, scent hounds, sight hounds, army dogs (also used as guard dogs or personal protection), and terriers (for pest-control and hunting small game).

Dragon: *Varanus sp.* A large monitor lizard related to the un-named species found in Greece from the Pleistocene. Typically four to six feet long at maturity and venomous. Their bites hurt like fire.

Elf: *Homo sp.* Another human species or subspecies. Although the idea of a second native Eurasian human was suggested to me by the existence of Denisovans, I made no attempt to give elves specifically Denisovan characteristics.

Gharial: *Gavialis sp.* A freshwater crocodilian specialized for eating fish. Similar to our Indian gharial, but smaller (seldom more than ten feet long) and even more aquatic. Some never come to land except to breed.

Giant: *Australopithecus sp.* A very large, ape-like hominid with thick body-hair. Males can be twelve feet tall. Females are seldom more than ten, and often shorter. They do not wear clothing or use fire, depending on hair and subcutaneous fat for warmth in the winter.

Griffin: Woolly rhinoceros, *Coelodonta antiquitatis*, a rhinoceros species whose remains have long been associated with the mythical griffin-bird. In the world of this story, there are two subspecies, northern and southern, both found on or near open steppe or wooded savanna.

Horse: domestic horse, *Equus ferus caballus*, but only domesticated within the past five or six thousand years. They are therefore much closer to their wild ancestors. Only a single breed exists, though there is some variation in size. They are small, sturdy animals, often highstrung and stubborn.

Hydruntine: *Equus hydruntinus*, a species of wild ass, with subspecies in both the northern and southern steppes. Typically a pale or orangish dun in color with a white muzzle.

Kelpie: European hippopotamus, *Hippopotamus antiquus*. Our mythical kelpies are usually described as water-horses, and it's worth noting that the word "hippopotamus" is simply derived from the Greek for "river-horse." Hippos are strict vegetarians, but they are seriously dangerous.

Leviathan: sperm whale, *Physeter macrocephalus*. Actually, the term can be applied to any whale or even to very large fish, since Nonanye knowledge of marine life is imprecise, but sperm whale is the strictest definition.

Lion: Cave lion, *Panthera spelaea*, a large lion-like or tiger-like predator. Typical coat color is yellow-ivory. Males are larger than females but lack manes. They are slightly larger than African lions and gregarious, but only semi-cooperative in hunting.

Mammoth: Woolly mammoth *Mammuthus primigenius*, a grassland-adapted elephant species that has, by the time of this story, diverged into two distinct subspecies. The northern mammoth is very similar to the historical woolly mammoth, but the southern mammoth is smaller, less woolly, with blond rather than red-brown hair and larger ears.

Manticore: Scimitar-toothed cat, *Homotherium latidens*, a lion-sized big cat with very big teeth (not as long as a saber-tooth) and forelegs are significantly longer than the rear legs. Unlike lions, it does not roar and has a somewhat higher, almost musical voice. The fur is red, often with vague spots, and is shaggy and thick in the winter but shorter and thinner in the summer. The tail is very short and normally carried raised and slightly curved over the back, somewhat reminiscent of a scorpion tail. Hunts most often in well-coordinated groups, taking larger prey than lions can. The only animals the manticore can't kill are olifants and lions.

Metasequoia: One or more species in the *Metasequoia genus*, a deciduous conifer capable of reaching two hundred and fifty feet. Dawn redwood, in our world, is an example.

Noble Maple: Norway maple, *Acer platanoides*, a large, fast-growing tree.

Olifant: Straight-tusked elephant, *Palaeoloxodon antiquus*, an elephant-like animal up to fourteen feet tall at the shoulder. This means a big olifant bull could be twice the shoulder-height of a small southern-mammoth cow. The tusks aren't completely straight, but are usually straighter than those of similar animals. This is also the species that gave rise to some of the island dwarf elephant populations.

Orange Pine: Scots pine, *Pinus sylvestris*, an early-successional pine with orange bark on the branches.

Panther: Cave leopard, *Panthera pardus spelaea*, a subspecies of the African leopard. It is a little larger than its African relative and shaggier, with no spots on its belly. Note that "panther" was originally the name of a mythical animal.

Phoenix: *Leptoptilos sp.* A species of giant marabou stork standing up to six feet tall. Capable of flight for very short distances. Seeks out wildfires or areas that have recently burned so as to hunt animals confused or injured by the fire and to scavenge.

Red Deer: *Cervis elaphus*, is what we in North America would call an elk. Europeans use the word, "elk" for what we call a moose. Apparently Europeans gave European names to North American animals a little haphazardly. But red deer and North American elk are not identical, being either separate subspecies or closely-related species, and since this book has a quasi-European setting, it is the European animal I mean.

Roc: Teratornis, *Teratornis sp.* An extremely large eagle-like or condor-like bird with a weight of over thirty pounds and a wingspan of twelve feet. An active predator as well as a scavenger. Although in our world teratornis remains have only been recovered from the

Americas, so far, the possibility of an undiscovered Eurasian species is intriguing, since they could have been big enough to fly off with the calf of an island dwarf species of elephant.

Siren: Humpback whale, *Megaptera novaeangliae*. Although sirens are more commonly associated with manatees and dugongs, humpback whales sing. Also, humpback whales, unlike manatees or dugongs, are found in the Mediterranean, making them a better candidate for the origin of the myth.

Sheep: *Ovis aries*. Another recently-domesticated animal. There are actually two different breeds, each descended from a different wild subspecies of mouflon (*Ovis gmelini*). The eastern sheep is larger with greater milk yields, while the western sheep is easier to manage and more tolerant of hot weather. Both are small, less than three feet at the shoulder, both come in multiple colors and have two to six horns, and both naturally shed their wool in the spring—by brushing the animal early in the shedding process, most of the wool can be harvested without the guard hairs. Some have wool that can be spun, some can be used only for felt.

Tarpan: *Equus ferus ferus*, a wild, never domesticated horse. Small, stocky, and variable in coat color.

Unicorn: *Elasmotherium sibiricum*, an extremely large (shoulder height up to eight feet) rhinoceros with a shaggy coat and a single large horn set high on the head, over the eyes.

Water-Hound: *Megalenhydris sp.*, a species of giant otter six to twelve feet long. Although it primarily feeds on fish, crustaceans, and shellfish, it is capable of killing large animals and can run at more than twenty miles per hour for short distances—meaning it can out-run some horses. They are territorial and live in family groups. Kill one member of the family, and the others will take revenge.

Yeti: cave bear, *Ursus spelaeus*, similar in size, shape, and color to a large brown bear (arctas), but lives mostly on fruit, seeds, and carrion.

Recommended Resources

The Civil War [TV program]
1990. Ken Burns

Occidental Mythology (Masks of God, Volume III)
1964. Joseph Campbell
Penguin Books

Grant
2017. Ron Chernow
Penguin Press

Life in Ancient Rome
1976. Frank Richard Crowell
Penguin Publishing Group

The Science of Open Spaces: Theory and Practice for Conserving Large, Complex Systems
2015. Charles G. Curtin
Island Press

Abraham Lincoln
1940. I. d'Aulaire, E.P. d'Aulaire
Beautiful Feet Books

Grant and Sherman: The Friendship that Won the Civil War
2006. Charles Bracelen Flood
Harper Perennial

Memoirs and Selected Letters: Personal Memoirs of U.S. Grant, Selected Letters 1839-1865
1990. U.S. Grant
M.D. McFeely, W.S. McFeely (Editors)
Library of America

Lincoln's Generals' Wives: Four Women Who Influenced the Civil War—for Better and for Worse
2016. Candice Shy Hooper
The Kent State University Press

Why Is This Happening? Live with Chris Hayes and Rachel Maddow [TV program]
2024. Chris Hayes, Rachel Maddow

A Short History of the Irish Revolution: 1912 to 1927
2007. Richard Killeen
Gill Books

Julius Caesar: The Making of a Dictator [TV program]
2023. A. Leith (Producer)
E. Frank, R. Pearson (Directors)

City: A Story of Roman Planning and Construction
1983. David MacAulay
Clarion Books

Nature's Temples: A Natural History of Old-Growth Forests (Revised and Expanded)
2023. Joan Maloof
Princeton University Press

And There Was Light: Abraham Lincoln and the American Struggle
2022. Jon Meacham
Random House

Fierce Patriot: The Tangles Lives of William Tecumseh Sherman
2014. Robert L. O'Connell
Random House

Grant and Twain: The Story of an American Friendship
2005. Mark Perry
Random House

Memoirs of General W.T. Sherman
1990. William Tecumseh Sherman
C. Royster (Editor)
Library of America

Sherman's Civil War: Selected Correspondence, 1860–1865
1999. William Tecumseh Sherman
B.D. Simpson, J.V. Berlin (Editors)
The University of North Caroline Press

The Practice of the Wild
1990. Gary Snyder
Farrar Straus & Giroux

How Civil Wars Start: And How to Stop Them
2022. Barbara F. Walter
Crown

The Myth of Progress: Towards a Sustainable Future (Updated Edition)
2023. Tom Wessels
Brandeis University Press

The Hidden Life of Trees: What They Feel, How They Communicate: Discoveries from a Secret World
2016. Peter Wohllenben
T. Flannery (Forward), J. Billinghurst (Translator), S. Simard (Contributor)
Graystone Books

Lincoln's Religion
1970. William J. Wolf
Pilgrim Press